THOUGHT GAZER

THE YDRON SAGA 2

RAYMOND BOLTON

WFP
WordFire Press

ISBN: 978-1-61475-666-8

Cover design by Natasha Brown

Cover artwork images by Natasha Brown

Kevin J. Anderson, Art Director

Published by
WordFire Press, an imprint of
WordFire, LLC
PO Box 1840
Monument CO 80132

Kevin J. Anderson & Rebecca Moesta, Publishers

WordFire Press Trade Paperback Edition 2018
Printed in the USA
Join our WordFire Press Readers Group and get free books, sneak previews, updates on new projects, and other giveaways.
Sign up for free at wordfirepress.com

❀ Created with Vellum

ACKNOWLEDGMENTS

Thanks to both social media and this author's propensity to travel, the hands that have helped craft this work into the product you are holding hail from several geographic locations.

In 2009, I began attending the Pacific Northwest Writers Association's summer conferences in Seattle, WA and met Canadian published author and sometimes book editor, Kate Austin, at the first one I attended. She helped me whip an early version of *Thought Gazer* into sufficient shape to enter it in PNWA's 2010 literary competition. And while the manuscript did not make it into the finals—perhaps because of stiff competition—both of us were confident it could have been a contender. The version you are holding is all the stronger because of her guidance.

Thought Gazer's cover was created by Colorado author and graphic artist, Natasha Brown. As was the case with my debut novel, *Awakening*, Tasha used her talent for combining strong images into a statement of the novel's core story.

Feminist artist, graphic novelist, cartoonist, and California Berkeley-ite, Maureen Burdock, turned my sketches into *Thought Gazer*'s map.

Santa Fe, New Mexico's culture photographer, Jennifer Esperanza, shot the portrait you will find at the back of this book.

If you are reading an electronic version, it is thanks to the technical expertise of author, formatter, and Californian, Clare Ayala.

Manuscript formatting for IngramSpark was performed by Italian resident, Janet Tallon.

Fantasy authors Robin Lythgoe (Utah)—*Dragonlace, In the Mirror,* and *As The Crow Flies*—and Matthew Stevens (Illinois) —*One in the Chamber*—agreed to serve as beta readers. Their invaluable comments, suggestions, and criticisms helped me eliminate weaknesses in the storyline and characters.

I will always be grateful to *New York Times, USA Today,* and Amazon best-selling author and Maryland resident, Melissa Foster, without whose websites fostering-success.com/ and worldliterarycafe.com/ I would have never found my way into print. If you, too, are seeking to be published, you would do well to make use of them.

Finally, I abhor typographical errors and do all that I can to present my readers a truly clean manuscript. My wife and line editor, Toni Bolton, and proofreader, Marlene Roberts Engel, leant their critical eyes to the initial self-published edition. I have Jonathan Miller to thank for editing the WordFire Press edition you are reading now.

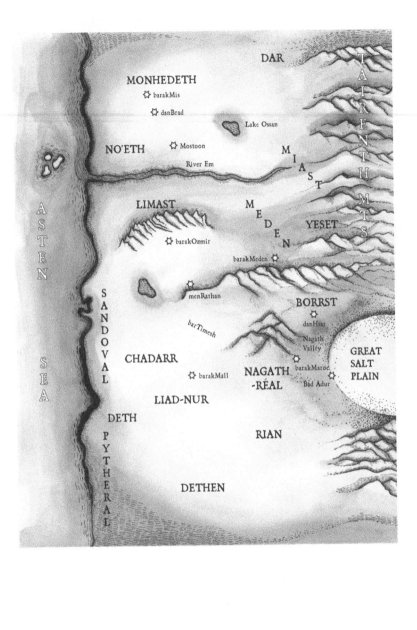

PREFACE

In this newly transformed world, where all the inhabitants are now telepaths, information flows so freely one might think books would no longer be necessary. In fact, with such an abundance of knowledge to sort through, much becomes lost in this vast sea of thoughts. As a consequence, books have become a convenient way to isolate important matters and preserve them for present and future generations. Here, then, is one account of certain events that preceded our world's awakening.

Before there was a kingdom named Ydron, before its sixteen provinces were demarked and united under a process we would one day refer to as The Joining, there was a period that historians would call The Great Conflict.

During its nearly fifteen years, anarchy ruled and almost every land was at war. Family set upon family, brother murdered brother, and ruler attacked ruler. Obah Sitheh, who would eventually change his surname to Tonopath, or Conqueror, cut a swath through the chaos. Slaughter, petty rivalry, and confusion all came to a halt because, in the end, no one was brave or foolish enough to challenge him. Fortune had so smiled on all his campaigns that he never lost a battle. His troops were feared as no others had been, and he was revered almost as a god. When he finally claimed dominance, there was none who would contradict him. Certainly he was brilliant, but there were many unchronicled events that repeatedly turned unfavorable circumstances to his advantage and would eventually fashion him into a legend.

The account I am about to relate occurred midway through that period and pertains to certain events peripheral to his campaign, but that nonetheless affected it. At the time of this telling, Obah Sitheh had not yet been tested in any great battle, only minor skirmishes.

I have gleaned the information I am about to impart both from historical documents, as well as from the minds of many scholars, with each thinker's permission, of course. I have only included accounts that agreed with one another, because, after the almost two hundred fifty years that have since elapsed, there is no way to determine the accuracy of differing interpretations.

The Chronicle of Ages
   Regilius Tonopath, Last Prince of Ydron

CHAPTER ONE

Bedistai Alongquith squatted beneath the dripping boughs of a falo'an tree. Its massive trunk and outstretched limbs had provided shelter from the storm. So large was this specimen, it was doubtful any force of nature could have moved it. Indeed, hollowed out, it would have been nearly as commodious as his home. Protected so from the full force of the wind, Bedistai had waited out the tempest's passing. As he nestled among the roots of this venerable old giant, he quietly chewed a moa root. Its mild narcotic properties kept away any cold, hunger, or thirst during the nearly two days he was forced to remain in this posture, and it prevented his muscles from cramping, despite such prolonged immobility. Now he began the ritual deep breathing exercises he had learned long ago. These would gradually restore normalcy to his metabolism and circulation to his limbs. To move before he had completed these efforts and restored himself surely would have resulted in strain or injury, so, with the practiced patience of a hunter, he breathed and offered the required prayers of thanks, meticulously following the twenty-one Acts of Renewal his people, the Haroun, had observed for untold generations.

This was not the first time he had performed the Acts. The hunt always took him far from home and for extended periods. A tent or shelter-cloth would have added unnecessarily to his endath's load, and a fine hunting endath was far too valuable to squander as a mere beast of burden. If the creature were to carry him across rough terrain in quick pursuit of quarry, it needed all its reserves at any given moment. So, out of respect for the one on whom he had depended for so much and so often, he brought only those things he could not do without: the clothes on his back, his weapons and tools of the hunt, medicine for treating injuries, a water skin, salt for curing meat, and some starter for his bread whenever he could trade for flour.

Bedistai, in fact, was not given to any form of excess. Even his appearance belied his talents. Most hunters of his ilk wore the talons, fangs, quills, and pelts of dozens of successful take-downs. His clothes, on the other hand, were of simple sandiath skin. Except for a solitary tooth suspended from a cord around his throat, he wore none of the ostentation of his calling. The significance of the tooth was that the creature who bore it, a beyaless cath'en, had killed all but one of a fully armed hunting party numbering a dozen. Bedistai, the sole survivor of the attack, had managed to slay the cath'en. It had been his first hunt, and while the accomplishment had elevated him in the eyes of his peers to master hunter, the tooth served more as a reminder than as a boast.

Aware that her rider had begun to stir, the endath approached. Her smooth muscular body moved with a grace that strongly suggested her true speed and power. The muscles of her four legs, of her long graceful neck and tail, as well as her powerful loins, all twitched with anticipation.

As the ritual concluded, Bedistai stretched and flexed his

back, breathing deeply with each tentative motion. Eventually he turned his head to greet her and smiled at the streamer of steam the wind carried off from her solitary nostril. She, like all of her kind, had an extremely high body temperature, brought about by an incredibly fast metabolism. Bedistai had grown accustomed to the fact she never seemed to sleep. He had learned through careful observation during their long association that she slept quite often—several times an hour—but only for instants. He even suspected she dozed mid-stride, but she never stumbled or hesitated, if in fact she did. Hers was an odd biological cycle, duplicated nowhere else, and it served both to protect her from predators and render her a perpetually alert, perpetually rested companion.

He arose from his haunches and stretched his arms and legs. He was hungry. The storm that had passed made hunting impossible, and he had not eaten during all of the time he had spent here.

"Come, Chawah," he beckoned. "Let us find breakfast."

The endath tossed her head and flicked her tail at the sound of his voice. Then she did the thing he loved most, the thing no other of her kind ever did. She met his eyes with hers. Her clear gaze fixed upon him and the living spirit inhabiting that magnificent body reached out to meet him. Bedistai wished she could speak. He strode up to her and rubbed her neck with strong affectionate strokes while he spoke to her in soft soothing tones. Only after he had examined her body and assured himself all was well did he place the saddle upon her and secure his few arms and possessions behind it. He hesitated for an instant before mounting, listening for sounds on the wind. Then, with no visible effort, he leapt onto her back and took up her reins. His seat touched and she took off as though their will were one.

The Expanse of No'eth is not flat as are the plains of Rian or Dethen. It undulates in a series of rises and falls so that quarry a short distance from pursuit finds easy concealment.

Sound does not carry well and the thickets that erupt in the lee of the many hillocks serve as further cover. Scent is as likely to reveal the upwind presence of hunter to prey as the reverse, so only by disciplined scrutiny of the details of the terrain and disturbances of the brush and grasses would Bedistai find success.

The rains had washed away all but the freshest tracks, and those impressions he encountered were clear and easy to read in the soft wet soil. Although he was looking for the spoor of a jennet or umpall—both large swift herbivores—this morning he would have settled for a rodent such as a marmath. Skewered, it would make a fine breakfast and his stomach rumbled at the thought.

Several times he dismounted to examine evidence of some creature's passing. Each time, however, he was forced to return to his endath's back with no useful information gained. The occasional broken branch or crushed shrub indicated the damage had occurred several days earlier. The stems were dried at the break and the leaves were browning at the torn edges. Then, as he came over a crest, he spied the fresh and unmistakable impressions of an umpall's cloven hooves. They were clear and evenly spaced. This beast was in no hurry and Bedistai knew if he proceeded with care, he could soon overtake it. He maneuvered to remain downwind from the trail and below the concealing ridgelines. Several times he had to backtrack because the creature's unpredictable wanderings took it down a different ravine from the one he had expected. Due to the endath's smooth gait, however, Chawah's footfalls were almost inaudible, and lost time was easily made up without revealing their presence.

Chawah turned her head into the wind and a quiver ran through her loins. The gust struck Bedistai and he smiled. It was rich with umpall scent. With a gentle tug on the reins, he slowed the pursuit. Now, instead of paralleling the quarry's trail, they followed it. The soil held deep impressions and the matted foliage made a path any child could follow. Still unable to see the beast, but hearing its snort, Bedistai slipped to the ground, bow in hand. He released the reins and gestured to Chawah to remain where she was. Drawing an arrow from the quiver, he fitted it to the string. He had nearly circled the mound separating him from his prey and was about to skirt a clump of brush when he heard muffled hoof beats just ahead. The wind in his ears had nearly masked them, but he recognized them for what they were.

Raising and tensioning the bow, he stepped into the open. The beast turned to face him as he emerged. Its ears were up, and its nostrils flared as it sensed the danger. In that seemingly long pause between the creature's perception and its reaction, Bedistai drew the bowstring, bringing the arrow's fletchings to his ear. As he took a slow, deliberate breath, his fingers released ...

He never saw the arrow reach its mark because, in that very instant, Chawah's panicked cry filled his ears and snapped his head around. The sound tore at him. Without thinking, he scrambled toward her as fast as he could. Clasping his bow, both arms pumping, he ran with all his might. She cried out again and he drove his feet harder into the ground, digging for every extra bit of speed he could muster, cursing each time he slipped. Without thought for his own safety, he burst into the clearing where he had left her.

No'eth is an empty land with sparsely scattered villages, so Bedistai was startled by the sight of four strangers swarming around his companion and clutching at her reins. Chawah's eyes were wide with fear. Finding nowhere to retreat, she tried to rear onto her haunches, but the youngest intruder had thrown a rope around her neck. When she rose onto her hind legs, he hung with his entire weight. Her fragile neck could not support him so, bellowing in pain, she lowered her head and dropped back onto her forefeet.

"Release her!" shouted Bedistai. "Move away from her now!"

The four turned to face him. The nearest one, startled at first, smiled and reached for the sword slung from his hip. Bedistai dropped the bow and reached for the knife at his own. With a sweeping underhand toss, he delivered it squarely into the man's belly. The stranger dropped his weapon, eyes wide with surprise. Grasping for the haft, he took two halting steps forward and fell face first onto the soil.

Bedistai leapt over the fallen figure toward the young man with the rope. The youth's nearest companion, also armed with a sword, drew it and moved to interpose himself between the two. As the hunter came within reach, the swordsman swung. Bedistai ducked beneath the arc of the blade and heard the metal resonate as it clove the air above his head. Before the blade could finish its swing, Bedistai closed in on his attacker. He captured his opponent's sword hand with his right and punched hard with his left until he heard ribs crack, then punched some more. When the man would not release his grip, Bedistai pivoted, and with both hands brought the man's forearm down upon his knee. The weapon fell to the ground, and Bedistai drove his left elbow up into the man's face, retiring him.

Out of the corner of his eye, Bedistai saw a flash of color hurtling toward him. He dodged, but not quickly enough, and he doubled over in pain. Enveloped in rage, he opened his mouth and a roar rose from deep within. One hand went to his side and he felt the warm wetness of his own blood. He pulled a pointed shaft from his side and kicked hard at the cause of his indignation.

The man, spear in hand, dropped to his knees, mouth agape, all breath gone from him. Bedistai, bent in agony from the effort, straightened and took a step forward. Tearing the spear from the man's grasp, he turned it end-for-end and drove it deep into his foe's abdomen. The man froze in position, twitching reflexively. Bedistai gave the shaft a twist, and when the man jerked in response, he extracted it and let the body topple.

Now there was only the lad holding the rope. While his Haroun upbringing and life on the frontier had taught Bedistai to react quickly and without mercy to danger and injustice, he was inclined to dismiss even the most foolish acts of the young. Despite the fact this one still held the neck of his friend in a noose, because of the lad's age, Bedistai considered releasing him.

"Leave her alone, boy, and go," he said. "Go back to your home."

The young man stood his ground. Not a movement nor expression on his face revealed his intentions.

"Release the endath and I will let you go unharmed."

Perhaps it was the speed with which his three friends were dispatched that caused him to distrust these words, but the youth tugged the rope and began to force the endath to follow as he backed from the clearing.

"You must not do that," instructed Bedistai, pointing the spear to emphasize his earnestness. "She will not leave with you. I will not allow it."

If the youth thought his next course of action would elicit fear or hesitation, he severely miscalculated, for he made the worst and final mistake of his life. With his free hand he reached for the dagger suspended from a cord around his neck. Pulling the knife over his head, he cried, "Follow me and I'll kill it!"

As the boy moved the blade towards Chawah's neck, Bedistai hurled the spear. The throw was effortless and unerring, and the young man died where he stood. When he fell, he became of no further concern, and Bedistai, without giving the body so much as a glance, strode deliberately towards his friend.

Chawah was visibly agitated. Trembling, she glanced nervously from side to side and her long tail thrashed violently.

Bedistai extended a hand to her and called in a slow incantation, "So, so, so, Chawah. So, so, so." The words were unimportant, only the soothing repetition and the tone of his voice.

Little by little, her breathing slowed and her manner calmed. Her eyes gradually stopped darting about the clearing, looking for danger. Eventually they settled onto Bedistai's placid familiar form. He waited until the blind panic in her eyes completely subsided before coming close enough to touch her. Before that, had her muscular tail, which was twice the diameter of his torso at its base and longer than her neck and body combined, lashed out in his direction, it could have broken his back or a limb or worse. It might have killed him. It would have been an unintentional act, but the danger was real. Bedistai considered it a small wonder she had not maimed the boy. Now, however, her eyes met his and the two connected. The meeting was palpable, and he saw she felt it too. Her body relaxed and her entire posture reflected calm. Her tail settled nearly to the ground. Her neck was no longer rigid and even sagged a bit. Her breathing slowed and the pupils of her eyes gradually contracted. Only then did he begin to stroke her neck.

"Oh, Chawah. They are gone, now. No harm. They are gone and you are safe."

She looked into his eyes, and after examining his countenance, gently brushed his arm with the side of her face.

"Good girl," he said and caressed her cheek with his hand.

Then, satisfied she was truly calm, he began to walk around her, his hand always on her so she would not be startled by an accidental touch. As he proceeded, he examined her for injuries. Her legs, from each tripod of toes to her shoulders and rump, bore no sign of injury. Though her chest still heaved, her breathing was regular. He could not see her back, an arm's reach above his head, but her movements gave no hint that it troubled her. Nonetheless, he would examine it later to be certain. In fact, except for the place where the noose had chafed her neck, from her heart-shaped head with its solitary nostril and great blue eyes, down the slender neck which equaled her dun colored body in length, to the tip of her long, pointed tail, everything about her appeared as it should. He breathed easier. Only now would he tend to himself.

The saddlebag he wanted was beyond his reach. As often was the case, Chawah anticipated him. She reached back and, with her mouth, plucked it from the saddle and gave it to him. Inside, he found a packet of herbs that would congeal the blood. Breaking it open, he poured the contents into his palm, then flinched when he applied it to the wound. Fortunately, the effects of the moa root had not yet vanished, or else the pain would have been intolerable.

Holding the medicine in place, he returned to the nearest body. Hoping it would not be flushed away by his blood when he removed his hand, he tore two lengths of cloth from the man's clothing. One he folded into a pad to contain the remedy and absorb the blood. The other he used to bind it in place. Satisfied it was secure, he decided to investigate what had happened.

He could not discount the possibility there were others nearby, so he turned his attention to the immediate area and tried to determine how the quartet could have surprised her. Chawah would never have allowed them to approach under ordinary circumstances. His eyes went from signs of a scuffle left in the soil when they had captured her to a rise not far from the origin of those marks. Its summit was a little higher than her head and was a likely spot for an ambush. Still, they could not have known in advance he would come to this place any more than he. So how had this occurred?

He was not about to investigate, armed with only the spear, so he returned to where his first victim lay. He extricated his knife and wiped the blade on the man's tunic before returning it to its sheath. Then, he picked up the discarded bow, slung it over his shoulder, and a moment later was standing atop the knoll. On its summit, footprints, handprints, and grass flattened by what was surely a prostrate form told a partial story of someone who had climbed to the top, had fallen briefly onto his belly, then scrambled to his feet and jumped. That one, likely, had landed upon the animal to be joined in the clearing by three more, one of whom had followed the first, leaping down the face, while the other two ran down its side.

But what had brought them to this remote spot in the wilderness? That was still unclear. He scanned the surrounding area, looking for anything unusual. For a while, nothing appeared out of place. A flock of chur soared overhead and a few other birds winged from tree to tree in their morning quest for food. Grasses and brush moved softly in the gentle breeze. Then he spied, protruding above the vegetation, what appeared to be a portion of a wooden structure.

He paused to examine the bandage and was pleased to see it was not saturated. The blood was no longer flowing. If he was careful, it would hold until he could sew the wound.

He turned and called, "Chawah!"

She craned her head and met his eyes.

"Stay here," he said. "I will be right back."

Her eyes half blinked in acknowledgement and Bedistai, satisfied she understood, turned and scrambled down the opposite side of the mound. He made his way down the slope and through the underbrush until he neared the place where the curious object stood.

In this wild place, anything constructed by man was suspect and he could not be certain there were no other marauders. He listened for the sounds of conversation or careless movement, but at first detected nothing. Then, as he approached, he heard soft rhythmic noises he could not identify. He slowed his approach even more, listening carefully. The sounds repeated in a pattern he could not attribute to any animal, but neither were they sounds of speech. A loud snort came from directly ahead, but it was separate from the utterings that had caught his attention. He drew his knife and peered through the brush. He saw several large hairy forms moving and heard the sound of hooves shifting stance. He circled to his right, keeping some distance between himself and whatever creatures they might be. Then, as he peered through the branches, he smiled. In a clearing stood an ox in harness and four horses saddled as steeds. The ox shifted and snorted as Bedistai emerged and the sound confirmed this was one of the noises he had heard. But now the puzzling murmuring which had drawn him here had grown clearer, coming from a place directly behind this great beast.

As he circled the ox, four wooden corner posts revealed the presence of a cart. Numerous smaller bars showed it to be a cage. Curious as to what it might contain, he approached. There, within the bars and resting on a bed of soggy straw, was a small wet pile of what appeared to be fine cloth. Well, "resting" was perhaps not the word, for the pile shifted and heaved in a pattern coinciding with the soft repetitions—too high in pitch to belong to any animal he knew. He stepped up to the cage, yet whatever was moving within the pile did not react to his presence. Carefully, he extended an arm through the bars, far enough to reach the mound of fabric. He grasped a fold between his fingers and tugged. At once, the pile rose up and he stepped back, pointing his knife. He found himself face to face with a woman whom, under other circumstances, he might consider beautiful. She was sobbing and trembling and, from her pallor, he could see she was deathly ill.

CHAPTER TWO

She awoke to a rich warm taste and someone speaking.

"That's good. Take another sip, child," a woman said.

She did as she was told and savored the warm flavorful broth that filled her mouth and soothed her throat. All at once, she was desperate for the taste and could not get enough, as if she had not eaten for days. But when she attempted to take in more, the cup was withdrawn and her lips came together futilely.

"Not too much. You have to go slowly. Your stomach isn't ready for too much food at one time," a woman instructed.

Someone wiped her chin and she realized she did not recognize the one who was speaking. Nor did she know where she was. In a panic, she tried to sit but was too weak to manage. She opened her eyes and the image before her gradually resolved into the face of someone older than she. As her perceptions clarified, she began to notice details. The woman's long, silver hair was drawn back from her face with combs made of either ivory or bone before it cascaded to her shoulders. Her eyes, an uncommon shade of blue without any trace of gray, were set in a face lined by years spent outdoors. She wore a

12

complex beaded necklace draped over a tan blouse of animal skin, and half a dozen or so silver bracelets on each of her wrists.

The older woman smiled.

"So, you have decided to return to the world. That is good. We have all been quite concerned about you."

"You *all?*" she asked, and was surprised at how weak her voice sounded. "I don't understand. Who are you and," looking about, she found herself forced to ask, "where am I?"

"I am Salmeh. You have already met my son, Bedistai. You are a welcome guest in my home. This is the village of Mostoon in the land of our people, the Haroun. Some call this land No'eth."

The younger woman nodded as she began to comprehend. She tried again to sit. This time she placed both hands against the mattress and pushed. Pain shot through her right hand, causing her to cry out. She held it up and saw it was bandaged, with a gap where the third finger should have been.

Salmeh set aside the cup she was holding and stood by the bed. "Here," she said, as she slipped her hands under the younger woman's arms. "Let me help."

Salmeh assisted as she struggled to come fully upright. Since the bed lacked a headboard, Salmeh propped her back against the wall. Then, before she released her, she arranged one pillow for her to rest against and a second behind her head. Exhausted from the effort, she sagged against them.

"That will do for now. Are you comfortable like that?"

She nodded, admiring how strong Salmeh appeared to be. The entire act had seemed so effortless, as if she weighed nothing.

"Someone severed your finger. Your hand became so bad we were afraid you would lose it. Do you remember how it happened?"

She shook her head, then paused, finally nodding as she

recalled the ambush. Her face must have reflected it, because Salmeh looked concerned and asked, "Can you tell me about it?"

"No," she said, averting her eyes.

Despite the circumstance, she was not ready to surrender her trust.

"Very well," Salmeh replied.

She noticed how Salmeh studied her as she returned to her seat, curiosity reflecting on her face. Now that she was awake and upright, she too was curious. Regarding her surroundings from this improved vantage, she was now able to assess the place where she found herself.

The room was dimly lit, but neither by windows nor torches. Instead, light appeared to be entering from above, perhaps through a skylight situated beyond her perspective. The walls and ceiling were constructed of long narrow logs and the spaces between them appeared to be caulked with clay. Larger logs formed the corner posts, studs, and rafters. The furniture, while fashioned from roughly hewn wood, appeared well constructed. A few hassocks and cushions were strewn about, but there were also two chairs of a more conventional design as well as some tables. Animal skins covered many of these, and the bed on which she lay was blanketed with various kinds of furs. The room had little by way of ornamentation, but those decorations she noticed, such as bouquets, were taken from nature and the air smelled of herbs and flowers.

The young woman turned to Salmeh and asked, "How long have I been here?"

"It has been nearly a week since Bedistai found you."

"A week!"

Salmeh nodded then mused, half to herself, "I've never seen him so frightened." Looking the younger woman directly in the eye, she added, "Nothing frightens my son, but in your case, he was terrified. He believed you might expire at any moment.

Although his own house is nearby, he would not leave your bedside for more than three days until your fever broke. You were delirious. He slept there." Salmeh pointed. "On those cushions beside your bed. Fortunately for you, Bedistai's knowledge of herbal medicine is considerable. The tincture he administered, he gathered and prepared himself. It was only on the fourth day, when at last you rested peacefully, that he allowed himself to return home. I don't think he slept much before that."

Salmeh picked up the cup and offered it again.

"You say your son's name is Bed ..."

"Bedistai. Bedistai Alongquith," Salmeh pronounced carefully.

As she was speaking, someone drew back the skin hanging across the doorway. Light flooded the room, and Salmeh turned to see. The young woman looked as well, but made out no more than a silhouette against the brilliance.

"How is she, Mother?" a man inquired.

He released the skin, obscuring the sunlight, and again her eyes took time to adjust.

"See for yourself," Salmeh replied. "She sits," she said, beaming and gesturing towards the bed. "You have wrought a small miracle."

"She is recovering?"

"Perhaps you should ask her yourself, Bedistai," Salmeh gently rebuked.

The young woman squinted at the approaching figure. Salmeh's son was a large man. He was muscular and, like his mother, wore his hair long. It was straight, dark in color, and he wore it drawn back from his face. But unlike Salmeh, he tied it into a neat single tail which hung below his shoulders. His face was rugged with angular cheekbones and jaw. And though she did not find him handsome in the way she regarded the men of her own culture—fair-skinned with softer turned features—she found his looks appealing. Moreover, his eyes had the look of fierce intelligence.

Unlike the men where she came from, who covered their bodies in fabric, Bedistai was nearly naked, wearing only a tanned skin belted to his waist and some animal's fur draped about his shoulders. Moreover, a fang, which must have belonged to a beast of impossible size, hung from a cord around his neck. She found herself blushing at his lack of attire and noticed how Salmeh tried to conceal her amusement. It was then that she noticed his bandaged side.

When he reached her bedside, he squatted and asked, "How are you feeling? We have been worried about you."

The admission brought a smile.

"I am feeling a little better, thank you. I am still weak, but your mother's broth is restoring my strength."

"Ah!" He seemed pleased and nodded. "That is good. Mother is a fine nurse."

"I understand you are a rather fine doctor," she countered.

Bedistai averted his eyes downward, apparently embarrassed by her candor.

"That is not a bad thing," she asserted.

Returning his gaze to meet hers he admitted, "No. It is not."

Still holding the cup, although she no longer offered it, Salmeh moved to the side of the bed opposite her son and asked, "Are you strong enough, child, to tell us who you are and how it is you came to No'eth in such a state?"

Uncertain whether to trust these strangers, or how much she should reveal, she paused to regard each of her hosts, studying each face carefully. She decided a minimal account would suffice, so after a moment, she replied, "I am Darva Sitheh from the land known as Liad-Nur. My brother is Obah Sitheh."

"You come from Liad-Nur?" Bedistai sounded startled.

"That place is far to the south, at least two weeks from here as an ox can draw a cart."

"I don't remember much of the journey but, yes, we had been traveling for some time."

Bedistai considered this for a moment, then asked, "You say your brother is Obah Sitheh?"

Darva nodded.

"The Haroun have little to do with the affairs of others, but his name has carried this far. He commands a large force of fighting men, does he not?"

"He does," she answered. "By now it has become a small army. All of the lands, save perhaps No'eth, are at war. There is only chaos. In order to protect his own lands and those of his neighbors, he has been compelled to pick up the sword against those who would either destroy or subjugate us. Our people have rallied to his side. To his credit, he has amassed no small number of followers, and for the moment we are holding our own. As for how I came to this place, that is not a simple tale, but I will try to make some sense of it."

She sighed deeply and continued.

"Hath Kael is the warlord who controls the land called Chadarr and he is trying to bring all of the southern lands under his fist. At the moment, his eye is on Nagath-réal and Rian. Those two regions control all of the goods which come to us from far to the east, across the Great Salt Plain. To save themselves, they have given their allegiance to my brother, and as our land lies between them and Chadarr, for the moment they are safe.

"In his attempt to make my brother step aside or surrender, Kael has enlisted the aid of Sabed Orr, who controls Monhedeth."

"Wait," Bedistai interrupted. "I don't understand. Monhedeth lies to our north. Why would Orr care to involve himself with the affairs of Chadarr?"

"Kael knows that Orr covets all of the northern lands," explained Darva. "Even though Kael will likely never be satisfied until he has forced even those places under his control, he has offered Orr the lands he desires in exchange for his assistance. Most specifically, in return for his aid, Kael has offered to help Orr conquer Limast. Since No'eth, which lies between the two, has no armies of its own, once Orr has occupied Limast, his arm will extend southward without interruption. He will have No'eth without lifting a finger. All that will remain for him to take is the tiny region called Dar. No one has decided who will conquer Meden. I suspect that point is moot. Kael wants it."

Bedistai cocked an eyebrow, started to speak, then paused for a moment.

"That doesn't explain ..."

"How I got here?" Darva anticipated him.

"Yes."

Her strength was flagging. Nonetheless, she sighed deeply and continued.

"Orr arranged for my abduction. I am to be taken to Monhedeth, far from my brother, where I will be used as a bargaining chip. Should Obah yield to Kael, I may live."

"May?"

"There are no guarantees in this life," she said, with an earnest look at Bedistai.

"How were you taken?" Salmeh asked.

"A large party of armed men intercepted me as I traveled with my bodyguard. We were outnumbered three to one. My guards fought bravely and, to their credit, they did not stop until the last of them perished. Although they were so overwhelmed, they managed to kill all but the ones who captured me. Had I but one or two more in my company, I am sure those four would have died as well."

She paused a moment, then turned to Bedistai.

"Now it is my turn. How did you find me?"

Bedistai smiled.

"I did not find you. The men who held you prisoner found me."

"So you simply killed them?"

She was trying to envision how that might have happened, not yet understanding who her rescuer might be.

"I killed three. I left the fourth one injured and I suspect that he will have run back to Orr by now. Had they not attacked my friend, or had they set aside their weapons when I asked them to, they would still be alive." He breathed deeply, then let out a sigh. "I would have preferred to have sent them on their way, but they left me no choice."

"Your friend?" she asked. "From what little I remember, you were alone."

"I have an endath," he explained. "She was waiting beyond the place where I found you."

Darva's eyes widened at the creature's mention.

"An endath? I have heard of them. People say they are marvelous!"

"Yes," he agreed. "They are, indeed. Chawah is more special than most."

"Is that his name? Chawah?"

"Yes, it is. But Chawah is a girl."

"You love her very much, don't you? I can see it in your eyes and hear it in your voice when you speak of her."

"She is my best friend. She has taken care of me almost all of her life, and I of her."

Darva was ignoring the broth so Salmeh set it aside.

"You are still quite feeble," Salmeh said, "so I am sure you will need to remain with us a while longer. But once you have recovered, what then?"

Without hesitation, Darva replied, "While I am most grateful for all your care and hospitality, I must return to my brother. So long as Obah believes I am imprisoned, all he has fought for is at risk. I must deliver myself to him, safe and sound, so he can give Kael the justice he deserves. As soon as I am strong enough to leave this bed, I will be on my way."

"Even if you are strong enough to stand, I wonder if you will be strong enough to make the journey," said Salmeh.

"Should I arrive in my brother's camp at death's door ... No! Should my corpse be delivered to him, he will be free to pursue his fight. There are more lives at stake than mine, so I will leave as soon as possible."

"We will not keep you prisoner," Bedistai assured her. "But we will counsel against too early a departure. What if you die along the way and your brother never learns of it? You will have accomplished nothing."

Salmeh gave her son a stern look and it did not go unnoticed.

"Yes, Mother," he answered her aloud. "Do not fear. I will not allow her to make the journey alone."

Darva propped herself upright with her hands, shaking from the effort.

"No, thank you. I do not require your assistance. You have already done more than I have a right to expect, so I will go by myself."

Bedistai responded with a gentle voice and a smile. "I have saved your life. In my culture, I would be throwing it away if I were to allow you to make such a perilous journey alone, unarmed and in frail health. Now, please rest. Some days hence, when you have regained sufficient strength, I will accompany you on your quest. I will leave your side only when you have seen it through and I will hear no further argument."

Before she could reply, he rose to his feet and departed. Darva, having exerted herself to the limits of her strength, collapsed back onto the pillows.

"You sleep, child," said Salmeh. She rose and drew the furs up about Darva's chin. "You need all the rest you can get."

She turned away and retrieved the forgotten cup.

She was about to depart, when she paused and added, "I can promise you this. You will certainly accomplish what you intend, young lady. There is no one like my son. When he makes a promise, nothing can prevent him from fulfilling it. Of all the places you could have alighted, you have found the best. Sleep soundly. All will be well."

CHAPTER THREE

Low clouds scudded toward Nagath-réal as the West Wind flattened the grasses of Liad-Nur's plains. Tented encampments standing in the lee of barakMall, the northwestern fort, strained against their guys while their canvas panels boomed and shuddered. Banners and guidons flapped and danced while grooms and stablemen scrambled to blindfold and calm horses and oxen against the uproar. All around, men were digging long broad trenches, planting row upon row of sharpened stakes within them. Deadlier by far than any moat filled with water, the stake pits would control the flow of the attack upon the fort should the fighting reach its walls. Farther out, lines of ox-drawn wagons, bringing provisions from Nagath-réal and Rian, meandered in unbroken lines from the southern and eastern horizons to the fortress. Drivers leaned into the gale and strove to see through tightly drawn hoods or, having abandoned the frustrating headgear altogether, squinted against the afternoon glare and the convoy's dust.

Obah Sitheh and his senior staff stood atop the main wall, watching the processions.

"Is everything arriving as planned, generals?"

"Yes, my lord," said General Kahn. "My observers assure me the last wagon will arrive just after dark. If we continue to work throughout the night, we can have everything stored by this time tomorrow, or by dusk at the latest."

"Excellent."

"Pardon me, lord," asked General Barral. "You sound optimistic, but you have been wearing that grim mask for days. May I ask what is troubling you?"

"I have recently learned that Hath intends to split our forces. He has enlisted the aid of Lord En of Borrst to supplement his main army and create a second front. Although their number is not so great as Kael's, an attack out of the northeast through the Nagath Valley will be difficult to defend against without weakening our position here."

"I wish you had brought that to my attention sooner," said General Kahn. "It will take some time to organize them, but Nagath-réal maintains two infantry battalions you might use to mount a defense. They are newly formed and lack discipline, but my sources tell me that they are highly motivated. They hate Kael and fear that if you fail, he will continue straight through Liad-Nur and into their land."

"What do you suggest?"

"I believe you have more than enough tested officers here to command your cavalry, your ground troops, and the fortification. With your permission, I would like to take two of your colonels with a brigade under each and ride to barakMaroc. If we intersperse them among their battalions, we can use them to train the Nagath-réali and have them ready in short order. With any luck, we can have them battle-ready before En can mount an attack. Although barakMaroc is still under construction, its walls are completed and will offer better protection than any other location Nagath-réal has to offer. Furthermore, standing as it is, where the Nagath Valley curves around the Han'nah mountains, it is perfectly situated."

"Two brigades are a lot to lose, General. Take one and divide it."

"Very good, my lord. With your permission, I would like to leave quickly."

Before Obah could answer, two soldiers dragged a prisoner onto the parapet.

"Pardon the interruption, my lord," said one, saluting. "Our captain thought you should talk to this man."

They threw the prisoner onto his knees at Obah Sitheh's feet. The man, although bound at the wrists, pushed himself upright and grinned at the warlord with a mouth that had been bloodied.

"Why was he beaten? Was that really necessary?" Obah demanded. "Doesn't your captain understand I can't take time to examine everyone he captures?"

"My lord," the first soldier replied. "This one claims to have news of your sister."

"Darva?" Obah asked, eyeing the man with changed appreciation.

"He has brought something he claims is proof."

The soldier reached under his breastplate and produced a leather pouch. Obah cocked his head as he first eyed the sack, then the prisoner.

"What would you know of my sister?"

The man looked at him and sneered.

"Orr has her. Be good to me if you wish to see her again," he chuckled. "You should tell your men that if they give me more of this sort of hospitality, she is likely to receive the same." The prisoner spat blood onto the battlement walk. Then raising his face to look Obah squarely in the eye, he finished with, "My lord."

Obah regarded him closely, then turned to the soldier who

offered the pouch in an outstretched hand.

"What is that?" Obah asked.

"He says it is hers. My captain instructed me to give it to you, my lord, although I am not sure you want to see this."

Uncertain what the soldier intended when he said, "it is hers," Obah accepted the offering and hefted it.

"Thank you, corporal."

He loosened the drawstring that secured the bag's opening. When he peered inside, his mouth tightened, and, for a moment, he closed his eyes and was forced to turn away. Then, drawing a breath, he withdrew the severed finger.

"It is Darva's," he admitted.

Two swords resonated as one as Kahn and Barral drew their blades.

"Let me give you his head," said Barral, as he seized the prisoner by the hair.

"Say but the word," growled Kahn, engaging Lord Sitheh's eyes with his own.

His weapon's point was already indenting the man's neck, sending trickle of blood down his chest, when the warlord shouted, "Stop!"

"My lord?" asked a puzzled Barral, even as Kahn glanced from the prisoner to his commander.

When both generals kept their weapons poised, begging permission with their eyes, Lord Sitheh demanded, "Leave him." Then, in a quieter voice, he explained, "Killing him won't undo the damage." He held up the finger to illustrate. Although visibly shaken—even now, his own hand was resting on the pommel at his hip—he nonetheless ordered, "Put them away."

He was trembling with anger as the generals sheathed their blades. The prisoner had started to grin when Lord Sitheh rounded on him.

"How do I know she is alive?" he growled.

The prisoner recoiled, raising an arm to protect himself.

When the warlord did not strike, he grinned again, even broader than before.

"I guess you don't, m'lord. You will just have to take my word for it."

"And if I don't?"

"Then she will not be alive for long. You will have to take—what do they call it?—a leap of faith."

"And what am I supposed to do to ensure she remains alive?"

"Surrender, my lord. Just surrender. My master has decided to make your task a simple one. All you need to do is lay down your arms and open the gates and he will return your sister alive and well."

"Minus a finger."

"Well, you wouldn't have believed me if I simply gave you my word, now would you?"

"What will you have us do with him?" asked Kahn.

"We will keep him prisoner for now."

"As a hostage to ensure her return?" Barral asked.

"No. I suspect neither Orr nor Kael regard him very highly. I may have another use for him. Meanwhile," Sitheh said, breathing quieter than before, "I have to decide how I will reply." He paused a moment, then turned to one of the soldiers. "Corporal."

"Yes, my lord."

"House our friend. The stockade will be good enough. Give him his own cell. Feed him and have a physician look in on him. I want him strong enough and well enough to carry my reply to Kael, should I choose to do so."

"My lord," Kahn interrupted. "He said that Sabed Orr holds Darva. Should we not reply to him?"

"Orr didn't do this on his own. It would have been beyond his thinking. Make no mistake. Kael conceived and ordered this plan." He turned to the prisoner. "You will remain our guest until I decide what to do with you."

"I wouldn't take too long, m'lord. You can never tell what can happen while you are thinking things over." He chuckled.

"And you should worry what will happen to you if anything unfortunate befalls my sister." Sitheh turned to his men. "Take this garbage away. Remove him from my sight before I forget myself."

The prisoner's face darkened and he glared over his shoulder as the soldiers dragged him back down the stairs.

When he was well out of earshot, Barral asked, "How can you be sure the finger is hers? It could belong to anyone."

"The ring." Obah displayed the digit to show the ring it still bore. "It was mother's. It fit Darva a bit too snugly, which is probably why it hasn't fallen off."

"I'm still concerned," said Kahn. "They may yet harm her. She may be dead, even as we speak."

"I doubt it. Kael isn't about to discard the one threat he holds over my head without good reason. He will keep Darva alive until he gets what he wants. The problem is, once I comply with his wishes, should I choose to, he will no longer need her and that is when he is apt to kill her."

"Pardon me, lord, if I am out of line, but what do you think Kael will do if we surrender? He doesn't take prisoners and he never forgives an enemy. What happens to all these men?" His arm panned from the fortress out across the surrounding plain. "What happens to the villages and towns? Too many lives are at stake."

"I know, General. I need to find another solution."

"What about your sister?" asked General Kahn. "I can put together a rescue party."

"And take them where? I do not mean to belittle your concern, but we don't know where she is." He clenched his fists. "I trust that criminal's words as much as I trust Hath, but there is nothing we can do. Sooner or later, he will try to force our hand. Until then, we continue with our plans. General Barral and I will continue to fortify our position and you will take your colonels and the brigade of your choice to barakMaroc. Once there, you will ensure that the fortification is as strong as you can make it and is provisioned for a long and bloody campaign. In the meantime, I will decide what to do about Kael."

CHAPTER FOUR

Bedistai! Bedistai! They killed them!" cried the youth as he leapt from his endath's back and ran towards the hunter.

Bedistai was stretching an umpall hide across a wooden frame to prepare it for curing. He cut the length of gut he had used to secure the skin, then placed the knife on a small table next to the scrapers he would use to clean the hide of fat and connective tissue. He finished knotting the cord as the boy's feet pounded the compacted earth. When the young man arrived, gasping for breath, Bedistai turned to regard his tear-streaked face.

"They killed them! They killed them!" the boy gasped as he sobbed.

Grasping his shoulders, seeking to calm him, Bedistai told the youth, "Slow down, Dorman. Catch your breath."

The boy took a few deep breaths but, despite his effort, could not stop the tears.

"They're all dead, Bedistai. They killed every one."

His body convulsed with each sob.

"Who is dead?" Bedistai asked, brushing the boy's hair from his face.

"Everyone in my hunting party. We were just returning—Seddah and me—with three of the initiates when strangers on horses burst through the underbrush and surprised us. They threatened us with crossbows, and when we tried to ride away, they wounded Radistai. He fell from the saddle and we couldn't just leave him."

"Of course not. Who are these people? Did they say what they wanted?"

"I've never seen them before. They asked about a woman. Seddah and me thought they might be talking about the one you had rescued, but when we told them we didn't know anything, they insisted we were lying. That's when they cut Seddah's throat."

Bedistai drew in his breath. He remembered the one he had left alive the day he stumbled onto Darva and wondered if he might be the source of their information. But since the place where he found her was scores of miles removed from the village, and because no outsider had visited Mostoon for decades, he dismissed the possibility as unlikely.

"Did they say how they knew?"

Dorman shook his head. "But they described Salmeh's house," the youth replied.

There was no way any outsider could know that except ... he did not like the reason that sprang to mind. *Impossible,* he thought. The stories providing that explanation were largely relegated to the realms of fables and fancy. Even so, because rumors and folklore were sometimes rooted in fact, he never completely discounted them. Since there was no other likely explanation, he was forced to consider it as possible.

"How many were there?" Bedistai asked.

"At least twenty, maybe more. We couldn't have overcome them. Please believe me."

"That is not why I asked, Dorman. You have never shown weakness or cowardice."

The boy's face softened. Bedistai had asked because he was trying to determine how badly Orr wanted this woman. Although four had proved insufficient to bring her to Monhedeth, twenty might suffice.

"How did you escape?"

"No one was telling them what they wanted to hear, and they were becoming very angry. After Seddah, they slit Borroh's throat and started to do the same to Haiat. I was next, and I think Tabur knew it," said Dorman, referring to his endath. "He broke free from the man who was holding his reins and ran toward me. When I saw Tabur swing his tail at the one holding me, I managed to slip free and duck. When the man flew through the air, I leapt into the saddle and never looked back. We rode here as fast as we could."

"Where were you when they came upon you?"

"At the edge of the marsh where Salmeh gathers her potting clay."

"And they were riding horses?" asked Bedistai.

"Yes."

"That is good. We still have some time to prepare," Bedistai said. "I want you to ride to the common house. My brother, Tahmen, will be there. Tell him what you told me, then sound the Horn. I must go to my mother's and take the woman away from Mostoon."

"All right, Bedistai. I will do that."

"Good. Now hurry."

Bedistai arrived at his mother's just as the Horn began to sound. She had come to the door and was peering out.

"Bedistai! What is wrong?" she asked. "Has the peace been broken?"

War had never come to this part of the world and it was almost unheard of that intruders or vandals would ride into

Mostoon. Yet, those were the only reasons the Horn would ever be blown. In fact, the last time it sounded was but a dim memory. Nonetheless, everyone knew what to do when they heard the blast. The women were to gather their children, along with foodstuffs and water, and take them to caves near the village's edge. The men and initiates were to take their weapons and endaths to preordained locations from which they were to guard Mostoon. Fortunately, there were no hunts underway and all the able-bodied were available.

"Riders have come looking for Darva," he said. "I suspect they are Orr's. They have killed four of our youths and will arrive here soon."

"Then you must take her to safety."

"Is she able to ride?" he asked.

"She is still recovering, but I believe she is strong enough. I would have told you to begin your journey in another day or two in any case. Today she will manage."

"Good. Then I will begin packing," said Bedistai.

"No. It is better that you fetch Chawah and find an endath for the girl."

"I have already found one."

"Then saddle them both," said Salmeh, "and Darva will be ready by the time you come back. I will pack food, medicine, and whatever else you will need."

He placed a hand on his mother's shoulder and kissed her cheek.

"I will return shortly."

CHAPTER FIVE

D arva inhaled the crisp morning air and sighed deeply.
This was her first opportunity to step outside. She
had been confined for more than a week since
awaking and was glad to be out in the open, glad for an opportunity to survey the place that had sheltered her.

Dozens of small low houses were arranged around a large
circular space where the communal work was performed. All
around it were pots for boiling tallow and frames for curing
hides. Meat hanging from poles was drying in the sunlight.
Smoke curled and rose from various chimneys and each home
boasted a well-tended garden of vegetables and herbs. Against
this tranquil tableau, women shouldered bundles and hurried
their children along pathways between the houses. An occasional toddler screamed in protest at being rushed, while men,
young and old, sporting bows, arrows, knives, and axes ran
through the village towards its perimeter. Despite the urgency,
their countenances reflected only purpose, not fear.

Darva regretted she had been unable to spend even a few
days getting to know this community. Even so, she was glad to
be leaving. She had been growing more anxious with each

passing day, knowing that, as time passed and her fate grew more uncertain, her brother might be tempted to make an ill-fated decision. Then, without warning, the opportunity to go tumbled down upon her and it was all she could do to get ready.

Her own dress was ruined. Even were that not the case, it was unsuited for the journey that lay ahead. Salmeh had approached several households for whatever they might offer and assembled several items she might elect to wear. Darva declined the traditional dress Haroun women wore and opted for leggings, the better to ride with. Since the days were turning cooler and the nights colder still, she chose a shirt and jacket made of sandiath skin. It was a Haroun favorite, because it wicked away perspiration, yet was remarkably waterproof.

She broke her fast with porridge, and when she stepped outside, she found Bedistai waiting at the door with Chawah and another endath he called Chossen. She had never seen an endath and had only heard of them in tales, so she regarded the creatures with amazement at first, then with caution, for she found their size intimidating. Still, they seemed friendly enough, almost affectionate, and with Bedistai's help she was soon astride Chossen and ready to embark.

As he completed their preparations, securing the last bag in place, Darva noticed they were bringing very little.

"Is this all we're taking?" she asked, studying what was hanging from the cantle of the oddly elongated saddle.

"This is all we will need for now," he replied. "I will gather more as we require."

He offered nothing further by way of explanation, but when she considered how well he had cared for her, she decided to leave any further questions unasked.

"You should go now," Salmeh urged, looking anxiously beyond the village.

"Do not fear, Mother. The strangers will not harm Mostoon," Bedistai said. "They will know we have gone the moment we depart. They have come for Darva and want nothing else. Besides ..." He raised his hand and halted Salmeh's protest before she could voice it. "They are too greatly outnumbered. They will find pursuing the two of us far more attractive than a direct assault on the village."

"I don't understand. How will they know you are gone?" Salmeh asked.

"Do you remember the story of Assan Bey?"

She paused to consider the question, then changed her expression. The cryptic reply seemed to satisfy her, because she pursed her lips, smiled thinly, and nodded.

"Do you think that is why they have come?"

"I do," he replied.

"Then go while there is still time. If you are right, they will indeed follow."

As he reined his own endath around, Salmeh bade him farewell.

"Take care, my son. I love you."

He turned in the saddle.

"I love you too, Mother," he said, adding, "I will return before Jadon has circled Mahaz."

It was a reference to the binary suns: Mahaz, the orange giant, and its companion, the hot white dwarf, Jadon.

As the endaths broke into a canter, Darva found herself leaving with scarcely time to thank Salmeh or to say a proper goodbye. She settled into the saddle and was immediately taken by the comfort of the ride. The jarring gait of a horse, the steed she knew best, would have drained all her energy over the course of even a healthy day as she leaned and braced against every jolt. Perched atop this endath, however, she was as relaxed as she would have been on a sofa. She was barely aware of Chossen's footfalls or its body's articulations, and she decided she might manage the journey after all.

They were soon beyond Mostoon's limits, out upon the

Expanse, a terrain unlike any she knew. And though she was out of her element, not yet recovered and uncertain how she would fare, she still believed the journey should be hers alone.

"Bedistai," she asked, "are you sure you should be leaving, instead of staying behind to help?"

"Mostoon is well defended. I doubt they will have any trouble with the strangers, and your departure will give our pursuers reason to pass them by."

"But how will they know we have gone?"

"The same way they knew you were there."

"Is that what you meant when you referred to the story of ... What did you call it ...? Assan Bey?"

But his attention had shifted. He was looking into the distance, scouting for something, she thought, so for the moment she decided not to press. They were on their way and she was grateful for it.

CHAPTER SIX

They had traveled well beyond Mostoon's borders when Bedistai sat up in the saddle, craning his head and scanning the terrain.

"What's wrong? What are you looking for?"

"Riders," he said.

"What do you mean? Surely they haven't had time to circle your village."

"If there were but one group, no. But if I were after you and not looking for a fight, I would have split my party to improve my chances, especially if I had guidance. If I am right, we will encounter one of those parties soon. If I am wrong, the endaths will quickly outdistance them."

"Guidance? What kind of guidance are you talking about?"

"They arrived near Mostoon so soon after I found you, it was apparent they had not been searching very long. And Dorman, the boy who brought me the warning, told me they seemed certain you were living with us. They were acting as if they'd been told, in possession of details no stranger should have. They even went so far as to describe Salmeh's house."

"But who would have known I was with you? Your people would not have betrayed me, would they?"

"No, not the Haroun. The one who is helping is one of their own."

"One of ... How would any of them know? I don't understand."

"There is a tale, a rumor—I am surprised you haven't heard it—of people who can look into the minds of others. They are called thought gazers. The tale I referred to is such a story."

"Of course I have heard the stories. Everyone has. But you don't believe them, do you? They are children's tales."

"Until now, I have been very skeptical of mind readers, or at least the extent of their abilities, although endaths possess an awareness that strongly suggests that possibility. But tell me, if you were to deny the existence of such persons, what other reason could you offer that explains how they found you?"

"Well," she paused to consider. "None, really."

"So we must acknowledge the possibility."

Something caught Darva's attention. Her eyes turned from Bedistai and widened while her expression shifted from curiosity to alarm.

"Bedistai! Look."

They had ridden into the middle of a steeply walled ravine, when six mounted swordsmen appeared at the gorge's far end. The endaths reared onto their haunches, forelegs pawing at the interlopers, nearly unseating Darva as she clung to the saddle's pommel. Bedistai glanced back and saw four more behind them. Flanked by earthen walls, they were trapped by both riders and terrain.

"Let us have her, Haroun, and we will let you live," said one of the men in the forward group. When Bedistai was slow to respond, he added, "I won't ask twice."

Darva looked imploringly at Bedistai. "You don't have to do this," she said. "Save yourself."

He ignored her, turned sideways in the saddle, and with his hand on his knife, studied the groups before and behind them. Their horses were agitated, moving constantly, as if they might be easily spooked. And while a few of the riders exuded confidence, seeming eager to attack, others were clearly nervous despite their overwhelming number.

"I will not surrender her," Bedistai replied. "You will have to take her from me." He paused to emphasize his last three words. "If you dare."

"If we dare?" The one who had addressed him sounded incredulous. "If we dare?" He surveyed the men in his company. "There are ten of us. You number how many? One?" He laughed and a few of the riders joined him.

Bedistai did not answer, replying instead with a long steady gaze.

The speaker scowled and called one of the four at the rear.

"Cosmin!"

There was the rasp of steel as the rider unsheathed his sword. He gave a sudden cry and dug his spurs into his horse's flanks. With wide-open eyes and nostrils flaring, the beast hurled itself towards Bedistai and Darva. It had closed to within a few strides when Chawah's tail lashed out, striking the animal's neck and throwing it to the ground as effortlessly as one might swat an insect. The horse landed on its head and shoulder, and its body and legs flopped to the ground as if it were a rag doll. Chawah's tail swung the opposite direction and caught the dismounted rider as he was struggling to his knees. She flung him against the ravine's wall and Cosmin stuck for a second—mouth and eyes agape—before falling lifeless to the gully floor.

Darva cried out in alarm while Bedistai remained unperturbed, surveying the remaining marauders. The only other sounds were the wind across the canyon, the beat of horse hooves, and the jingle of bridles as the animals, threatening to bolt, jerked their heads against the reins.

The group's leader stared at the bodies, then lifted his head to study Bedistai. He turned to the five riding with him, tightened his mouth and raised his sword before shouting, "Get her!"

As one, the forward five drew their swords and spurred their horses. Their mounts gathered themselves, then broke into a gallop as Bedistai climbed into a crouch atop Chawah's back. When the lead horse approached where the endaths were standing, Bedistai hurled himself in an arching leap. He embraced the foremost rider and, as he dragged him from his saddle, Bedistai's hand went to his knife and backhanded the blade into the haunch of the second rider's horse. The beast bellowed in agony and stumbled to its knees, launching its rider forward and over its head.

Bedistai and the one he was holding tumbled to the ground. The man landed on his back with Bedistai atop him. Before the man could react, Bedistai delivered a head butt, tore the sword from his hand, and leapt to his feet.

The third horse, leaping over the one that had fallen, struck Bedistai as it passed. Thrown against the side of the ravine, Bedistai dropped the sword he had taken. Then, when he arrested his fall, he recovered it and glanced up at Darva. She was still atop Chossen, but the rider whose horse had collided with him had a hand on her leg and was trying to unseat her. Since Chossen's height put Darva above him, she brought her knee to her chest, kicked hard, and drove her heel into his face. Two more kicks unseated him. Before he could rise, Bedistai arrived beside him and clove the man in two.

A fourth rider was reaching for Chossen's reins. As the endath backed away, Bedistai spun and backhanded his sword into the man's side. His victim halted, face filled with surprise, then fell to his knees as he grasped at the gaping wound.

The rider who had catapulted from his horse was shaking his head as he rose to his feet. When his face sobered and his eyes regained focus, he pointed his sword and ran at Bedistai, attempting to impale him.

Turning in time to see the man coming, Bedistai arched his torso and avoided being skewered. He bellowed at his attacker and parried the strokes that followed. As his fury grew, his blade clashed ever louder, until one strike flung his opponent's sword into the air.

The two stood, staring, panting hard. Without further preamble, Bedistai buried his blade in the man's belly.

The fifth rider leapt from his horse onto Bedistai, knocking him to the ground. They landed hard, the rider atop him, and the horseman began delivering punches to Bedistai's head. Raising both arms in defense, Bedistai seized the man's wrists. When his assailant attempted a head butt, Bedistai jerked his own aside. Planting his palm against the attacker's face, Bedistai curled his fingers into the man's eyes. Jerking away, but remaining astride him, the assailant unsheathed his knife and stabbed at Bedistai's head. The Haroun caught his wrist, and with his free hand punched the man's side until ribs broke and pain halted the assault.

Bedistai shoved him aside, just as another took hold of his feet and tugged. Bedistai snatched the knife from the fallen man's hand, and without looking to see who was pulling, kicked hard and connected. Drawing his feet towards his buttocks, Bedistai sat upright.

The bloody face before him belonged to the first rider, the one he had dragged from the saddle. Bedistai kicked with his right foot and his heel broke the man's nose. He kicked again with such force that it toppled the man onto his back. The man's arms flopped like a rag doll's. His chest rose and fell twice before it stilled. The remaining assailant threw himself onto Bedistai. With no more patience to waste on this struggle,

Bedistai returned the knife he had taken, burying its blade in its owner's chest, then climbed to his feet and looked about for the rest.

The endaths were thrashing their tails to fend off the rearward three. He sought out the commander, and saw him still mounted on his horse, scowling and staring, appraising the one who had defeated his entire company. Abruptly, the man wheeled his mount and spurred it to a gallop. When he had disappeared into the brush, Bedistai turned to deal with the trio at his rear, only to find they were gone as well.

"Bedistai! Are you all right?" asked Darva as she climbed from the saddle.

"I'm fine."

"No," she insisted as she dropped to the ground. "You're hurt." She ran up to him and placed her hands on either side of the crimson streaming from his belly. "We have to take care of this."

"It appears worse than it is. It's a shallow cut. I have some medicine in my bags."

Darva looked at the bodies. "Are they all dead?"

Bedistai nodded.

"Then maybe we will be safe," she suggested. "Maybe they will leave us alone."

"I doubt it. They will follow at a distance, hoping to come upon us while we sleep."

"What will we do? We have to sleep."

"We will sleep while we ride," he said. When she gave an uncomprehending look, he explained. "I will show you how to secure yourself to the saddle. The endaths will outpace them and by morning we will arrive in Meden."

CHAPTER SEVEN

For the remainder of the morning, Darva napped in the saddle. When she awoke, she assured Bedistai she felt confident she could see the journey through. To while away the hours, Bedistai told tales of his people's history and their relationship with the land, so that, for a while, she was able to forget the urgency of their mission. One matter nagged, however, so eventually she felt compelled to ask, "I am sorry, Bedistai, but aren't we going the wrong direction? Unless I am mistaken, we are riding to the east and Liad-Nur lies south of here."

"We are indeed, and so we will continue for the rest of the day. Only by morning will we be able to change direction." As he spoke, the endaths ascended a rise and Bedistai gestured to their right. "Behold our obstacle, the river Em."

She followed his hand and her eyes and mouth fell open.

"Darmaht protect me! I had no idea. I had always heard ..." But her voice trailed off without completing the sentence as she took in its magnificence.

Its roar had been with them longer than she could say, but the terrain had always concealed it from view. Now, however, as they crested this rise, the fabled river displayed its fury. Its waters were brown with the mud and silt it had gouged from the countryside and the torrent churned white with spume. At this point, as it coursed between its banks, the Em stretched nearly three hundred yards from shore to shore.

"By the time it reaches the sea, it will be six times as wide, a full mile in breadth," he said.

Darva was amazed. "I can't imagine how we will ever cross it."

"You may not remember, but you crossed it before you entered No'eth. In fact, by land there is no other way from the south. Your cart clearly could not have managed such a difficult transit, so I suspect your party traversed it at the foot of the Tairenth Mountains, nearer its source, where the Em is quite narrow and tame. Fortunately for us, we will not have to travel that far out of our way. The place I have in mind, though quite wide, is shallow enough for the endaths, and the waters are somewhat quieter. The crossing, while difficult, will bring us into Meden days sooner than the route you took, although it is also where our journey will become dangerous."

"Wait. You mean we will not cross into Limast?"

"No. And I must tell you that is why Orr will never realize his ambition. Limast cannot be conquered from the north for the same reason No'eth has never been conquered from the south." He gestured at the river. "Nor do I think No'eth will ever be taken by Monhedeth, although for an entirely different reason." Darva shook her head and furrowed her brow, so he explained, "Look behind you at the terrain we have crossed."

She turned in the saddle to see.

"It's very rough," she remarked.

"So rough no army could ever see whom they were attacking, nor keep track of its own force's locations. And that is why I believe that Orr is a fool. He can never have what he has been promised, and if only he took the time to think, he would realize it. As it is, greed dominates his thoughts and enables Hath to use him."

"But were he to capture Meden, he could then attack Limast. It's on the same side of the river."

"The Em would still be an obstacle. Even at the place I have in mind, it cannot be crossed except slowly and with great care. A small force situated on the opposite shore could easily cut down advancing troops before they could reach them. Further, it would be nearly impossible to maintain supply lines over the distances involved, especially across No'eth where there is no easy road."

"He is a fool then," she said.

"Yes, and an easy pawn. I suspect, should he realize he is being used, he will react with all the irrational anger such individuals inevitably bring with them. Fools are dangerous."

"How long do you think it will take us to reach Liad-Nur?" Darva asked.

Bedistai turned in the saddle and thoughtfully appraised her. "You look well. Your skin has good color and you sit upright with ease. I would have thought you would have required more time to recover, so it is good you have come this far so soon.

"Ordinarily, in more peaceful times, we could complete our journey in little more than a week, probably in as few as eight days, depending on how long you could ride each day and provided we rode only by day. An endath can travel much faster than a horse, certainly faster than ox in harness. These days, however, there is no telling what obstacles or dangers we might encounter along the way, so I cannot venture a guess. Let us hope the road is neither too long nor fraught with too much danger."

"Bedistai, I see riders again," she pointed. "Oh! They just disappeared below a rise."

"I suspected they would follow. But since they will need to stop and sleep, by morning we will have left them far behind."

"Won't that put too much strain on Chawah and Chossen?"

"They don't need sleep the way we do," he replied. "Even now, at the end of the day, I think we can manage to put more distance between ourselves and our pursuers." He patted his endath's neck, leaned forward and said, "Chawah, let's make the horses work to keep up."

She turned her head, gave a snort of understanding, and moved quickly into the trough below the rise. Chossen followed with no apparent prompting. Now they were moving much faster than before, and as her endath gradually caught up and drew alongside, Darva was smiling broadly.

"My!" she exclaimed. "I didn't realize they were so quick."

"They have not even begun to reach their ultimate pace," he replied.

"And mine didn't even require coaxing to follow you."

"As I said before, we believe these wonderful creatures are empathic. Time after time, they seem to understand us without our indicating what we want."

"So, they read our minds?"

"No. I don't believe they are telepathic—nothing that direct or literal—but they are sensitive to our desires."

"If you don't mind, may I ask one more thing?"

Bedistai laughed. "This is going to be a long ride. If you don't ask questions, we will have little to talk about. Of course, you may ask. What do you wish to know?"

"Earlier, you said that you and Chawah had taken care of each other all of your lives. Is that really true? I mean, how long have you two been together?"

Before he answered, Bedistai stroked the endath affectionately. "We have been together a long, long time. Haven't we, girl?"

Chawah tossed her head, snorted, and flicked her tail, and Darva laughed at the apparent acknowledgement.

"The Haroun and the endaths have enjoyed an enduring

symbiotic association for as long as anyone can remember. We are the only people who hold such a relationship with them. Perhaps it is because they know how much we respect living things that they trust us as they do. But don't misunderstand. We have not domesticated endaths as people have domesticated oxen and cattle. It is entirely because they choose to engage in this relationship that it exists at all. They are not under our control. We are friends."

And though Darva regarded him askance, having difficulty with the concept that these beasts might have a conscious role in their relationship, he went on.

"Every spring, about the time our children reach their seventh year, our parents take us to a special place, a large clearing halfway between Mostoon and Lake Ossan. Children from all the villages converge in this place. We know when the day arrives, not by any calendar nor astrological event. We simply know when the time has come. When we arrive, the endaths will have brought their young to the clearing as well." When he saw the question that was forming on her lips, he explained, "This has happened since we began to count time. No one can say when or how it began. It simply is."

"Once all are assembled, the endaths step back from their young and the Haroun from theirs. It is then that the children begin to circulate among each other. Gradually, over the course of the day, the Pairing occurs."

"So you, along with all the other boys, were paired by your parents with the endaths they ride" Darva suggested.

He shook his head.

"Your statement implies two errors in your reasoning," Bedistai said. "First, it is not just male children who are brought to the Pairing. Our girls participate fully. Salmeh, my mother, was one of the finest riders in her younger days. She participated in many hunts. Although hunting is primarily a man's activity, in our culture, we do not distinguish between which activities a woman or a man may participate. While men and women tend to gravitate to certain activities—a man's greater strength lending itself to the hunt, a woman's greater emotional sensitivity, coupled with her biological role, better suiting her to the task of caretaker—if an individual's skills and desire set him or her on a nontraditional path, then he or she is free to pursue it. For example, as you saw earlier, while we generally rely on our men to defend our land from invaders, throughout our history certain women have also risen to the call. Over the years there have been many famous women warriors."

Then, returning to his point, he said, "The second error is that you imply we choose the endath with which we will pair. That is simply untrue. At my Pairing, I had my eye on another, a male. But Chawah kept interceding, placing herself between the two of us. She had determined I was to be the one for her, and eventually the male moved off and I also relented. We have been together ever since."

Darva considered this declaration for a moment, then offered, "But then there are obviously endaths, like Chossen, who are never paired."

"No. All endaths are eventually paired with a Haroun."

"Then, where is Chossen's rider?"

At this question, Chossen became momentarily agitated. Her tail thrashed and she bobbed her head up and down.

"He was killed during a hunt three years ago. Like many, Chossen is now alone."

"Will she not pair again?"

"No. It is once and for life. There is never a second Pairing. When an endath's Pair dies or is killed, the endath grieves for a year or longer. Afterwards, the others of its species take care of it. Endaths are social creatures and can never live alone. Occasionally, however, a need arises for a riderless one to carry someone, such as now. When it became apparent you would need one of them to carry you, I asked all of the riderless if any would consent to help. After a few days, Chossen came forth. She considered you carefully and found you acceptable."

Darva's eyes opened wide as she regarded Chossen.

"We never compel them to do anything to which they do not consent. She does not carry you by chance. You were chosen," he said. "This is no small undertaking. By so agreeing, she has consented to give her life for you, should the need arise."

Darva looked at the endath in silence. After a very long minute, she said, "Thank you, Chossen."

In response, the endath tossed her head and flicked her tail.

CHAPTER EIGHT

They awoke at dawn and dismounted. Bedistai prepared a fireless repast to avoid alerting their pursuers to their location. Even so, he suspected Orr's men already knew. When they had finished eating, they mounted again and turned towards the river.

"Darmaht protect me!" Darva swore when they arrived at its bank. "You don't mean you intend to cross it here."

Her eyes were wide as she looked to Bedistai for reassurance. While calmer here than when she had first seen it, the Em was by no means tame.

"There is no other crossing for another day's journey east. And while an endath can manage here, if it is careful, no horse can ford waters this deep. If we hope to find rest, we must cross now."

"I don't know if I can do it, Bedistai."

"You don't have to."

Darva sighed.

"Chossen will do it for you."

Clearly, that was not what she had intended, and she looked about as if for assistance or for another way to present itself.

Finding none, she turned to Bedistai and he began instructing her.

"Hold the pommel firmly while you cross and don't look at the water."

"Where else can I look?"

"Fix your eyes on the opposite shore."

"I think I will close them."

"No. You will need all of your balance every moment. Keep them open and stay alert."

"But Chossen's gait is so smooth."

"This is different. This is not dry land."

She suspected he was not simply stating the obvious. Although she did not like to consider what might cause the ride to roughen, a stumble perhaps, she swallowed and nodded grimly.

"All right," she said, resigning herself to what lie ahead. "Let's go."

Again without a prompt, the endaths moved forward. When Chawah stepped into the water she reared onto her hind legs for an instant, startled by the cold, then settled down. Chossen hesitated when she saw her reaction, but as Chawah proceeded, she followed cautiously. Every step for the beasts became tentative, as they placed their feet onto an unseen bottom. They craned their heads, looking in vain where the next step would take them.

This is very different, thought Darva. *Very different, indeed.*

Midway across, the waters had become so deep her feet became soaked. And while the endaths were not swimming, they were struggling hard against the current. The water roared past, brown and muddy, and waves broke against the animals' flanks, bursting into spray. Each beast's wake was a swirling white eddy, furiously streaming away with the current.

Darva's hands ached. She was holding the saddle so tightly her knuckles had become the color of the foam. Furthermore, her injury was not yet healed, and she wondered how well her right hand could hold if it had to. She could hear nothing above the waters and she knew, if she needed to call out to Bedistai, her words would be lost in the tumult.

Without warning, Chossen lurched forward. All but her head, neck and saddle were submerged.

"Chossen!" cried Darva, her voice all but wiped away by the wind and water's roar.

With powerful lurching efforts, the endath struggled to find bottom. Darva clung to the pommel, desperate to keep her seat. It was all she could do to hang on with her left hand and thighs as Chossen nearly tumbled onto her side, fighting against the current to maintain balance. Stretching her neck against the direction of the fall and thrashing her tail violently, the endath righted herself and continued her battle against the river. Darva gripped with her legs and hugged Chossen's back with her body, clinging to the saddle, ignoring the pain in her hand.

"You can do it," Darva shouted to be heard. "You can do it. Don't give up."

By now they had drifted far downstream from Bedistai and Chawah. The river had deepened so much that Chossen had long since lost her ability to walk and was swimming hard for the opposite shore. Ahead, the land streamed past with ever increasing speed because the Em had narrowed and deepened, its waters churning with increasing violence. And though the bank grew nearer with each of the endath's strokes, Darva worried if the beast could hold out. Chossen's neck bobbed hard with every effort and she had begun using her tail to propel herself forward. Darva could not remember ever hearing Chossen breathing, even as she had sped ahead of their pursuers. Now her breaths came in deep rumbling gasps, audible over the crash of the waves and the roar of the wind.

Just when Darva believed this creature could go no farther, Chossen rounded up and rose above the wave tops, climbing onto a shallowing patch of river bottom. With terrific heaving efforts that threatened to throw Darva from her back, Chossen fought for foothold after hard-gained foothold. Sensing how near the beast was to success, yet how close she was to defeat, Darva urged her to fight onward. In response, Chossen fought ever harder, until she was standing knee-deep, dry land only a few yards away.

As Chossen climbed onto shore, Darva could feel the animal's exhaustion. Her sides moved in deep, heaving breaths and she trailed her tail in the water, rather than extending it parallel to the ground as she was accustomed. When she finally arrived on dry land, Chossen halted, gasping, reluctant to take another step.

"You did it, girl," Darva said. She shook out her hand, then patted and stroked the endath's shoulder. "Thank you. You saved us both."

Chossen snorted weakly, then began walking upstream to join Chawah and Bedistai.

CHAPTER NINE

Bedistai and Darva agreed to proceed with less urgency until Chossen had recovered, and for a time, events cooperated.

After the crossing, they arrived on new terrain, passing from No'eth's jumble onto Meden's fertile plains which spread flat and unbroken, seemingly forever. Here, in times of peace, the rich alluvial soil had supported abundant harvests. All manner of crops had been produced in this region, making it one of the wealthier lands. Now, however, in this time of war, Meden had become a sought-after prize. Whoever captured and held it would also acquire its hills and mountains where, in their southernmost reaches, mines delivered up precious metals and gemstones.

They struck out across the fallow farmland, hoping to turn the level terrain to their advantage and to put as much ground behind them as possible. There was no cover here, and though the mountains far to the east, in Miast, might have helped conceal their progress, they were another day out of their way. Also, because of the rough terrain, the going would have been slower. Here, although exposed and vulnerable,

Bedistai and Darva were making excellent time. Chossen showed signs she was recovering, so without being prodded, the endaths strode effortlessly across the fields at a pace horses could only replicate at a gallop. The land and the hours flew by and the two did not pause but once to take time to eat.

Eventually, however, Meden would present new problems since, unlike No'eth, this land was at war. Columns of smoke in the distant west served as reminders of the conflicts raging around them. And though the land through which they coursed presented a face of peace and tranquility, they were not deceived. Still, if it struck either of them as curious that they had thus far encountered no troops, neither mentioned it.

They spent the night in an abandoned barn, and in the morning set off again, barely allowing time for breakfast or conversation. As they rode, the fields became an expansive valley surrounded by low-lying hills.

By the time evening was near, Bedistai led them up a hill to its crest. Once atop, they were able to view the next stretch of their journey. The scene below was not promising. Companies of troops were traversing the plain before them, moving from the west to the east. Numbering in the hundreds, perhaps even thousands, there was no single body, nor was there any urgency to their step.

Darva leaned onto the pommel and watched the seemingly endless parade. After several minutes, she turned to Bedistai and asked, "Is there some other way around?"

He shook his head.

"I don't believe so. My guess is they are returning to either Yeset, Meden, or Miast after battling with Limast. No banners identify them, so I cannot determine their origin with certainty. Still, they are moving without haste. If they were mounting an attack, they would be in formation and their pace would be urgent. These men appear to be tired and going home. I expect we will encounter many more, both to the west towards Limast, as well as towards the east."

"Then, tired as they are, they should pose us no danger," Darva suggested.

"On the contrary," he replied. "They will automatically distrust anyone they do not know. Their first reaction will be to take us as prisoners until they can determine who we are and the nature of our mission. If we do not allow this—and we will not—their second reaction will be to kill us. They must assume we are enemies."

"If that is the case, do we wait for them to pass?"

"If we knew when that would be, it might be an option. But remember, not only does your brother need us, but we are still being followed, or we should assume that we are."

"I don't see how we can manage. There are so many, and you could not begin to fight them all."

"We have endaths. That alone gives us a tremendous advantage." She tossed him a skeptical glance, so Bedistai explained. "You must have noticed the unusual shape of your saddle by now."

"Yes," she answered. "It is unusually long. I assume endaths carry two or three riders on occasion."

"The saddles are indeed long but for a very different reason. When we descend into the plain, you will be riding far faster than you have ever experienced and Chossen will maneuver far more abruptly than any horse you have ridden. If you are upright, she will hurl you from her back when she turns. So you will ride prone, with your body pressed tight against her. You will also insert your feet into the rear set of stirrups all the way to their arches and extend your legs to the rear, pressing hard."

He ignored the puzzled look she gave him, asking instead, "Do you see the strap which runs around her chest at the front of the saddle?"

Darva looked down, then nodded.

"You will run your forearms under it, so it secures them, and you will grasp the pommel firmly with both hands. In this manner, you will be secured to her back."

"But, how will I see?"

"That is unimportant," he replied.

Darva didn't like what he was telling her.

"Chossen will not allow herself to be caught," he explained. "In fact, it is of the utmost importance you give Chossen her head. If you aren't sure you can do this, then drop the reins altogether. You must allow her absolute freedom."

Darva opened her mouth to object, but Bedistai interrupted.

"You must trust me in this."

"I don't understand. This is contrary to everything I have ever been taught. At a gallop, the rider crouches forward, standing in the stirrups on the balls of her feet with her knees bent. She never drops the reins."

Losing patience, but trying to maintain his calm, Bedistai explained, "That is because a horse's gallop is jarring. One absorbs the impact with one's knees. An endath's stride produces no shock whatsoever. Further, a horse is an incredibly stupid beast compared with these creatures. One needs reins to control it. By the end of this ride, however, you will come to believe that Chossen is every bit as smart as you are, maybe smarter."

Chossen tossed her head, as though to agree. Darva smiled but resolutely clung to the reins, clearly torn between a lifetime of experience and what he was now instructing her to do. For the first time since she had known him, Bedistai showed real anger.

"Drop the reins," he ordered.

Still reluctant, Darva held on.

"I said drop them!"

He had never spoken harshly before. Caught by surprise, Darva complied.

"Now, insert your feet into the stirrups as I instructed."

Although distrustful, she obeyed.

"Now, run your arms under the strap and grasp the pommel."

She did this too, extending herself forward until she was lying flat atop Chossen's back.

"Extend your legs rearward until you are pinioned fore and aft."

Only when she had done so, was Bedistai pleased.

"Now you are secure. We ride!" Then, to his own mount, he called, "Chawah! Forward."

CHAPTER TEN

As the Haroun assumed an identical posture, Chossen turned down the grassy slope, accelerating effortlessly to a pace Darva had never experienced nor imagined. This time she followed Chossen's lead, and it seemed as though there were no upper limit to what was possible. They were moving at easily twice the speed she had ever experienced on a horse. Now thrice that. Now more. Darva was nearly breathless as the ground rushed beneath and behind her into the distance. Never in her life had she traveled at such velocity and she realized Bedistai had been right. Aside from the undulation of Chossen's back muscles, there were none of the jolts she would have expected on a horse, merely the soft thuds of Chossen's feet and no other sensation than speed.

They descended into the valley and it was not long before certain soldiers became aware of their approach. A cry went up and every helmet turned in their direction. Every weapon was raised. The warriors no longer appeared weary, but seemed ready and willing to do whatever was necessary to thwart the unknown riders.

The endaths were hurtling towards a space in the field

where the fewest soldiers were amassed. As they ate up the intervening ground and the troops moved laterally to close the gaps between them, Darva began to doubt they could escape either capture or death. While the animals raced forward, rapidly closing the distance between, the soldiers closed ranks to form a nearly unbroken line.

It was then, when the endaths were almost on top of them, both creatures turned sharply right in unison, so abruptly that, although Darva gripped the pommel with all her strength, the maneuver almost tore her from the saddle.

The soldiers were becoming a blur, and Darva gasped as, suddenly, and once more in unison, the endaths executed another abrupt turn, this time to their left. They broke through a gap in the line and for the moment were in the clear.

She glanced around, trying to locate Bedistai and found him and Chawah beside her and to her right. All around, soldiers were scrambling, raising weapons and positioning themselves to intercept them.

Directly ahead, another body of troops was amassing, as orders Darva could not understand were being issued. Archers at the front of the formation had dropped to a crouch, nocking arrows to bows, while lancers and soldiers with battle-axes stood poised behind them.

At the first volley of arrows, Chossen swung left. Darva glanced everywhere, but could not locate Chawah. Looking over her shoulder, down the length of her torso, she was dismayed to see Bedistai and his endath disappear into the distance. The beasts had turned in opposite directions, and Darva's heart sank. But with soldiers maneuvering to intercept her, there was no time for regret; all the while Chossen was scrambling, continuing to evade them.

As the endath passed one group, she suddenly accelerated, and a volley of arrows sailed just behind. Just as abruptly, she dug her feet into the soil. Coming almost to a halt, she turned sharply left towards the archers. At the instant she veered, a second volley passed close enough for Darva to hear their hisses. Chossen wailed. Darva realized, had Chossen not braked, then turned as she had done, the salvo would have killed them.

Once again, the endath hurtled towards the soldiers and Darva gripped the pommel, trying to prepare for whatever this wondrous beast might do next. One minute they were nearly on top of a group and the next, while the archers were drawing shafts from their quivers, they were soaring above them. Chossen's speed provided great aerial velocity and she landed well to their rear, somehow absorbing much of the impact when she contacted the ground.

The landing was not entirely without effect, however, and though Darva's strapped forearms prevented an aerial launch over Chossen's neck and head, she had forgotten Bedistai's caveat to tension herself with her feet. As a result, the impact freed both her feet from the stirrups, leaving only her hands and forearms to hold her in place.

They had passed through the force's main body whose numbers, by now, were diminishing. Even so, she and her steed were by no means in the clear. Realizing that Chossen's next turn or leap would surely eject her, Darva fumbled to locate a stirrup. The instant before the endath maneuvered to avoid another group, she found it and inserted her left foot.

Anticipating the turn, she pressed her leg rearward, and by sheer dint of luck was able to remain in the saddle. Had the endath turned left instead of right, she realized, she would have been tossed.

No more could she rely on good fortune. Consequently, when Chossen's course straightened, Darva hunted for the stirrup's pair. She smiled when her fingers found it swaying gently below her right foot. Had she been on a horse, it would have been bouncing and flailing madly. Now, however, thanks to

Chossen's gait and its lack of concussion, her foot found it easily and she was secure again in seconds. Able now to brace against whatever maneuver might come next, she vowed never again to repeat that mistake.

Eventually, she and her endath left the army behind. As they began to ascend from the valley into the surrounding hills, Chossen's pace slowed and Darva once again assumed an erect seat in the saddle.

In the valley below, the neat lines of troops were already disassembling into the less orderly array she had seen at the outset. They were making no obvious signs they intended to pursue, so Darva sighed in relief, then caught her breath.

Where was Bedistai?

She rose in her stirrups and scanned the terrain for any evidence where Chawah might be, but there was no sign of her. The meandering soldiers and their lack of urgency were certain indications that Bedistai had vanished. Darva was alone now, alone in a land at war. Nonetheless, she still possessed a purpose. She would return to her brother regardless of the cost. Instead of panicking over her new situation, it was exhaustion that overtook her, and her body sagged. Not caring where she was or where the endath was taking her, she lay back in the saddle and let Chossen set their course.

Chossen found a way up, into and between the hills, following a ravine that wound through groves of damass trees. She ascended ever upwards, until the ravine joined a gulley through the center of which ran a brook. The endath, likely thirsty by now, slowed to a walk, approached the water, and halted at its edge. Before drinking, Chossen paused and looked back over her shoulder.

Darva smiled.

"You're right, Chossen. How rude of me," she said and slipped from her back. "You've been carrying me long enough."

Once Darva had alighted, the endath knelt by the stream

and consumed gallons of water. Dusk was approaching and though the surrounding hills concealed the suns, Darva surmised from the sky's deep green coloration that Jadon had already set, and before long Mahaz would follow suit. With no small appreciation of how Chossen had saved them, she stroked the endath's flank.

"Thank you," she said.

With a hand on her protector's hide, she began circling the animal to examine her.

She is smarter than I, Darva thought.

Following the contours of the endath's body, she ran her hand from Chossen's haunch, past her flank and ribs, to her shoulder. When she reached Chossen's chest, about to turn away and get a drink for herself, she noticed a purple patch she was certain hadn't been there earlier. In fact, she did not recall either animal displaying any distinguishing marks. So, trying not to disturb Chossen as she drank, she moved to a point where she could see better.

"Mastad!" she gasped. Placing both hands over her mouth, she stepped back into the water. There was a gash across the chest with blood seeping from it, sheeting in a swath down her breast. "Chossen. What happened?"

In fact, Darva knew very well what had happened. She had heard her bellow the instant she had avoided the arrows. At the time the shriek had been meaningless. Now, she recognized it for a cry of pain. Chossen had avoided death perhaps, but not injury.

Darva gathered her wits. Her friend was hurt. As Chossen finished drinking, Darva came closer. In the fading light, she tried to assess the wound's depth. The blood made it difficult to determine how grave it was, so she decided to wash it clean.

"Hold still, Chossen. I need to do this," she said, hoping the endath would understand.

She squatted, scooping a handful of water from the brook,

and placed her cupped hand against the gash. A quiver ran through Chossen, but the endath held still.

"I know it is cold, but the water will help."

She took another handful, then another and another, all the while speaking soft words of comfort. As the water thinned the blood, the extent of the injury became clearer. It was a long gash, running almost the entire breadth of Chossen's breast. While it didn't appear to be deep enough to be life threatening, the bleeding continued.

After a while, Chossen backed away, as though sensing Darva's ministering was futile. She strode to a place a short distance from the stream, where she reclined beneath a damass tree's gray-green boughs.

Darva had no idea what more she could do. She had no medicines, no bandages, nothing whatsoever with which to alleviate the endath's discomfort. She would have cried, but she felt doing so would indicate she had given up. So, as darkness closed in around them, she placed her arms around Chossen's neck and pressed her cheek against it. Then, as night descended, she offered silent prayers her friend would be all right.

CHAPTER ELEVEN

A forceful shaking woke her. Half asleep, Darva placed her palms on the ground to either side of her, hoping the act might quell the disturbance. She opened her eyes and tried to focus, while her sleep-muddled brain struggled to determine the cause of the tremors. Then, as her head cleared, she understood.

"Chossen!" she cried as she sprang to her feet and turned to see.

The endath was shivering uncontrollably. Her entire body trembled, convulsing with intermittent shudders. Darva had no idea how long she had been like this, and though she would have been as helpless during the night as she found herself now, by light of day, she felt overwhelming guilt at having slept while her friend had lain suffering.

She dropped to her knees and examined Chossen's breast. The entire area surrounding the wound was discolored and swollen. She did not know what she might do to help, but it occurred to her to look through the saddlebags. To her dismay, all her rummaging produced were packages of food. She would want sustenance later, but at this moment, food was the last thing she required.

There must be something I can do, she thought, *but what?*

An idea came to her. It wasn't much, but it was something. She untied a saddlebag and emptied it, whereon she carried it to the brook. She immersed it, filling it with water, all the while hoping the leather would not leak. When she withdrew it, she was relieved to see the bag retained most of its contents. She hurried back and Chossen sniffed the offering, then swallowed the contents with a single gulp. Tears welled in Darva's eyes and she smiled at having done something useful. She ran back and refilled it, making several trips before Chossen turned her head, indicating she had drunk her fill.

Next, Darva set about releasing the bridle and saddle, as well as the one remaining bag. There was no need for Chossen to be encumbered. After she had done everything she could think of to ease the animal's discomfort, there was nothing left to do but sit by her friend, stroke her, and speak words of comfort. Chossen continued shivering while Darva prayed she would not die.

She had been sitting thus for more than an hour when she thought she heard a voice. A gentle breeze had arisen and had set the leaves to rustling, so she could not be certain. Since her legs and feet had grown numb, she decided it would be wise to restore sensation in the event she needed to move quickly. With a gasp, she stood upright, wincing as blood began to course through her veins. She stamped one foot, then the other, and flexed her toes until the tingling abated and she could move about with ease.

She listened again, but heard nothing. When she turned to regard her companion, she saw Chossen now lying with her head and neck extended. The endath had closed her eyes, so Darva despaired and began to cry.

She had been sobbing for several minutes when she heard

the voice again. She fought back her tears and quieted her breathing in order to listen. For the next several seconds nothing disrupted the stillness of the woods. She was about to dismiss the voice as a product of her imagination, when it arose again. It was a man's voice. It had grown louder and clearer and she worried who it might be until it called, "Darva!"

Borlon's eyes! she swore. *It sounds like ...*

"Darva!"

Bedistai!

"Bedistai! Bedistai!" she called.

Something crashed through the brush and branches parted. Chawah pushed through with the hunter riding on her back.

"How did you find us?" she cried as she ran to him.

"Chawah found you. Is everything all right?"

"No. No, it's not. Chossen is hurt," she answered, gesturing urgently towards the endath. "I'm afraid she's going to die."

At the sight of the ailing beast, Bedistai dismounted.

"What happened?"

"An arrow cut her across the chest. I tried to wash the wound, but when I woke up this morning, she was like this. I don't know what to do."

He regarded the endath. She was obviously distressed, but from where they were standing, her neck obscured her injury. He approached, uttering soft assurances. When he was standing beside her shoulder, he squatted and examined the wound. He shook his head.

"It's not good," he said.

He went to Chawah's side, opened a saddlebag, and produced a packet wrapped in leaves, as well as a shallow ceramic dish.

"Mother packed some medicine. The wrapping identifies it. It won't be enough, but it is a start. I want you to gather tinder."

"How will we light it?" she asked, standing frozen to the spot. "We have no spark stone."

"I can do it," he replied. "But we haven't much time. So, go. Find tinder and dried grass while I look for larger fuel."

Darva required no further prompting. In almost no time, her hands were full, and she returned to the clearing the moment Bedistai appeared with an armful of branches. Clearing a rough circle of earth with his foot, he dropped the wood at its edge and placed one piece in its center.

"Hold what you've gathered until I tell you otherwise," he ordered.

She nodded, and he rushed to where Chawah was standing. Bedistai retrieved his bow and arrows, then returned to the bare patch of earth. He squatted, setting the quiver and bow beside him. Unsheathing his knife, he grasped its hilt, pointing the blade downward, then pressed its tip against the heartwood where the piece had broken off in a wedge. Repeated twists produced a depression, after which, with a backhand flick of his wrist, he tossed the knife. As it flipped half a rotation, he seized the haft, this time holding the blade parallel to his thumb.

Drawing an arrow from the quiver, he severed the head from the shaft. Placing the arrowhead within easy reach, he whittled the shaft into a point and placed it beside its severed tip.

"May I have some dry grass?" he asked. "A small amount will do."

This he arranged around the hollow. Next, he reached for one of the branches he had set aside, simultaneously testing the edge of his knife with the thumb of his other hand. Satisfied with its sharpness, he began shaving off slices, so thin they curled as they fell. Once he had produced a few of these, he resheathed the blade and arranged the shavings around the grass.

Taking the bow, Bedistai flexed it and untensioned the

bowstring, unwinding it two turns at either end. He placed the arrow's shaft against the string and gave it a twist so the string encircled it midway along its length. He inserted the pointed end into the hole, removed one of his shoes, and with its sole protecting his left palm, he pressed the arrow into the hole in the heartwood. As he held the bow with his right hand, it looked to Darva as if he were holding some bizarre musical instrument.

Gradually, he tested the arrangement, moving the bow to and fro, spinning the arrow in the hollow, first one direction, then the other. Dissatisfied, he quickly rearranged the grass and shavings so that they encircled the arrow more closely. Then, he began bowing rapidly, spinning the arrow's shaft within the hole, creating heat with its friction. Ever faster he worked, his body bent to the task. The bow's great size would have made it unwieldy, were it not for Bedistai's strength.

Darva was fascinated. She had heard of this technique for fire-starting, but had never seen it applied. So, with more hope than skepticism, she wished for his success as drops of perspiration began to bead across his brow. She watched as Bedistai worked. His skin glistened and his muscles tensed as he concentrated on the hollow in the heartwood. Minutes passed as he labored. Then, at the moment she thought he must surely give up, a faint wisp of smoke began to curl up and away from the scraps. He continued in this manner for several more seconds, until gradually the smoke grew to a healthier plume. Then, he set aside these implements and, with care, to avoid undoing his accomplishment, he picked up the smoldering bundle of grass and shavings. Holding it between his fingers, he softly blew on it once, twice, three times. All at once, the bundle burst into flame. Carefully, lest he drop the precious packet, he replaced it on the wedge and added more shavings to the flame.

"Tinder," he said with urgency. "Small twigs."

She placed them onto his palm and he accepted them

without removing his eyes from the fire. One by one, he arranged them into a careful structure that surrounded and arched over the flame. They caught, and he demanded, "Branches."

Darva gave him the balance of her load. Once these were in place, he arose and gathered the larger pieces he had set by the circle. He placed some of them over the fire, arranging them to create a draft, before setting the rest nearby. Only now did he remove his eyes from the blaze. He retrieved the ceramic dish and leafy packet and handed them to her.

"Partially fill the dish with water and place it on the fire. I have arranged the branches to create a place on which to rest it."

He pointed.

"When the water begins to simmer, carefully remove it. You may need to use two pieces of wood so you can lift it without burning yourself or spilling it. When you've done so, add the contents of this package and mix them until you've created a thick paste. This you will work into Chossen's wound."

Darva nodded.

"I do not mean spread it over the wound," he said. "I want you to work it into the gash with your fingers."

Darva cringed. She was about to object when Bedistai said, "It will not be pleasant for either of you, but this you must do exactly as I instruct. It is important you work it into the places where the foul yellow discharge is forming."

She bit her lip and nodded.

"I am going to search for medicinal herbs. Don't let the fire die while I am gone."

"Won't someone see the smoke?"

"That is the least of our worries. Besides, while I was searching for you I spotted several cottages scattered throughout these hills. If anyone sees the smoke, perhaps they will believe it comes from one of their chimneys. In any case,

Chossen's life is my first concern. If I am fortunate and find something useful, we will need fire to make another poultice." He paused a moment, then insisted, "Do not allow it to die."

He was emphatic, as he spoke that final instruction.

"I will attend to it," she said. "How long do you think you will be gone?"

"I hope to return within the hour, but I cannot say for sure. It will take however long it does."

He retensioned the string and slung the bow and quiver over his shoulder. After pausing a moment to study the hills and the gully, he set off downstream, eyes scanning both the banks of the brook, as well as the groves of damass and barrel stave trees that filled the hollow.

Darva noticed that Chawah, on her own initiative, had moved to Chossen's side and had lain down beside her, lending her body's heat. It was comforting to see how one cared for the other. That, in turn, reminded her how remarkable a man Bedistai was. She was struck by how, on one hand, he could be such a fearsome fighter, yet on the other, he could be so caring and so tender. In this darkest hour, that thought evoked a smile.

She set about her task, going to the stream, then filling the dish before following the instructions Bedistai had given. She had never prepared a poultice before, but a life was at stake and she was determined she would complete this task correctly.

CHAPTER TWELVE

By all above us, what are those?"

Darva spun to face the intruder. She had been working the paste into Chossen's wound, with no thought to anything but the task she was performing. Caught unawares, she almost dropped the dish.

The speaker, she saw, was an elderly man. He was bearded, attired in a knitted cap and clothes of homespun wool. Leaning on a staff for support, he did not appear threatening. Nonetheless, she was wary.

"Who are you?" she demanded.

"I believe I might ask you the same," he replied. "After all, you are the stranger here."

"My name is Darva," she answered, deciding to reveal only what was necessary.

"I see." His gaze was on the beasts instead of her. "Well, that certainly tells me nothing." When she did not expand her response, he changed his approach. "Would you mind telling me what kind of creatures they are?"

"They are endaths."

"Endaths! I have heard of them, but have never laid eyes on

one." He drew nearer. "And what are you and your endaths doing in these woods?"

"This one is ill. I think she is dying and I am trying to save her."

The old man came within a few feet and studied the animals carefully. Pointing at Chossen, he observed, "It appears to have been injured."

"Yes, sir. She was."

"Would you mind telling me how that occurred? The wound looks nasty."

Darva hesitated, then decided he was only a local resident. He was certainly no soldier and she chided herself for considering, if only for a moment, that he might be a spy. In any case, there should be no harm in disclosing this much, provided she kept the conversation to a very narrow footing.

"She was grazed by a soldier's arrow."

"In that case, I'm not at all surprised she's doing poorly," the man said. "Many of them foul their arrow heads with filth so that, if they don't kill you outright, you will die nonetheless from the wound's contamination." He shook his head. "Poor beast. What are you doing to help her?"

"I washed her wound earlier and my companion gave me powder for a poultice. Now, I must figure out how to keep it in place."

The man nodded. "I see. And may I ask where your companion is now?"

"He has gone to gather herbs to prepare more medicine."

"Since he made the first preparation, I suppose he is knowledgeable in these matters," he suggested in an inquiring tone.

"He is a Haroun," Darva said, then wondered if she had volunteered too much.

The man grinned broadly and clapped his hands. "Ah! I should have guessed as much when you said these were endaths." He looked her up and down, adding, "Except for your complexion, your clothes say the same about you."

She decided not to respond.

"Well, he certainly will be knowledgeable, but I suspect he will not find all he is looking for on this side of the river."

"Why do you say that?"

"Medicinal herbs, like many other plants, are often found only within certain locales or specific environments. Just as this region is very different from No'eth, many of our herbs differ as well.

"As for your endath, she doesn't look well at all. I think it may take more than the small amount you've applied."

Darva nodded. "My companion said it wouldn't be enough."

"From the look of her wound, he is right. The preparation may not be strong enough, either. If you don't mind my telling you, I have something in my cottage which may serve the animal better. With your permission, I'll go fetch it."

"Please, sir. If you would," she said. "I will be most grateful."

He started to turn, but paused. "Your fire is dying. You will need to attend to it if we are to make use of the medicine upon my return."

She saw he was right. "Thank you. I had nearly forgotten."

The man gave her a kind look and suggested, "She will likely do better if you don't worry about her to the point of distraction. Pardon me if I tell you to keep your wits about you."

"Yes, sir. Thank you ..." She hesitated. "I'm sorry, but I don't know how to call you. What is your name?"

"Ah! Yes, I had forgotten. How rude of me. My name is Ruall."

"Thank you, Ruall."

"Don't mention it, ah ... Darva, is it?"

"Yes. My name is Darva. You have it right."

"Good. Now, don't you forget the fire. Keep it alive."

With that, he turned and walked away.

She watched him wend his way up the hill and into the trees. When he was gone, she placed more branches on the fire. Once it had grown into a healthy blaze, she returned her attention to the wound. Its discoloration was somewhat subsided, she thought, and the trembling not so severe. She considered she might be deceiving herself, but no matter. For better or worse she would do whatever she must, determined not to allow Chossen's condition to further overwhelm her.

Collecting her thoughts, she retrieved the saddlebag she had used earlier and refilled it. After Chossen had drunk her fill, she offered some to Chawah. To her disappointment, Chawah looked away, then rose to drink directly from the stream, perhaps to show she was quite capable of taking care of herself. After she had finished, she returned and settled once more beside Chossen.

Initially, Darva felt hurt, then decided her knowledge about endaths was too limited to allow any inference from Chawah's behavior. *After all*, she thought, *they are just animals.* Even so, she said, "Sorry, Chawah. I didn't mean to offend you."

When Chawah looked her way and tossed her head, Darva found herself smiling and was glad she still could. The old man's appearance was also reassuring. He seemed to possess knowledge Bedistai might lack, and she took comfort from the encounter.

CHAPTER THIRTEEN

D arva, who is this?"
    She smiled at Bedistai's voice. While she and
    Ruall were busy tending to Chossen, Bedistai had
come upon them unannounced.

"This is Ruall, Bedistai. He has been helping me."

Ruall turned to meet the new arrival. He arose slowly, and
his effort produced a groan.

"Mastad!" he swore. "These bones are unforgiving. Every
day becomes more difficult."

In obvious discomfort and with a hand on his hip, he drew
himself erect and studied Bedistai.

"From the look of you, young man, you won't understand my
complaint for many years to come. You must be the Haroun
this lovely lady has been telling me about."

Bedistai, in turn, scrutinized Ruall, whose patched clothing
and worn leggings bespoke a man of little means. He nodded
but chose not to comment, regarding the man with obvious
suspicion.

"Bedistai," said Darva, in an effort to break the tension, "it has only been a couple of hours, but Chossen already seems to have improved."

She gestured towards the animal and Bedistai turned to look. Although Chossen was still lying prone, her head was raised and her trembling had abated. Chossen returned Bedistai's gaze, and flicked her tail. Before approaching her, Bedistai took a moment to greet Chawah, who was still lying beside her wounded companion.

"Ho, Chawah. I see you've been concerned."

The endath returned his gaze, blinked slowly and deliberately.

"That is a good thing. I'm sure Chossen is the better for it."

Bedistai came nearer. When he was directly in front of Chossen, he squatted.

"I want to see how you are doing," he told her.

Taking her muzzle into his hands, he examined her eyes, then turned her head from side to side, carefully regarding it before placing his cheek against her nose, then upon her forehead. Chossen snorted forcefully through her nostril, as if to express discomfort at the proximity, but allowed him to continue his examination. He lifted her head so he could peer below her neck at her chest. He released her head, keeping one hand underneath it until it was clear she was supporting it on her own. Once her strength was apparent, he stood and moved along her neck until he could step between her forelegs. There he knelt and got onto his hands and knees. Leaning forward, he eyed the wound closely. He nodded once, then extended a hand and palpated the area around the gash.

Bedistai looked past his shoulder at Ruall and said, "This is good. She does not recoil from my touch and the swelling has begun to subside."

Rocking back onto his haunches, he wrapped an arm around her neck, partly for balance, but obviously to also express affection.

"I have never witnessed such a rapid turn for the better. What have you given her?"

The look of concern on Ruall's face, while he awaited Bedistai's verdict, softened a bit.

"I made a tea of wartwood, diamass, and greasebark. It took quite a bit of coaxing to get the poor beast to drink it. Thank the Powers she trusts this lady." He glanced at Darva, who smiled at the acknowledgement. "I don't think I could have gotten it down her on my own. I don't like the taste or smell of the stuff either, but it breaks a fever pretty quick. Helps an infection, too." Glancing at the bundle of foliage Bedistai had placed on the ground, he said, "It appears you've found something while you were away. What is it?"

"We call it witch's nettle. It is a very fine healing herb."

"I didn't think you would find much of anything you would recognize on this side of the river, especially this far south." Ruall scratched his head. "I've heard of it, but I'm surprised you found any. I didn't think it grew in these parts."

"The birds like its seeds," said Bedistai. "They help scatter it, and little by little, its range is increasing. Its stalk and root are the useful parts, should you wish to try working with it. When you forage, you'll find it growing on sunny slopes near running water."

"Thank you," Ruall replied. "You've taught me something I can use."

The exchange pleased Darva. Ruall's posture had relaxed and Bedistai also seemed more at ease.

"I want to tell you," the old man continued, "that normally I'm not the presumptuous sort, so I hope you don't mind my tending to your animal. I just couldn't see I had much choice, especially in view of how poorly she was doing."

"This is not my endath," said Bedistai. "She belongs to Darva. It was for her to decide, but I thank you for your kindness nonetheless.

"Darva," said Bedistai, turning towards her. "The poultice is starting to dry. If you can keep it moist and perhaps find a strip of fabric to wrap around it, the mixture will continue to benefit her."

"I brought back some cloth and a pot to boil it in," said Ruall. He pointed at the larger fire they had built. "I had to cut up a bed sheet to make strips large enough to wrap around the beast. The water should be boiling soon."

Bedistai nodded his approval. "You didn't have to destroy your possessions. Nonetheless, I am grateful."

"I thank you, too," added Darva.

"I must admit," Ruall said, "I wasn't thinking how I'd replace it when I cut it up. Even so, it's a small effort on my part."

When Ruall went to the fire to examine the pot, Bedistai asked in a quiet voice, "How did he come across you?" His voice carried a note of distrust.

"I ..." Darva paused to consider how he had happened on them, then answered, "I really don't know. One minute I was alone, tending to Chossen. The next he was here." Looking at Bedistai askance, she asked in a whisper, "You're not suggesting he means to harm us, are you? He's a harmless soul. That much should be obvious."

"These days, I question everyone. Appearances can be deceiving."

"By Borlon's eyes, I would have given you more credit than that. I would have thought you would have given me more credit as well." Unable to contain her indignation, she raised her voice. "I may not know the woods or herbs as do you, but I know people and I must tell you there is no deceit in his heart. He has not pried into our affairs and has only tried to help. How could you think of him so?"

Ruall glanced briefly over his shoulder, then pretended to ignore them.

"Until I know the man, almost as I know myself, I will not easily lend my trust," said Bedistai. He had opened his mouth to add something further, but he caught himself, then relented a bit. "He could be just as you say."

"No one could have known we would pass this way," Darva insisted, trying to lower her tone to something less audible. "Even we did not know until we found ourselves here."

"I agree. On the other hand, while he did not expect us, he may be hoping to better his lot by passing information to whichever warlord controls this region. I have known a few who play the friend quite convincingly while they scheme for better things. Further, poverty often leads to the kind of desperation that will push even an honest man to act as he might not in more fortunate times."

He appraised Ruall for a moment, then added, "Still, things are as they are and cannot be undone. I will only caution you to guard your tongue and reveal as little about our purpose as possible. As for your friend, it will be better for him, should he truly be honest, if he knows very little about us. If our pursuers follow us here, he can protest his ignorance convincingly."

"I see what you mean. Very well, I will guard my speech. I don't believe I have revealed anything crucial, but thank you for the caution."

Bedistai placed his hand on hers and she smiled at this small reassurance. He returned it with one of his own before withdrawing his touch.

Once the fabric had boiled, they helped Ruall remove the strips, careful to keep them from touching the ground. As they wrapped the cloth around Chossen, Ruall commented, "I must say, I've never seen medicines actually worked into a wound. I would have thought that would lead to complications."

"For you and I and anyone but an endath, you would be correct," said Bedistai.

"Ah!" Ruall chuckled. "So this is not another piece of folk wisdom I can use."

"Not unless you choose to treat endaths."

They all laughed.

Once the bandages were in place, nothing remained to be done but decide how to spend the night.

"Unless you feel you need to stay with the animals for some reason or other," said Ruall, "I'd like to invite you into my home." Nodding towards the endaths, he added, "They look as if they will be fine by themselves. As for the two of you, my cottage is warm, and I have food enough for the three. What do you say? Will you join me?"

Before Bedistai could object, Darva replied, "I would love to sleep under a roof again, if only for one night." Without stopping to see if Bedistai agreed, she added, "We would love to, Ruall. We accept."

She was pleasantly surprised when Bedistai agreed.

"Thank you for your hospitality," he said.

They reassured themselves that the animals required no further attention, then Darva and Bedistai gathered those items they thought they would need and followed Ruall into the woods.

CHAPTER FOURTEEN

Ruall's house was an odd conglomeration of logs and planed boards which, he explained, was the result of an unreliable supply of materials.

"Only the rich have access to boards like these," he said, pointing at the finished ones. "Do you see the holes here and there along their surfaces? They don't appear to have any bearing upon the house's structure, do they?"

Darva and Bedistai agreed they did not.

"That's because all of them were once part of a wrecked sailing ship. Someone long ago brought all of this lumber inland and built a fine house with these boards. Years ago—I suspect when all the battles began—warring parties destroyed the house, reducing it to rubble. By the time I came upon its remains, most of the house had already been broken up and carted off. I got my hands on as much as I could in hopes of building this one. I had a wagon then and an old horse who's no longer with us. I carried away two loads of pretty decent stuff. But the third time I returned, someone else had carted off the rest. I had to finish with small trees and saplings." Ruall chuckled. "It's not much, but it keeps out the weather."

"Nonsense!" said Darva. "It's a fine house."

Bedistai spent a moment regarding the walls and their supports, running his hands over their joinings. "You chose good materials and the workmanship is excellent." He looked at Ruall. "You have nothing to be ashamed of."

Ruall's face flushed. "Thank you," he managed.

Darva and Bedistai helped him prepare the evening meal. As before, Bedistai gathered dry branches while Darva searched for tinder. Ruall attempted to ignite kindling by striking a piece of tanass, or spark stone, against a piece of metal. When his efforts proved unsuccessful, Bedistai once again untensioned his bow and soon produced enough heat to start a blaze. Before long, the small clay stove was warming and Darva helped Ruall cut and peel the roots and garden vegetables that were destined for the pot. After their host had ladled water for stew and prepared a pot of tea, Bedistai returned to the stream with buckets to refill the cistern. Supper was on the table almost an hour before dusk, early enough to eat and clean up without requiring any of the precious lamp oil.

When Darva had finished the last of her meal and set her bowl upon the table, she thanked her host. "That was delicious," she said.

Ruall nodded and blushed.

They cleaned up the dishes while their host told them about himself.

"It's been nearly eight years since we moved from the flats up into the hills," he said. "It was a move we never planned, but sometimes life takes you down an unexpected path."

"You said 'we.' Who do you mean by 'we'?" Bedistai asked.

"Eflyn and myself. Eflyn was my wife. I think life up here was too hard for her, so she finally gave up and died." His lips pursed at the mention of her name and he paused briefly before continuing. "That was just over three years ago.

"Before that, we tended a small flock of sheep we kept for

food and wool. Since that kind of work is too much for one person and I couldn't watch them properly, little by little they wandered off, until I realized it was a losing proposition. I finally let the last of them go. Now I just tend my garden, forage a bit, and drop a line into the brook for cappies. It's not much, but I eat."

"If life here is so hard, why didn't you return to the flats?" asked Darva.

"We didn't return for the same reason we left: we didn't have much choice," Ruall answered. "When the armies began to scour the land for soldiers and supplies, any folk living in the valley who were too old to be of use, like us, were simply killed. Our own warlord, Harven Goth, gave us no protection at all. Oh, we tried laying low and out of sight whenever word came round they were moving through the region. But you can only get away with that strategy so long. Once, when they came through at night, they almost caught us abed. We barely got out of the house and into our hidey-hole. We spent the night there and part of the next day, until they gave up on finding us. That was just too close, we thought, and soon after we gathered whatever we could fit into a cart. Then, as hard as it was to say goodbye to what had been our home for all those years, we made ourselves scarce. Never thought we'd be leaving for permanent. Always thought that, after a few years at most, the trouble would clear up and we'd be back home farming the land. It never did though. Things are still bad, and I don't see any sign they will ever improve.

"You two are actually passing through in relatively peaceful times. One of my neighbors recently traveled to danBashad. He really didn't expect he could get there at all, but he had to try. Although he had to travel pretty much by starlight or close to dusk, he not only made it there, but got back home as well. Even a few months earlier, there would have been too much fighting for him to go anywhere. He never would have made it."

"We almost didn't make it ourselves," Darva offered.

"Naturally," the man agreed. "You were traveling by day. No one does that any more. You were lucky you weren't killed."

She and Bedistai nodded in agreement.

"There was a lot of movement over the plain we crossed," said Bedistai. "Do any soldiers ever come up into the hills?"

Ruall wiped his lips as he, too, finished eating. He put his plate aside and emitted a quiet belch.

"They used to when we first moved here. It's been years, though, since we last saw any sign of them. It's not likely they'll come up here after you, if that's what you're getting at."

"Yes. That was my concern."

"I really wouldn't worry about it too much," Ruall reassured. "Now, if you will pardon my asking, which way are you going when you leave?"

"We are going south," Darva answered. She had calculated this answer would be vague enough to satisfy Bedistai and she was relieved when he didn't react.

"Then, when it's time for you to go, might I suggest a path of egress?" When his guests sat awaiting his suggestion, he continued. "Yesterday, had you been able to continue your journey, the contour of the hills and mountains would have taken you past barakMeden. There, you either would have perished outright, or else would have been taken prisoner and kept until Lord Goth had no further use for you—with the same outcome. But fortune has looked kindly on you. Not only have you found refuge for your endath, but you have stumbled upon a modest," he winked, "and very knowledgeable guide."

They grinned as he continued.

"There is a path leading up from the brook where your animals are resting, to a meadow where our sheep used to graze. From there, a trail winding east of barakMeden goes over the Tairenth Mountains and eventually into northern Borrst.

Depending upon where in the south you wish to go, at that point, the world opens up to you.

"However, there is that conflict between Chadarr and the lands east of its borders. Although, as you are probably figuring out, borders don't mean very much these days."

With a smile and a wink, Ruall hinted he suspected more about their destination than they had revealed. He began to collect their bowls and cups and it was clear he did not intend to ask them to confirm his suspicions.

For the first time since they had met their host, Bedistai gave Ruall a warm smile.

"Thank you," he said. "We want to avoid taking any dangerous routes, especially until Darva's endath is fully recovered. With luck, that route will provide another day or two for her to heal."

"You can have all the time you need," replied Ruall. "I know this place isn't much, but I can fix two comfortable beds against the wall and you can stay here as long as you wish."

"Again, I thank you," said Bedistai. "Make but one bed for the lady. She will be forced to sleep on the ground more days than she will care to before this journey is over. As for me, I will spend the night with the endaths. I seldom sleep beneath a roof and will feel more at ease out of doors.

"As for the remainder of your offer, matters press us onward. We do not have the luxury of time. Thanks to your ministering, Chossen will be well enough to travel if we do not push her too hard. Endaths are a hearty breed and of unique temperament. I know them well enough to say they will be restless by morning. Their agitation, if they are prevented from traveling, will slow her recovery. Still, we could not have fared as well as we did without your kindness. We are much in your debt."

"Indeed," added Darva. "I certainly would have been at a loss over what to have done in Bedistai's absence, were it not for you. I will never forget you."

"Nonsense," said Ruall. "You would have done just fine. Bedistai would have returned with his nettle and the animal would have done well. She was already improving when I found you."

"You broke her fever," Darva insisted.

"And I did not bring enough poultice," Bedistai added. "No, my friend. You did much we could not have done on our own. We thank you."

"I only did what was needed."

"Our point exactly," Darva replied. "You did what was needed. I think Eflyn was a fortunate woman."

Ruall's eyes teared a bit. He paused to regard both his guests.

"Thank you," he said.

CHAPTER FIFTEEN

I tell you again, sir. I have no knowledge where they went, and I did not accompany them to their steeds, so I cannot even say if they rode off to the east or the south or the west."

"I don't believe you," said Harad and slapped Ruall hard across the face.

Tears began to stream from the old man's eyes.

"I don't know! I don't know!" he cried. "I can't tell you anything."

Harad released his grip on Ruall's hair and the old man slumped forward. He had been tied to a chair in the center of the room for nearly an hour. Harad had asked the same questions repeatedly and Ruall had provided consistent answers. Between interrogations Harad and his companions had taken turns beating him, hoping brutality would either change his story or reveal any lies.

Harad turned to Peniff, who was seated behind Ruall, beyond his range of vision.

"What do you say, Thought Gazer? Do you still say he's telling me the truth?"

"In essence, he is," Peniff replied with an exasperated sigh. For the past hour he had given Harad the same confirmation. Still, he repeated, "He did not tell them where to go and he only provided them with general information. Truthfully, I do not expect we can gain anything else from this man. As for me, I could serve you better if you would just let me step outside so I can ascertain their direction of travel without all this distraction."

True to the name people gave him, Peniff could see Ruall's thoughts. In this time of war, the old man had either known or heard of others like Harad, and he understood that, however he answered, his fate would remain unchanged. In all likelihood, he would die. He also understood if he helped Harad locate Bedistai and Darva, their fates would be no kinder. Consequently, the old man had resolved to dig in his heels and hold his ground. He was not going to provide even a stitch of satisfaction. If frustrating Harad and his companions was all he could do in return for the beatings they gave him, that was what he would do.

While Peniff also saw that Harad's intentions verified Ruall's conclusions, he hoped he could persuade him to be lenient. Like Ruall, he too was a prisoner. And while the restraints that bound him to this service took the form of a threat hanging over him, they were no less real than the ones that lashed Ruall to the chair.

By now, Peniff had grown tired. He was frustrated and yearned to end this quest and return home. Even more, he was becoming increasingly annoyed at Harad's unwillingness to take the advice he was bound to provide. Harad's obsession to control every aspect was stifling. The thoughts in the cottage overwhelmed to the point of suffocation and he could perceive nothing beyond its walls. If only he were allowed to step into the open, where he could isolate the thoughts of the couple they were chasing, perhaps even enter their heads and see the world through their eyes, he could not only learn where they were, but also what route they were taking. He could end this ordeal. To Peniff's misfortune, Harad was a man who believed he held all the answers, regarding everyone else as fools. As a result, they would plod unnecessarily.

"This old man cannot tell you anything, but maybe I can, if you will just allow me outside," Peniff repeated.

"Shut up!" Harad shouted. "When I want your advice, I will ask for it." Turning to the others, he declared, "We are done here. Burn the place."

As Harad's three cohorts rose to obey, leaving the old man tied to the chair, Peniff stammered, "W—we will free him first, will we not? He has done nothing wrong. You can't just kill him!"

"Did I ask for your opinion?" growled Harad. Then he ordered the others, "Set a fire and get out."

As Peniff watched in disbelief, they took burning brands from the hearth and touched them to the bed, the pantry, and other parts of the hovel. He tried to stop them, but two of them seized his arms and dragged him outside. After several small fires had begun dancing, a third man tossed his torch aside and joined the others. Harad lingered a moment, oblivious to the flames, then, turning his back, departed with Ruall's shrieks following him through the door.

He strode to the small stand of trees where the horses were tied. As he went, he threw a studded glove to the ground and Kord—one of the four who had kidnapped Darva—picked it up. When he caught up with his leader, he tried to return it. After several paces, Harad snatched it away without acknowledgement.

Harad halted and stared into the woods. All at once, rousing himself from his reverie, he whirled and demanded, "Where is Peniff?"

"I'm right here," the thought gazer answered.

Harad's head snapped around. Peniff was directly behind him, still in the grip of Tonas and Ward.

"Let him go," said Harad, suddenly sounding drained.

They began to release him but Peniff shook free. He strode up to Harad, put his face within inches, and shouted, "That was not necessary. You didn't need to kill him, let alone burn him alive."

Harad stood unblinking, as if unaware of the world around him. Peniff studied his thoughts as he vacillated in and out of the present, one moment enrapt with the old man's horrific demise, the next fraught with anxiety over his failure to catch the pair. The thought gazer had never met anyone so unstable.

"Why?" Peniff demanded when Harad returned to the moment.

Harad's eyes focused. As if seeing him for the first time, he shoved Peniff away, saying, "I wanted to show you how I treat people who are less than honest with me." He cocked his head and studied Peniff. In a voice that showed he was now fully present, he said, "And what I will do to your family should you fail to keep your promise."

"That poor man cooperated. You did it solely for pleasure."

"And now you know who I am. But I should have thought you would have already figured me out. Perhaps you are not really what they say you are. You certainly haven't accomplished what I hired you to do. They're still out there," he said, gesturing towards the hills with a sweep of his arm.

"You're right. I haven't. But we are right behind them."

"We should have caught them by now."

"Had you let me do my job, we might already have them."

"Are you blaming me?"

Peniff sighed, "You would never have located the woman on your own, nor been able to follow her this far. Yet we caught up with them in No'eth. Now, according to my senses, we are still on their trail. If you will start trusting me and allow me to do what you've asked, we may intercept them yet."

Harad opened his mouth to speak, but Peniff cut him off. "There was no need for *any* of this," he said, gesturing at the nearby inferno. "Neither the questioning, nor your ..." Peniff paused. He bit his lip, shook his head as he tried to come to terms "... little bit of fun. The hour that you wasted has also cost us. As it is, it's going to be hard to catch up."

When Harad opened his mouth to speak, Peniff anticipated him.

"They are somewhere up there." He pointed. "Through the trees. If we leave now we might have a chance."

Harad looked up the hill, then back at Peniff, angry he might be right.

"Mount up!" he said. Then to Peniff, "Do your job."

CHAPTER SIXTEEN

The morning sky acquired a bluish tinge as white Jadon led the solar procession. It would gradually transform to its more customary green as Mahaz, the orange giant, rose and added its coloration. Until the suns had climbed above the surrounding hills, the ravine would retain the night's chill, so Darva clutched her cloak to her breast and looked skyward, content with the knowledge it would be warmer at the summit of the draw they were ascending.

Chossen, she noticed, was doing well. Her breathing was not at all labored. She held her head erect and flicked her tail from time to time, as if she was enjoying the climb. When she bounded up short rises in the trail, it suggested she might even be impatient with Chawah's cautious pace.

It was not long before they climbed into the light. They paused while Bedistai surveyed the terrain from the improved vantage. As Chossen drew alongside, Darva pulled back her hood and shook her hair to free it in the warmth of the suns.

"At last!" she said, as she took in the view.

From the west through the north and around to the east,

the land called Meden extended to the horizon, uniquely beautiful, deceptively tranquil.

"This is lovely," she beamed, wishing they could linger. "When we have accomplished our mission, I would like to return. I have never seen such beauty and I'd dearly love to enjoy it again. I would also like to bring Ruall a present to thank him for his kindness and hospitality. I ..." She halted.

Bedistai was scowling.

"Did I say something wrong?" she asked.

"You will never have that opportunity."

"Of course I will. The lands will not always be at war."

"That is not what I meant. Look," he said, pointing in the direction from which they had come.

It took a few seconds for her to understand. The canyon seemed peaceful enough. A thin morning fog filled the vale. Between the treetops that poked through the mist, occasional columns of smoke rose from the chimneys of the homes nestled in the hollow. Nothing seemed amiss. Then, she noticed one of the plumes, darker than the rest, was widening into a thick billow of black.

Fire! she thought.

"They have followed us," said Bedistai.

"Followed? Here? No, Bedistai. That isn't possible. How could anyone follow us here? We have covered so much territory and no one could have predicted our path. They would have had to read our minds, and no one can read minds."

"As I told you, a thought gazer is among them."

She was regarding the smoke when another thought occurred, and her eyes widened.

"They wouldn't kill Ruall, would they?"

The question was rhetorical. All lives were at risk, Ruall's no less than any other. As Bedistai gazed at what was fast becoming a conflagration, first Chawah, then Chossen started, as if at an unexpected touch. Fire did not easily spook these creatures and Bedistai suspected what had caused them to jump.

"They have located us again," he said. "We must ride."

Without questioning, Darva pulled her hood over her head, took the reins, and turned Chossen south. The instant they touched the endaths with their heels, the beasts accelerated along the ridge line.

They rode all day, for the most part in silence. Bedistai, hoping to put even more distance between them and their pursuers, kept the endaths to a pace that would not tax them, but was more than a horse could sustain for any length of time. By the time Mahaz had begun to set, Bedistai reined Chawah to a halt. Chossen drew alongside and Darva assumed they were stopping to set up camp. He rubbed Chawah's neck with long affectionate strokes and spoke to her softly.

"Chawah, my good girl, you have done well today," he said. "We have only a little farther to go before nightfall."

He patted her twice, then leaned back in the saddle and drew his knees almost to his chest. He pivoted in the saddle, then slid down her side. When he alit, he touched her gently with his palm, and Darva could see how great was his affection. He maintained that touch for a moment, then placed his other palm against Chossen. The endath turned to look.

"Ho, Chossen," he greeted her. "How are you doing after such a long day? I would like to see your wound," he said and stepped around to obtain a better view.

"Do you still hurt?" he asked, before placing his hand on her chest.

She quivered at his touch.

With his hand still upon her, he looked up and asked, "Does that hurt, or did I startle you?"

The quivering subsided, so he studied her a moment longer.

"I'm going to press," he said, then did so.

She did not react.

"No?" he asked. "That does not hurt?"

He pressed harder and Chossen remained calm.

"Good," he said. "That is very good," he repeated and removed his hand.

He stepped back and told Darva, "You have done well. I believe she has healed."

"You speak to her as though she were a person."

"She understands," he replied. "She is a conscious entity. All living things are aware. Those who have intelligence enough to comprehend words and can respond to affection understand more than most people are willing to accept. We Haroun treat all living things—endaths especially—as if they understand us. In turn, the endaths have demonstrated repeatedly that they do. Just because they cannot answer, don't consider them stupid. You survived the battlefield because of her intelligence. Credit her, then, a little more."

Without waiting for her to reply, Bedistai turned and walked towards the edge of the ridge they were following. As he stared into the declivity, wind rushed up from the valley below and turned his hair into streamers. He remained gazing for several minutes. After a while, he turned to face her.

"I think this is a good place."

"I'm sorry, Bedistai," Darva said. "I don't understand. This is a good place for what?"

"We will go down from here."

"What?"

The statement startled her, and she laughed. Twisting in the saddle, she craned to see what might have brought him to that conclusion. Seeing no indication of a trail, she looked at him for an explanation. He returned her stare placidly. Hoping she had either missed an important clue or else misunderstood, she peered into the chasm but saw nothing helpful. Bedistai's face showed no trace of humor, so she was at a loss how to react.

Faced with the possibility he might really be serious, she said, "It's a sheer drop."

When he did not respond, she leaned towards him, placed both hands on the pommel, and studied his face. All at once, she realized he was serious.

"No!" Darva said. "We cannot. Are you mad?"

"Today, we left our pursuers a good distance behind," he replied. "Under ordinary circumstances, I would be content with that result and we would camp here until morning. The darkness of night would make it all but impossible for them to follow. Then, at first light we would mount up and leave them behind for good. But these are not ordinary circumstances."

He paused until she acknowledged with a nod.

"With a thought gazer among them, darkness will not deter them. Rather, it will conceal them until they are on top of us, coming upon us while we sleep. We have only two courses to choose from if we are to stay ahead. The first is to continue without stopping, sleeping in the saddle. Normally, that would pose no problem. Since endaths do not sleep as we do, they could carry us indefinitely. But Chossen has only now recovered from her wound. I suspect she is still recovering, although if that is the case, she will give us no indication. I have spoken of the respect I have for these animals. Since she cannot speak and will not give us any sign she needs rest, I will advocate on her behalf and assume she will soon need to stop. Continuing onward, then, will provide none of the respite she needs, even though it provides some short-term advantage.

"Our other alternative is to descend to the valley floor by the most expeditious route possible."

Before Darva could speak, he raised his hand indicating she should hear him out.

"I will not unnecessarily jeopardize the endaths, and they will not follow me blindly to their death. You should also understand that I have lived with them all my life, so I understand their abilities completely. You also know I have tried to take the best care of you and I hope you can find no fault with my efforts."

He paused and again she nodded.

"You must trust me, then, when I tell you that Chossen and Chawah can easily negotiate this slope, even though you and I never could on our own. It is very steep, but not, as you put it, a sheer drop. You must trust me when I assure you that you will be safe if, once again, you do exactly as I instruct."

Darva was wary, but continued to listen.

"If we follow this course of action, we will arrive at the valley floor before dark and our pursuers will not be able to follow. Even if they choose to continue along the ridge, they will not have the benefit of our presence before them to serve as a beacon through the darkness. They will have to continue at a crawl, guessing which way to go, or be forced to stop and make camp until morning. Even when morning does arrive, they will still not be able to follow, except by the longest, most circuitous route. They will fall ever farther behind until—the gods willing—we arrive in Liad-Nur at your brother's camp. Then what can they do?"

Darva hesitated a long moment. Finally she said, "Everything in my nature screams out against it, but, yes, you are right. You have taken wonderfully good care of us all, so I trust you." She took a deep breath. "Let's go before I change my mind."

"Good," Bedistai said. He leapt, and his foot found a stirrup. Again in the saddle, he turned to instruct her. "Now, slide forward so your pelvis is against the pommel. It will serve as your seat during much of the descent. When Chossen follows Chawah over the edge, lean as far back as you can. Keep your feet in the forward pair of stirrups and your legs straight, completely extended before you. Make sure you are sitting squarely. You may hold the reins, if it serves to reassure you or aid you to balance, but as before, you will not use them. Focus on this task and Chossen will do the rest."

"All right. I can do that," she said, despite her anxiety.

He stroked his endath's neck. "It grows dark, Chawah. Lead the way. We go down."

Chawah tossed her head and flicked her tail. She stepped to the brink, then disappeared over the edge. Chossen followed and Darva held her breath as her endath appeared to step into space.

And then, there was no turning back.

Darva had expected a long, slow, cautious descent to the valley floor, but she was gravely mistaken. Chossen began down the cliff at a rate that took her breath away. As soon as her hind legs left the ridge, Chossen shifted into a squat, sitting back on her haunches. Extending her tail for balance and holding her head and neck rearward, she accelerated down the scree-covered surface like a sled. All the while, her feet were continually moving to compensate for irregularities in both surface and resistance.

The valley floor was far below and the route to it neither straight nor regular. Nonetheless, Chossen's reflexes were such that she never lost control. Whenever the ravine took a turn, she would either lean into the new direction when the curvature was gentle, or she would pedal rapidly through a sharper one until she had left it behind.

At certain points, the surface would level somewhat and Chossen met the change in terrain smoothly, adjusting to a run that matched her previous pace, until, when the surface dropped off again, she resumed her slide. At no time did she show any sign of fear or indicate she wanted to stop. And though she sent a continuous shower of stones before her, Chawah and Bedistai were far enough ahead they were never in danger of being struck.

They plummeted like this for several minutes until Darva

began to acclimate to the pace, growing exhilarated, almost forgetting her fear. When, at last, the slope started to shallow, Chossen rose from her haunches and shifted to a loping gait, gradually slowing to a walk as the ground leveled altogether. Darva looked ahead and saw Bedistai and Chawah waiting.

"I see you survived," said Bedistai with a chuckle.

"Hah!" Darva blurted, erupting into laughter. "I am sorry for once again doubting you."

"It was the endaths you doubted."

"You are right." A bit self-consciously, she told Chossen, "I am sorry. I will not doubt you again." When Bedistai cocked an eye at her, then glanced at Chawah, she added, "And I am sorry for doubting you, Chawah."

Both endaths responded with their customary half blink.

"What now?" Darva asked.

"It's almost dark," he said. "I do not believe we will find a better place to rest than this. I see a depression in the rock face that should keep us sheltered from the wind. We will set up camp and have something to eat. We should sleep directly after, so we can rise early. In the morning the endaths will find water for us."

"I suppose I should trust them in this, as well."

Bedistai smiled. "You learn slowly, but I see there may be hope."

Darva accepted the jab graciously, and the two led their mounts towards a hollow in one of the canyon walls and prepared to spend the night.

CHAPTER SEVENTEEN

We have lost them," said Peniff.

"What do you mean? How can we lose them?" demanded Harad. "Are you trying to tell me you don't know where they are?"

"I know exactly where they are," he replied evenly.

"So how can you say we have lost them?"

"They went down there."

Peniff gestured with his thumb at the precipice. Harad looked at the place where their quarry had descended and reacted with the same incredulity as Darva.

"Impossible!"

"On the contrary. It is quite possible. They are riding endaths."

Harad dismounted and walked to the same place Bedistai had stood. He peered over the edge into the darkness.

"I don't believe it."

"Whether you believe me or not," said Peniff, "you will have to find another route. I won't go down there, and you will have to wait until morning if you care to attempt it." He held his torch aloft and dismounted. "I have had almost no sleep for the last several days. After I find a place to tie up my horse, I am going to lie down. I suggest you do the same. We have many long days ahead of us if you still intend to catch them."

"Oh, we are going to catch them," Harad said. "You can depend on that."

He watched Peniff dismount and lead his steed away, angry he had to depend on this man. He would ignore his insolence for now, but when this all was behind them, he would make the thought gazer pay dearly.

"MASTAD!" Peniff swore, gasping and clutching his side, curling into a fetal position.

"Get up!" When Peniff did not respond, Harad shouted, "If you don't get up, I will kick you again."

The pain made moving difficult, but Peniff straightened, placed both hands on the ground and pushed himself erect. He was not moving quickly enough to suit Harad, however, so Harad kicked again. Peniff perceived his intention, so, before the boot could connect, he grabbed Harad's ankle and held it.

"I'm moving," Peniff said as he rose to his feet.

"Let go!" Harad ordered.

Peniff knew how much the man resented being controlled, so he maintained his grasp, lifting Harad's foot until it was nearly level with his shoulders.

"I said let go!"

"Gladly," said Peniff as he shoved and released.

Harad fell onto his rump, much to the amusement of his companions. His face contorted, and they broke into laughter.

"Shut up!" he shouted. He pointed at Peniff and snapped, "Don't ever do that again. You are a long way from home and I promise a lot of bad things can happen before you see your family." As he struggled to stand, he corrected himself. "*If* you see your family."

Peniff knew he had transgressed. After all, Harad was a bully and, like all bullies, he needed to maintain a sense of superiority. Peniff also knew, should he fail to come out on top in this exchange, he would be in danger for the rest of this journey.

"You're right," he said. "We are indeed a long way from home, but we also have a long way to go before we catch up with the Haroun and the woman. I'm certain you can't find them. Do your worst, if it suits you, then explain to Sabed Orr how I died before you could fulfill your mission."

Harad was angry, but his face showed he had not considered that result. He needed Peniff and he knew it.

"If you kick me again," Peniff said, trying to look as menacing as possible, "don't go to sleep."

"We are holding your wife and children," reminded Harad.

"No. You are not," Peniff countered. "Sabed Orr is holding my family and he has no idea what's transpiring here."

"Are you willing to risk their well-being?"

"That is my concern. As for you, it occurs to me that if something were to happen to you, and I were to return to Monhedeth alone, I could catch Orr unawares and secure my family's freedom."

"Then why don't you?"

"I don't because, in the attempt, there is an inherent degree of risk. So the question you must ask yourself is: how far will you have to push me before I am willing to accept that risk? Certainly, if I am faced with death or even serious injury to myself or my family, I will be willing to risk far more than I will if we proceed amicably. It's up to you to decide on what footing we proceed."

Actually, despite sounding confident, Peniff was unsure if he was willing to endanger his family at all. On the other hand, having played that card, he could not allow Harad or the others to sense he might be bluffing. Since they did not really know the full extent of his abilities, he would be safer the more credit they gave him.

"I don't think you want to test me," he emphasized, looking at each of them. "Now, where is the food? I'm hungry."

PENIFF BROODED as they rode out after breakfast. This was not the mission Harad had promised. When Orr's men had taken his wife and children hostage, Harad had explained they were searching for a woman whose family posed a threat to Monhedeth's sovereign. Further, he said, once they captured her, they would only imprison her. It was never their intention to kill her. They had no intention of killing anyone, Harad explained. Moreover, at that time Peniff could tell Harad believed what he said. However, after learning how unstable he was, Peniff also understood that Harad was capable of complete self-deception. And while he knew from the outset Orr's men all were evil, he did not anticipate the full extent of their depravity until they had murdered the Haroun youths. He cursed himself for not probing deeper. That was the least he should have done. After all, Orr and Harad had enlisted him because he was a thought gazer.

He considered what that label meant to the world who had bestowed it on him and others like him. It implied they were able to examine thoughts as one regards one's image in a mirror. In actuality, while most who were given that label rarely, if ever, achieved such a degree of clarity, other thought gazers did possess the ability to touch minds and glean certain information.

In truth, most thought gazers could only skim another's thoughts myopically, perceiving vague images or intuiting certain feelings or inclinations. And although their perceptions might be vague, many postured themselves as seers, claiming a prescience none actually possessed, while attempting to eke out a living telling fortunes. The few who possessed greater clarity were often feared and perceived as threatening. As a result, they tried to conceal their difference. Certain of them, unable to achieve anonymity, were sought out by the powerful or aspirants to power, in hopes of gaining an advantage over their opponents. Those savants involuntarily entered into a servitude from which they could not escape. Sometimes, due to the imperfect nature of their abilities, their service brought them death when they could not deliver the information their masters sought.

Among all of these, Peniff was unique, endowed with a clarity of perception beyond what even the masses believed. Still, he never inhabited a person's thoughts in the way that individual did, perhaps because he feared this immersion might someday cause him to lose his own identity. Nonetheless, whenever he chose to, he could see what another thought or intended. And while these perceptions rarely manifested as words, the images he perceived were so clear, so vivid, they often embarrassed him. In fact, because he never actively sought to invade the sanctum of another's mind, whenever one was laid open, he would hurry to extricate himself. Unintentional intrusion into another's privacy was unsettling to the point of embarrassment, and Peniff strove to avoid it. He would try to forget it, pretending to himself he was like everyone else.

Ultimately, however, he could not hide from the truth. So he attempted to isolate himself by living as reclusively as possible, never employing the full extent of his abilities. Curiously, it wasn't until the moment he had threatened Harad that he realized how great was the power he possessed. For, by anticipating others, he had the ability to change his future. The possibility he had voiced was more than hypothetical, and he realized he could neither run from it nor ignore it. None but he could save his wife and children. In fact, he knew with certainty that once he had completed his appointed task, Orr, having no further need, would dispose of them like so much garbage. Peniff knew he could not allow that to happen.

And his situation was more complex than that. Not only did he need to keep his family safe, but it was plain that whether he helped Harad or not, other lives would depend on his choices, including the pair they were pursuing. In good conscience, he could not allow any harm to befall either of them as a result of any fear or weakness. So he elected to help them, although matters would grow dangerous should Harad perceive his intention. He did not know how he would accomplish any of this, but he knew he must. There was no other way.

CHAPTER EIGHTEEN

Northern Borrst was emerging from the long shadows of first light. Low clouds in the distance produced scattered flaws of rain. Eshed, dur, and barrel-stave trees forested the hollows between the low rolling hills; and the land, tinged faintly blue with the morning's glow, appeared devoid of habitation. Absent were the columns of smoke one would expect from fireplaces or cook fires, so Bedistai knew this peaceful scene was illusory. Since the many small villages between here and danHsar, far to the south, should all be preparing their first meals, he was certain they were deliberately concealing their presence. This suggested that the inhabitants were either engaged in warfare, or else were preparing for it.

He scrambled from his observation perch and returned to the night's encampment. The endaths would be craving water, so he and Darva needed to break camp immediately to allow them to find it. Since they had nearly exhausted the provisions they had brought, he would spend most of the morning hunting. He was optimistic he could acquire whatever food they needed, since the lush countryside promised water in abundance and, therefore, game.

By the time he returned to their encampment, Darva was awake. She had already dressed, folded their bedrolls and had nearly finished packing their gear. She waved when he arrived, smiling as he approached.

"Good morning," she called.

"Good morning to you," he replied. "I am sorry if I worried you."

"Why should I be worried?"

"I was gone when you awoke."

"I expected you would be scouting ahead. Was I right?"

He smiled, pleased with her awareness. "You were."

"What did you see?" she asked.

His smile faded. "We will need to be careful. It is what I didn't see that worries me," he told her, explaining his reasoning. "As the day unfolds, we may learn if I am right. For now, we will attend to Chawah and Chossen."

As was his custom, he took a moment to greet and examine Chawah, then he checked to see that the saddles and equipment were properly secured. Everything was in order, and he complimented Darva on the job she had done. She smiled a "thank you," but when the fond look in her eyes spoke of much more than gratitude, Bedistai felt naked, wondering if she could see his own attraction. Embarrassed, he turned away and told her to mount up. Almost immediately, worrying that he had offended her with his brusqueness, he turned back to apologize. To his relief, he saw she was smiling.

As they exited the canyon, Bedistai again instructed Darva to give Chossen free rein.

"They will locate water more quickly if we do not interfere," he explained.

The endaths set off on a different course from the one he had established. A short while later, they were all drinking from a swift-running brook. Once Bedistai had drunk his fill, he set about filling the water skins while the endaths continued drinking.

The rivulet ran through a broad lush meadow of knee-high cymbal grass, a relative of the scythe grass populating the coast. The undulating blades, gently agitated by the morning zephyr, gave rise to pleasant music reminiscent of wind chimes. A dense wood surrounded the meadow on three sides and most of the fourth. In the space between, above the grass, flitting orange and white specks marked the mating dance of thousands of lace flies, whose wings reflected the colors of the suns.

While Bedistai studied the glade and the surrounding hills, the endaths left the stream to graze. After a while, Chawah finished her meal and raised her head to search for him. She spotted him restringing his bow, ambled to his side, and nudged his shoulder with her head.

"Ah!" he said. "Are you ready at last? I will be, too, in a moment."

He finished his task with several wraps of gut and a knot. He released the compression he had placed on the bow and examined the new string's tension. Satisfied, he slung it across his chest, then turned to his friend.

"You are right. The day is slipping away, and we have much work to do. Let us see what we can find."

Chawah flicked her tail and Bedistai shouldered his quiver and secured a water skin to her saddle's cantle. When he had mounted, he turned to Darva.

"You should be safe while I'm gone, but don't stray too far from Chossen." To Darva's alarmed look, he added, "Chawah hasn't indicated any danger. I am just being cautious." Her expression relaxed, and he said, "This feels like a good morning for a hunt. With any luck, we will return soon with game."

"Wait," she said.

Bedistai paused, curious about what she held as she ran to Chawah's side.

"I have something for you."

He reached for the offering and examined it. "Flatbread!" he exclaimed.

"It's the last of what Ruall gave us. You haven't broken fast. You should eat before you go."

"Do you take care of your brother like this?"

"I take care of everyone like this," she said, and he thought he saw her blush. "Good luck this morning and, please, be careful."

No woman, save his mother, had ever taken such care of him. While he was unsure what to make of it, he was beginning to enjoy the attention.

CHAPTER NINETEEN

It was almost midday when Bedistai returned. As he emerged from the forest, he called out to Darva, who was busying herself with some task. She turned, and he lifted the gray shape that was slung across his lap. He grinned and held it aloft, displaying the morning's reward. It was a jennet. Holding the small hooved herbivore in one hand, he dismounted.

"This one has enough meat to carry us for almost a week," he said.

"It won't take that long to get home," she replied in a hopeful voice.

"Not if everything goes well. In that case, I will have enough left to carry me part way back to Mostoon."

"Oh," was all she could manage. Her smile disappeared as she asked, "Will you not stay even a little while after we arrive?"

He had not intended to disappoint her, but neither did he intend to remain at barakMall any longer than necessary. Her brother was preparing for a war that was not his to fight, if in fact it had not already begun. On the other hand, he was in no hurry to leave her. While the predicament was troubling, the outcome was unavoidable.

"I can remain a few days," he allowed.

When she still appeared distressed, he dropped the jennet's carcass and took her hands into his.

"That is not my life. Please understand. As much as I might want to remain with you, I cannot. I am a Haroun and must eventually return to No'eth."

Darva hesitated before replying. "No. No, of course not. There would be no reason for you to linger."

When she looked away, he placed a finger beneath her chin, turning it until she was facing him. Her lower lip quivered, and tears began to well.

"I will stay as long as I can," he said, smiling tenderly.

She tried to return his smile, but could not hide her disappointment. She bit her lip and changed the subject.

"Look, Bedistai. See what I found," she said, pointing to a cloth spread open on the ground.

"Ha!" He laughed when he recognized what it held. "Are those marberries?"

"They are," she said triumphantly, her enthusiasm returning. "We will have more than meat for at least a couple of days. That is, if I can figure out how to pack them."

"We will find a way. I love marberries. You have done well."

"At the price of my hands," she said, rubbing them together. "I wish they didn't have such brambles."

He took them into his and smiled. "Your hands are lovely," he said. "They heal and take care of others."

When she pulled away the disfigured one and held it behind her back, he reached around and brought it where he could see it.

"Don't," he said, putting it to his lips and kissing the gap.

She started to cry, then looked at him. He had a smile on his face and she returned it through her tears.

Bedistai spent the next three hours cleaning, dressing, and salting the jennet, packaging the meat in the leaves of a plant which, like the berries, also grew near the brook. Preserving the meat required all of the salt he had brought. After thoroughly rinsing the bag that had once held the condiment, he found it was large enough to hold most of what Darva had collected. They made a supper of the rest.

Once they had packed, he said, "There are about six hours of useable daylight left. I would like to see how much ground we can cover before nightfall. I am sure our pursuers have used most of today making up for lost time. Perhaps we can take back some of what they've gained.

"But, Darva, I am a stranger to these parts. Now that we have come so far south, do you have any idea where we should go from here?"

She answered, "I have had it in mind to head towards the city of danHsar, then on through Nagath-réal before turning west towards Liad-Nur. That way should keep us clear of my enemies. I believe the city lies a bit west of due south. When we clear these woods and hills I should have a better idea."

"Are we ready to go?"

"I am ready when you are."

They mounted their endaths and set off through the trees. Sunlight filtered by tree limbs dappled the forest floor. It was not a particularly dense wood and did not impede their progress, but without any landmarks and because of the meandering nature of the valley floor, the direction they were heading grew increasingly uncertain. Certainly, Bedistai possessed a fine sense of direction, but under normal circumstances, day or night, the subtle cues the horizon, the stars or the landscape provided, verified, and reinforced what he might have suspected. Here, there was none of that. So after nearly three hours' progress, he ordered the endaths up a slope to an imposing hill's summit. From there, he assessed their progress.

"Good," he said, as he surveyed the landscape below. "We have deviated only a little from our intended course. I am glad we checked. After a while, even a tiny deviation can turn into an error of many miles."

"I think we chose well," Darva said. "That small range of mountains in the distance are the Han'nah and I can just make out the rim of the Great Salt Plain to their east. danHsar lies roughly midway between the two, a few miles to their north."

"In that case," said Bedistai, "the canyon below us should be the wisest course."

He indicated a stretch of forest extending towards the horizon from the foot of the hill atop which they were standing. It wandered only slightly as it led south.

"We will follow it until it is time to camp. Once morning arrives, we will only need to follow it a few hours more before we come out of those trees onto the plain. Let us descend while we still have light."

CHAPTER TWENTY

They had been making good time through the woods until the endaths began to slow. Chawah and Chossen were both growing skittish and craned their necks in all directions, as if looking for something unseen, listening for things unheard. Their tails flicked, and the muscles of their flanks twitched until Bedistai and Darva could tell something was amiss.

"What is it, girl?" asked Darva, stroking Chossen's neck, trying to calm her with touch. "What do you hear?"

Bedistai was also stroking his mount. He was assessing their surroundings and peering through the branches when, suddenly, a figure dropped from the branches and landed behind Bedistai. As the man tried to wrap his arms around him, Bedistai twisted and drove an elbow into his ribs. He felt bones break and quickly followed the first blow with three more, driving the attacker off.

"Run!" shouted Bedistai.

The endaths took off as men began emerging from behind trees. An arrow hissed behind Bedistai's head and two flew past Darva. One pair of attackers flung a net at Chossen. She tossed her head and it fell harmlessly past. Chawah vaulted someone who had stepped into her path, attempting to raise his bow. As others emerged ahead, Chawah veered left, traversing the rise walling this cleft in the hills. Chossen mirrored the tactic, veering to the ravine's opposite slope. The valley ran straight without branching, giving small chance they would become separated.

Fighters continued to materialize in numbers, but after the initial group, they were no longer hiding and were traveling en masse. Bedistai and Darva had accidentally overtaken a column of soldiers who turned in surprise at the endaths racing past. Some lifted weapons, most belatedly. The arrows they fired flew into the woods or else struck intervening trees.

As Bedistai considered their growing number, then looked across the valley at Darva, he realized they should not be separated. Here, in this corridor, with so many either between them or positioned above them on the slopes, it would be all too easy for a mishap to occur. He shifted his weight, telling Chawah his desire. She turned sharply right and ran straight through the column. And though the troops responded by raising lances, pikes, and swords, Chawah was swifter. She broke through their lines, darting to avoid them or leaping above their heads. Soon, she had traversed to the canyon's other side, arriving at last beside Chossen.

This should have provided comfort, but the clamor was escalating. By now, everyone ahead had turned in response to the commotion they were causing. Bedistai searched for an avenue of escape, but by now the canyon walls were almost vertical. Turning back was not an option. The troops they had passed had created a blockade that contained them from the rear. In response to orders from their commanders, the soldiers around them had begun closing ranks. Too closely packed to ride through, too many men to vault over, shoulder to shoulder from one wall to the other, the human barricade had become impenetrable.

Chawah and Chossen slowed, uncertain which way to go. Eventually, they were standing on the only piece of unoccupied soil, a tiny mound backing onto a canyon wall. Cornered, they lashed out with their tails, attempting to hold the hundreds surrounding them at bay.

Bedistai wondered who these soldiers might be. While they clearly intended to be an army, none were in uniform, and Bedistai was impressed how this ragtag assembly had responded so quickly. One man, dressed finer than the rest, with epaulets stitched to the shoulders of his shirt, wore a visored cap adorned with a feather. As he stepped through the ranks and approached them, Bedistai assumed him to be an officer.

"Who are you to ride through Borrst without permission? Identify yourselves," the officer demanded.

"I am Bedistai Alongquith of the Haroun," he replied, sitting upright and returning the officer's stare. "This woman was separated from her brother and is returning home. In these dangerous times, I could not allow her to travel alone."

He knew that anything untruthful would show in his voice, but until he could learn who these men were and where their allegiances lie, he omitted any details that might jeopardize their safety.

Turning to Darva, the officer asked, "What is your name?"

"I am called Darva."

The name was common enough and most, save the Haroun, lacked surnames, so Bedistai thought her reply would be safe enough.

"Tell me, Darva," the officer said, cocking his head inquisitively, "Where do you and this brother of yours call home?"

"I am returning to Liad-Nur."

"Liad-Nur, is it?" The officer stroked his chin. "Well, you're nearly home."

"We are, indeed," she smiled. "As you can see, the two of us pose you no danger, so won't you kindly let us pass?"

"Tell me, Darva. You surname wouldn't be Sitheh, would it?"

She paused, and her hesitation provided the confirmation he needed.

"I thought so," he smirked. He turned and ordered two soldiers by his side, "Kill the endaths!"

"Wait!" cried Bedistai. He held up both hands, turning left and right in an effort to control the situation. "These creatures aren't your enemies. Please let them go. I beg you. We will come with you. Please."

"Well of course you will come with us," the officer said. "You will come with us or we will leave your bodies here." He laughed at his perceived wit.

"Certainly. You are right," said Bedistai, trying to avoid irritating the man. "But please, sir, let these animals live."

"Do you see how they endanger my men? Those tails could kill someone, and I won't risk my men's lives."

"The beasts are afraid," he replied. Then, to the endaths, Bedistai said, "Chawah. Chossen. These men will not harm you. Quiet, now. Still your tails. Don't hurt them."

The animals relaxed, and their tails drooped.

"You see," said Bedistai. "They are quite tame. Let them live. They will not harm you."

Still suspicious, the leader sheathed his sword and approached Chawah, extending his hand as he came. Although she twitched nervously, she allowed him to stand beside her and stroke her neck.

"She is quite tame, after all," the officer observed. "The other as well?"

"See for yourself. She stands calmly."

"You are right. I like them. I will keep them," he said. "Dismount and come with me."

Darva looked to Bedistai, unsure how to respond. When he gave her a nod and a look that said, "trust me," she dismounted.

The officer grinned and took the endaths' reins in his hands.

"Sergeant!" he called to one of the two by his side. When he stepped forward, the officer handed him the leads. "We are going to put the man and woman where we put all troublemakers. Bring the endaths with you."

"Yes, sir."

The sergeant loosely saluted and started leading the animals away.

When Chawah looked back at Bedistai, the Haroun assured her, "It will be all right. I promise."

Glancing back as they went, Chawah and Chossen allowed the man to lead them away.

The officer returned to his captives. "I hope you will like danHsar. Garmak En will be interested in both of you," he said, referring to Borrst's warlord. "You most of all," he told Darva. "He has no great love for your brother and I believe he will find you very useful," he said, leering at her, his eyes roaming the contours of her body.

Darva ignored his stare, asking instead, "Are you saying that En has thrown in with Kael?"

"He has certainly offered more than your brother."

"More than safety through alliance?"

"In exchange for helping him defeat your brother, Kael will give him Nagath-réal and we will all be rich," the officer replied.

"Do you really believe that Nagath-réal has that much wealth? It is a trading hub and wealth travels through it. Very little remains.

"For that matter, do you really believe Kael will honor his promises to you when he has seldom kept his word to others? I thought you looked smarter than that."

The backhand compliment appeared to perplex him. His

mouth fell open as he attempted to formulate a reply. Unable to do so, he scowled and motioned to a nearby group of soldiers.

"You men, take these two. Bind their wrists and follow your sergeant. Make sure they don't escape."

He frowned at Darva, then turned on his heel and strode off.

The soldiers grabbed Bedistai and Darva's arms. One had the presence to seize Bedistai's bow and arrows. Seeing this, another took his knife. Then they bound the pair, tying their hands behind them.

Once the soldiers had the couple secured, they joined the rest, keeping pace with the march to danHsar. When the canyon's walls began to shallow, widening into a broad valley, the column spread out, and the group that accompanied Bedistai and Darva relaxed, breaking into easy conversation. Bedistai seized the opportunity. He whistled. The sound was loud and piercing and the endaths turned to look.

"Run!" he commanded. "Run!"

Chawah and Chossen tossed their heads, jerking the reins from their handler's grasp. With a sweep of their tails, they cleared the space, then broke into a gallop and disappeared between the trees.

One of the men holding Bedistai punched him in the face. He staggered back then turned to face him. Darva gasped at the blood running from his nose.

"Why did you do that?" the man demanded, gesturing towards the vanishing beasts.

"This is a political affair," Bedistai explained. "Whatever you feel about us has nothing to do with endaths."

Bedistai snorted and the resulting spray peppered his assailant's face. The man wiped it away and raised his fist again. Instead of striking him again, he gazed towards the trees through which the endaths had disappeared, then at Bedistai. He lowered his hand and opened it.

"The captain's not going to be happy with you," he said and punched him again.

Darva hurled herself at the soldier, but with her hands bound and her slighter weight, the gesture was ineffective. The soldier shoved her aside and she tumbled to the ground.

"You'd best behave," he snapped, then grabbed her by the arm. He pulled her to her feet and said, "You have a long walk ahead of you. It'll be even longer if you force me to hurt you."

CHAPTER TWENTY-ONE

B astard!"

Peniff dodged and the cup flew past his head and shattered against the wall.

"Monster!"

He ducked, and the vase exploded into shards of glass.

"Do you think you're clever, you little turd?"

"No, Mother," he replied, barely louder than a whisper.

"If you couldn't read minds, you would be nothing. Nothing! You know that, don't you?"

"Yes, Mother," he said, trying to appease her as a tear coursed down his cheek.

Childhood memories rarely surfaced. Peniff stored them in the place where he kept all his tears. In his youth, he had learned not to cry. He had seen how frightened and insignificant his mother felt in his presence and how she disguised her feelings with shrieks and screams to hide her pain and inadequacy. Initially, he would cry because he felt things as she did, but she ridiculed his empathy, so he stopped, learning to present a placid façade.

In fact, as he grew older, he had learned everyone was

afraid. Not only of him, but of each other. The fears he perceived were overwhelming, and he learned it was often fears that molded them into the kinds of people they became. They lied and cheated and stole from one another because of fear, and made the world the way it was with wars brought on by their hatred, mistrust, grief, and greed.

He understood that, ultimately, fear was the reason Orr held his family hostage and had sent him in search of the woman and the hunter. Peniff had no choice but to feign cooperation. It was a dangerous game, and if he did not play well enough, people would die. His wife and children, the woman, the hunter, and others would die, just as the boys and the old man had.

The dream faded; he hovered, neither asleep nor awake, trying to fathom how he might escape his dilemma.

"Wake up!" Harad shouted, yanking Peniff upright by his neck. "Get on your feet!"

Peniff's hands went to his throat and found a leather collar.

"Can't read minds while you're sleeping, can you, Thought Gazer?"

Harad held a leash and his three cohorts laughed. When Peniff remained sitting, Harad kicked him in the ribs.

"Don't EVER threaten me again," Harad said, and kicked again.

Although he did not possess the most agile of minds and it took him a few days to realize Peniff's threat was hollow, once he had arrived at that conclusion, it did not take Harad long to decide how to respond.

"Did you think you would beat me so easily?" Harad glared. When Peniff failed to respond, he said, "Now listen. You are going to find the woman and you will find her under *my* terms." Another kick. "Even then you still may not return to see your family." And another. "Now get up." One more. "Move!"

Peniff staggered to his feet, or tried to. The pain in his right side dropped him to one knee and his inability angered Harad. As Harad stepped towards him, threatening to continue, Peniff held up his hand.

"I'm rising," he gasped.

"By the Powers you are. I'll make sure of it."

As Peniff brought the kneeling foot under him, Harad yanked hard on the leather strap and pulled Peniff forward, dumping him onto his face. With both hands, Peniff pushed himself to his knees and scrambled to stand before Harad found another opportunity.

"This is not the way to secure my cooperation," he said when he was standing.

"Don't tell me what is or is not the way!"

"I cannot do my best when I am in pain."

"You will learn to do your best when and how I tell you. Do you understand?"

"Please understand I want to find them."

Harad strode up to him and punched him, knocking him onto his back.

"Please understand," Harad sneered, putting as much sarcasm into the words as he could manage, "that *I* want to find them. What you want does not matter."

He pulled on the leash until Peniff was again sitting upright, then stood astride him, bending until his face was only a hand's breadth from Peniff's.

"And if you fail, I will ..."

"... make sure my family dies horribly," Peniff finished for him.

Harad's face twisted into a smile of satisfaction. "Ah! You see. You can still read minds, even like this."

He spat in Peniff's face, then laughed, looking to see if his men appreciated the joke

Of course, they laughed.

"I am tired of traipsing around the countryside with only

your vague 'They are in this direction' or 'They are in that direction.' What I want to know is where are they, exactly? Can you tell me that? Can you tell me exactly where they are at this moment?"

"I don't know," said Peniff, wiping the blood from his mouth. "That is, I am not sure, but I can try." He looked Harad in the eyes. "Do you suppose you can give me a little room to breathe and to think?"

Harad looked puzzled.

"What I am trying to say is, you have all of your men to catch me should I attempt to run. I am but one man, bound and alone. I cannot escape."

Harad appeared to consider the statement.

"Please step back," said Peniff as he wiped the trickle of blood running from his nose. "If you want that degree of specificity ..." When Harad did not seem to understand the word, Peniff rephrased, "that degree of accuracy ..."

Harad nodded.

"Then I must have a few undisturbed minutes in which to locate them."

Harad eyed him suspiciously.

"They are a long way from here, so they are not as easy to find as if they were around the bend in the road."

Harad snorted through his nose. "Don't go wasting my time," he said, then stepped back, still holding the leash. "I will wait right here," he said, gesturing towards a fallen log. "But I have very little patience."

He dropped the leash, then went to the log and sat.

Actually, Peniff had lied. It wasn't hard to locate them. Once he had touched anyone's mind, he could find him almost at once, whenever he chose. Each mind had what Peniff thought of as a unique voice that stood out amid all the other thoughts, once he had learned to recognize it.

But Harad had unwittingly touched on the underlying truth

that made his request difficult to fulfill. Peniff's sense of where they were was purely directional. So, if all one wanted to do was to find any person, then it was only important to know in which direction to proceed. Precise location was entirely different. To determine that, were it possible at all, he would have to enter the individual's mind and see the world as they saw it, as well as enter the minds of the people around them, assuming there were any—people he had never touched before. That was the hardest part, although it was not impossible. If he were lucky, those minds—the ones he sought—might even give up more than sensory information and emotions. They might provide thoughts containing specific details about their situation.

Hoping this morning would bring him luck—he did not wish to endure another beating—Peniff walked towards a tree near the edge of the precipice and sat at its base. As he drew up his legs and crossed them, the pain in his ribs grabbed him and forced him to gasp. Even so, he set the pain aside, as he always had done, and set about locating the pair.

He found the hunter almost immediately and was surprised by his state of mind. On past occasions, he had found him serene, confident, and unshakable. Now, however, he was angry and concerned for the safety of—ah, yes—the woman. The two were still together. The man's thoughts, however, were not centered on their destination, so Peniff removed himself and nestled in among hers. She was afraid, both for herself and for the hunter, but also for her brother and her people. Peniff, who had not yet concerned himself with the full depth of her story, did not yet understand the reason underlying these fears. For the moment, he avoided these particulars and instead turned his attention outward to see the world through her eyes.

She was surrounded by trees. And men. A great number of men. He decided to glean what he could from one of them. Under other circumstances, he might have taken time to inves-tigate the people with whom the pair were traveling, but since

Harad would soon grow impatient, he didn't have that luxury. Instead, he flitted from mind to mind, frequently leaving each one bewildered by the sensation of another's thoughts merging then departing.

For a while, this strategy seemed fruitless. All were preoccupied with thoughts of war and the attendant emotions of fear and exhilaration. None seemed concerned with the couple, nor with where they were headed. None, that is, until he touched one whose mind held a very specific purpose.

Peniff stilled himself until the confusion caused by his initial brusque intrusion had subsided and the man's thoughts calmed again. When they did and the man's focus returned, it became apparent he had stumbled upon the one in charge. Unlike the rest, who were content to be herded towards some nebulous conflict, this one knew precisely where the battle would occur. It was at the forefront of his thoughts and fairly dominated them.

Peniff smiled, because mixed in with this knowledge was an irritation over the pair's recent intrusion. They were an unwanted presence and had interrupted his purpose. He intended to dispose of them. Did that mean ...? No. He did not intend to kill them. He was going to deposit them somewhere.

"Well?"

Harad's shout interrupted Peniff, abruptly returning him to the encampment.

"Are you just daydreaming, or do you have anything useful to say?"

Momentarily disoriented, Peniff rubbed his face and tried to comprehend Harad's words.

"Well, have you?"

At first, it was all he could do to suppress anger over Harad's stupidity. Had this interruption occurred even a few seconds earlier, all his efforts would have been for naught. As it was, at the very last second, the officer's mind had yielded the gem for which he had been so carefully mining. While he would have enjoyed castigating Harad for his insensitivity and lack of timing, he realized how providing anything apart from what he had been asked would be counterproductive.

Setting aside his feelings, he looked Harad in the eyes.

"Yes," he said, enjoying being cryptic.

Harad waited. Then, when nothing more was forthcoming, he demanded, "Is that all? Yes? I would like to hear a little more than yes."

As Harad curled his hand into a fist, Peniff grinned. The information he had gained almost made up for the pain in his ribs.

"The couple have been captured by a fighting force of several hundred men."

That revelation stopped Harad and his fingers uncurled.

"Don't look surprised," said Peniff. "All the lands are at war. I would have been far more surprised had they managed to elude all of the armies in their path."

He grinned, enjoying keeping Harad dangling.

"Have no fear. You will not have to extricate them from the midst of so many. They find them a burden, so they intend to part with them in danHsar."

Peniff could see he had taken Harad to the limit of his patience. The man was about to punch him regardless of what he said next. Consequently, he found it particularly satisfying to reveal, "It should be no trouble whatsoever for you and your men to extract them from lemekUven."

Harad's mouth gaped. In all the world, there was no other prison as secure.

CHAPTER TWENTY-TWO

To say Harad was relentless is to understate the rage that drove him. He had pushed his party mercilessly until eventually one of the horses, driven to exhaustion, fell and refused to rise. When Harad began flogging it, Peniff tore his leash from Kord's grasp, strode up to Harad and grabbed him by the wrist, arresting the whip at the top of its arc. Harad turned to glare.

"You will kill it and still it will not rise." In a soft, but deliberate tone, Peniff went on. "In fact, if you continue to deny the other horses rest or sleep, you will kill them all. Then what? Do you expect us to walk all the way to danHsar?"

Harad's face became a mask of hate, but Peniff persisted.

"Even now, the man and the woman are entering the prison. Do you expect that somehow they will run away and evade us? I promise you, they will not escape any time soon. Look at your men. Even should we stumble on the pair in the next minute, they would be too exhausted to act."

Harad was breathing heavily, but he opened the fist he had formed with his free hand and lowered it.

"We all want the same thing," said Peniff. "Even this poor,

dumb creature wishes to rise and avoid your wrath, but it cannot. Look at its eyes. They are filled with terror, but the animal is spent. It can do no more and neither can we."

Harad could not deny the truth. The horse's chest heaved, its mouth frothed, and the whites of its eyes showed how deeply it feared the next strike of the lash.

"Very well, Thought Gazer," Harad said as he looked from the horse to his men. "We will rest, even sleep if you like, but not one minute past Jadon's rising. I intend to arrive at the city's gate tomorrow."

"And this poor beast will carry you there, if you but allow it to sleep the night, then feed and water it in the morning."

As the two stood staring, it was hard to say who was in charge: the one with the whip, or the one with the collar around his neck.

"There are some things even you cannot simply will into being," said Peniff.

Harad stared a moment longer, then threw the whip to the ground.

"All right," he hissed, before returning to his normal voice. "The thought gazer has declared a holiday. Rest, if that's all you are good for. But I promise, in the morning we will cover ground as we have not done for days."

By morning the West Wind had risen to a level none had seen since the journey began. They were camped in a valley that paralleled the one Bedistai and Darva had taken. The valley's north-to-south orientation reduced the gale's impact, but the wind's ferocity still prevented lighting a fire.

"All right," said Harad. "It's cold food this morning. Not only serves you right, but it won't take as long to clean up. Eat up, all of you. I don't intend to wait here all day."

The men grumbled as they folded their bedrolls and shoved whatever they could into their mouths. The change in mood did not elude Peniff and he carefully went from one mind to the next to learn what he might.

When these men first came upon him, they had been united in purpose. This morning, however, dissension had begun to set in. It had not reached such a level that any would yet dare voice it, but Kord, Tonas, and Ward were clearly unhappy. Peniff resolved if there did come a time when he might turn even one against Harad, he would be ready. The tactic would be risky, but the reduced size of the party certainly improved his chance of success. Harad had split his force outside Mostoon, bringing it from twenty to ten, and the hunter had halved their number again. A defector would put the odds at two against three, rather than one against four, so from this point onward, Peniff resolved to be watchful.

They were soon underway. The wind howled, branches shook and creaked, and all five raised their hoods against flying debris. No one spoke as they wended their way south. The tension among the men remained palpable, and now acquired an added dimension. Although the terrain was becoming easier and they were making good time, everyone understood new difficulties would begin in danHsar. Rumor had it lemekUven was thickly walled and heavily guarded. Situated near the city's center, it would be difficult either to approach or to leave undetected.

By mid-morning, they were emerging from Borrst's wooded foothills onto gently rolling countryside where the land sloped down towards the plains of Nagath-réal. In these higher elevations, herders tended flocks of sheep, while in the lowlands, farther south, below the walls of danHsar, cattle and oxen ranged. That land was open, devoid of concealment, and was as sparsely settled as these foothills.

The five galloped on without interruption, veering only to avoid troop movements as Peniff steered them wide of any encounter. They arrived at the city as dusk was falling, exhausted, bone weary, and their horses were once again ready to drop. Although finding and releasing the two prisoners would likely take time, were it possible at all, Peniff wondered how would they manage to leave danHsar if they succeeded. The gate was well guarded and the sad beasts they rode would be incapable of eluding anyone.

Harad, however, appeared buoyed by their arrival, oblivious to the state of the animals.

"I say we camp outside until morning," he said. "What say you, Thought Gazer?"

"I would prefer to be within its walls," he replied.

"I thought you would contradict me."

"That is not my point. The horses need water and better feed than they can find grazing. Further, I have a great deal of reconnaissance to perform, many minds to examine before we decide what to do."

"We?" Harad raised his brows.

Peniff turned in the saddle. "Do you intend to try to carry this out on your own?" he asked. "If you don't care to consult with me, then my work is finished, and you should tell Kael to send a pigeon to Monhedeth instructing Orr to release my family. Otherwise, I need to study Lord En and determine his intentions. Then, I will examine the prison and its guards to determine what difficulties we are facing. And when I have accomplished all of that, I will advise you which course of action should yield the most favorable results. If you don't like this strategy, why have me along? Your eyes and ears work as well as mine. If your basic senses are all you intend to rely on, you don't need me. Do you?"

Harad ignored the men's snickers as he regarded the walled city. Through tightened lips he concluded, "All right. We're going in."

CHAPTER TWENTY-THREE

Although danHsar was the capital of an agrarian region and by no means a center of commerce, it was far busier than the five had anticipated. Merchants and mercenaries, herders and vendors, craftsmen and artisans, a parade seemingly without end, poured through its rough-faced, closely-fitted stone walls. Lord En was preparing for war, and his army required goods of all sorts. Since there were wages to be earned, craftsmen were converging in droves. The press of men and animals throughout danHsar's cobbled streets made navigation difficult and the noise filling the canyons between the buildings was overwhelming and oppressive. Accents, dialects, and various tongues assaulted the ears, while anxious beasts added brays and bellows to the tumult.

To make matters worse, the cacophony compounded the deluge of thoughts cascading over Peniff, so he sat huddled on his saddle, holding his head. Until now, he had forgotten why he avoided crowds, let alone big cities. danHsar forced him to remember. The world was populated with many latent telepaths, unaware of their abilities and unable to control them. In large enough numbers—an inevitability in a city like this—

their thoughts assailed him to such an extent he could not keep them out. Their random outbursts pummeled him until he believed he would surely go mad.

Amid this cacophony, he thought he heard someone calling. Cupping a hand to his ear, he glanced around, trying to determine its source. On the horse beside him, Harad was mouthing something.

"What?" Peniff called, shaking his head to indicate the difficulty hearing.

"We need to find lodging," Harad shouted all the louder. "And I need to find a place where I can think."

Relieved, for a change, that Harad shared his discomfort, Peniff nodded. "We all do," he shouted back. "Let's try a side street. Perhaps we can find a local who can tell us about the city."

Peniff gestured towards an alleyway and Harad nodded. The horses were becoming skittish. Since they were threatening to rear and throw their riders whenever they were jostled, the men dismounted. Leading them on foot for better control, they maneuvered towards the edge of the river of bodies and found side streets an improvement. Peniff sighed when the congestion abated. The rest of his party also seemed relieved. Tonas and Ward began making pleasant conversation, and Harad managed an uncharacteristic smile.

Following Peniff's suggestion, they began making inquiries whenever they found someone who would listen, but were surprised to find almost everyone was a stranger like themselves. Occasionally, however, they encountered a resident willing to provide suggestions. Even so, their quest for lodging took longer than expected. Most hostels were full, and it was well after dark before they located an inn with both rooms and stables to let. Fortunately, its location was a quiet one, offering Peniff the possibility of accomplishing his appointed task.

The innkeeper led them to the two remaining rooms. Harad

took one and ordered Peniff to share it with him, while assigning Kord and the others the adjoining one.

When they had deposited their belongings, Harad announced, "I'm famished. Let's find something to eat."

"I'm sorry," Peniff replied, as he tossed his bag onto the floor beside the nearer bed. He sat upon it and apologized. "But I intend to stay here. I'll eat later. You can go on without me."

"So you can escape? I don't think so," Harad objected.

"That isn't what I meant."

"No?" Harad asked.

"We have lost most of the day. Now that we're situated, I need to get to work. I need to find Lord En. I need to locate the prison. Most of all, I need to determine where En is keeping the couple."

"Aren't you too tired for that?" asked Kord. "I can't believe you're not exhausted.

Peniff nodded and said, "That's even more reason to avoid eating. With a belly full of food, let alone drink, my mind will be sluggish and I may miss something important. Go eat if you want. The quiet will help me think."

"Do you think me stupid?" asked Harad.

"Of course not," sighed Peniff. Harad's paranoia was beginning to wear, but he was too tired to engage the man at length. "Leave Kord, if that will keep you happy, but I need to get to work. It will take time to locate them precisely. That said, do you have any idea how hard it will be to determine a means of entry, or how we might extricate them after we find them—if getting them out is even possible? That strategy will require a great deal of time and patience to work out, and I promise it is not the sort of information one can acquire in a pub."

Harad appeared torn.

"Leave him," said Kord. "Where can he go? We can order the stableman to hold the horses until you tell him otherwise. If the thought gazer tries to run for it, he will have to do it on foot. Besides, he hasn't any money. If he wants to sit here and starve, then let him. My stomach is growling."

That seemed to satisfy Harad.

"Be here when we return," he ordered. "Don't make us come looking for you."

"As your man said, I haven't any money. I will be here."

Harad nodded. Turning to the rest, he said, "Come on, boys. Let's wash away the dust."

They closed the door behind them and their muffled laughter and jibes followed them down the corridor.

Peniff slumped when they had gone and ran his fingers through his hair. Indeed, he did have a great deal to accomplish. This was the opportunity he had been waiting for, and he hoped he had enough time, let alone the strength. He stilled his thoughts and reached outward.

Finding Ganeth En turned out to be easiest. So many minds in the city were focused on the warlord that Peniff was able to locate him almost at once. After he had occupied En's mind, determining his plans for the pair was also easy. En had only recently been apprised of their capture and had ordered them detained within the last hour. Consequently, the pair were at the forefront of his thoughts.

He had decided to hang on to the woman to leverage his standing with Kael. If he were going to risk setting his army against Obah Sitheh, he wanted Nagath-réal as his reward. If anything would induce Kael to keep his promise, it would be the girl. Kael could keep Rian and everything else in the south, En reasoned, but Nagath-réal would add immeasurably to his wealth and would open the door to the east. Controlling the gateway would elevate him from overseer of a land of shepherds, to a lord with real holdings. The Haroun, on the other hand, was of no real use. He would dispose of him by morning and be done with him.

That last bit of information alarmed Peniff. From his earlier contact, Peniff knew the hunter planned to return home, and he intended to accompany him. Traversing battlefields on his own would be far too dangerous and he did not wish to contemplate what harm might befall him were he forced to attempt it on his own. He stifled his agitation. If his emotions got the better of him, he would certainly fail, so he set his fears aside and focused on acquiring information about the lemekUven. As he began, however, En's attention became diverted and that knowledge was soon buried under newer, more pressing matters.

Carefully, meticulously, in order not to unsettle the warlord and thereby compound the difficulty of his task, Peniff trod between those thoughts until he located the pertinent memories. He was not concerned with the prison's location. He could easily learn that later. Most residents would likely have some idea where it was, and he could make a simple inquiry on the streets if he had to. What he needed most was how to gain entry and who controlled access.

En, however, was growing agitated over news he was receiving about the forces in Liad-Nur. His thoughts were becoming turbulent. Nonetheless, after half an hour's effort, Peniff found what he needed. He spent the better part of the next hour learning about the prison's entrances, its guards, how it was laid out, as well as on which floors the pair were being kept.

When he believed he knew how to locate their cells, at least in approximate terms, he checked to see how Harad and the others were doing. When he found them, their thoughts were so disjointed and muddled he had trouble believing he had succeeded. Then he understood. All of the men, except Kord, were blind staggering drunk. To make matters worse, Harad had left the dining hall and was returning.

Peniff was not about to allow a drunkard to jeopardize his mission. The Haroun's impending death demanded immediate action. Rising from the bed, he pulled on his cloak and started to leave. He was reaching for the handle when the door flew open.

"I missed you, Thought Gazer," Harad slurred as he swayed, holding the doorjamb for balance. "Oh!" he said, as he strained to see through the alcoholic haze, and saw Peniff was dressed to go out. "Did you miss me, too?"

"I was getting hungry and thought I'd try to find you," Peniff lied.

Harad's face darkened and twisted to a scowl. "Are you sure tha's what you were up to? You haven't any money. Remember? How were you going to eat?"

"I was hoping you would have saved something for me."

"So you were jus' going out to find us."

"I had learned what I needed, so there was no reason to remain. Besides, I thought you wanted me to join you. I wish you would make up your mind. Were you expecting me to just sit here all night and hope you would return?"

"Tha's 'zac'ly what I 'spected," Harad slurred. "You were s'posed to sit here and wait. You had your chance to join us and you missed it."

Looking back over his shoulder, Harad lost balance and stumbled into the corridor.

"Kord!" he called, as he slammed into the corridor's opposite wall.

Before he lost footing altogether, Kord stepped up and caught him.

"What should I do with this pile of manure?" Harad asked, this time barely comprehensible.

"Let's get out of the hallway," Kord suggested, bracing himself against Harad's weight.

Harad would not be put off. "What do you say, Kord?"

"Whatever you wish," Kord said, struggling to keep to his feet. "Slit his throat, perhaps."

"I have a better idea," said Peniff. When Harad tried to focus, he suggested, "Come back inside and I'll tell you."

Kord grasped Harad's shoulders and gently but firmly walked him into the room.

"Let's hear what he has to say."

"Is it only the two of you?" Peniff asked, looking back down the hallway.

Kord nodded. "Tonas and Ward are busy eating and drinking, although to be honest, it's more drink than food. I thought one of us ought to come with him."

Harad was losing his ability to stand, so Kord deposited him onto a bed. Harad struggled to return to his feet, but lacked the balance and fell back, nearly tumbling onto the floor. His eyes widened. Too late, he put his hands to his mouth. Unable to staunch the sudden upwelling, he vomited all over himself, the bed, and the floor.

Kord jumped away, barely in time to avoid being soiled.

"This room is going to be pleasant," he observed.

"I'm not planning to spend the night," replied Peniff.

The remark caught what little attention Harad still possessed, although he was rapidly losing consciousness and could not respond. His head came up, then stared vacantly, and Kord spoke for him.

"So, he was right. You're running out on us."

"Not at all," said Peniff, sizing him up.

While he had known Kord was not entirely Harad's minion, he could tell he was not Harad's friend either. There was an underlying current of animosity between Kord and his leader, so Peniff decided to see if he could turn it to his favor.

"As I said, I was on my way out to find you," he explained. "I wanted to share what I have learned, although it is obvious you are the only one who is still coherent."

"They will all be fine come morning."

"We don't have until morning. En has ordered the couple

killed at dawn," Peniff lied. "The prison is almost full, and I don't believe he knows the full value of his prisoners."

"What are you saying?"

"What I am saying is, either with you or without you, I am going to try to effect their escape. If we wait until morning, all our efforts will have been wasted."

Kord glanced at Harad as he toppled onto the floor, where he lay motionless in the puddle of vomit. Although not as drunk as the others, Kord was not completely sober either and Peniff needed him to focus.

"The only question I have is whether you are coming with me."

"You can't leave him like this."

"What do you suggest? If the woman is killed, my family dies and our mission has failed. While I hold no love for any of you, my wife and children mean everything to me. I will do whatever I must to fulfill my part of the bargain. So tell me: do you plan to stay here with this drunkard, or will you join me?"

Kord looked from his leader to Peniff, weighing his dilemma.

"Make up your mind, Kord. The sand in the hourglass is draining and I am on my way out the door."

As Peniff turned to go, Kord gave Harad one last look.

"I'm coming."

CHAPTER TWENTY-FOUR

Rather than undertake the arduous process of gleaning lemekUven's location from the minds of the citizenry, Peniff elected the more direct method of asking passersby. As luck would have it, the first one he asked pointed the way and gave directions. To Peniff's good fortune, both the prison and the inn where they were staying were close to one another. In a matter of minutes, he and Kord found themselves standing before it.

A monolithic block, rising five stories above the pavement, nearly as wide at its base as it was tall, lemekUven lived up to the rumors. While most buildings in the city fronted narrow streets and lanes, the prison was surrounded on all sides by broad well-lit avenues, making undetected approach impossible. Featureless except for two rows of small and widely spaced windows, high above the street, and a great metal door at street level, it appeared to be a solid block of stone. In addition to the pair of sentries at its entrance, guards were posted at each of the prison's corners, commanding uninterrupted views of its perimeter, while lookouts stood watch atop its roof.

As he and Kord stared perplexedly at the prison's façade, a

unit of four guards turned one corner, while a similar patrol rounded from the opposite direction. They crossed paths directly before the main door, then disappeared as they marched towards IemekUven's rear.

Seconds later, Kord turned towards Peniff.

"I can't tell you how many jails I've seen. I could pick most of their locks with a bent pin in less than five minutes." He shook his head. "But I've never seen the likes of this. What do you propose we do now?"

"I'm not sure. Allow me a minute to learn what I can," Peniff said.

Closing his eyes, he began seeking information. The task took considerably longer than the minute he had asked for. He stood motionless for several minutes before reopening them, then smiled at the revelation. The guards stationed at the rear gate had provided the insight.

"We have one possible entry, but we must act quickly. Food and other goods are delivered through the rear. The wagon which is scheduled to deliver grain for tomorrow's porridge has yet to arrive. I located the driver at a nearby pub. He and his helper have finished drinking and are preparing to complete their delivery. If we hurry, we can intercept them and possibly use the wagon as our way inside."

"Do you know where it is?"

"I know the direction. Let's hope it's not far."

"You lead and I'll follow."

Peniff ran back down the lane from which they had come, glad that Harad was not here to controvert or impede him. He crossed two streets, then turned down a third. A short while later, he and Kord arrived at an intersection across from the one brightly-lit building in the vicinity. On the street before it, a wagon drawn by horses was hitched to a post topped with a lantern serving as a street lamp.

"I think that's it," said Peniff, gesturing towards the box-like conveyance. "If it is not locked, we can climb inside before anyone sees us."

Boisterous voices and laughter issued through the public house doors.

"Quite a party," said Kord. "Let's hope the noise works in our favor." He stared at the wagon and added, "It looks empty. Shall we try it?"

"The driver and his partner are still inside. We should go before they come out."

They were about to break for the wagon when a pair of celebrants, waving to others inside, stepped onto the sidewalk. They shouted something indecipherable, then stumbled towards the wagon. One man unhitched the horses, while the other climbed onto the driver's seat and took up the reins. When his partner climbed aboard, the driver gave a whistle, shook the leads and the team of horses clomped down the cobbles.

"Voreth's horns!" Kord swore. Tearing off his cap, he threw it into the street. "There went our chance."

He was turning away when Peniff grabbed him by the shoulder.

"Wait."

In that instant, the wagon halted.

"I won't be but a moment," they could hear the partner say. He leapt to the curb, nearly falling when he landed. "I'll be right back," he said and tottered up the street towards the pub.

"This is our chance," Peniff said. "I don't think they are in much better shape than Harad."

While they were waiting, a pair of young lovers strolled by. Peniff decided they were too enrapt with each other to notice much else. So, when the partner disappeared through the public house doors, Peniff hissed, "Go!"

They dashed across the street on tiptoes. The driver was

busy complaining to the horses, but they were afraid their boot heels on cobbles would alert him.

At the back of the wagon, Kord tested the latch and grinned when it released.

"They didn't lock it."

Peniff grinned back. "Nobody steals porridge," he whispered. Then, keeping watch for the driver's companion, he urged, "Hurry. Get inside."

Kord started to climb in, then stopped.

"There's no room," he said.

Peniff looked inside and saw the wagon was full. He was starting to panic, until he looked closer.

"There's room on top of the sacks," he said. "Get in before the other one comes back."

Kord climbed aboard, wedging himself between the cargo and the wagon's roof. Peniff followed, and the two struggled to situate themselves, almost dislodging two of the bags as they fit themselves into place. When Peniff attempted to pull the doors shut, to his dismay, there were no inside handles or inner latch.

"I'll have to hold them," he said as he gripped the doorframes with his fingertips. "Let's hope they stay shut."

In a short while, the partner returned. Once again, the driver whistled to the horses. When the wagon lurched forward, the doors flew open and Peniff hurled himself toward them. Kord's fingers dug into his calves. But despite his fears, Peniff sighed when he managed to keep the doors from swinging irretrievably apart. Praying to gods he did not believe in, he drew them shut and tried to calm his pounding heart.

"This is crazy," he whispered.

"We're crazy," corrected Kord. "What kind of idiots break into a prison?"

Peniff had no answer, but he knew Kord was right. This whole endeavor was insane. Even worse, he had been so focused on getting inside, he had no idea what they would do if they finally succeeded.

As he listened in the darkness to the clip-clop of hooves, he tried to formulate a plan. But when he examined the men who were making this shipment, he found little to encourage him. They were so intoxicated, and their thoughts were so muddled, he could only glean incomplete images of what lay within those walls.

Armed with only scraps, he told Kord, "When we arrive inside the gate, keep your hand on me and do as I do. We will pass into a courtyard. If all goes well, when the gate closes behind us, we will jump out and find someplace to hide. Pray it goes smoothly."

The wagon continued for several minutes, but eventually halted. They heard muffled conversation and what sounded like a laugh before the wagon started off again. This time Peniff watched the wagon through the eyes of a guard. As they passed through the entrance and the gates came together, he threw the doors open and leapt out. Kord landed beside him as Peniff struggled to secure the latch. When the wagon passed into the ring of light cast from the loading dock's lantern, he aborted the attempt and they hurried to lose themselves in the shadow of lemekUven's wall.

They watched as the horses halted and the two men climbed down. The driver stumbled up a short flight of steps onto the loading dock's platform. He muttered as he yanked a cord hanging beside the door. A bell rang, and shortly thereafter, a uniformed guard appeared. While the two stood there chatting, the partner went to the wagon's rear.

"Someone's been inside!" he shouted.

When the guard rushed to look, the driver called out, "I wouldn't get my dander up. It's just Wil. He forgot to lock them again, same as he did last week. Remember?"

The guard nodded and slapped Wil on the back.

"Gotta be more careful," he said. "Somebody's gonna come along and steal all that cereal. Then where will we be?" He laughed at his own joke.

Peniff was starting to wonder how long they would take, when the guard echoed his concern. "From the look of you, I'm willing to bet you stopped off for a dram. I better lend you a hand, or you'll be all night with the unloading."

The guard stepped onto a rung below the wagon's doors, hooked his fingers inside the doorway, then groaned as he pulled himself aboard.

"You're gonna owe me," he called over his shoulder.

Grabbing a large sack of grain, he pulled so it toppled to the ground, then climbed down after it. The driver and Wil followed suit, making jokes at each other's ineptitude. For the next fifteen minutes, the three continued to work, stopping on occasion to catch their breath or tell another joke. Then, calling noisy goodbyes, the driver and his partner climbed back on board and turned the wagon around. The guard, apparently as careless a man as Wil, left the loading dock door ajar as he disappeared inside.

When the wagon reached the gate, the driver put his fingers to his mouth and whistled. The portal opened, allowing the vehicle to pass before the gate shut behind it.

When the crossbar thudded into place, Peniff and Kord emerged from the shadows and Kord gestured towards the door.

"Is it safe?" Kord asked.

Peniff paused to consider, then nodded.

"The guard's gone well inside. It should be fine for a while."

As they approached the stairs, Kord whispered, "I guess you're happy Harad was too drunk to join us."

"Why do you say that?"

"You two don't get along."

"That wouldn't be an important enough reason." When

Peniff could see Kord was perplexed, he explained, "It is not necessary to like one's partners. It helps, but it is not important. It's only important he trust them. Even though I don't like Harad, I know I could count on him to see this project through. He has too much at stake not to finish it. Actually, I would have preferred that he and the others had been able to come along. Five are better than two in a fight. I only decided to go it alone because too much could have gone wrong if they came along drunk."

CHAPTER TWENTY-FIVE

As they approached the loading dock door, the two men fell into silence. Kord drew his sword, then hesitated, looking at Peniff.

"Where is yours?" he asked. "Don't you have something to defend yourself?"

"You mean a sword?" Peniff asked, then shook his head. "You know Harad doesn't let me carry one."

"You should have taken his before we left."

"Back home, I'm never armed. Old habits are hard to break. If you're afraid, I can go it alone."

"I'll come," said Kord. "But I should lead the way."

"Then I need to tell you the first room we'll come to is empty."

Kord nodded and stepped through the door with Peniff close behind. The room was dark, illuminated only by exterior light and a torch on one wall. It appeared to be a storage room filled with stacks of boxes, piles of sacks—some full, some empty—and several barrels scattered about in no particular order. There were doors in two of the walls, through one of which came a distant lamp's glow.

"Do you know where we're going?" Kord whispered.

"I know the layout in broad brushstrokes, but not every detail. They are holding the Haroun on the third floor, so we must find a way up."

"What about the woman?"

"I'm not as sure," Peniff lied.

He knew exactly where she was, but it was important they find the hunter first. With Bedistai free, he and the hunter could overcome Kord, if it became necessary. Then Peniff and the couple could leave together. On the other hand, if Darva were freed before the Haroun, Kord could take her at sword point and Peniff would be powerless to stop him.

They continued inside, trying to be silent and listening for sounds as they went. When they reached the next lighted doorway, they paused, standing to either side. Beyond, a woman hummed softly to the accompaniment of a soft, rhythmic scratching. Peniff peered inside and saw she was sweeping. Her back was turned. So, putting a finger to his lips, he raised his other hand and gestured to Kord he should wait. She paused, left a small pile of debris, then moved to a new location and resumed. As soon as she turned away again, Peniff slipped around the corner and rushed towards her, motioning Kord to follow. As she turned at his footsteps, Peniff covered her mouth and pulled her against him. Kord emerged from the shadows, brandishing his sword.

"Keep quiet and we will not harm you," said Peniff.

Her eyes were wide with disbelief, so he tried to calm her.

"We don't want to hurt you, but we have to make sure you won't alert anyone to our presence. We are going to put you inside that closet." He indicated with his head. "If you remain quiet and give us no trouble, nothing bad will happen. Can you do that?"

She nodded vigorously.

"We are going to barricade the door to make sure you stay

inside, but I am going to put the oil lamp on the floor outside. It contains no more than an hour's oil. When the crack under the door goes dark, you can make all the noise you want so the guards can find you. Do you understand?"

Again, she nodded vigorously and produced what sounded like an affirmative whimper. Once they had put her inside, they stacked boxes to hold the door shut.

"Do you think she will give us away?" asked Kord. "I'd rather slit her throat and be done with her."

"When you brought me along, you promised no one would die," Peniff said. "Twice now, you have broken your word. First, it was the boys, then the old man. If we have to kill guards, that is one thing. But touch one hair on this cleaning woman's head and ..."

"And what?" Kord pointed towards the door with his sword. "I don't trust her."

"She won't give us away. She's too afraid."

When Kord asked, "How can you be sure?" Peniff tapped his head with a forefinger.

"You could be wrong. My way is certain."

Kord tried to step around him, but Peniff barred his way. Kord grabbed his tunic and Peniff exhaled.

"You're right," he said. "I have no way to stop you. But unless we can trust each other without hesitation, the guards are sure to discover us. And then what? We won't be able to rescue anyone because we'll either be prisoners ourselves or, more likely, we'll be dead."

Kord considered this, then put the edge of the blade to Peniff's throat.

"Step aside," he said.

"You'll have to kill me to get to her. Do it my way or try explaining my death to Harad and Kael, because that is the only way you'll get by me. Then explain how you failed, because without me you have no chance of finding anyone. You need me. I'll do everything in my power to stop you from hurting her, and you don't dare harm a hair on my head. Put down your sword and let's finish this."

When Kord hesitated, Peniff added, "I want to be perfectly clear. From this point on, it is my way or nothing. There will be more than enough killing ahead. But for now, I call the moves. Put away your sword and let's get on with it. Either that or everything is finished here and now."

Kord stared for a moment, then, breathing heavily, resheathed his blade.

"Fine," said Peniff. "Let's go."

CHAPTER TWENTY-SIX

Save for the pots and cauldrons, the kitchen was empty. After they passed through it and approached the building's heart, activity increased, and the way was better lit. Guards came and went, either singly or in pairs, and although Peniff and Kord were repeatedly forced to duck into side passages or hide behind walls, with the thought gazer always on the alert, they were able to avoid detection. Even so, some locations offered no concealment at all. If someone were to encounter them out in the open, they would be finished.

They had ducked into a closet near one set of stairs. One hinge was broken, and the door hung ajar. Footsteps and voices at the flight's summit indicated a handful of guards. Since the activity was constant, Peniff and Kord huddled, waiting for an opportunity to move. As the minutes dragged by, Kord began to fret.

"It's late," he said. "It should be quiet. What's going on?"

"Shift change coming up," said Peniff.

"And we're stuck here?"

"We'll be fine for a while. The guards on this floor are occupied elsewhere. The floor above is several hands short, so the ones coming down will be few."

"The night's old. I don't intend to spend the rest of it hiding." He started to leave.

"No!" Peniff whispered and grabbed him by the shirt. Yanking him back, he said, "Wait."

Kord had started to object when two guards wearing heavy boots descended.

"When I get home," one was saying, "I am going to fall into bed before the old lady starts in. She's fed up with these hours and my coming home like some old man."

"I know what you mean," his partner replied. "My wife is tired of these long shifts as well. She's even threatened to find herself a boyfriend." He snorted. "As if she could find anyone with her looks."

They were still laughing when another set of footsteps ascended from below. The first guard greeted one of the newcomers.

"Bolo, we thought you was gonna miss your shift."

"So did we," Bolo replied. "The captain decided to give us boys a lecture."

"What about?"

"If he don't say something before you go home, I'm sure you'll hear about it in the morning. Lord En is going to begin executions tomorrow. He wants to add as many guards to his army as possible. He thinks most of the prisoners here are dispensable and doesn't want to keep any more of us on duty than he has to."

"You mean he's planning to recruit us for that war of his? Voreth's horns! I'm no soldier."

"Me neither, but it seems he don't care. You're in his service for better or worse. Argue and he's apt to execute you, as well."

"Mastad!" the second guard cursed.

The four complained heatedly for several minutes before

the first pair headed home, too engrossed with the news to notice Peniff and Kord. Meanwhile, their replacements disappeared up the stairs.

"You were right," whispered Kord. "If we'd waited till morning, they both would be dead."

Peniff frowned as the lie he had concocted was coming to pass. He told Kord, "It's best if we wait until they finish changing shifts. After that, we can do what we need to."

A short while later, when most of the activity subsided, they left their hiding place and ascended the steps. When they reached the top, they halted. They had expected the stairs to continue from the second floor to the third but, instead, they ended here. A short distance beyond stood a duty desk. And though the guard who manned it was occupied, eyes glued to the desktop, they would have to pass before him to reach the next flight.

"We can't stay here," said Kord.

Peniff nodded and considered what to do. "I'm going to try to get close and draw his attention. Either he grabs me or I'll grab him. While we're struggling, you jump out and we'll repeat what we did with the cleaning woman." He looked Kord in the eyes as he added, "Only this time, you won't just show him your sword."

As Peniff prepared to make his move, a shout from a corridor caught the duty guard's attention. When the guard glanced toward the commotion, it was Kord who dashed toward him, ending his move in a crouch beside the desk. The guard turned at the sound of his footsteps and set a stack of papers aside. As he stepped out to investigate, Kord rose from his crouch. The guard was rounding the duty desk when Peniff hurled himself across the room and into the man's middle, upending him. As the guard fumbled for a truncheon, Kord arrived and tore it from his hand. He struck the guard's head and the man became still.

"That should do it," Kord said.

Peniff climbed from the body, listening with his mind and ears. The clamor the duty sergeant had responded to was growing in volume. Shouts from both prisoners and guards filled the air.

"We need to go," he said.

"Let's at least drag him behind the desk," suggested Kord.

"No time," replied Peniff. "We need to go."

"But if someone sees him ..." Kord started to say, but Peniff was already heading towards the stairs.

CHAPTER TWENTY-SEVEN

Abandoning caution, taking three steps at a time, Peniff ran up the stairs with Kord right behind him. He did not know what they would do if one of the guards were to see them. To make matters worse, it was becoming hard to think clearly. The farther into the prison they went, the clamor of thoughts grew until they were becoming almost unbearable.

They halted at the top, arriving in a room where several corridors intersected, radiating out like the spokes of a wheel. Cells lined each passage with doors spaced so closely it was evident each room was no wider than the span of two arms.

Kord grabbed Peniff's arm.

"Where do we go from here?"

"I'm not sure."

Kord's eyes opened wide. "What do you mean you're not sure?"

"It will take a minute," Peniff replied.

"We don't have a minute."

As if in reply, voices rose on the floor below.

"Everything is going wrong!" cried Kord.

"I will do what I can," said Peniff.

Even as Kord looked back in a panic, Peniff found himself growing unexpectedly calm. Here, in the place where he needed to be, the place he had struggled against so much adversity to find, was the solution to his problem. The guards below were debating what to do about the duty desk guard, so he took a minute to reach out. He located a guard on this floor, hoping his mind might hold the key.

"Ah!" he said softly, as the answer presented itself.

He walked to a corner between two corridors.

"Here they are," he said and took a ring of keys from a hook fastened there.

As he held them in his hand, an idea what to do with them presented itself. As the shouting below grew more urgent, he began fingering the keys one-by-one.

"What are you doing?" Kord's eyes darted from Peniff to the stairs and back again. "Let's go! We don't have any time!"

Oblivious to Kord's urgings, Peniff passed each key between his fingers, carefully touching their surfaces while Kord began to bounce up and down, unable to contain his panic any longer. Peniff had never done this before and smiled at the ease of the task. The technique was not unheard of. Thought gazers who made their living as entertainers often used this method to "magically" glean information from personal articles owned by members of their audience.

"This one," Peniff said, holding one key apart from the others.

As more voices joined the chorus and feet pounded up the stairs, Peniff held the key at arm's length, aiming it down one corridor, then down another, and another still.

"What are you doing?" Kord's eyes were wide. He was shaking and perspiring, half mad with fear and ready to bolt. "I can't stay here."

"This way," Peniff said, and proceeded down a corridor, eventually breaking into a run.

"Thank Siemas!" Kord swore, running after him.

They had nearly reached the corridor's terminus when Peniff halted, holding the key towards one door, then, as he turned completely about, towards its opposite.

"This one," he said.

He inserted the key into the lock and turned. When he tugged the door's handle, the door swung open and Kord's mouth fell agape.

The cell was unlit, and at first, he was unable to see. Then, as his eyes adjusted, he made out the shape of a man sitting cross-legged.

"Who are you?" the man asked.

"We are here to help you escape," said Peniff. "You and the woman."

"Who are you?" the man repeated, this time with emphasis.

"We are friends," Peniff replied.

"By the powers," said Kord, looking back down the hallway. "We don't have time to explain. They are coming. Get up. Show us where the woman is, so we can get out of here."

"I'm sorry," replied Bedistai, climbing to his feet, "but I don't know."

"I can find her," said Peniff, smiling broadly.

Kord glared. "I thought you said you didn't know where she was."

"I lied."

As Bedistai pushed past and stepped through the door, Peniff looked back at the approaching guards.

"This way," he said and turned the opposite direction. "Hurry."

When they reached what Peniff assumed to be the prison's outer wall, he turned down a corridor that ran the perimeter until he reached a spiral staircase leading up. Sensing no guards were immediately above, he climbed and probed the floor for the woman. In doing so, he located another jailor and learned where the fourth-floor keys were kept. They emerged and Peniff turned to Bedistai.

"You find your friend and I'll get the keys. I'll join you shortly."

"And if I cannot find her?" said Bedistai.

"Then I will," he assured.

Bedistai cocked his head and studied Peniff. When Peniff returned his gaze without hesitation, Bedistai nodded.

Bedistai and Kord set off, calling for Darva through the bars of every door. As they did, Peniff ran towards the intersection's terminus. There, he located a hook similar to the one on the floor below and began fingering the keys.

One indicated Darva. It said she was near. That was fortunate, because the guards on this floor were rallying like the others. Looking back down the corridor from which he had come, he saw his companions approaching.

"Kord!" he called. "I've found her."

As the voices and footsteps behind them grew louder, he led them to her cell. When Peniff threw the door open, Darva flinched and raised her right arm as if to ward off a blow. She had been sitting in total darkness, so she squinted at the light.

"Darva!" exclaimed Bedistai.

At the sound of his voice, her arm came down and her expression softened. They could see that the guards had done more than imprison her. Her face was discolored, and the right side of her mouth was swollen, covered with a mass of dried blood. Her left hand secured the severed front of her leather shirt.

"Bedistai!" she exclaimed as she struggled to her feet. Her top fell apart when she threw her arms around him. "How did you ...?" she began, but Peniff cut her off.

"There is no time for explanations. If we have even a chance of escape, we must go at once."

"Which way?" asked Bedistai as he removed his shirt and draped it around her.

"Down spiral stairs at the end of this passage." Peniff pointed. "The confusion is too intense for me to tell what we'll find at the bottom, but we can't remain here."

Kord was already on his way.

"Follow me!" he called.

CHAPTER TWENTY-EIGHT

They descended from the fourth floor to the third. At the foot of the stairs, Kord announced, "This is as far as we can go by this route. I only know one way down and it's right in the middle of things."

His description could not have been better. Even as they approached, it was obvious the stairs had become a focal point. Near the place where the corridors converged, a guard was unlocking cabinets stocked with truncheons and swords, axes, and pikes. The ones who were joining him chose from this arsenal.

Kord unsheathed his sword, then reached past Peniff and handed his dagger to Bedistai.

"It's better if I'm not the only one with a weapon."

Bedistai hefted it and tested its edge, then nodded his approval.

"This will do," he said. "But with luck, perhaps I can find something more effective."

Kord was starting to reply when bells and gongs began sounding, alerting the prison an escape was underway. He turned to Peniff.

"I don't think we stand much of a chance. Is there anything helpful you can tell us?"

Peniff shook his head. "There's too much commotion. It's going to be luck that gets us out."

Kord nodded grimly. "Then let's pray we have it."

"Wait!" Peniff said. "I have an idea. We need to add confusion to the mix."

"Isn't there enough already?" asked Darva.

"Not nearly. If we are the only ones trying to escape, the guards will surely seize us. There need to be others." When they met his remark with vacant stares, he said, "I still have the keys." Holding them aloft, he explained, "They will be trying to round up everyone by the time I've finished."

He went to the nearest door and unlocked it.

"Everyone," he repeated with a wink.

As his company watched, he proceeded down the corridor, unlocking each door as he went. Initially, most prisoners stared dumbly Then, as they rose and began stumbling from their cages, some began crying, "I'm free!"

Understanding spread like wildfire until, as Peniff unlocked each new one, the inmates burst forth without prompting. By the time he had freed half the corridor, those still locked in their cells were banging on their doors, demanding freedom. He handed the keys to one of the newly liberated, instructing him to continue the task. The man grinned and picked up where Peniff had left off.

"Now, it's not just us four. They have dozens to corral. More every minute."

As the trickle of escapees began swelling to a stream, then a river, then a flood, Peniff realized it would not be long before the rising tide would be too overwhelming to contain. Even now, at the hub where the corridors converged, clubs and swords rose and fell as uniformed arms struggled to control what they soon could not. A multitude of hands seized the jailors. Helmet crests sank and disappeared beneath the deluge. Each time another guard fell, a cry went up and the crowd surged forward. By the time Peniff and company reached the stairwell, it had become the conduit for the exodus.

The press had become so great they had no choice what to do. Congested though it was by a mounting logjam of wounded and dead, the onslaught carried them into it. Guards at the foot of the stairs were hacking at the ones leading the advance. As those bodies fell, the ones following either trampled them, or else, tripping and falling themselves, were crushed by the ones coming after. It was all Kord, Peniff, Bedistai, or Darva could do to remain upright, grasping those around them for balance and support, treading on those unfortunates under foot.

Escapees spewed onto the second floor. As the jailbreakers spread across the area surrounding the duty desk, guards wielding truncheons, maces, and swords dove into the fray. Kord and Bedistai were attempting to use their blades, but the prisoners, seeing one more way to arm themselves, attempted to wrest away their weapons. Now, instead of fighting guards, they were compelled to stab, punch, and elbow, even bite the ones inadvertently aiding their escape. More than one prisoner fell to the sword and dagger as Kord and Bedistai slashed, punched, and pushed their way free of the throng. Even Peniff and Darva found themselves grappling with those who struck at their liberators with the same anger and hatred they directed at their captors.

Bedistai grabbed a guard by the tunic and wrenched away his sword. But when he attempted to hand the blade to Peniff, the thought gazer only stared.

"I'll take it!" cried Darva and grinned at her prize. With hardly a pause, she began clearing space around them.

"This way. We need to go this way," shouted Kord, shouting above the tumult and pointing the way.

As they moved through the rooms leading out of the prison's

core, Darva recovered a club from one of the fallen. This time, when she handed the weapon to Peniff, he accepted it, bringing it down on the head of a man attempting to knife Bedistai.

Felling guard and prisoner alike, they descended to the ground floor, then fought through a series of rooms until, suddenly, they were on the courtyard cobbles. The gates had been forced open, so as the confinement that had given cause to the struggle ceased to be, the mob flowed past and fled through the opening. They allowed the flow to carry them with it until they were back on the streets where the stream of escapees disintegrated into a disorganized mass moving in all directions. It was hard not to become separated for all the jostling, so the four separated themselves from the crowd.

They were trying to decide how next to proceed when they heard someone call, "Kord!"

Peniff froze at the voice just as Kord turned to face the speaker.

"Harad," he called back. "Thank the powers you're here."

"Thought you would double cross me?"

"What? No. You were drunk and I ..."

Harad cut his explanation short with a blade to Kord's middle.

"No!" Peniff cried, staring in horror as Harad withdrew the sword. "What have you done?" he demanded as Kord fell upon his face.

"I gave him what I do to anyone who betrays me."

Peniff felt blood rushing to his face. "He was doing what you were too drunk to do. We learned that En intended to kill all his prisoners, so he was saving these two while he still had the chance."

Harad regarded the body at his feet, then looked up at Peniff.

"You're lying."

"Kord was loyal. He would never have betrayed you. You are a fool who can't tell his friends from his enemies, so I will make matters clear. *I* am the one who is betraying you. The hunter and the woman are leaving with me," Peniff said.

He raised the club to make his point and his companions stepped up beside him.

"Did you learn nothing in No'eth?" asked Bedistai. "I advise you to take your friends and leave while there is still breath within you."

Although Harad, Ward, and Tonas each held a sword, they made no move to challenge as Bedistai continued, "If you wish to see another morning, I would advise you to leave."

Harad stared at Darva and scowled. After so much time and effort, after coming so close to capturing her, he was clearly outmatched. Flanked by his cohorts, both of whom were looking to him for direction, he tensed as though preparing for a fight, then lowered his blade.

"Run," he told the trio. "Run and hide if you can. We will be close behind you every step of the way. Don't close your eyes. Don't turn your backs or go to sleep, or I promise you will pay dearly."

With that, he and his men sheathed their weapons, then turned and disappeared into the crowd. Only when Peniff, Bedistai, and Darva were certain they were gone did they put away their own.

"Was that who I think he was?" Darva asked. Then, turning to Peniff, she said, "For that matter, who are you?"

"We ought to go," he replied, casting glances at the open prison door. So far, only prisoners had been exiting into the courtyard, but he felt it would not be long before the first guard showed his face. "Let's find someplace safe and I'll explain everything."

As they turned to go, Bedistai knelt beside Kord and unfastened his scabbard. He caught up with Peniff and Darva, fastening its belt as he arrived beside them.

They wound their way through danHsar's streets, through the pandemonium of guards, soldiers, and escaped prisoners, perhaps eluding notice because they did not resemble the prison population. Fearing someone would order the city gates closed, they made directly for them. And though they worried the authorities would detain them when they attempted to leave, by the time they reached the outer wall, word from the prison had not yet arrived and they were but three among an exodus of hundreds.

A short while later, they departed the main road, then trudged across a meadow and up a hill, before disappearing into a stand of trees. Ten minutes later they emerged into a glade surrounded by woods where they decided to spend the night. When they were certain no one had followed, they sat upon a log, whereupon Peniff sighed deeply and began his account.

"You asked me who I am, by which you mean why have I come to set you free? I am afraid your question has no simple answer, but I will try to relate the events that have brought me here."

He paused for a minute, remembering the day.

"It began like this," he said.

CHAPTER TWENTY-NINE

His first recollection was of peals of laughter. Broodik was chasing Halli across a meadow of sweetgrass and wildflowers covering the knob overlooking danBrad, the city he and his family called home. He and his wife, Miened, were delighting in their children's play. Halli wore the pink dress Miened had finished sewing the day before and her golden curls bounced and danced about her shoulders as she ran. Although Broodik could have easily caught his sister, he pursued her at a pace just sufficient to sustain the chase and the fun.

It was Sa'amas, the Day of Contemplation, and earlier that morning, the family had climbed to the hill's summit to escape their cares. Small clouds scudded across the deep green sky. The red roofs and white walls of danBrad spread across the valley below. As Peniff chewed on a blade of grass, reclining and watching how Miened followed their children with loving eyes, he found himself at peace, unable to imagine a finer day.

All at once, he sat upright.

"Miened! Get the children. Riders are coming."

Miened, caught up in her own delight, was unable to

comprehend his sudden alarm. She turned slowly from the objects of her joy and with a casual smile asked, "Who did you say is coming?"

Peniff, however, was now transfixed, oblivious to her voice as he gazed unseeing into the distance. While his posture suggested he might be listening for faint, distant sounds, he was trying to detect the inaudible. Indeed, the footfalls of the horses he knew were approaching would have been unde-tectable until they topped the rise, so instead, he was extending his mind towards the riders he knew were nearly upon them.

"Sabed Orr's men," he replied as if in a trance. He rose slowly. Then, as his consciousness returned to the meadow and the moment, his tone grew urgent and he repeated, "Sabed Orr's men are coming. Hurry, Miened! Get the children. We must go. They mean to harm us!" he cried, even though he knew running would be futile.

"Halli!" called Miened.

Over the course of their marriage, his wife had grown to trust the odd and sudden declarations he made from time to time. And though she still did not understand the why or the how of it, she had learned he was often aware of things she could never foresee and that he was always right. So, with no comprehension but a great deal of trust, she scrambled to her feet and ran to collect her daughter as Peniff ran for Broodik.

"Mama!" the girl cried, for at that moment she saw the first rider appear on the meadow.

Eyes wide and screaming, she ran to her mother, who caught her and lifted her into her arms. Peniff had already picked up his son, so together the family watched as a dozen or so riders topped the hill and surrounded them. Heaping recriminations upon himself for failing to notice the danger sooner, Peniff listened to Miened's panting breaths and the children's sobs and whimpers.

As the riders slowed their mounts to a walk, they rode

around them, appraising their quarry. One halted directly before them while his comrades maneuvered until they were five abreast, one row before and one row behind, hemming the family in. The leader nudged his horse forward until Peniff could feel its hot moist breath on his face.

"Peniff!" gasped Miened, and Halli began to cry. Broodik, intimidated by the beast's proximity, buried his face in his father's shoulder. He wrapped his legs around Peniff's chest and clung to his neck.

"Are you Peniff, the thought gazer?" the rider asked in an impassive tone.

"My name is Peniff," he replied, holding his son protectively.

The rider, angered by his incomplete response, demanded, "I asked if you are the thought gazer."

The very afternoon seemed to take on the man's anger. The breeze which had been tousling his son's hair and ruffling his daughter's dress now rose in force as if in concert with the riders. It whipped their clothing about them and beat the grass into a frenzy.

"I have been called by that name," Peniff acknowledged cautiously.

The man turned to one seated to his left.

"Take the boy," he commanded. As the man he had ordered attempted to wrest Broodik from Peniff's arms, the leader said to the riders on his right, "Take the woman and the girl."

"Leave my family alone," shouted Peniff, clinging to his son. "They have done nothing. We have done nothing."

He realized at once how foolish that had been, but it was too late. The lead rider turned his mount sideways and struck Peniff with the pole of his lance. The shaft hit the arm holding Broodik and Peniff, staggered by the blow, dropped to his knees, barely hanging on to the boy.

"No!" Miened cried, in no position to help.

She clung to Halli as two men dismounted and pulled at the

girl. Another approached Miened from behind. He grabbed her arms, tugging them apart, while his cohort seized Halli and tore the girl free. The one who had struck Peniff wrapped his reins around the saddle's pommel, swung a leg over, and, with the casual ease of one who had spent all his life riding, dropped to the ground. He strode up to Peniff and snatched away the boy, telling one of the others, "Here, Kord. Take this squirming brat before I squash him."

Peniff dared not speak. He knew if he did, the leader would make good on his threat, so, to his surprise, he was actually relieved when Kord took Broodik. Kord, however, showed little regard for the boy's safety, because he tucked him under one arm and held him like a sack of flour with his head and feet dangling.

Peniff, with eyes fixed on his son, climbed to his feet and prayed Kord would not drop him. Then, he turned to the one who had struck him and repeated, "We have done nothing."

He was breathing hard, and knew any show of emotion would only increase his disadvantage. He stilled his breath, and in the most even tone he could manage, asked, "What do you want of us?"

The rider's lip curled into a sneer. Then, as though he were making a perfectly polite request of a merchant or craftsman, his expression softened, and he said, "My lord requires your services."

Peniff was aghast. Forgetting himself, he demanded, "Is this how Sabed Orr contracts for all of his work: with intimidation and barbarism?"

"Watch how you speak of your lord, Thought Gazer. You hold your family's well-being in your hands. If you wish them easy treatment, you would do well to remember your respect."

This was not a battle Peniff could win. Even though he raged inside, he bit back his anger and again asked as calmly as he could, "What does your lord wish of me?"

The man smiled at the victory. "One of my lord's enemies, a woman, has fled his grasp, aided by a savage, one of the Haroun. As you may know, those people are very elusive. It is my lord's wish that they do not escape, but are recovered and returned to his justice as quickly as possible. To this end, he requires you to help us in our pursuit." His voice lost its pleasant tone and slipped into almost a growl as he dropped his pretenses and concluded, "These are his words."

"Your lord should understand that my skill is an imperfect one. Sometimes I can readily touch another's mind. At other times, especially when that person is some distance removed, I cannot."

The man's face darkened, and he shouted, "Then it is time you begin perfecting your craft." He paused, then resumed in a quieter tone, "Your skill is already better than most. You knew Sabed Orr sent us without my telling you."

Peniff opened his mouth to speak, but the leader snapped, "Don't try to tell me you knew because this is Monhedeth. We could have come from anywhere—Dar, Yeset, Meden —anywhere."

Peniff's face fell when he realized how he had slipped.

"If you are unable to locate the woman, your loved ones will pay for your inability."

"Why? How can this be?" Peniff asked. "You would not expect the same of any other. Certainly I will do my best. I promise I will do everything in my power to succeed. But you speak as though I would deliberately put my family at risk. I hold no loyalty to the ones you seek and I love my family dearly, so why would you harm my wife and children if I cannot do what no other person can?"

The leader folded his arms and replied, "These are my orders, Thought Gazer, and I have as much power to change them as I have to change the tides or the seasons."

He turned to the ones holding Miened and the children.

"Take them to barakMis," he ordered, naming Orr's fortress. As his men placed their prisoners on their saddles, he turned back to Peniff. "You will see them alive again when you complete your mission. Until then, bid them goodbye."

As Peniff watched, the men rode off. That was the last he had seen of them. He then recounted the events of the pursuit right up to the moment he opened Bedistai's cell and how, in fact, his loyalty had shifted.

"How did they know where to find you?" asked Bedistai.

"That has left me wondering, too. All I have been able to glean from Harad's mind was that someone at the palace told him."

"I find that odd," Darva said.

Peniff nodded and brooded for a minute over this missing puzzle piece.

"Now that you both are free," he said, returning to the present, "there are only two things left for me to do: Take you to your brother as quickly as possible," he said to Darva, then to Bedistai, "and free my family."

CHAPTER THIRTY

Peniff awoke shivering. Forced to sleep on the ground with only the clothes on their backs for protection, he, Darva, and Bedistai had huddled together for warmth, nestled within a cluster of bushes. As he grew more aware, he realized that Darva, who had spent the night snuggled between the men, was no longer beside him. He sat upright, drawing his knees to his chest and clasping his arms around his legs for what little warmth that provided. Perhaps if he had eaten something since yesterday's breakfast, he thought, he might have staved off the cold. An empty stomach, he knew, is good for very little, especially in severe weather, and his was growling its displeasure. It occurred to him that movement might generate some warmth, but his muscles reacted stiffly as he attempted to rise. His hip stabbed him after pressing all night against a rock. Still, he forced himself to complete the act. He climbed to his feet and, with another effort, straightened.

Once he was standing, he noticed Bedistai also had vanished. Afraid they had deserted him, he panicked until he paused and reached out to find them. It took only seconds to touch each one, and another moment to determine where they were. He sighed with relief. Bedistai was foraging in the woods, and Darva was standing on a nearby bluff. He set off to join her.

He found her near the place where they had slept. Her arms were crossed, and she was gazing across the plain below. She was wearing a guard's leather jerkin, one that Bedistai had picked up as they exited the prison after she had insisted he take back his shirt against the chill.

Peniff cleared his throat to avoid startling her. She jumped, nonetheless, and glanced over her shoulder.

"Good morning," he said. "Did you sleep well?"

Darva hesitated, then mustered a smile before her battered mouth forced her to grimace. "I did," she said as she touched it. After another pause, she added, "Thank you." As if it required an explanation, she added, "For rescuing us. You risked a great deal."

"You are welcome, but the act was not as heroic as it may have appeared. Had I not acted when I did, I would have attempted it this morning, possibly at knife point."

"Nevertheless, your decision was both noble and perilous. Besides, you could have simply left the city and run back to your family. Most likely you would have beaten ... what was his name?"

"Harad."

"Yes. Thank you. You would have beaten Harad. You would have known his thoughts and could have avoided him."

"Perhaps. And, then again, in spite of my talent, he may have covered ground faster. My deed was not so noble as it was foolish, and had I failed, Sabed Orr would have put my family to death. If he learns what I have done, he still may."

Peniff eyed her bruises and was almost tempted to ask if they hurt. Since he despised small talk and begging the obvious, he said nothing and Darva turned away. The silence felt awkward, but he stood beside her, regarding the plain as she continued to gaze.

After another moment, without turning to face her, he said, "You seem troubled."

"I am studying troop movements. With so many below us, I can't see how I will be able to return to my brother." She turned to face him. "But why do you ask? I should think you would know my thoughts already."

He shook his head. "I try not to intrude unless I need to."

When she cast a questioning look, he replied, "Here, or when I am at home with my family, I try to live inside my head as any other man does."

There was another awkward silence while Darva studied him, as if trying to comprehend something.

"You thought we left you!" she blurted.

Peniff's mouth twisted. He looked away, then nodded.

"I'm sorry," he said.

"I see," she said. The space between her eyebrows creased. "Is that why you were unable to detect them in time?"

"Who do you mean?"

"The horsemen who took your family. You were keeping to yourself, instead of reaching out."

Peniff grimaced again. She had confronted him with the guilt he had been trying to suppress, an emotion that still surfaced unbidden. He could have prevented everything, he kept telling himself, questioning the ethic that honored others' privacy. If only he had put his own needs first, they still might be together.

"You were doing what every man has the right to do," said Darva. "You were enjoying your family. You couldn't have foreseen what would happen. How could you know that day would be different from any other?"

He turned to her, probing her eyes, as if she could somehow remove the sour feeling.

"Our circumstances are actually quite similar," she said.

"One minute, I was riding towards a meeting with an arms merchant."

She looked away for a moment, apparently caught up in the memory.

"Hah!" she laughed. "I had even planned against what actually happened, or so I thought. I had brought my bodyguard—not one or two, mind you—but a company of ten. Even they were not enough, and you had how many?"

Peniff studied the scuffs on his shoes.

"Your wife and children," she answered for him. "Do you see what I mean? I was prepared because I knew I was headed into danger, although, granted, the danger I was prepared for was less than what I actually encountered. But you, Peniff ..." She touched his chin with her fingertips. "You had no reason to be on the lookout for anything. You were spending a day with your family."

He smiled tentatively at the chance she was right, at the chance he was not to blame. He wanted ... no, he needed to believe her. When the silence once again became awkward, he changed the subject.

"Do you know what your friend is doing?" he asked. "The morning is almost gone, and I suspect we should be on our way."

"He is looking for food and water, although I am at a loss as to how we will cook any food or carry any water. We are in a fine mess. We are armed, but aside from our weapons, we have absolutely nothing else to help us survive."

"And if the nights grow any colder," Peniff added, "sleeping in the open like this, I'm afraid we may all become ill."

They stood in silence, watching the columns of troops streaming southward towards Nagath-réal and Liad-Nur, wondering aloud how they could pass through them undetected.

Just when they thought they must surely go crazy speculating, Bedistai broke the silence.

"I have found breakfast," he announced.

Peniff and Darva started at the interruption and whirled to see him standing bare-chested, gripping his shirt with both fists and holding it like a basket. It was obviously laden, but with what Peniff could not tell.

Bedistai offered his prize, saying, "We will have nuts and wild tesberries."

As the Haroun dropped to his knees and laid his treasure on the ground, Peniff noticed Darva casting him a glance. The smile flickering across her lips helped alleviate his guilt, if only for the moment. That she would ignore her own pain, brought about by a violation he could only imagine, in order to comfort him, touched him all the more.

"I have also found three brush hen eggs," added Bedistai, as he fished inside the bundle before producing one. Triumphant, he displayed it between his thumb and forefinger.

"Eggs?" said Darva. "How will we cook them?"

"We don't need to," he replied. Then, holding the egg pointed-end up, he drew his knife, and with a sharp, deft flick of his wrist, sliced off the tip. "You simply drink them," he explained as he put the opening to his lips, sucked out the contents and swallowed. "Ah!" he gasped. "Good. Here, try one," he said as he bent to retrieve another.

"You can't be serious," said Peniff. "I can't do that."

Bedistai paused and looked up. "Why not?"

"Because I don't eat raw eggs."

"Why not?" Bedistai repeated, furrowing his brow.

"Because I don't."

Bedistai shook his head, picked out another and offered it to Darva.

"Would you like to try one?"

Darva wrinkled her nose, then stepped forward and extended her hand, regarding the egg as if it might explode.

"How do I remove the tip?" she asked.

Bedistai grinned. "I will do it for you." He did as he had done to the first, then handed the egg to her. "If you are afraid of the taste, tilt your head all the way back and the contents will go straight down your throat."

She nodded, eyeing it askance.

When he added, "That is how we teach our children," Peniff stifled a grin.

Darva's eyes narrowed and she studied Bedistai's face, clearly uncertain about the comment's implication. When his face remained placid, as if nothing was intended, she accepted the offering. After glancing at each of her companions, she put the egg to her mouth. Exhaling through her nose, she tipped her head as Bedistai had instructed and sucked hard, swallowed even harder, and shuddered as the contents went down her throat.

"See?" Bedistai encouraged. "Not so bad."

"If you say so," she said with a distasteful edge to her voice.

"It will help you get through the day. Are you sure you won't try one?" he asked Peniff.

Peniff considered the proposition and the lingering expression on Darva's face. "I don't suppose we will be sitting down to a full meal any time soon," he said and extended his hand.

Obviously pleased at convincing him, Bedistai retrieved the last egg, removed its tip, and presented it. Peniff accepted it with a nod, determined he would not embarrass himself. He took a deep breath, and in a single motion, tilted his head, and sucked the contents into his mouth. He swallowed, then paused to consider the taste. As he lowered his eyes to meet the Haroun's, he conceded, "You know, it really wasn't all that bad."

Bedistai threw his head back and howled. "You have the makings of a Haroun."

They all laughed together, and Peniff tried to remember the last time he had done so.

Bedistai sat on the ground and spread his shirt to display its contents. As the three ate their breakfast, they discussed the best way to proceed towards Liad-Nur.

"The troops I've been watching appear to be moving towards barakMaroc, a fortress still under construction," Darva said. "Since there is no way to avoid it on the way to Liad-Nur, I suspect my brother will have already garrisoned troops there in anticipation of their arrival. Even though En has offered overtures of friendship, over time it has become clear his ambitions exceed what his lands can provide. His recent attacks on the villages at the northern edge of the Great Salt Plain have already demonstrated his determination to acquire whatever he can, however he can. We have long discussed the possibility he will turn against us. Now, with Hath Kael preparing for war, it appears En is taking advantage of the opportunity in hopes of catching my brother between Kael's forces and his own."

Each man was nodding.

"Ordinarily, I would have suggested losing ourselves among the caravans arriving from the East. So many strange faces come and go with those convoys, it would be easy to hide among them. But if a battle were to arise before we could cross the Nagath Valley with one of them, the only way into Liad-Nur would be a lengthy journey south through Rian, then back again, several weeks out of our way. On the valley's west side, however, there rises a small range of mountains called the Han'-nah. If we cling to their edge as we swing around their southern face, we can avoid the Nagath Valley altogether and make directly for barakMall, where Obah will be organizing his main defense and counterattack. Do you agree?"

The question was unnecessary. Bedistai and Peniff were strangers here and deferred to her judgment.

Bedistai added, "Not only will the terrain provide concealment, but it is apparent, even from this distance, those slopes are heavily forested. We should find food there and, in all likelihood, several streams will be running down their sides. Before we leave, however, there is a small brook near here. We should drink our fill. Although we will probably find more water today, we may not find it as soon as we would like."

CHAPTER THIRTY-ONE

They descended from their observation point, traversing the hillside on a course paralleling the troops. But as the suns rose ever higher and the day became warmer, the three began to grow thirsty. While they could tell they would reach the Han'nah by nightfall and observed a waterfall's silver thread cascade down the distant slopes, there was no indication where its stream reached the valley and they had yet to encounter another source of water. Hours passed with no sign of even a trickle and the uneven terrain involved as many steep climbs as it offered descents.

"Bedistai," Peniff gasped, as he struggled up a grade. "We need to find water. I hate to complain, but I am starting to feel dizzy."

"Me too," said Darva. "If we only had a little, I think I could manage."

"It may be a while," replied Bedistai. "You have to be strong."

Darva started to object, but Peniff raised a hand. He saw an encouraging sight directly below on the valley floor. With a hand on Bedistai's shoulder, he brought him to a halt.

"Look at that," he said, and pointed.

Drag marks carved into the soil ended at a broken-down supply wagon. Its team of horses had pulled it away from the parade of troops and two soldiers were examining its busted wheel. One of them stood and threw something at the ground, then stared at the countless others parading by and ignoring their plight.

"Do you think they might help us?" Darva asked Peniff.

"It is possible. I don't see why not, if we approach them carefully. I can concoct a story, but I suggest only Darva and I go. You are an imposing man, Bedistai, and I think they may perceive you as a threat. And if they realize you are a Haroun, my explanation will fall apart. We should also give you our weapons to avoid raising their suspicions."

Bedistai agreed. "But I will be watching in case you need me."

They headed towards the breakdown as Bedistai waited, then followed at a distance. One soldier noticed when they emerged from the brush. He nudged his kneeling companion, who interrupted his examination of the wheel. When Peniff smiled, raising a hand in greeting, the second one rose and stood by the first.

"Can you help us?" asked Darva.

In response to their stares, Peniff said, "We were ambushed by Obah Sitheh's men." Darva gave a harsh glance, but allowed him to continue. "They took all our possessions and we were lucky they left us with our lives," he concluded, hoping Darva's beaten face would lend credence to his tale.

"You dress like a Northerner," the one who had been kneeling observed. "What would bring you so far from home during times like these?"

"We are on our way to Bad-Adur to join our uncle," said Peniff. "He sent a pigeon with a message asking us to join him."

"He lives there?"

"No. He is a trader whose business brings him there. Despite the difficult times, he is transporting a shipment of sandiath pelts from Sandoval which he hopes to sell in Mitheron. With their rainy climate, they are always looking for anything waterproof. We both speak Mitheroni, and he needs us to translate. Now, however, it will be nearly impossible for us to join him. The bandits took our horses and carriage, everything but the clothes on our backs."

Darva jumped in. "Do you suppose we might prevail upon you for even a water skin? We have nothing with which to pay you but I, for one, would be most grateful," she added, giving her sweetest smile.

The one who had been speaking raised his hand, as if to say payment was unnecessary. He returned Darva's smile and said, "Certainly, dear lady. It appears we are not going anywhere soon and the water we're carrying will just sit here as the food spoils. Can we offer you some dried meat to go along with it? It's not much of a meal, but it will keep you from going hungry."

"Oh, sir. I cannot begin to thank you enough."

As he went to the wagon to fetch what they needed, his partner asked, "Do you think you'd be willing to show me some gratitude?"

He grasped Darva's arm and planted his mouth on hers. In an instant, Peniff grabbed his elbow and tugged.

"Get away from her!" he demanded.

Still holding Darva, the soldier whirled and drew his knife.

"Do you really think you can stop me?" He grinned as he pointed the blade at Peniff. "Everything has a price, and I intend to collect."

Eyes wide, Darva looked beseechingly at Peniff.

"Don't!" she pleaded. "I'll be all right."

But when the soldier put his blade to Darva's throat, Peniff moved instinctively. Acting on what felt like a long-forgotten memory, he grabbed the man's jaw and twisted his head around to face him. Putting his face right up to the soldier's, Peniff stared into his eyes. What he intended was different from merely reading thoughts and required a different entry. He couldn't say why it did, or what was causing him to act in this manner, but once he had begun, he felt driven to finish what he had started.

He entered through the portals of the soldier's eyes, delving deep, searching for the man's core, for the vital essence. What he learned when he thought he had found it both startled and repelled him. This was a man who knew no kindness, who delighted in other people's misery. For him, causing pain or instilling fear was cause for excitement.

Peniff gazed down a long tunnel of memories and saw how the man's life had been filled with pain and anguish, with beatings by his father, eventually leading to abandonment. He might have felt sorry for this soul, were it not for the twisted way it had developed, finally becoming like the father who had spawned it. Now, it was a monster bent on tormenting everyone it met. The possibility it would not only harm Darva, but might even kill her, was something Peniff could not allow.

Peniff was struggling with his conscience over what to do next, when he realized the man was attempting to break free. Angered by the confusion and inability to act caused by Peniff's mind lodged inside his, the man was struggling to regain control. His mounting anger was leading to murderous thoughts, directed at both Peniff and Darva.

As the man tightened his grip on the knife and tried to will his arm to move, Peniff struck. With no weapon to wield, save for thoughts, he began calling forth the man's demons—his buried fears and long forgotten pains.

The soldier convulsed. He released Darva and started to sob. His mouth contorted into a hideous shape, something between pain and terror. Then he opened it and uttered something guttural, neither a cry nor a moan but something primitive and bestial. While the man fought to avert his gaze, Peniff delved ever deeper, seeking whatever else he might unleash. In response, the soldier dropped the knife and raised his arms to push Peniff away. Peniff retaliated by stifling all the man's thoughts. The man froze, unable to complete the act. Instead, he began trembling violently. His legs started to buckle, and he sank to his knees.

A voice intruded. "Peniff! What are you doing?" cried Darva.

She tugged at his arm, trying to pull him away, trying to make him stop. But while Peniff was aware of her, he maintained his focus. For another full minute, he bent over the man, driven to continue until the soldier had curled into a ball.

"Peniff, please," she begged.

This time Peniff relaxed. He stepped back while the man crawled away, his entire body trembling. The soldier gave Peniff one backward glance, then struggled to his feet, staggering for several steps as he retreated. Then, as his steps became more certain, he ran out among the passing troops, running into several at first, eventually disappearing into the throng. His comrade, who had been watching, had dropped the things he had gathered. Then he, too, turned and ran, leaving Darva and Peniff alone by the wagon.

"Peniff," Darva gasped, unable to raise her voice above a whisper. "What happened? What did you do?"

He stood for a moment, staring after the soldiers, before turning to face her. At first, he didn't know how to answer.

"I don't know," he started to say. "I have never done that before." Then, as a shred of a memory began to emerge—something old and forgotten—he changed his response. "No. That is not right," he muttered, disbelieving what he had done. "Something tells me I have. Once. But I can't remember when. I think it was a long time ago."

"But, what did you do? I have never seen anything like it."

185

He paused, reflecting, then met her eyes again. "I reached inside him. I reached inside and ... How should I say this? It felt as if I grabbed his soul and twisted it with my hands," he said, growing puzzled at his own admission.

Now it was he who was shaken. He sat on the ground and looked up at her.

"I think I could have killed him. I believe I would have, had you not spoken."

"But, why?" she asked.

"He wanted to hurt you. I was unarmed. I'm not as strong as he and I could not think of what else I could do to stop him." He paused. "And then, I knew how to do it and I acted. I don't know what to say except that I am very much afraid." As he looked up at her, he said, "And I am sorry."

She stared at him a moment, her face full of distrust. "I do not think I can continue traveling with you," she said.

"Oh, no!" he gasped. "I did not wish to frighten you. I would never do such a thing to you. Please believe me. I would never ..."

"Are you all right?" Bedistai asked. He was standing beside her now.

She regarded Peniff, then turned to the Haroun. "Did you see that? Did you see what he did?" When Bedistai nodded, she said, "I think we should continue alone."

"Please," Peniff begged. "You may still need my help. And," he paused again. "I certainly will need yours."

Darva shook her head. "We will be fine on our own, Peniff. Go home. Help your family. There are supplies enough on the wagon for all of us. Take what you need and go your own way. We began without you and we will manage the rest of our journey by ourselves."

Peniff was at a loss how to fix things. He knew he would never hurt either Bedistai or Darva, but he could not think of a way to convince them.

"I am sorry," she said. "I don't mean to hurt you, but if you are as uncertain as you say you are about what you did, that does not inspire confidence."

"No. Of course it doesn't. I'm sorry. I only meant to protect you."

"Of course you did," she replied, sounding unconvinced.

Peniff bit his lip, dismayed he could offer no better assurance. "Gather what you need. I must take my time. I need to think for a while to understand it better." When they remained where they were, he insisted, "Go. I will be all right."

Bedistai and Darva went to the wagon and began gathering supplies. Peniff watched as they filled two skins with water and two other bags with food. They also took blankets. Bedistai made sure Peniff was watching when he placed a sword and scabbard on the ground beside the broken wheel. After one last goodbye, they turned away and climbed back up the hillside.

Peniff was crushed and not a little afraid. Certainly, he still feared for his family, but he was also frightened by this newfound ability. To make matters worse, he was not at all certain it was something he could control. Had Darva not interrupted, he would have taken the soldier's life. That was the one thing he knew. What might he do, he wondered, if Darva or the hunter or—the thought terrified him—one of his family angered him? Would he now try to kill them as well? Would anyone be safe with him after today? A great black dread filled him, and it was nearly dark before he picked himself up. He collected the supplies he would need and followed the two into the mountains. He did not have a plan, but he felt they might still need him and hoped he might eventually prevail on the hunter to help save his family.

CHAPTER THIRTY-TWO

Evening had arrived and Mahaz and Jadon had descended behind the Han'nah. Darkness enveloped the range's eastern slope whose shadow stretched across the Nagath Valley to the Great Salt Plain, an ivory rim on the edge of the visible world.

Despite the breathtaking vista and crisp evening air, Peniff trudged onward, mired in wretchedness and despair as he followed the couple, desolated by the monster he saw himself becoming.

By the time it became so dark that he had trouble seeing, Bedistai and Darva had discovered a cave in which to spend the night. Caught between his ethics and his need not to lose them, he reached out and perceived they were settling down to sleep. With only starlight for illumination, finding his own place to bed down would pose a challenge. He repeatedly tripped over unseen obstacles, but eventually he located a cluster of bushes that would break the wind gusting up from the valley floor. After depositing his provisions and assuring himself they would not roll down the mountain, he cleared a space of rocks and twigs, then swaddled himself in the blanket. Unearthing the water skin from among his supplies, he took his first sip of water since morning, then closed his eyes as it ran down his throat. After two more swallows he considered his situation.

He realized, for the first time since he had set off from the wagon, how truly alone he had become. It wasn't the hunter or the woman he missed, although it wounded him when they had left him. In his heart he knew they were right. They could not trust him, and until he understood his own actions better, he could not trust himself. While whatever had compelled him to hurt the soldier continued to baffle him, he was certain it was not the first time he had acted in that manner. At the bottom of his soul lay the memory of that first event, and he believed if he could somehow resurrect it, an important door would open.

None of this caused his emptiness tonight. Instead, his broken heart longed for its missing pieces: his wife, Miened, and his children, Broodik and Halli. Although he missed them constantly and longed for their company, he had avoided reaching out to them lest he break down over their absence and find himself immobilized, unable to finish what he needed to accomplish to set them free. His betrayal of Sabed Orr also haunted him, as did the possibility that something or someone might convince Orr he no longer needed a thought gazer. Certainly, if his duplicity were uncovered, the warlord would deal with his hostages as unwanted garbage.

As Peniff shivered, huddling to keep warm, tucking thoughts of his family away, he stopped. Tonight he needed to feel them. Cautiously, so as not to disturb—for of all who walked the lands, his family nearly always knew when he touched them—he reached out to Monhedeth and located them almost at once. Gasping at how quickly their thoughts filled him, he withdrew abruptly, savoring the sensation, holding his breath as their presence overwhelmed him. After another moment, he exhaled, then filled his lungs again and smiled. They were alive and they were well. For now, that tiny certainty would have to suffice, yet a tear ran down his cheek as he forced back the flood he had been containing since their abduction.

Since losing his composure would not serve him, he drank again, then stoppered the skin and set it aside. He opened the rest of his provisions and munched on a carefully rationed portion of dried meat and cheese, trying not to gorge.

He continued to stare across the valley until the last shred of light vanished. As determined as he was he would not fail, he was at a loss how he could ever regain Darva or Bedistai's confidence.

CHAPTER THIRTY-THREE

P eniff's eyes opened. Before he was even awake, he was sitting upright. In the instant he became conscious, he knew something was amiss. He stared into the darkness and attempted to identify the sudden flood of thoughts. Since the moment he had set off after Bedistai and Darva, he had violated his major caveat by leaving his mind open. Now, he could sense not only the couple, but others—inhuman minds of evil intent—converging on the sleepers. Tossing aside the blanket, he fumbled for his sword. The scabbard was still fastened to his belt, but he had forgotten to ensure that it still held the weapon before he fell asleep. He panicked until his hand found its hilt. Reassured he was armed, he established the cave's direction, then, fixing the couple's location, he struggled uphill, arms extended before him like an unassisted blind man.

As he crashed through the underbrush, stumbling and falling more than once, he feared he would reveal himself to the entities in the cave. But when he realized the things stalking Bedistai and Darva were focused solely on their prey, he charged forward, heedless of the noise he was making. His greatest fear now was not of being heard, but of sliding down the hillside, only to end up farther away, injured and unable to reach them before his worst fears came to pass.

And though they were encamped but a short distance above the place where he had been sleeping, the climb seemed to take forever. Brambles tore at his leggings and stones slipped beneath his boots, as if the rocks and vegetation were conspiring against him. Time and again he had to disentangle himself from branches and it seemed he could not move fast enough. Then, as he rounded a corner of the mountain's rocky face, a faint amber glow revealed the cave's opening.

He listened, but heard nothing. The creatures' thoughts told him they had not yet reached the sleepers. Before plunging inside, he assessed his condition, wondering if he were prepared for what lay ahead. He felt strong. He was gasping for breath, but not winded. His life as a miller had not prepared him for this climb. Rather, it was his trek with Harad that had hardened him. Angrily suppressing such perverse gratitude, he grasped the rim of the cave's narrow mouth and pulled himself through, arriving in a surprisingly large cavern.

Dying embers in its center provided scant illumination, but in the semidarkness, he could discern two prostrate forms lying near the fire's remains. He could also see several openings punctuating its walls, and it was through these he detected the ones approaching.

He knelt by the sleepers, intending to arouse them, but when he reached for Bedistai's shoulder, the hunter whirled and grasped his wrist. Lurching upright, he put his knife to Peniff's throat.

"What do you want?" he hissed, his eyes boring into Peniff's.

Arching his neck from the blade, Peniff pointed towards the cave's wall and uttered the only word he could muster.

"Samanal."

The clatter of stones snapped Bedistai's head around, as a

lizard larger than either man slithered from a waist high opening and dropped onto the floor.

"Darva!" cried Bedistai.

He sprang to his feet and positioned himself between the samanal and the woman. Until now, Peniff had only heard tales of these creatures. His eyes went from the lizard's dagger length claws to its mace-like tail thrashing from side to side. Milling grain had never prepared him for such a chilling encounter, but when he felt the first hint of fear begin to blossom, he suppressed it. If any harm were to befall these two, his family would perish as well. So, as Darva began to stir, glancing around without comprehension, Peniff unsheathed his sword and stood beside the Haroun.

As the red glow of embers glinted off scales of indiscernible hue and amber eyes studied them, Bedistai moved to his left, away from Peniff. The samanal's tongue flicked out of its mouth and in again, tasting their scents. Bedistai tested the arc of his sword to insure there was room enough to wield it. Without needing to be told, Peniff accommodated his swing by stepping away to his right.

By now, Darva was sitting upright and rubbing the sleep from her eyes. She only became aware of the creature when the samanal hissed. She froze.

"Darva!" called Bedistai. In a low even tone he ordered, "Get up slowly and pick up your sword."

His words broke her trance and she nodded. With her eyes fixed on the beast, she reached for her weapon and stood. Finally alert and in possession of her senses, she began circling to expose the creature's flank. Even while she maneuvered, two more emerged from adjacent passages. As if rehearsed, she and her companions altered their positions to confront each lizard individually. In an unexpected show of intelligence, the reptiles countered by sidling around the chamber as if trying to encircle them.

Bedistai was holding the nearest one at sword point, when three more hurtled into the chamber. Legs splayed, tongues flicking the air, they hissed and bared their fangs. If the claws and spiked tails were not statement enough, the rows of needle-like teeth made it evident how deadly a moment this had become.

The trio widened their stances and poised themselves, waiting for the first samanal to attack. The one nearest Darva pounced. She evaded it, moving back and to one side. Her blade followed its arc as momentum carried the lizard past. She struck, and her sword caromed off its scales. The lizard rasped its reply. When it landed, it turned and swiped at her with a foreleg, barely missing as another samanal leapt. Whirling to confront it, Darva lunged and managed to pierce its shoulder. It cried as it turned away, but she was forced to duck the spikes that it swung.

The pair facing Bedistai attacked head-on and in unison. The one nearest Peniff tried to decapitate him with its tail. Peniff dropped to the ground as Bedistai sidestepped the duo. Tossing aside his sword, the hunter leapt onto the nearer one. Rotating in mid-air, he landed head to head upon its back. With one arm wrapped around it, he knifed first one eye, then the other. Blinded and screeching in agony, the beast bucked and shuddered, trying to dislodge him. As the second one lunged, mouth gaping to devour him, Bedistai rolled from the blinded one onto the cavern floor. Finding his cast-off sword, he turned to face his newest attacker. The floor was uneven, and when his heel caught on a rocky edge, he stumbled backward.

The lizard leapt and would have landed on top of him, were it not for the fact the blade was aimed up at its soft underside. Holding on with both hands, he buried its length into the lizard's belly. Impaled, it writhed in agony, tearing the weapon from him. As it showered him with blood, he drove his knife repeatedly until its thrashing started to lessen.

When all motion ceased, he shoved its carcass aside and climbed to his feet, grimacing and wiping the blood from his eyes.

The blinded samanal was still flailing its tail, forcing Peniff and Darva to retreat to opposite walls. One random swipe tore another lizard's flank apart, and its organs burst through the wound. A second blow struck the wall beside Peniff, sending an explosion of shards through the air. The one dragging entrails turned on the blind one. The two grappled, assailing each other with claws, teeth and tails.

Caught up with avoiding their struggle, Peniff failed to notice a third lizard creeping up until almost too late. Alerted by its thoughts, he whirled. With his sword in both hands, he struck its face and the impact lifted him from his feet. The lizard recoiled, then bared its teeth, even as blood spurted from the gash. Before it could reply, Peniff severed its neck. The body remained standing until its legs collapsed and it toppled to the floor.

The grappling pair were nearly finished as well. Their assaults diminished in both strength and frequency as they, too, began to die.

Near the far wall, Darva was holding off the remaining two. With her legs spread for balance and her sword in both hands, she pointed first at one and then the other, in an effort to hold both creatures at bay. In spite of this, the pair were advancing, forcing her to retreat. In an instant, Bedistai was upon one lizard's back and Darva used the diversion to strike at the second.

With both hands to drive it, Bedistai thrust his blade into the base of the samanal's skull. Darva drove hers into her attacker's mouth. The samanal bit down hard, and with a shake of its head, tore the weapon away. Roaring in anger, it advanced. In wide-eyed retreat, desperate for a weapon or avenue of escape, Darva backed into a wall. When she collided she flung her hands outward, feeling unbroken stone as the lizard flicked its tongue and crouched.

Peniff saw her situation. With no time to think, waving his sword overhead, he ran as the samanal leapt.

For an instant the creature was airborne. Then it crashed into the wall, with the hilt of Peniff's sword protruding from its neck. The strike, coupled with the lizard's momentum, tore the sword from his hands and sent Peniff spinning. It was a moment before his head cleared and he had the presence of mind to return to his feet. He groaned as he forced each limb to move, testing each one in turn to determine if anything was broken. When all seemed in order—scraped and bruised, but intact—he came fully erect and gasped.

Bedistai was climbing from the one he had killed, breathing hard from exertion. Darva was in tears, trying to avoid the corpse beside her.

She was opening her mouth to speak when one more beast sprang from a passage and ran towards her. As it did, Bedistai leapt onto its back and, as he had done to the others, stabbed it repeatedly. Absorbed with finishing it, he failed to see the lizard that followed. It raked him with a claw, tearing gashes across his side. Horrified, Peniff bounded over two reptile bodies, recovered Darva's sword and was on the beast almost before he knew it. He drove the blade into its back, and when it turned its head to bite him, he slashed at its face and neck until, after several more efforts, the samanal collapsed.

CHAPTER THIRTY-FOUR

Amid the reptiles' dying gasps and hisses, Darva glanced at Bedistai. Blood poured from his side as he tumbled from the samanal, grasping at his wounds. He looked at her and mouthed something inaudible. She shook her head.

"My bag," he gasped. "There are bandages, medicine."

For an instant she stood immobile. Then, her eyes fell on the satchels he had brought from the wagon, now some distance from the spot where they had slept. She ran to them, rummaged and withdrew a large bundled packet. Someone had marked it with the symbols of an apothecary, indicating that, indeed, it contained something medicinal.

"Here," she said as she hurried to where Peniff was standing. She handed it to him. "Open it. My hands are shaking."

He carefully unfolded it and found it contained a quantity of powder.

"Apply it directly to my wounds," gasped Bedistai. "Hurry."

Peniff held the packet over Bedistai's side and began to sprinkle.

"Generously," the Haroun urged, gasping as the powder fell upon open flesh. "Hurry. Please."

"Let me," said Darva.

She took it, and ignoring Bedistai's cries, poured its contents over the gashes. When the packet was empty, she smeared blood and powder together, combining them into a paste.

Bedistai's face contorted in agony, but despite this, he managed to instruct her.

"Don't let it run off. Hold it in place. It will stanch the flow. The blood will gradually congeal. Once it does, wrap the wound with whatever you can find. But not before, or the paste will adhere to the bandage and not to the wound."

She cupped her hands to hold the mixture in place and kept them there. One did not have to be a thought gazer to see how worried she was, Peniff thought. Caught up with watching her ministrations, he started when she spoke.

"Can you detect any more?" she asked.

He extended his mind, examining the passages. Eventually he replied, "No. There are no more." Feeling the need to do something to assist, he asked, "Do you have a water sack? After losing so much blood, he needs to drink something."

She looked about and shook her head.

"There was one where we were sleeping, but I don't see it."

In fact, the few remaining embers provided very little light. They were continuing to dim, making it all but impossible to see. The battle had scattered them about the chamber and those that had retained any heat were nearly out.

Peniff realized he could not allow them to extinguish. Working quickly, lest the last ones die, he scraped as many as he could into a pile, hoping to concentrate their heat. He blew, and when they showed promise, he searched for something to ignite. He scrambled between the corpses and found some sticks Bedistai had probably gathered earlier. He placed them near the coals, then dropped to his knees and arranged them into a structure arching over them. Bending close, he blew, but this time felt nothing. His few moments spent searching had allowed the embers to cool. Verging on panic, lest the chamber grow too dark for them to see, he encircled them with his hands to contain what little heat they might possess. He blew again gently, fearing if he blew too hard, he would cool them even more.

To his relief, this strategy helped. Each gentle breath increased their glow until, after several efforts, he felt heat against his hands. Encouraged, he kept to his task until they, at last, glowed brightly. One more breath and the sticks he had arranged burst into flame. Although the fire was small, it cast enough light for shadows to appear. He knew the flame would not last, but now that it was burning on its own, he rose and looked for something substantial to add.

It was difficult to search for all the corpses lying about, so he trod between them. The floor was becoming wet with blood, but eventually he located three dry branches. Two were nearly as thick as his wrists and the third was the diameter of a finger. These weren't enough to fuel a long-lasting blaze, but he placed them as well as he could, hoping the tiny flame he had created would ignite them.

He was relieved when the flames lit the smallest one. Soon after, the larger two caught. The fire was now generating both light and heat, so he left the cave and stepped out into the night. By the soft illumination cast through the cave's opening, he found a quantity of dry brush he could add. After bringing the fuel inside, he searched for the water sack. When a small dark object caught his eye, he rose to retrieve it. When he returned, Darva was sitting with Bedistai's head on her lap. Peniff removed the skin's stopper and put the sack to the hunter's lips, tilting it until he began to drink.

Eventually, he turned away.

"Thank you," said Bedistai, gasping with relief.

"How are you feeling?" Darva asked.

"The wounds are not so deep they will kill me. Now that the bleeding has stopped, if I can rest, I believe they will heal." He looked up at Peniff. "Thank you, my friend, for the water and for waking us. I am deeply indebted."

"It's my fault you are hurt. I wasn't paying attention. I should have sensed the last two."

"How could you?" said Darva. "You were fighting for your life. Really, Peniff, you take too much responsibility for things beyond your control and not enough credit for the good that you do. Without you, we would be dead."

Peniff surveyed the chamber. "We need to make a place where you can rest," he said. "And we need to remove these bodies. We will stay with you until you are better."

"That will take many days, and you," said Bedistai to Darva, "must get to your brother. I cannot see you to the end of your journey." He turned to Peniff. "That is for you to do." Before Peniff could object, he added, "If you can leave me food and water to last a few days, and if I remain immobile, I can manage. I am not so weak I cannot feed myself, but I should not travel. That's for the two of you. Continue on to barakMall. Once you are there, you can return by horse with a physician. I should be all right until then."

"What if you start to bleed?" Darva asked. "Is there more powder?"

Bedistai hesitated, then replied, "I will have to make sure that doesn't happen, won't I?" He winked. "And you will have to travel quickly."

Peniff stood. "Before I go, I am going to drag these lizards as far down the passages as I can. Otherwise, in three more days the stench will make you wish you were dead."

Bedistai's lips formed a smile.

This was hardly a laughing matter. Bedistai, though seemingly invincible, was, in the end, a man. He could easily bleed to death and his avoidance of Darva's question underscored the fact. Nonetheless, Peniff knew if he dwelled too long on the matter, fear might overtake him. Instead, he put his back to his task. As Darva began cutting apart her leather shirt to fashion a bandage, he grabbed a samanal's tail and began dragging it out of the chamber.

"If this doesn't exhaust me first," he huffed. "I had no idea how heavy these things are."

"When I'm finished, I will help," said Darva. "We need to close off those tunnels, then get under way. It is still early. If we don't lose too much time, we can cover a great deal of ground before nightfall."

By the time he returned for a second one, Darva had completed her task. Clad in the leather jerkin, she added her strength.

"We'll do it together," she said, as both of them leaned into the effort and pulled.

CHAPTER THIRTY-FIVE

T his is stupid."

"What did you say?" Harad snapped and whirled to face Tonas.

"I said, this is stupid. I'm not taking another step."

Having made that declaration, Tonas halted. He was struggling for air and the sweat running down his face streamed from his nose and chin. His shirt was soaked through and clung to him. As he fumbled for the water skin's strap and struggled to pull it over his head, his hands trembled. Then, when he lifted it to his mouth, a trickle ran onto his tongue, then disappeared.

"Mastad!" he swore and hurled the sack to the ground. "The water's run out. What are we going to do now?"

Ordinarily, Harad would have struck him. But he was faring no better himself. In fact, all three were stretched to their limits from the pace he had set. Normally self-confident to the maniacal extreme, Harad was growing uncertain, almost desperate, though he would never voice it to the others. The trio they were chasing had gotten tangled in the city's mass exodus— something Harad hadn't counted on. So great was the number of escapees, he lost track of the three almost at once. His pursuit had come down to a guessing game that reduced his ability to cover ground rapidly. If he lost them before they reached barakMall, he would be dead. Kael had never threatened him. He didn't have to. Harad knew what kind of man the warlord was and how great were the stakes. Even so, this was the first time he had allowed himself to admit it.

"F–face it," Ward stammered as he caught up with the pair. Portlier than his comrades, he had been lagging behind, and his face was scarlet from exertion. "We have lost them."

"We have not!" snapped Harad.

Ward glared. "It's nearly three days since we last saw them. Since then, we've not glimpsed so much as a footprint. We don't know where they are or where they are going."

Harad rounded on him. "Now it's you who sounds stupid. We know exactly where they are going. They are making for barakMall and the safety of her brother's arms."

"But there are thousands of square miles between Borrst and Liad-Nur," Ward objected. "How do you expect to find them?"

"I am not trying to find the exact route they are taking, although it would certainly help if we did. But if I can reach the fort before they do and intercept them, I can still accomplish what I need to." Harad turned to Tonas. "Are you honestly proposing we forget all we've been through? Are you suggesting we simply sit down and give up?"

Tonas, who was bent nearly double with his hands on his knees, was beginning to breathe easier. He raised his head and looked Harad in the eyes.

"That is exactly what I'm proposing. There comes a time when it is better to cut your losses and take the wiser course."

"Well thank you for that," said Harad. "And this may come as a surprise, my friend, but I believe I will take your advice. I have virtually carried you all this way by myself. I have prodded, cajoled, begged, and pleaded in order to get you off your pathetic ass every day and somehow keep you moving. Enlisting you were certainly the worst mistake I ever made, so you are right. It's time to cut my losses."

With that, Harad drew his sword, and with one sweeping motion, brought it around and down through Tonas's neck. Tonas's eyes were still open as his head bounced at his feet. Even before his legs had time to buckle, Harad gave the skull a mighty kick and sent it sailing over the precipice, where it caromed down the hillside.

He turned back to Ward. "So, what do you say? Want to join him? Or do you think you can help me see this through to its end?"

At first, Ward could not reply. He stared into the chasm, then at the jumble of torso and limbs. Blood was streaming from the body, pooling and turning the earth beneath it black.

"I will come," he muttered.

"What did you say? I couldn't make out your words," said Harad as he raised his sword.

Ward paused to take a breath. He then repeated in distinct syllables, as loud as he could manage, "I will come with you. I will see this through to the end."

"Good," said Harad. He wiped his blade on Tonas's clothing, then replaced it in the scabbard. "That is very good."

He started to turn, but paused and gave Ward a deliberate look, burrowing into his eyes, until he was certain he had the man's attention.

"Make no mistake, dear fellow. Although we have grown fewer—just we two now—I can complete this mission on my own if I have to. I cannot afford any further mistakes. I cannot afford any hesitation on your part." He paused for emphasis. "None whatsoever. If you are unsure if you can do what I tell you, it will be better if you pack up while I am sleeping and slink away. I have better things to do than chase after you. Leave while you can. For the moment, I will pretend my sword arm is tired. Run away if you're not up to it, but heed my words when I promise you, as sure as we are standing here, I will not hesitate to cut you down—even as we capture the woman—if I sense you are not fully committed. Do I make myself clear?"

Ward returned Harad's gaze while he considered his words. He took a deep breath as he replied, "I am in it to the end. I promised as much when I joined you. I meant it then. I mean it now."

Harad cocked his head. The reply surprised him. He was unaccustomed to direct answers, but he could see from Ward's look that the man really meant it.

"Good," he said and clapped him on the shoulder. "Better two men with courage than a dozen craven cowards. Let's find some water."

They soon found a stream and drank their fill. They replenished their water skins, along with the one Tonas had discarded. Once rested, they continued on for perhaps two more hours, by which time dawn had begun breaking. Jadon and Mahaz were rising in tandem, throwing shadows in long dark pairs. Due to their angle, the landscape became a riot of confusion—patches of orange and white punctuated by deep purple shadow—causing Harad and Ward to strain as they scanned the terrain.

All at once, Ward placed his hand on Harad's shoulder and brought him to a halt.

"Look," he said, pointing toward the ridgeline before them.

Harad attempted to follow Ward's arm, but saw only a jumble of color.

"What are you talking about?"

"Look carefully—high upon the next hill, moving along the crest. Two figures. A man and a woman. They are just about to top its rise. Do you see them?"

Harad squinted, not seeing anything at first. Then, "Yes!" he exclaimed. "I see them. But why are there only two? Do you think those are the right ones?"

"I don't know. Perhaps something happened to the third. Then again, perhaps he has already descended and gone on ahead. As for whether they the right ones or not, there is only one way to find out. Shall we run to catch up?"

Without waiting for Harad's answer, Ward took off. Harad was grinning and was hot on his heels. He could smell blood and the scent of it renewed him.

CHAPTER THIRTY-SIX

Obah Sitheh was grouchy this morning. He had been eating poultry three meals a day for longer than he cared to consider, but then, so had everyone else. It was not because other meat was unavailable. Rather, it was because the fletchers were working overtime to create an arsenal his archers could not easily deplete and the quantity of feathers the task called for required hundreds of dead birds. He could ill afford to let all that meat go to waste, and that left him with little choice. All he could do was hope the arrows would be ready before he lost his appetite altogether.

Spitting a piece of bone onto his plate, he turned his mind to other matters and almost found a smile. Although En's forces were continuing to fill the Nagath Valley between barakMall and Hath's encampment, Obah's situation held more promise than did his menu. The thing that delighted him was the new weapon he had found. Perhaps it was more accurate to say it was a new take on an older one, but one of his archers had come up with the concept. When the man demonstrated its capabilities, Obah immediately seized on its worth and ordered the invention into production. *This will take the wind out of Hath's sails*, he smirked, because the device rendered an old tactic useless. In conventional warfare, the unsuccessful arrows fired by one side could be reused by the other. Since many missed their mark, it was a simple matter to pick them up and use them against the ones who had shot them.

This new invention, which the inventor termed "the overdraw," enabled the use of shorter arrows than could be fired with a conventional bow. The overdraw was a guide mounted on an archer's wrist, upon which the shorter arrow's tip rested. When the bow was fully drawn, the shaft did not have to extend all the way from the string to the bow because the tip rested on the guide. Since the other side lacked similar devices, they would not be able draw the bowstring fully if they attempted to reuse Obah's shorter arrows. Consequently, they could not shoot them any appreciable distance.

On the other hand, in addition to the new ones the fletchers were fashioning, Obah's archers could still return Hath's. Moreover, the new arrows were lighter and flew farther and faster than their heavier counterparts. Not only would it take them longer to exhaust their arsenal, Obah's archers could take down targets long before Hath's could do the same.

If only the new arrows were ready so he could use them, he mused. Turning to other more urgent matters, he turned to the man beside him.

"General. Is there no word of my sister?"

"No, my lord, not yet."

"Something is bothering you. I can see it on your face."

"My lord, please forgive what I am about to say. I mean no disrespect but, yes, I am deeply troubled."

"Have no fear, Barral. You may speak freely."

It had been years since Obah called his old friend by his proper name. Discipline and protocol were what held his army together through these difficult times, and with Hath's forces gaining strength, these days were among the gravest. Nonetheless, Obah broke form and recognized Barral for the old friend that he was, not the general he had become.

"Tell me what worries you."

"We cannot afford to wait any longer for news of your sister. The men assembled here," Barral gestured towards the fortress and the nearby encampments, "have entrusted you with their lives. Until now, we have had a numerical advantage, but as new forces continue to arrive at Kael's encampment, that advantage is starting to dwindle. I am no longer sure we can easily defeat him, and soon we may have no chance at all. I know how much you love her, but are you willing to throw away all these lives, as well as the lives of the villagers and townspeople who rely upon you, for Darva's sake?"

He paused for Obah's reaction. When none was forthcoming, he said, "I also must ask what makes you certain Kael will not kill her, even should you meet his demands? Were you to ask my advice, I would council you to attack now."

"Are you saying you will not follow orders?"

"My lord, I will follow you to the edge of the abyss, even into its depths, should you to command me to. But I would be neglecting my duty as general of your army were I not to share my thoughts with you."

Before Obah could reply, trumpets sounded. He and Barral looked from the parapet to see a large mounted force sweep over a ridge, directly towards a small party of reinforcements galloping towards barakMall from the southwest. The smaller contingent, who bore the colors of Pytheral, a recently declared ally, had no chance at all. Hath's fighters, who outnumbered them three or four to one, rode through them, felling rider after rider, leaving nothing but bodies in their wake.

"It looks as though Hath is trying to force the issue," Barral observed. "How do you intend to respond?"

"It appears he wants words with me," Obah replied.

He inclined his head towards the opposing encampment

where a soldier, carrying a banner adorned with Hath's colors, emerged from the main body of warriors. When he arrived at a spot roughly midway between Hath's army and the fortress, he reined in his horse and waited.

"Find an appropriate emissary and fit him with armor, a steed and a flag. We will hear what their man has to say, although I expect we already know."

"Yes, my lord."

Obah watched as Barral descended to the courtyard. There, he intercepted a passing captain. An animated but inaudible conversation ensued, after which the captain saluted, then turned and hurried towards the stables, shouting orders as he went. After several more minutes, an armored soldier emerged, and a saddled horse was led from the stables to the courtyard's center. The captain and General Barral spoke with the soldier briefly before Barral led him to the parapet's stairs. When Obah met him at the bottom, he appraised the man approvingly.

This was no raw recruit, but a seasoned fighter, and his bearing exuded all of the confidence the warlord could hope for. The armor the soldier wore was newly made, polished, and by its look, had been created by the finest craftsmen in the lands. His appearance stated that Obah was no pauper and his men were well equipped and ready for war. It was the face Obah wanted to present and it would influence how Hath's messenger would regard his counterpart and the forces he represented. Obah hoped the same regard would be apparent in the emissary's tone and choice of words when he subsequently spoke to Hath Kael.

"Are you ready, soldier?" Obah asked.

"Yes, my lord." The soldier saluted and held the pose until Obah returned the salute and released him. "What will you have of me?"

"I need to learn what message Hath Kael is sending. For the moment, I need nothing more. If he demands a reply, you will tell him that I may choose to respond once I have considered his words. No matter how urgently he presses for a response, you will tell him that I will not be rushed. Is that understood?"

"Certainly, my lord. That is most reasonable."

"Good. Then go."

With a final salute, the soldier turned and went to his mount. He was helped into the saddle by two grooms who were standing at the ready. Once in the saddle, they handed him a lance crested with Obah's sigil. The captain called to a sergeant who was standing nearby.

"Open the gates," he ordered.

When the sergeant saluted and echoed his order to the gate-keepers, the fortification's massive doors slid back upon rollers and the soldier drove his spurs into the horse's flanks. The animal started at the prod, then gathered itself and galloped onto the plain.

"Let us see how this meeting goes," said Barral, looking askance through the opening.

They watched when Obah's man arrived at his destination, at which time the emissaries entered into a lengthy dialogue. While Obah's soldier remained calm, Hath's grew increasingly agitated until, apparently exasperated, he hurled his flag to the ground, pointed his finger at Obah's soldier, then at the fort. Next, he rode close to the emissary and did something that Obah could not see. Whatever he had done caused his man to double over and drop his lance, while Hath's wheeled his mount and galloped back to his encampment. Obah's man turned his horse around, and with hands on his belly, loped slowly back. He was swaying in the saddle and it was obvious something was amiss.

The captain sent another rider to assist him. This one whipped his steed to the fastest gallop it could muster until, as he approached the injured rider, he leaned back in the saddle, reining his steed almost onto its haunches. When his mount slid to a stop, the rider turned the horse and grasped the other horse's reins close to the bridle. Obah watched the two men speak. When the emissary nodded, the second rider led his horse back at a canter, eyeing him repeatedly. As the two cleared the gates, the second rider hailed the gatekeepers.

"Get a physician!" he called. "Get a physician and close the gates!"

Obah was already there by the time the two entered. He hailed them as they entered and was about to ask what had happened, when he spotted a hilt protruding from the emissary's stomach.

By then, soldiers were surrounding the riders. At General Barral's direction, two of them eased the man from the saddle. He grimaced, suppressing a groan as he slid into their arms. Once they had placed him onto a litter, the emissary spotted Obah.

He extended an arm towards the warlord and gasped, "My lord, Hath Kael demands that you surrender by first light." He grimaced, then added, "Should you fail to do so, he says he will destroy you."

He closed his eyes and his body went limp.

Barral looked at Obah. "Hath is making your decision for you."

Obah nodded. He had no choice and he hoped Darva would forgive him.

CHAPTER THIRTY-SEVEN

There! Peniff, do you see? I can't believe my eyes. It's barakMall!" exclaimed Darva.

Nearly exhausted from two days' forced march, Darva and Peniff had topped a rise overlooking the southern end of barTimesh, the long plain running from menRathan to Liad-Nur. The fortification, a lone structure amid a sea of troops, stood perhaps one mile from the foothills.

"I will be home by evening!"

"That will be good," said Peniff.

He studied the encampments. Although no details were discernable at such a distance, from whatever movement they could see, it was evident both camps were bustling.

"One doesn't have to read minds to see a battle is forming," he said. "I would like to reach your brother before the fighting begins."

"Can you manage the rest of the way without stopping?" she asked. "I want Obah to know I am well."

"I will manage. The road goes down from here and the thought of hot food and a warm bath will keep me going."

213

"Good," she said. "Let's go."

"Not so fast, my dear," a man said behind them.

Darva turned to look. She did not recognize the voice, but knew his face at once.

"You!" she exclaimed.

"Yes," said Harad. "Your expression almost makes up for all I've been through. Ha! I can see you didn't think I would find you."

His smugness soured her stomach and she glanced towards her brother's fortress, as if looking would carry her there.

Harad gloated. "So near and yet so far. Isn't that how the saying goes? I guess you will be finishing your journey with me after all."

She put a hand on her sword, hoping Peniff would reach for his. Instead, he strode towards Harad, balling his hands into fists.

"No, we won't," Peniff said.

Raising his right hand to strike, each step coming faster, he was almost at a run when Darva screamed, "Look out!"

Peniff pitched onto his face and lay still at Harad's feet. Darva's hands went to her mouth as she froze, unable to decide what to do. Harad grabbed her arm, yanking her up when she bent to look after him.

"Thank you, Ward," he said, as Ward tossed aside the rock.

"My pleasure. He has been such a nuisance ever since you brought him along. I finally got tired of his whining."

"You animals!" shouted Darva. Her eyes went from Peniff's crumpled form to the pair standing over him. "You could have killed him. Do you ever think of anything but killing and hurting?"

"Frankly, my dear, not a lot else. Ward, help me."

As blood began to well from the wound on Peniff's head, Ward took Darva's arm while Harad held the other.

"Come along," said Harad, as they led her down the slope. "We're nearly there."

"Where are you taking me?"

"Well, since we haven't had any success taking you to Monhedeth, we are going to do the next best thing and take you to Hath Kael himself."

CHAPTER THIRTY-EIGHT

P eniff probed his head. There was a lump, and his hair was matted, sticky, and wet. When he brought his fingers to his nose, they carried the coppery tang of blood. He wiped his hand on his pants, then pushed himself onto his knees, spitting out dirt and wiping particles from his mouth and face with his sleeve. He had no idea how long he had lain there, unconscious. Stars specked the heavens and torches along the fortress's battlements illuminated its walls. Ringed by islands of light—the campfires of Obah Sitheh's forces—it stood as a brilliant sentinel against a sea of darkness. Nothing, however, indicated what time it might be, so he opened his mind and searched for Darva and her captors.

He located them almost at once, pleased to find they were still in the foothills. Catching up would be difficult, but he believed he might yet have a chance. He recalled how the hillside below was sparsely vegetated and sloped easily towards the valley, not at all like the one the endaths had negotiated the week before. Despite the scant illumination the stars and tiny moon provided, Peniff hoped he could recognize a drop-off before it was too late. Deciding he might manage after all, he breathed deeply, steeled his resolve, and left the trail.

The first hundred yards proved easy enough and he was able to maintain his footing as he navigated between scrub and boulders. Farther down, however, the grade steepened, and he fell back onto his rump several times until he questioned the wisdom of his decision. One fall sent him sliding amid a torrent of earth and gravel before he collided with a rock.

"Mastad!" he swore as the impact blinded him with color.

Several minutes passed before the aching subsided and he could drag himself onto his knees. When he attempted to stand, the injured hip refused to cooperate. Inhaling deeply, he willed his leg to move and cried out as he brought the limb under him. Dreading the consequence, he put his full weight upon it, wondering if it would support him. Much to his relief, it held, and he climbed fully to his feet. When he attempted a step, however, another jolt of pain halted him abruptly. Although he managed a second, he cried out as the hip stabbed him again. He looked for some place to rest, then realized how ludicrous sitting would be. Time was slipping away and with each passing minute, so was Darva.

"Borlon help me," he prayed, as he looked to the heavens. The god did not respond, nor did he expect he would. He rebuked himself. "Peniff, if you were ever good for anything, you will suck up the hurt and do what you must. There will be time enough for tears in the morning."

He took another step and, although his knee tried to buckle, he refused to let it collapse. The next step also hurt, but was somewhat better. So was the next and the next until, as he began to make progress, he grew confident he had broken no bones. Little by little, he gained momentum until he was moving nearly as fast as before, determined nothing short of death would stop him.

By the time he had descended to the foothills, the pain had

all but vanished. He reached out with his mind and located Darva. Through her eyes, he could see that she and her abductors were passing onto the plain. Torches on the battlements and campfires outside barakMall's walls indicated the trio had begun skirting the fortress. He switched his attention to Harad and was pleased to learn he had slowed their pace to avoid detection.

Overtaking them might be possible after all. But could he do so before they crossed onto the battlefield? Buoyed by the possibility, he found new strength that, minutes earlier, he would have sworn wasn't there. He started to run, but with a pronounced limp. He ran nonetheless, praying for a miracle, praying his leg would hold out, praying he would not fall and injure himself again. And as he did, he prayed for other things: that a chance patrol would happen upon the three he was chasing; that Harad or Darva would come up lame.

And he despaired because he knew the things prayed for were useless flights of fancy. For, as the minutes went by and he considered the distance between them and his halting, ungainly progress, he realized he could never run fast enough or long enough to catch them. Even if he could, the fact remained he was but one against two. A cripple with a sword and a poor hand at that. Harad would cut him down because, having captured Darva, Harad no longer needed him. After he was dead, Sabed Orr would kill his family.

In the same instant he arrived at that conclusion, his hip grabbed and brought him back to a walk. He could no longer ignore his burning lungs and how his legs were threatening to betray him. He halted, as a new idea came to him.

He didn't need to catch them after all. Stealth had slowed the trio to the point it would take them at least two hours to circumnavigate Sitheh's troops. After that, they would need another two to reach Kael. Yet, if Peniff were to turn immediately and make for the fort, Darva's brother was no more than a quarter hour away. It could be Obah, or at least Obah's soldiers, who would run Harad down. They had the necessary numbers and, further, they were armed. All he needed to do was to convince the warlord he was telling the truth. And how could he not? Only those party to the kidnapping would know of it. His real problem would be to convince Lord Sitheh he was a friend and not an abductor. If he couldn't ... He didn't want to consider that possibility. This was the chance he had to take. It was his only chance and that cinched it. He turned and hobbled down the last few yards of the lower foothills. Holding his side and limping, he headed onto the plain.

CHAPTER THIRTY-NINE

H alt!" a soldier commanded, raising his torch to illuminate the ones approaching. "What's that you've got?"

"Caught ourselves a spy," said one of the pair.

"Aw, I wouldn't say he's a spy," his partner corrected. "Ran right up to the gate he did, saying something about Lord Obah's sister."

"What kind of things? Insults?"

"Naw. Nothing like that," said the partner. "Some kind of drawn-out story. We don't have time to figure it out, so we're going to let him cool his heels until morning. The sergeant can sort through the details after breakfast, assuming he has an appetite for anything else after he's eaten."

They laughed, but the news alarmed Peniff.

"After breakfast?" he blurted, struggling against their hold. "That will be too late! Kael will have her by then. Please. You have to let me speak to someone now, while there is still time."

"Listen, friend. I assume you are a friend," said the first of the pair. "No one has time to sit and chat. We are preparing for battle."

"And that is why I must get my information to your lord," pleaded Peniff. "It has to do with the battle. He needs to know what I have to tell him before the fighting begins." He tore free and grasped the soldier's collar. "Please."

The soldier removed Peniff's hands and took hold of his wrists. "I've grown tired of you," he said. "I have been as civil as I can, but this finishes it. You are going to the stockade. Maybe someone will listen to you when the battle is over."

He began to drag Peniff across the compound as his friend hastened to assist.

"No!" cried Peniff, digging in his heels and trying to stop them. "I have to tell someone."

Despite how he argued, they were deaf to his pleas. Peniff looked for anyone else he might enlist. To his dismay, the entire fortress seemed preoccupied with carrying arms and supplies to the battlements and he was unable to capture anyone's attention.

A wagon laden with provisions crossed their path, forcing the trio to halt. After it passed, Peniff noticed a man clad in artfully crafted armor, who had not been there the instant before. Its lustrous polish and ornate decorations were not at all like an ordinary soldier's, and Peniff realized, if anyone here could help him, this might be the man. He reached out to inquire as to his identity, and the mind he touched revealed him to be a general.

"General!" called Peniff. "General!" he called again, but the man did not respond. Peniff was nearly out of earshot when the general's mind also gave up his name.

"Barral!" Peniff shouted.

His voice must have carried above the clamor because the general halted. He turned to see who was calling. Encouraged, Peniff cried out again.

"Barral!" Tearing one arm free, he waved it frantically, calling, "Barral. Barral. Barral."

He shouted and waved until the general's eyes focused. In turn, Barral raised his voice and called to Peniff's captors.

"Halt! You with the prisoner. Stay where you are."

The pair halted at his command. They maintained their grip as they came to attention, restraining Peniff as securely as they could.

As Barral came closer, ignoring their salutes, his eyes fastened firmly on Peniff and his face was full of undisguised curiosity. When he was standing near enough to see clearly by torchlight and lanterns, he studied Peniff's face.

"I don't believe I know you. How do know my name?"

Suspecting any explanation he could offer would raise more questions than he had time to answer, Peniff replied, "General, I know where Lord Sitheh's sister is. Darva is not far from here and you can save her, if you act in time."

Those words were probably the last thing Barral had expected to hear because his eyes widened, he cocked his head and probed Peniff's eyes.

"What do you mean?"

"As we speak, her abductors are taking her to Hath Kael's encampment. They are skirting your forces on foot. If you hurry, you can intercept them. I beg you, do not delay or they will cross the battlefield and Kael will have her."

"And how do you know these things?"

Again, deciding the complete truth would not serve his purpose, Peniff replied, "I was accompanying her here when two men intercepted us. They overpowered me and took her."

Although his bloody clothes and fresh head wound should have lent credence to his words, the general nonetheless asked, "Why should I believe you?"

"General, with all due respect, how many people know Darva was abducted, let alone can claim to know where she is? You should believe me, because if you do not, she will soon be irretrievably beyond your grasp. You should believe me because, frankly ..." he paused to lend weight to his words. Returning the general's stare with equal intensity, he concluded, "You can't afford not to."

Peniff could see the many questions the general wanted to ask, but he also knew Barral finally suspected he was telling the truth.

"Release him," Barral said. When the soldiers were slow to respond, his expression darkened. "I said, release him!"

The pair stepped back and Peniff rubbed his arms while Barral studied Peniff.

"It is dark outside these walls. Even if I were to send a rescue party, they might not be able to locate her."

"Let me accompany your men, General. I can find her. I know where they left me and I know where they are going." Barral raised an eyebrow, but Peniff continued. "If you think I am simply trying to escape, send enough men that I cannot. And if you think that I am lying about the woman, you certainly have means enough at your disposal to make me regret wasting your time. So believe me when I say I'm not lying and that Darva's life depends on how quickly you act."

That was enough.

"Captain!" Barral called to the one who had dispatched Obah's emissary earlier. "Mount a dozen armed men and ride with them to wherever this one tells you," he said, gesturing towards Peniff. "He will accompany you and explain your mission as you go."

The captain eyed Peniff curiously before catching himself.

"Yes, General," he replied crisply.

"You will not regret this decision," Peniff told Barral.

The general nodded. "I don't know who you are or how you arrived here, but I expect a full explanation when you return." Then, as Peniff turned to follow the captain. "One more thing," he said as Peniff halted. "If you do not find her, it will be better if you do not return."

"I understand. You will see Darva shortly."

CHAPTER FORTY

The gates closed behind the riders and Peniff indicated the direction Harad and Ward had taken. He had not yet explained the nature of their mission—only where they were going—but the soldiers spurred their horses to a gallop at his command. As for Peniff, who had rarely ridden, he clung to the reins with one hand and the pommel with the other as he spurred his steed onward, fearing he would be thrown from the saddle. Yet again, Peniff realized if he allowed fear to overwhelm him, he would lose them. He shoved the anxiety aside, cleared his mind, and began searching.

When he located them, he could see that the three would soon be rounding Sitheh's army's last encampment. They would then move onto the plain that separated the opposing forces. Once they crossed into the open, both the searchers and the abductors would be exposed. Peniff did not want Darva—or himself for that matter—to become the first casualties of the impending battle. When the horses had closed the remaining distance between them, Peniff signaled to the captain to bring his squad to a halt. Once the soldiers had reined their mounts into a circle, Peniff addressed them.

"Gentlemen, we are pursuing two men and a woman. The men are kidnappers, and the woman is Lord Sitheh's sister, Darva." Murmurs arose, and the horses began tossing their heads and shifting stances, as if in response. "I don't need to tell you to protect her, but you should also understand that the ones who are holding her will have no compunction about killing her if they feel there are no other options."

"And where might these kidnappers be?" the captain asked.

"They are directly ahead of us, about one hundred yards away and on foot."

The captain stood in his stirrups and stared into the night. The encampment's campfires revealed silhouetted warriors, as well as picketed horses, but nothing more.

"I can't see anyone. Are you sure they went this way?"

"Do you see that pyre, Captain?" Peniff pointed towards a large bonfire at the edge of Kael's encampment. "They are moving towards it in a direct line from us."

"Oh, really?" cried one soldier. "It's so dark tonight, how do you know they're not fifty yards ahead? Or three hundred? Or maybe off to the left a bit?"

As he paused for effect, chuckles, then stifled laughter began to erupt.

"Or maybe they've turned around and are making for Nagath-réal," the soldier finished.

The laughter was now undisguised, and Peniff was forced to wait until it subsided in order to make himself heard. He raised his voice.

"Your name is Rogert. You have served in Obah Sitheh's army since Thirdmonth four years ago. Your wife's name is Sannah. You have no children. The one you had hoped to have died in her womb. I am sorry to say you have both given up on having another. You had chicken and deleth fruit for breakfast, but declined to have lunch. Now you're regretting it and are hoping to end what we're doing here so you can return to the barracks and have your supper. Have I missed anything?" Peniff asked.

There was no response, but the troop fell to murmuring and the words "thought gazer" emerged above the clamor more than once.

Peniff turned to the commander.

"I will admit I am no soldier, Captain, but I feel it would be to our advantage if you were to dispatch half of your men to cut them off. If the riders you send can position themselves about two hundred yards ahead of us, we can contain them. I will leave what comes after that to you. Can you think of some way the men you dispatch can signal us when they are ready?"

The captain gave Peniff a long thoughtful look, then called two officers to come forward. As the captain discussed strategies—proposing a signal torch be lit, then extinguished—Peniff reached out once again with his mind.

CHAPTER FORTY-ONE

"Get up," Harad ordered.

Darva had tripped on an unseen obstacle and fallen face first. As she raised her head, she regarded the hundreds of campfires blazing. On her left, tantalizingly close, were her brother's battlements, illumined by dozens of torches along its walls and parapets and by dozens of campfires at its base, spreading out into hundreds more across the plain. She briefly considered running toward them, then discarded the thought. She knew she could never run fast enough or far enough. Harad would catch her. She began to despair, less concerned for her own well-being than the prospect of her brother's capitulation.

She chastised herself. He was better than that. Through the course of her journey, her unvoiced objective had been to stand before him and set his mind at ease, to let him know she was alive and unharmed. It was never to prevent him from throwing down his arms, for she knew he would never forsake the people who relied on him. No matter how much he loved her, despite whatever momentary lapses he might have, in the end he would do what was right and protect them. Their thousands of lives would outweigh any blood tie. She would have been gravely disappointed were it otherwise.

She looked to her right where hundreds of other campfires burned. These marked the encampments of Hath Kael's army. Harad and Ward were keeping to the dark swath between the opposing armies, having argued about the problems they might encounter when, finally, they were forced to pass through Kael's troops.

"We need some light. We'll break our necks out here," Ward had complained.

"And if some upstart lieutenant recognizes who we're bringing and is looking for a promotion, what then?" Harad demanded. "He'll take her and present her to Kael as if it was he who found her. Then where will we be?"

"And how do we find this warlord of yours? Does he put up a sign? Something like 'Behold! This is Hath Kael's tent'?"

"Open your eyes," said Harad. "Do you see that blaze?" He pointed to a massive pyre a hundred yards off, in the midst of Kael's encampments. "There's your sign. We'll make our way toward it when we have the least ground to cross." He looked down at Darva and told her, "You had strength enough to find your way back to your brother. You can find enough to carry you to Hath. Get up."

He grabbed her wrist and yanked her to her feet, nearly pulling her shoulder from its socket.

"All right!" she cried.

Despite her intention to maintain a stoic façade, tears welled in her eyes, born less from the pain Harad had caused than by the prospect of never seeing Obah again. Regardless of what her brother decided, she knew Hath Kael would never return her, let alone allow her to live. Furthermore, Kael would make sure Obah knew of her death. Her brother would have to lead his troops into battle regardless of his loss.

"I'm coming," she said.

Harad had begun hauling her in the manner one might drag a reluctant goat, when Ward called him.

"What is it?" he snapped.

"Did you hear something?"

"No," Harad said, pausing to listen. "What do you think you heard?"

The question was answered by hoof beats.

"Run!" Harad cried.

Surreal forms materialized around them as firelight glinted on polished armor and spear tips. Harad yanked Darva to his side with such force she cried out again. Voices were encircling them. Whirling at each new sound, Harad clasped her against him like a shield. Each time she stumbled, he jerked her upright.

"Halt!" a voice commanded. "Stand where you are."

As the encircling silhouettes eclipsed the campfires, Harad drew his sword and Ward's resonated as it, too, left its scabbard.

"Throw down your weapons," the voice ordered. "Release the girl and raise your hands."

"That's not very likely," said Harad. "Let us go or she dies."

"Harm her and you will die where you stand. She is all that is keeping us from trampling you into the ground. Release her and you will live."

As the captain and Harad sparred with words, Darva noticed Peniff riding with them. Their eyes met as he slipped from his saddle and made his way to a spot a short distance off to one side.

"Kill the bitch," Ward urged.

"You are outnumbered," countered the captain. "Throw down your weapons."

"Let us go or I promise, I *will* kill her," shouted Harad, placing the edge of his blade against Darva's throat.

When one of the riders nudged his mount too close, Ward seized the opportunity and attacked. Hooves pounded earth and steel clashed with steel, golden glints marking the arcs of blades caught by firelight.

The skirmish was over in seconds, the soldier being the better swordsman. When he parried a thrust, deflecting Ward's sword to one side, in an economy of motion, he severed Ward's shoulder then cut off his head.

In the midst of the riders, there was a click and the flash of sparks as one soldier struck a tanass stone. He ignited a torch, thereby illuminating the scene, and the remaining riders tightened their circle around Harad. When several soldiers raised their arms against the unaccustomed glare, Harad used the distraction to drag Darva away. He shoved his way between two horses, nicking one with his sword when it refused to step aside. By the time other torches were ignited, he was nowhere to be seen.

Harad's disappearance meant nothing to Peniff. He sensed him running towards Hath's encampment, silencing Darva's first attempt to cry out with a fist to her mouth. The plain was flat empty grassland, so they ran unimpeded until Harad halted at a voice he knew well.

"This is as far as you go," Peniff said in a dry even tone.

Harad reached for his sword, but the instant he touched it, Peniff's hand was on his. With his mouth to Harad's ear, Peniff asked, "You've never tested me, have you?"

"Damn you!" Harad shouted.

Harad struggled to break free, but Peniff pressed closer.

"Release her," he hissed, feeling the heat of his breath coming off Harad's cheek.

"After working so hard to find her?"

"Release her!"

CHAPTER FORTY-TWO

A s the two men struggled, Darva broke free. When Harad reached out to catch her, the distraction allowed Peniff to unsheathe the man's sword and toss it away. Before Harad could react, Peniff grabbed him by the collar and with both hands forced Darva's abductor to face him. Far beyond angry with the man who had stolen everything from him, Peniff sought to cause him to suffer something far greater than what he had been forced to endure. He would never be a killer like Harad, but he was not above meting out pain. He intended to inflict something deeper than physical pain, and for that he needed to form a mental connection.

In the near black between them, Harad's head was only a silhouette and his eyes were barely discernable. Yet that was enough. Peniff delved into those portals, probing for something buried. At first, he encountered recent memories. He was as unconcerned with these as he was with Harad's anger or his desire to recapture Darva.

He had been considering the reduced size of Harad's party, how it had dwindled to just him and two others. Consequently, when he encountered Tonas' murder, it came as no surprise.

Instead, it was Harad's delight when he kicked the man's head that brought Peniff up short. So did the pleasure he had taken from Ruall's incineration. And while these recollections provided insight to the man's nature, Peniff was seeking something deeper still.

All at once, he stumbled on the darkness within. The night fell away and Harad stood revealed. The horrors this one had witnessed and the evils he had performed were all there for him to see. For the first time in his life, Peniff was dumbstruck. He had never visited the likes of this mind. Here was a monster who delighted in seeing and doing things that would horrify most men. He hated without cause and the things that gave him pleasure were the agony and torment he inflicted on others. But it was what Harad intended to do to his family that frightened Peniff most, and he recoiled at the images of rent flesh, of blood and broken bones.

As he had at the breakdown, he reacted instinctively. He reached deep inside and began to draw forth all the horrors Harad had inflicted on his victims. All of the fear and pain that had brought him delight now suffused his mind and his body so that he was no longer the doer. Instead, he was the victim. Harad's mouth opened in a protracted howl, something primordial and visceral. He did not will it. Rather, it emerged on its own. Enveloped by the visions, at the mercy of the sensations, like the soldier at the supply wagon, Harad began to crouch and curl into a fetal position, unable to tear his eyes away from Peniff's, unable to stop screaming.

How long this continued, Peniff could not say—it could have been minutes. It might have only been seconds—for he was as immersed in the process as Harad. It was a morbid fascination, how he could transform thought into reality. It was a power he had never imagined.

Removed though he was from the external world, Peniff began to hear something out of place. As if echoing down a long winding tunnel, someone was calling his name. When he focused, he began to hear it more clearly.

He began rousing himself from his reverie, torn between relishing Harad's pain and his desire to know who was intruding. With an effort, he extracted himself from Harad's mind, only to find the man crumpled at his feet. A hand on Peniff's shoulder shook him.

"Peniff!" shouted Darva. "Stop it! What are you doing to him?"

Though she held his shirt in both hands and shook him with all her might, he had been oblivious until he turned to meet her gaze.

"Please stop. I beg you," she cried.

Peniff came to his senses. Horrified he could inflict such pain upon another, shocked that he would not only invade the sanctum of another mind uninvited, but use its darkest secrets for dark purposes of his own, he let Harad go.

Harad was shuddering. He held his knees to his chest and rocked himself, as a mother rocks her child. All the while, his entire body trembled, and his mouth uttered soft incoherencies.

"You did it again," Darva said as she held onto Peniff. "You did it again."

Peniff buried his face in his hands.

"I'm sorry."

CHAPTER FORTY-THREE

Since the moment Barral had told him his sister was alive, Obah could think of nothing else. Over the weeks he had spent preparing for battle, Kael's extortion tore at him. Thoughts of her death or, worse still, the possibility of her torture made sleeping almost impossible. And while he did not know what choice he would make in response, almost to this minute, he knew Kael was not likely to spare her, especially if he were to elect war over surrender.

And what if Kael did not have her? The ring and the finger offered scant evidence of her capture. Even if it were hers, Darva was a fighter, a survivor, and the possibility she was still free and alive had burned bright in the back of his mind. Now, as her return loomed large, its imminence drew him to the parapet where he stared into the night, as if doing so would hasten her arrival.

"Horsemen, my lord."

A voice broke his reverie and his head jerked up. He looked past the wall at the approaching party's torches. At first, he could discern only soldiers and his heart fell at the prospect they were returning empty handed. Then, just behind the lead riders, he saw her in the saddle, sitting erect and looking about, scanning the fortification's battlements.

"Darva!" he called as he broke into a run.

Scrambling down, Obah took the stairs two, three, even four at a time. By the time he had reached the courtyard, all semblance of decorum had vanished. Soldiers leapt aside as he ran towards the gates, dodging man and beast with eyes for naught but his sister. By the time he had left the fortress, the search party had arrived.

"Darva!" he shouted.

She rose in the stirrups at his call. As soon as she saw him, she secured the reins, threw a leg over the pommel, and dropped to the ground. In the time it took her to land and run three steps towards him, he was lifting her into his arms and whirling her about.

"You're alive!" he cried. "By Siemas, you're alive! The gods know how I've missed you." He drew back his face to study hers. "I can't tell you how good it is to see you," he said as he kissed her on the cheeks and forehead.

"I've missed you too," she said, returning his kisses in kind. Then, burying her face in his shoulder she began to sob. "But I'm here now," she managed.

After a minute he returned her to her feet and examined her carefully, frowning at her bloody mouth, the bloodstained clothing, the leather jerkin, and the tattered pants made of skins.

"Are you all right?" he asked, touching her mouth with his fingertips. From there, his eyes traveled to her hand and he took it into his. Her finger was indeed missing, and he kissed the gap where it had been.

"Yes. Yes. I am fine," she assured.

"Does it hurt?" he asked as he held her hand.

A smile curled across her lips. "Not anymore."

"And this?" he asked, placing his fingers beside her swollen mouth.

"Well, yes. That does hurt." She grimaced at his touch. Then she chuckled. "Otherwise, I'm fine."

"Really?"

"I am, but I owe my life and my safe return to two brave men. One is here with me. His name is Peniff, and he comes from danBrad in Monhedeth."

Obah followed her eyes as she looked through the crowd that was swelling around them. He could see little else beyond the immediate press of bodies, so he returned his eyes to her.

"The other is a Haroun," she said. "His name is Bedistai Alongquith. He is hurt very badly. Even as we speak, he is lying wounded, perhaps dying, in a cave in the Han'nah." Her smile faded, and her composure began to crumble. Her voice cracked when she said, "Obah, I don't know what I will do if something happens to him. I owe him my life many times over."

"I will do something at once. Let me see if I can find an officer. I will make sure a rescue party leaves within the hour."

"Send a physician with them. His wounds are serious."

"I will send two."

Peniff had finally penetrated the throng, but when Darva introduced him, Obah thought he looked contrite, rather than pleased with his accomplishment. His head was down and he clasped his hands before him, as though bringing Darva home were something to be ashamed of. He avoided Obah's eyes when Darva introduced him.

"Obah," she said, placing a hand on the thought gazer's arm. "This is Peniff. He rescued me from lemekUven and from a cluster of samanals who attacked us in a cave. Just now, he rescued me from the man who was taking me to Hath Kael. I owe him my life."

Obah's eyes widened as he appraised him. Here was no

warrior, no man of obvious strength. Darva was not one to exaggerate, so this man had performed greater acts of courage than most warriors Obah knew. Yet here he stood, his clothes as bloody as his sister's, appearing to wither as if he yearned to shrink away.

"My friend Barral told me about him," Obah told her. "Not only is your friend a man of remarkable courage, he is quite persuasive." To Darva's questioning look, he explained, "Had he not been so convincing, two of my men would have jailed him."

"Jailed him?"

Obah nodded and related what he had been told. "How can I express my gratitude?" he asked Peniff. "My sister means more to me than anything else in this world. I am at a loss how to thank you. Ask anything and I will grant it, if it is at all within my power."

"I did what I had to, my lord," Peniff said. "I was as much Kael's prisoner as was your sister. In fact, I still am."

"I don't understand."

"Hath Kael is holding my wife and children prisoners in barakMis. Your sister makes me out to be a hero but, in truth, I was recruited by Sabed Orr to bring her to Monhedeth. That was what I was doing before I arrived in danHsar. Knowing the kind of man he is, I could not bring myself to finish my assignment. But once Orr learns how I have betrayed him, he will murder my family. There is no way I can return to Monhedeth in time to save them, so I have betrayed them as well. I mean no disrespect, my lord, but saving them would be the only way you could help, and that is clearly beyond your power."

Orr grimaced and nodded. "Even if I were to send an entire battalion, Orr would see them coming. I am sorry," he said.

"Don't be," Peniff replied. "The choice was mine. Ready your men for battle, my lord. That is all you can do. It will not be long before Kael learns of my treachery and then you will feel his wrath as well."

"What do you mean?"

It was Darva who answered. "We left Kael's agent on the plain. I am afraid that is my fault. Despite all he did to me, despite what he intended to do, I felt pity for him and at my request your men left him there. Even now, I suspect he is heading to Hath's encampment. It won't take him more than a couple of hours to find his lord and tell him the news."

"Then we must mobilize at once," Obah said. "General!" he called to Barral, who was standing nearby.

"Yes, my lord?"

"What is the general state of readiness?"

"The troops can be ready within the hour."

"Notify me when they are. We attack at once."

"What about your prisoner, my lord?"

Obah hesitated when his mind went to the one who had brought Darva's finger.

"Not now," he said.

"Weren't you planning to send him with your response?"

"Our attack is my response. I will deal with that scum when the fighting is over."

CHAPTER FORTY-FOUR

By the half light of dawn, the opposing forces were already engaged. Obah's advance had caught the enemy sleeping. But though surprised and despite their initial losses, they were far from beaten. Even from barakMall's parapets, Peniff could see that the fighting was fierce. The blare of horns resonating across the plain, above cries of the warriors, bespoke its intensity.

And now, unable to sleep, Peniff sat on the wall watching. He turned from the plain to regard the fortress around him. While by no means abandoned, the number of soldiers left behind to guard it was a fraction of what was here hours before. Obah refused to have his men contained within the battlements, preferring to carry the fight to Kael with as many as he could.

Feeling impotent in the face of what must surely follow his betrayal, Peniff extended his mind westward seeking Kael. Instead he found Harad whose mind was a cauldron of anger, fear, and loathing. He, too, had failed the warlord and did not yet know what consequence he would suffer. In the face of the ongoing battle, Kael was postponing that decision. Regardless of what Kael might choose to do when the battle was over, Harad had made up his mind. Even as Peniff watched through Harad's eyes, Harad penned the words that would seal his family's fate. He folded the scrap of paper and inserted it into a tiny canister. Container in hand, Harad strode between the tents to the hutches where the homing pigeons were kept.

Like everyone of power, Kael maintained large numbers of such birds and used them to communicate with allies great distances removed. When released, these messenger pigeons always found their way back to the places they were bred. With canisters attached to their legs, they were the most efficient form of long distance communication. Harad strode between the rows of coops examining the labels on each. He paused before a large group labeled Monhedeth. Apparently Kael communicated regularly with Orr.

Carefully, to prevent the bird from escaping before he was ready, Harad opened the door, reached in, and cupped his hand over its wings. Then, turning it onto its back and cradling it in his hand, he secured the cylinder containing two fatal words. When he was satisfied it could not be dislodged, he kissed the bird's head and tossed it skywards. In one week at most, Orr would read the words, "PENIFF TRAITOR." Harad smiled and Peniff watched as the messenger soared. Once aloft, it turned north, sealing Miened, Halli, and Broodik's fate with every beat of its wings.

The suns rose, illuminating the plain and the unfolding spectacle of troops locked in combat, but this morning's glory was lost on Peniff. It might as well have been midnight. Nothing could help him now. He sat brooding until a cry from one of the fortress's walls caught his attention. He thought he had heard incorrectly, but the shout came again.

"Endaths!"

CHAPTER FORTY-FIVE

Peniff rose to his feet, too afraid to be hopeful after Harad had sent the bird. It was too soon for Obah's rescue party to have fetched Bedistai and returned. Besides, they were riding horses. Only Haroun rode endaths.

He forced his bruised body down the parapet walk, behind the rows of archers stationed along it, then turned when he reached the wall's corner. He followed the next section, avoiding men bringing baskets of arrows, turning his back to the plain where the battle was being waged, and headed to where the cry had arisen. While most of the soldiers on the battlements, or in the courtyard below, were making preparations in case the fighting were to arrive at barakMall's gates, a handful were peering through the rear castellation's notches. The suspense was too much to contain, and he broke into a trot.

Joining the ones gazing downward, searching for the cause of the alarm, he spotted the approaching party almost at once. Accompanying them, surrounded by the men and physicians Obah had dispatched, were a pair of saddled endaths. Atop one of these, crouching over the pommel, rode a man with long, dark, disheveled hair that shrouded his face. He was clad in a loincloth and wore something else tied around his torso. His musculature was unmistakable and Peniff's excitement increased.

As they passed beneath the place where he was standing, the rider straightened and tilted his head skyward. He scanned the faces looking down at him until, when he recognized Peniff, Bedistai grinned and waved. His lips uttered something, but when Peniff indicated, with a shake of his head and a hand to his ear, that he could not understand, the Haroun raised his voice.

"I couldn't wait!" he called.

Peniff was caught between tears and laughter. For two days he had envisioned his newfound friend dying alone. That Bedistai was alive brought such great joy that the fears he had striven to contain condensed into torrents that flowed down his cheeks. All the weeks spent with murderers and scoundrels, all the weeks spent living in dread, descended and enveloped him.

Since his family's abduction, he had lived in isolation. He had not lived with his abductors, but merely accompanied them. How could he share his thoughts and feeling with those men? He had been a lone swimmer in a sea filled with serpents. Finding Darva had done little to alleviate his desolation, especially after she had grown to distrust him. Of all the people he had met since he started on this quest, this hunter from No'eth was the one person who believed in him, the one he could truly call his friend. Oh, how he needed one now. Waving with unabashed delight, he looked for a stairwell that would take him to Bedistai's side.

Battle horns were sounding as the gates opened to admit the new arrivals, and though none in the fortress could long afford to ignore the battle beyond the walls, all stopped to gape at the two fabled beasts that were entering. Few outsiders ever journeyed to No'eth. Of those who did, fewer still had seen an endath.

When most had returned their attention to the battle and the rescue party had halted, Peniff descended the last few steps and ran out to greet the new arrivals. The endath bearing the hunter knelt and hugged the courtyard floor as if knowing her rider could not easily dismount. While Bedistai eased himself from her back in obvious distress, men leapt from their horses and hurried to assist him. He slipped to the ground using the saddle's front rigging to slow his descent. The first ones to reach him took hold of his legs and arms, avoiding the bandage around his middle.

"Bedistai!" cried Peniff as he ran to meet him. "I am so glad to see you," he said as he encircled Bedistai's shoulders in an embrace.

"As am I," grimaced the hunter.

"I am so sorry. I did not mean ..."

"I am fine. You did not hurt me," said Bedistai, ruffling Peniff's hair. "It is good to see a friend."

"I didn't think you would be able to ride so soon."

"Actually, riding an endath is far more comfortable than sitting on that rocky floor. And, frankly, despite your well-intentioned efforts, those rotting lizards drove me out. It will be months, maybe years before anyone will be able to enter that cave again."

They both laughed.

"I trust Darva arrived all right," Bedistai ventured.

Peniff nodded. "She is a little more bruised than when you last saw her, but is finally with her brother."

"I should have known. A man such as you finishes whatever he begins. Someday, if I can persuade you to visit Mostoon, I shall have you named an honorary Haroun."

Peniff took a step back. "Is that done?"

"Not yet. You shall be the first."

They laughed until reality came crashing down on Peniff. His face darkened and he turned away.

"What is wrong?" asked Bedistai.

The thought gazer regarded his friend. "You need to rest. These men," he gestured at the physicians and the others who had gone to search, "are here to care for you. You should go with them. We can talk later."

"Please tell me. You are hurting too. I can see it in your face." Peniff began to object but the Haroun would not be put off. "I cannot rest knowing something is troubling you. Tell me what it is, then I will do as you ask."

Peniff sighed and tried to make light, but the impending horror of his family's now-certain fate was too much, and he broke down and sobbed as he explained.

When he had finished, Bedistai turned to the physicians saying, "Doctors. I need you to bind these wounds securely. I have a long journey ahead of me."

"No!" cried Peniff. "You must rest."

Ignoring him, Bedistai asked the men surrounding him, "Where is the commander of this fort?"

Before they could answer, a new voice called out. "Bedistai, you really are here. I can't believe my eyes."

Darva was running across the quadrangle, picking her way through the troops. Like Peniff, she could not conceal her enthusiasm, her genuine liking, but more, her genuine love for this man. And like Peniff, when she arrived at his side, she threw her arms around him. He concealed the pain when she grasped him and returned her embrace, drawing her to him, surprising them both by pressing his lips against hers, holding the kiss until she pulled away gasping.

"Bedistai!" she exclaimed, as Bedistai blushed.

Embarrassed by his uncharacteristic spontaneity, he changed the subject. "I've brought friends."

When she appeared confused, he gestured towards the endaths.

"By the gods!" she said, raising her hands to her mouth. "Chawah? Chossen? Is that really you?"

The endaths raised their heads and nodded. One stepped forward and brushed her cheek with its face.

"Chossen!" She exclaimed, wrapping both arms around its head. Without releasing the animal, she turned to Bedistai. "Where? How? ..."

"They came to me."

"They found you in that cave?"

"How could they not?" he said, repeating his description of the cave's aroma.

Darva laughed. All at once, the glow faded from her face as her eyes went to the blood-soaked leather binding his side. She had fashioned the padding from her shirt and the bindings to hold it in place from a strip running from the wrist of one sleeve, across the shirt's back to the opposite wrist. While the binding still held, it was clear it needed changing.

"How do you feel?" she asked, placing a hand on the bandage.

"I am still sore and a little weak, but the claws did not pierce as deeply as they could have. I will have some scars to remind me of our encounter. Nothing more."

"Good. I will make sure you get your rest while you are here and after a few days ..."

"Darva," he interrupted. "I must leave within the hour."

"What? No!" she blinked, shook her head and stared in disbelief. "What are you saying? You cannot go. I won't allow it."

"I must. A carrier pigeon has been sent to Monhedeth. When it arrives, Peniff's family will die. I must intercept it."

"How? That is crazy. You cannot catch a bird."

"Endaths run at nearly the speed a pigeon flies, perhaps

faster. And while the bird must stop at night to sleep, endaths can continue indefinitely. If Peniff and I leave now, we may be able to intercept it."

"How will you follow it? It is so small, and the land is so vast ..."

"Chawah and Chossen can do this if we leave soon enough. They can sense the bird's direction if it does not put too much distance between us. Peniff risked his life to save ours and I must return the favor."

"But ..."

"Please, Darva. Don't disappoint me. When all this is over," he gestured towards the battlefield, "we will see each other again. I have already told you I would return home after you returned to your brother. Granted, this is sooner than I planned, but the reason is too important to ignore. I need you to be brave. Everything will work out in time. You must believe that."

"But your wounds. You might die."

"I can rest as well on Chawah's back as well as I can within these walls. Perhaps more safely, once we leave the battle behind."

"That's just it, Bedistai. How can you return north while this battle is raging? You certainly can't go the way you came. As surely as Hath's forces are swarming over this plain, En's have made the Nagath Valley impassable."

"I have no intention of heading in either direction. Instead, if we go directly north, hugging the western face of the Han'nah, we should be able to avoid the battle completely. Unless your brother's forces are overrun at the outset, we should be able to follow the bird's course directly. But we need to leave soon if the endaths are to track it. So please, help us. Gather four or five days' provisions and fill some water skins. While you are doing that, the doctors will tend to my wounds."

She tightened her lips, but knew he was right. She relented with a nod.

"I am sorry," she said. "You must do what you have to, and I will help."

She kissed him hard on the mouth. Then, turning to hide her tears, she ran to the kitchens.

Peniff saw that Bedistai was not untouched either. A pained expression crossed his face, like the shadow of a cloud darkening the landscape, then vanished. There was clearly more to the stoic hunter than he let on. Peniff decided not to press, asking instead, "Do we stand a chance?"

Bedistai cocked his head at the question.

"I mean, can the endaths really locate the pigeon?" Peniff asked.

"Chawah. Chossen," said Bedistai. "Can you still sense the bird?"

As one, the beasts raised their heads, craning their necks northward as if listening, their heads panning slightly from east to west then back again. They stood motionless for several minutes. Occasionally a muscle twitched or tail tip flicked. At one point, concerned by their lack of response, Peniff looked to Bedistai. When he started to speak, Bedistai extended one hand and put a finger to his lips, indicating he should wait and be silent, all the while keeping his eyes on the two great beasts. After several minutes had passed, once again in unison, the endaths turned towards the men and blinked deliberately.

"They indicate they can," Bedistai interpreted, "but their response was so long in coming that I suspect the bird is at the very edge of their perception."

"Then we should leave at once. We can find food later," said Peniff, on the verge of panic.

"They have the direction. Even should it fly beyond what they can perceive, once we are on our way they will begin to overtake it and their sense of it will grow stronger. If they had failed to locate it when I asked them, I would be pessimistic about our chances. But pigeons home in a straight line. With its course established, we can confidently pursue it. Hunting for food will be counterproductive, requiring far more time than waiting for Darva to complete her task."

CHAPTER FORTY-SIX

W hat?" Peniff asked, waking from a dream.

He blinked his eyes and lifted his head from the saddle. He thought he had heard a voice. Certainly, something had awakened him. In the darkness, he shifted his awareness to the hunter, but Bedistai was deep in dreams. He rose onto his elbows and attempted to see the world around him. The countryside, dimly lit by starlight, appeared as a series of shadows passing against a darker backdrop and the muted, rhythmic footfalls of the endaths were the only sounds punctuating the night. Since sight and sound were of no assistance, he reached out with his mind for another's presence, but there was no one. Unsettled by the disturbance, he lowered himself against the saddle and tried to sleep. That also proved fruitless. He was now wide-awake as his mind latched onto the problem, refusing to quiet for nearly an hour.

This was their second night out. Yesterday, they had crossed the plain of barTimesh and, by Peniff's estimation, they should be rounding the menRathan plateau. If his guess was correct—he was relying on Bedistai's assessment of their progress—by morning they would pass into Meden. That, according to the hunter, would be the most dangerous portion of their journey. Limast and Meden would still be at war. Even so, he hoped that leg of their voyage would pass as uneventfully as had the first.

Departing Liad-Nur had not been as perilous as he had feared. As Bedistai predicted, the battle in its early stages was confined to the area northwest of barakMall. The armies concentrated on the plain between the fort and Kael's encampment, with battle lines clearly delineated. As a result, Bedistai and Peniff easily avoided the conflict and the first day out was an easy one, punctuated by brief pauses to eat and stretch their legs.

At the outset, Peniff had expressed misgivings about life in the saddle for days on end. Even though circumstances dictated the need and there was no real alternative, he had been apprehensive about how he would tolerate it. Contrary to his fears, the pliant material from which the saddle had been crafted proved such a comfortable bed that, on the first morning out, he awoke refreshed and in good spirits. And while he suspected he would eventually resent being confined to this perch, as the day transpired, the riding was pleasant enough that he found himself enjoying the passing terrain—places he had never seen, but only heard about—lands he would likely never visit again.

He was slipping back to sleep when he was roused again, alarmed at another mind's touch. The contact had an almost familiar feel, but he could not identify it. The visiting mind felt confused, inexperienced. Nonetheless, he could tell it was deliberately seeking him out. As it fumbled, not realizing it had succeeded, he recognized the consciousness for what it was: the transitioning mind of a latent. That was the name he gave a new power coming into its own.

His first experience with a latent had come when he was still a child. She was a prescient, not a telepath. And though she had no ability to communicate with thoughts, nor to direct them toward another, she was near enough, as her mind transitioned from latency to potency, that he could observe her mental activity during that process.

It was a confusing, disorienting time for her and she grew terrified as her potential unfolded. Many things beyond her understanding or control were happening. Eventually, however, her mind settled, and she grew accustomed to her new state of being. He grew disappointed, however, at the way she chose to use her new abilities once she had fledged, employing them almost exclusively to win at games of chance, with no thought of applying them to a higher purpose.

Over the course of the ensuing years, he became aware of an occasional other unfolding. A woman who dwelled to the south, in land of Deth, could foretell the future. Two others in distant lands and with even more unusual abilities, like telekinesis, had also come to his attention. He did not know how many latents there were throughout the world. For all he knew, the entire population might possess some potential. It had been years, however, since the last one emerged and this new contact startled him.

"Ah!" he gasped as it touched him again.

He broke off his reverie of times long passed. This mind felt almost hostile, even angry. And while it had an undeniably familiar feel in its transitioning state, it remained unidentifiable. Although its thoughts were garbled and unintelligible, the snippets he could discern made it increasingly evident the thinker was searching for him in particular. Like an insect in the dark, it collided with him time and again, fluttering off before returning. He could not imagine who this latent might be and it was not until the contact finally broke off that he wondered from which direction the probe had originated. By then, however, it was too late, and he chided himself for lacking the presence of mind to have at least made that determination.

CHAPTER FORTY-SEVEN

A low thin fog hung over Meden's grasslands and the chill that formed it gradually brought Peniff awake. He sat, stretched, then to his surprise, noticed the endaths were standing motionless, poised for something unimaginable. He turned to Bedistai and was about to ask what was happening, when the hunter, sitting upright in his saddle, motioned him to be silent. Peniff did as he was instructed and endeavored to remain as quiet and still as the morning.

This day was quiet indeed. Nothing stirred. No birds soared. No breeze ruffled the grasses. Bedistai, motionless save for the rise and fall of his chest, sat bow in hand, an arrow nocked, staring at a nearby copse of dur and eshed trees. They remained that way for another half hour, and Peniff was intending to dismount and relieve himself, when something small and brown flew from one of the trees. Moving faster than Peniff's eye could follow, Bedistai released one, two, three, four arrows, drawing, nocking and releasing them in a fluid blur of practiced motion until whatever had taken wing fell impaled to a spot beneath the blanket of mist.

Bedistai turned to Peniff and said, "There is your pigeon."

Peniff's jaw dropped. He was unable to speak as he stared first at Bedistai, then at the place where the bird had fallen, and again at the hunter. Bedistai responded to his amazement with a calm that suggested he had done nothing extraordinary.

Peniff slipped from Chossen's back, his bladder forgotten, and hurried towards a flighted shaft poking through the vapor. He trembled as he bent to retrieve the feathered corpse and gathered the still warm body into his hand. Not caring whether any life still remained, he fumbled for the canister fastened to its leg. Cursing hands that were threatening to drop what they held, he located and tugged the container free. Prying off its lid, he peered inside, tipping the cylinder to better catch the light. Sure enough, it contained a roll of paper.

Removing the sheet was almost too much for his vanishing dexterity, but he managed to extract it before he fumbled the bird. Shaking uncontrollably, he unrolled and attempted to read the message, staring dumbly as his mind refused to comprehend what his eyes revealed. Suddenly, his mind focused and grasped the words Harad had written. In angry triumph, he crumpled the dispatch and hurled it away.

"We did it!" Peniff cried as he looked across the meadow. Then, correcting himself, he said in a more humble tone, "You did it."

With that admission, his excitement evaporated, the tightness in his chest released and a sob welled in his throat. He opened his mouth and the emotions he had dammed burst forth in a wail. He stood like that, screaming his relief for several minutes with his hands balled into fists. Then he dropped to his knees and bowed.

"Thank you," he said to no one in particular, for he did not believe in gods. Then, raising his head and wiping away the tears so he could see his benefactor, he mouthed the words again. "Thank you."

Bedistai nodded. "Thank the endaths," he said.

When his emotions finally cooled, Peniff rose to his feet and walked to Chawah and Chossen, who by now had begun grazing. He placed his hand on Chossen's flank and she lifted her head from her meal to appraise him. She snorted softly and returned her attention to the dew dampened grasses and tender shoots.

Peniff looked up at Bedistai. "When do you think it would have arrived if you ..." he paused, not wanting to voice the possibility, then completed the thought. "If you failed to bring it down?"

"Perhaps four more days."

Peniff nodded, understanding how close they had come to failure.

"So, six days altogether. That would have been the number of days from the time it left until my family died." He considered that for a moment, then asked, "How much longer before we arrive at barakMis?"

"That depends on you. If you want to slow the pace and sleep on the ground at night, seven or eight days would be my guess." Then, seeing in Peniff's eyes the urgency that spawned the question, he added, "On the other hand, if you don't mind maintaining our present pace, we might manage the rest of our journey in no more than four full days."

"But can the endaths keep up this pace for that long?"

"My sense is they were enjoying the chance to run unfettered as they have not done since their youth. I suspect they would quite enjoy four more days of the same. What do you say to that, girls?"

Both creatures raised their heads and snorted, nodding vigorously. Peniff responded with an open-mouthed grin, incredulous they had understood.

"So then I must ask," said Bedistai, "what do you choose?"

"Ha!" laughed Peniff. "Why ... why, yes. I say let us continue as before," he replied, almost giddy at the prospect. Then, remembering Bedistai's injuries, he asked, "But how are you? Can you manage such a pace?"

"Except for drawing my bow this morning, I have been relaxing and healing myself. In four more days, I will have rested more than a week, if we also include the time between when you left me in the cavern and when I arrived at barak-Mall. I will be just fine." When Peniff grinned broadly, Bedistai suggested, "Let the endaths finish grazing, then let them find water. We need to fill our water skins as well. While they are digesting, I will see if I can increase our larder. We will need a bit more food for the next four days, even though Darva was generous when she apportioned our rations. I can roast the pigeon over a fire and that will be our breakfast. Do you have any objections?"

"No," said Peniff, grinning at the thought. "I think I will rather enjoy making a meal of that foul creature."

CHAPTER FORTY-EIGHT

Harad was growing increasingly paranoid. Ever since Peniff had attacked him, he had remained so shaken his confidence had all but vanished. It had further declined after his report to Kael, and with good reason, he admitted. He had failed the warlord utterly. Had Obah's sudden mobilization not catapulted Kael into the very conflict Darva's kidnapping was intended to avert, the warlord might have executed Harad the moment he arrived.

As it was, Kael had let him know he was in great disfavor and his fate would remain uncertain until the battle was over, a battle that was now going poorly. Even in these first few days, Obah Sitheh was gaining the upper hand and Kael's formerly superior numbers were declining. It would not be long—a few days perhaps—before Sitheh would either drive Kael back to Chadarr or obliterate his army altogether. Harad could only imagine what Kael would do to him then and his dread compounded with each passing hour. He knew he dare not remain in the encampment if he wanted to keep his head. And while he should have been imprisoned, Kael's failure to incarcerate him, he knew, was an indication of the extent of the warlord's preoccupation, not his beneficence.

Then there was the matter of the thought gazer. Unaccustomed to defeat as Harad was, his humiliation at Peniff's hand galled him ever deeper. True, he had sent word of Peniff's treachery to Orr, but thoughts of potential mishap plagued him, and he feared that the messenger pigeon would somehow fail to deliver its precious cargo. So it was that he found himself standing before the hutches a second time, pacing and debating with himself. He tried to reason away his misgivings, arguing that these birds were reliable, rarely if ever failing to return home. Then again, there were hawks and other birds of prey. He shook his head. Prudence brooked no chance mishap. Once again he removed one of Orr's pigeons, attached another message and tossed the bird skyward.

"That will do it," he whispered.

Then he shouldered the satchel at his feet and made his way out of the camp and away from the conflict to Sandoval's harbors and his new purpose.

CHAPTER FORTY-NINE

It was dusk as Bedistai and Peniff crested a rise east of barakOzmir. After an uneventful day's ride, they were hardly prepared for the sight before them. Bonfires blazed at regular intervals across the plain, revealing a convoy transporting stone. So massive were the flat hexagonally cut rocks, that more than a dozen men struggled to slide one from a wagon's bed, despite the rollers on which each stone rested. After tipping one edge-first to the ground, once they had it standing, they rolled it facet by facet, eventually fitting it beside others like it—another piece of a ribbon stretching to the horizon.

"What is it?" asked Peniff. "Some kind of road?"

"I am told that Malik Obed is building a causeway from Limast to Meden for the express purpose of transporting weapons and supplies for his troops and his intended conquest of Meden. After every successful engagement against his enemies, he extends it farther."

"There must have been many successes," Peniff concluded. "Why doesn't Meden, or Yeset for that matter, halt its construction?"

"Probably because they understand that the road can just as easily carry their own troops towards Limast. Furthermore, they don't need to waste men or resources building it." Bedistai chuckled.

"From the fires, it would appear they intend to work throughout the night."

Bedistai nodded. "We will have to circle to the east to avoid them. That will probably work in our favor. When Darva and I forded the Em, we attempted an ambitious crossing and the river nearly claimed both her and Chossen. I regret to say I misjudged the danger and I prefer not to repeat the risk. I intend to cross farther eastward this time, where the Em is narrower. That will be easier on the endaths and they should be able to make up much of the time the detour costs."

They turned their mounts and dropped below the ridgeline to avoid detection, then paralleled the crest, keeping the hills to their left. It was dark when they topped it again, then descended with the intention of proceeding towards Miast. Bedistai was pleased they had left the pyres far behind, now barely discernable in the distance. With any luck, he thought, the darkness would serve to conceal their passing.

It was well into the night and they were dropping off to sleep, lulled by the soft cadence of the endaths' pace, when Chawah woke Bedistai with a tap of her tail.

His head came up and he whispered, "What is it, girl?"

She had halted on a knoll overlooking the valley and Chossen drew alongside.

"Bedistai?" Peniff whispered as he too awoke.

When Bedistai did not reply, Peniff paused and extended his awareness outward and gasped. There were hundreds of men ahead. Several hundred. He felt to the left, then to the right and realized that they were almost surrounded. They had stumbled onto a sleeping encampment, by his estimation from Limast, not that it mattered. There were no friends in these parts. He maneuvered Chossen until her flank touched Chawah's, then leaned across to Bedistai.

"We are nearly surrounded," he hissed. "What shall we do?"

"Let us back away. Perhaps we can find a way around."

They were about to turn, when someone unshielded a lantern and shone its light towards them, illuminating their presence.

"Halt! Identify yourselves," the man challenged.

Without hesitation, Bedistai replied, "I am Bedistai Alongquith of the Haroun. My companion and I have been hunting far afield and we now seek safe passage north. We are not your enemies. We have no quarrel with you. Please allow us to pass."

"Haroun?" The guard sounded surprised. "What are you doing so far from No'eth?"

"As I said, we were hunting."

"How do I know you are not spies? Can you produce the game you caught as evidence?"

"A bear decided it wanted our catch. We didn't think we would win the argument, so we are returning empty-handed."

The watchman laughed. "My daughter could have done better."

Bedistai laughed as well, and Peniff forced a smile. Fear was beginning to embrace him, and it was not without effort that he struggled to maintain some fraternal appearance.

Holding his lantern high, the man regarded the intruders, then studied their saddles and baggage. His voice soured and he ordered, "Ride forward and dismount. My captain will have a look at you."

Peniff could tell that several soldiers were beginning to wake. Their thoughts ranged from bewilderment to suspicion. Fearing they would be unreasonably detained or worse, killed, he whispered to Bedistai, "If we dismount we are finished. I can't allow it to end here."

Before Bedistai could respond, Peniff drove his heels into Chossen's flanks and spurred her to a gallop, leaving the hunter sitting alone.

"No! Peniff, no!" cried Bedistai.

It was too late. Left with no choice but to follow, he reined Chawah around and chased after him.

"Halt!" cried the watchman.

Raising his lantern and swinging it overhead, the man signaled the army. As soldiers responded, cries went up amplifying and repeating the alarm. Although endaths are fast, sound travels faster, and soon troops were rising to their feet ahead of them.

Chawah dug hard, propelling herself until she drew abreast of Chossen. With their necks and tails extended, the endaths were like low flying missiles hurtling through the night, at times barely touching the ground. Peniff and Bedistai conformed their bodies closely to the saddle, their low profiles, arms and legs extended, providing little resistance as the creatures clove the air. All around, outraged voices threatened, then receded behind them.

Thin staccato hisses, barely audible, whipped past their ears. *Arrows!* thought Peniff.

At that very instant, a shaft pierced his thigh, just before Chossen made an abrupt turn to the south. Reacting less perfectly at night than by day, the endaths had once again saved their riders' lives, if barely.

Before long, satisfied they had passed out of range, Bedistai and Peniff resumed their eastward course. Ashamed he had panicked, Peniff attempted to apologize.

"Bedistai," he began, but Bedistai turned away. When he made an attempt to explain himself, the hunter snapped, "I don't want to hear about it," then lapsed into silence.

Hours passed and Peniff's leg began to throb. Despite his injury, he suspected they would not stop until morning.

Nothing could be done for him until it was light enough to see, and that would require either a fire or daylight. Fire was out of the question, so he clung to the saddle as the night dragged on. Feeling faint, he secured his arms under the cross strap. There was nothing to do but hang on.

CHAPTER FIFTY

Peniff cried out as a surge of pain jolted him to consciousness. Bedistai was easing him from Chossen's saddle while the endath knelt to assist. His head whirled and his limbs felt weak. As he looked about, confused by what was happening, Bedistai said, "You have lost a great deal of blood. As soon as you are lying on the ground, I am going to try to stop the loss."

Although Bedistai tried to be careful, Peniff cried twice more before the hunter laid him upon the blanket he had readied. He lit a fire, and once it was blazing brightly, he knelt by Peniff and began cutting the pant leg away.

"How are you doing?" he inquired as he worked, studying Peniff's eyes as he worked.

"I am all right, I suppose. Just weak."

"Hopefully, over time we can change that. First, though, I must stop the bleeding. I don't have the herbs I need to congeal the blood or prevent infection, so I must tell you in advance that what I am about to do will be very painful. You must also understand it is absolutely necessary."

He produced a leather strap and doubled it twice before handing it to Peniff.

"I want you to put this between your teeth and bite down hard. Otherwise, you may accidentally bite off your tongue."

Peniff complied. Were he not so disoriented, he might have been more alarmed by that statement. Caught as he was between delirium and consciousness, he regarded Bedistai passively.

"You will have to trust me," Bedistai said. "First, I have to break off the arrowhead. The barbs will not allow me to remove the shaft without causing unnecessary damage. It is imbedded deep in your thigh, so to do this, I will have to push the shaft completely through your leg. Are you ready?"

Biting down on the strap, Peniff nodded. The hunter grasped the flighted end and shoved. Peniff screamed through his teeth as Bedistai pushed the arrow almost to its vanes, until the tip protruded on the other side.

"There," said Bedistai. "That is the first part. Now, I must break off the head. This will not be pleasant, either. I will try not to hurt you, but from experience, I must tell you the shaft will move when I break it. And again, it will be painful."

He grasped the shaft with his left hand and the arrowhead with his right. With a sudden twist he broke off the tip, then tossed it aside. Peniff screamed when the shaft moved, and he began sweating profusely.

Next, Bedistai leaned towards the fire and picked up a firebrand. He studied it a moment, watching how it burned. Apparently satisfied, he again turned to Peniff to explain what must come next.

"I need to sear the wound completely, both to staunch the bleeding and to prevent contamination." He looked into Peniff's eyes to insure he understood, saying slowly and deliberately, "This will hurt a great deal, but there is no other way."

Peniff only partially understood what Bedistai was telling

him. His vision was tunneling and his color perception had all but vanished. In a world reduced to browns and yellows, he watched what the hunter was doing, barely comprehending as Bedistai used the brand to ignite the arrow. Despite his incoherence, Peniff stared wide-eyed as the flames grew brighter, slowly spreading along its shaft.

"I must make sure that the wood is quite hot and that your blood will not extinguish the flames prematurely."

Even in his semi-conscious state, fear took hold as the shaft began to burn and Peniff's eyes widened.

"Grasp the blanket tightly with both hands."

Peniff complied.

"Bite down hard on the strap and hold on."

Peniff did as he was told.

"Are you ready?"

Peniff shook his head in an adamant "no" as tears flowed down his cheeks. Nevertheless, he gathered himself, held on as instructed, then nodded once.

"Good."

Bedistai grasped the flights tightly and slowly drew the arrow through the wound. As the flaming wood entered Peniff's leg, accompanied by the sizzle and smell of burning flesh, Peniff screamed, his eyes rolled back in his head and blackness enveloped him.

CHAPTER FIFTY-ONE

The light was dim when Peniff opened his eyes. From the sky's coloration, he suspected it was still early morning. Pleased they had not lost much time, he propped onto his elbows and examined himself. Aside from the fact his pants now covered only one leg, the other leg sporting a bandage just below where the cloth had been cut away, his mind felt clear. His leg hurt beyond description, but from the color of the cloth wrapped around his leg, he could tell the bleeding had stopped.

"Good," he heard Bedistai say. As he turned his head to look, Bedistai asked, "Are you hungry?"

"Famished," Peniff answered. "I feel as though I haven't eaten in a week."

"Well, not that long. But it has been almost two full days, so I'm not surprised."

"Two days! What do you mean? It has only been since morning ..."

"Another morning has come and gone, and it is nearly time for dinner."

For a moment Peniff could not respond. He glanced around

and saw the horizon intersecting the upper portions of both solar spheres. Mahaz was leading Jadon and the two suns were setting.

"We have lost two days," he murmured.

"That is true. We have lost two, but you are still here and that is reason for thanks. Let me bring you something to eat."

Before Bedistai could turn away, Peniff realized from the tone of his voice, that Bedistai was controlling his displeasure.

"You are angry with me."

The hunter glared at him. "Yes, I am angry," he snapped. "You jeopardized all of our lives with your stupidity."

"I am sorry. I was afraid for my family."

"Look at yourself. Look what you have done to yourself. If you had died, how would that have benefitted anyone?"

"I didn't ..." Peniff began. He was about to explain how it was someone else who shot him, when he realized the idiocy of the explanation.

"You nearly got the rest of us killed as well!" shouted Bedistai. "What if we had died? Where would your family be then? You say you love them, but do you? You don't show it."

"I don't know what to say."

"Neither do I."

"Will you still help me?"

Bedistai stared at him through narrowed eyes. He was breathing heavily and Peniff could tell he was considering how to respond.

After a moment, Bedistai said, "I gave you my word I would help you, so I will keep it. I have certainly made my share of mistakes on this journey, so I am hardly one to give reproach. But listen. If you do anything else to unnecessarily risk Chawah's or Chossen's lives, I will forget my promise. I will wash my hands of you and your loved ones forever, and you will be on your own. These creatures risk everything for you, asking only to be safeguarded when that is possible. They will die to save you, but I will not have you risk their lives when there may be another way. Do I make myself clear?"

"Again, I apologize. I will be smarter next time."

Peniff hated the silence that followed, but he knew better than to speak. After a while, Bedistai relented.

"I accept your apology," he said. "Let us hope the endaths do as well." His voice softened. "We need to eat. I will see what we have while the animals are grazing."

He went to Chawah's saddlebags, then paused and turned.

"I hope you don't mind dried meat, bes, and parm," said Bedistai, referring to the coarse, country-style bread and savory cheese Darva had packed. "I had to douse the fire after I had cauterized your wound. It was too risky to keep it burning. Now that it's growing dark, a cook fire will be even more obvious."

"No. Of course not. I will eat anything. My stomach isn't very particular at the moment."

Bedistai returned with food and a water sack, placing them on the blanket where Peniff lay. The two ate in silence.

"Don't be so glum," said Bedistai, as he began to clean up. "In the state we are both in, we need the extra day. By the time we arrive, my wounds will have healed and you should be walking, although I suspect you will do so with a limp. Time is our friend. The more time we have to recover, our chance of helping your family increases. Furthermore, it has occurred to me that we can pass through my village on our way to Monhedeth. I can assemble a party of Haroun on almost no notice. We will not want too many to accompany us, lest we attract attention. But a small party—six or eight perhaps—can accomplish a great deal. I'm optimistic."

"I am glad," said Peniff.

"Care to try out that leg? I would like to see how well you can walk. Do you think you can manage a few steps? If you can get about, if you can climb onto Chossen—with help, of course —we can rest as we travel and sleep as we ride. While I am glad for this respite, you are partially right. We cannot allow too much time to slip away."

"I am not sure I can. My leg is weak. I'm weak," Peniff said. Then he saw Bedistai standing with his hands on his hips, and remembered how this man, wounded by a samanal, had, without hesitation, come to his assistance. "But I will try," he finished.

Bedistai nodded.

Getting to his feet was no easy task. He assayed several positions from which to rise before he found one that did not put too much stress on his wound. Once on his feet, however, he was pleased to find that he could move about unassisted, albeit slowly. He suspected he would do better after a few more days.

"It looks as if I can manage after all," he declared.

He smiled and Bedistai smiled back.

CHAPTER FIFTY-TWO

The nightmare grasped Peniff and would not surrender him to the healing balm of sleep. Terror engulfed him as his faults and failings paraded through his mind, a cavalcade of errors, weaknesses and missed opportunities. Long before those riders crested the mound on that pastoral afternoon, he had felt them approach. Their thoughts came to him like whispers from afar, an unease that he had shrugged aside in preference to the delight of Halli and Broodik's glee, the sparkle of Miened's eyes and the smile on her lips. Oh, what he would give to return to that time and sunder that illusion, to react to their presence sooner so they could flee from Harad and his thugs. So they could hide until those wraiths had passed and, finding no one atop that hill, fade into the shadows, disappear, and leave them unmolested. But he had chosen to ignore the warnings, subtle though they were.

He also understood what a foolish fantasy this was. Harad was not the kind who would have abandoned his mission so easily. He would have scoured the countryside, bribing or terrorizing the locals into revealing his family's whereabouts. He would have followed them home. Perhaps he would have been waiting at their doorstep when they returned from their picnic.

Even now, while Peniff rode across the countryside beleaguered with fears, his innocent children and the woman he loved were huddled in the dark holds of a distant keep, waiting for they knew not what.

Peniff realized a greater truth, something that had eluded him until now. Regardless of whether he succeeded or failed, their fate would likely remain unchanged. In the end they would perish. They lived for now, serving only as incentive, a hollow promise Orr would snatch away as soon as he learned which path Peniff had taken: either the capture and return of his quarry, or his failure and betrayal. And while the first course had offered faint promise his loved ones would be spared, they were now the certain victims of Peniff's conscience. Because he could not abide what Orr had intended for Darva, now these three, these dearest three would suffer for his treachery. Their faces loomed in the dream, smiling and loving, only to distort into screams and horrors, and it was all his fault.

A new face appeared, catching Peniff off guard. It was not one of theirs and did not belong in this dream. He struggled to recognize it, then saw it belonged to Harad. Peniff was traveling through Liad-Nur. Why was Harad here, visiting him as he slept?

Hello, Peniff. Thought you'd done me in?

Why was Harad speaking? This was wrong. It felt too real. It felt ...

Like I know what you are dreaming? Oh, but I do. I know exactly what you are dreaming and, no, you did not do me in. You see, I am like you now. I am a thought gazer too. I can see your thoughts. I can see your family's thoughts. I can even see the pigeon's thoughts. Not the one you killed. A second one. A bird I dispatched later. It's on its way to inform Orr of your treachery.

No! protested Peniff. *This is impossible. How ...*

How? When you went inside me, you did something to me. I don't know how to describe it and I know you didn't intend it. Why would you? Why would you want me like this? Nonetheless, you did it and I am just like you now. Well, no. That is untrue. I could never be like you any more than you could be like me. But I am alive and I am well and I am on my way to Monhedeth. Does that frighten you?

You can't be!

Oh, but I can. I can and I am. I am on my way at this moment and if Orr doesn't kill them, I will.

No! Peniff cried again. *No! No!* "No! No!"

"Peniff."

"No!"

"Peniff. Wake up. Wake up. You are dreaming."

Peniff opened his eyes. It was Bedistai. Under the starlight, dark as it was, he recognized his friend, riding beside him and seated on Chawah.

"It wasn't a dream," gasped Peniff. "It was real."

They reined in the endaths and dismounted to talk. Peniff told him what he saw, how it felt.

"Still, couldn't you simply have dreamed it? Simply manufactured the whole thing?"

Bedistai placed a hand on Peniff's forehead, then sat back again, clearly perplexed.

Peniff shook his head. "Right now, as we sit here speaking to one another, how do you know this is not a dream? You know because everything about this moment has substance. There is no question about its reality. That is how I know that he really spoke to me: from the substance of the encounter."

"What I want to know," said Bedistai, "is why Obah's men released him. He abducted their lord's sister. Wasn't that reason enough to imprison him?"

"Darva insisted they leave him alone. I think it was because of what I had done to him."

He explained how what he had inflicted on Harad was similar to what he had done to the man at the supply wagon.

"As for the ones who rescued Darva, when they came upon us he was a sobbing heap, clutching himself and trembling uncontrollably. They wouldn't have perceived him as a threat. He was pathetic, and they simply left him there. I think we all believed he was done for."

"Obviously he was not. But if he is following us, he will not catch us. We are moving too swiftly, and he will have to find a way through Limast as well."

"I don't think he is following. I briefly glimpsed the world through his eyes and it appeared he is heading westward."

Bedistai raised his eyebrows. "West, you say? Well, that is good. If he is going westward, the only route to Monhedeth is by sea. The Em is uncrossable nearer its mouth. He must first go to Sandoval, then find a ship owner willing to transport him. The seas, let alone the distance, will be too much for a smaller craft and passage will not be cheap. Even if he is successful, the journey will take many days, more than a week. We will be finished before that. I don't see him as a threat. Rest easy, my friend."

Peniff considered his reasoning, then sighed. "Thank you. That makes me feel better."

"Let us return to the saddle and tie ourselves in. We have a long way to go and we need to sleep."

They rose and remounted. But though Peniff tried to rest easy as Bedistai suggested, Harad's specter would continue to haunt him throughout the remainder of their journey.

CHAPTER FIFTY-THREE

H e's come back. Salmeh, he's come back. Bedistai has returned."

She looked up from the tallow she was boiling as Dorman, stumbling, nearly falling, ran to deliver the news. She could hardly believe she had heard him correctly. Jadon had yet to complete an orbit around Mahaz—the time her son had predicted his journey would require—and each day he was gone was more cause for worry. Almost daily, Salmeh had chided herself for her motherly concerns. After all, Bedistai, a full-grown man, was far more capable than most. Even so, she understood the violence of the times and knew that calling her fears motherly underplayed the gravity of his mission. But now ... She set down the stirrer and wiped her hands on her apron.

"Who did you say?" she asked, making sure she had understood.

"Bedistai, Salmeh. It's Bedistai." He collided with her and hugged her, in part out of joy, and in part to prevent both of them from falling.

"Where is he?" she asked, craning her neck in the direction from which he had come.

"He was entering Mostoon when I spotted him. I thought of you at once."

"You're such a good boy," she said, squeezing him.

"He should be here any minute."

He began to release her when Salmeh felt his body tense.

"Yes!" Dorman cried as he raised an arm to wave. "There he is."

Chawah's head and neck appeared as she emerged from behind a house, then the rest of her. As she rounded the corner, Bedistai looked in their direction. When his eyes fell on his mother, he grinned and raised his arm in a grand sweeping wave.

"Who is that with him?" asked Dorman as Chossen appeared. His arm dropped to his side and he squinted. "He's brought someone."

"We shall find out soon enough."

She untied her apron, then folded it and set it on the stool where she had been sitting.

Both endaths had turned the corner and were striding between the houses toward the common area. As increasing numbers of villagers realized what was happening, they began setting aside their work and encircled the pair, accompanying them and speaking to the riders with great animation. When the endaths halted before her, Bedistai leapt to the ground and embraced her. Then, as Chossen knelt beside them, Bedistai turned to help Peniff.

"You are injured," Salmeh said. Then, regarding each one in turn, she blurted, "Both of you. How did this happen?" Before Bedistai could reply, she turned to Dorman. "Find Nessra and tell her we need bandages." As the boy ran to do her bidding, she turned back to the pair. "Josah is heating water for soup. If she hasn't begun adding vegetables, we can use it to clean your wounds. Those rags you are wearing look awful." Noticing Peniff's limp, she asked, "Can I help you?"

"Thank you, ma'am. I can manage."

She cast an inquiring glance at Bedistai.

"Mother, this is Peniff," he explained. "He saved my life and helped me return Darva to her brother."

"Did you now?" she said, raising her brows. "I am honored to make your acquaintance. If you have helped my son in any way, let alone saved his life, you are welcome here. Consider Mostoon your home and us your family." She reached for a walking stick that was lying near the fire and handed it to him, saying, "I use this whenever my joints start to hurt. I'm doing better today than you seem to be. Humor me, please, and take it."

"Thank you," replied Peniff.

To Bedistai, she said, "Tell me about your friend while we walk to Josah's cook fire."

As they proceeded, he began recounting all that had happened since he had left home. When they found Josah, still chopping vegetables and setting them aside in bowls, Salmeh explained why they needed the water. Josah, in turn, ladled a portion into a large ceramic pot.

"I have a quantity of dried witch's nettle in my house," she said. Then, gesturing towards a smaller fire nearby, she handed the pot to Salmeh saying, "I was about to brown the meat. Heat this while I bring back the herb."

As Salmeh began stripping off the men's dressings, she appraised her son. "You have lost weight. Have you been eating?"

"Yes, Mother," said Bedistai with a grin.

"You promised you would be careful."

"I tried to, Mother. I really tried, but some things cannot be avoided."

Dampening the corner of her apron with some of the water, she dabbed at the area around Peniff's cauterization.

"You amaze me, young man," she said. "It is usually he who rescues the others."

"Ma'am, I only did what was necessary and, truthfully, he saved my life as well."

"Please call me Salmeh," she said. "How long will you be with us?"

"We must leave as soon as possible," said Bedistai. When her face fell, he explained about Peniff's family.

"Then your work is not finished. I understand." Turning to Peniff, Salmeh said, "Family is foremost in the minds of our people. How can we assist you?"

It was Bedistai who replied. "I need to ask Tahmen if he and his pod will accompany us," he said, meaning his brother and his hunting party.

Just then, Dorman and Nessra returned. As she draped the strips of cloth Salmeh had requested over a rack used for stretching hides, Dorman told Bedistai, "I know where to find Lorek and Samen. They were just about to leave for Bandoon. If I hurry, I think I can catch them."

"Go," said Bedistai. As Dorman turned away, Bedistai called after him. "After that, gather the rest and wait at my house."

"Once we've attended to your wounds," said Salmeh, "Nessra and I will begin preparing food for your journey."

CHAPTER FIFTY-FOUR

Are you sure you wouldn't rather wait until after the storm has passed?" Tahmen asked.

They had gathered in Bedistai's home. And though Peniff was impressed by the girth of the logs used to construct it, vaguely wondering how many men it had taken to cart and place each one, he asked, "What do you mean? The weather is fine."

"Clouds to the west presage something large. The sea birds arriving at Lake Ossan indicate how bad it will be. If it's as fierce as they predict, traveling to Monhedeth will not be easy."

"Nothing we've been doing is easy," said Peniff. "We did not race from Liad-Nur to No'eth to stop and take a nap."

Lorek, a young man, nearly as muscular as Bedistai, looked up from the knife he was sharpening. "You're in quite a hurry."

"If this were your family, wouldn't you be?" Peniff countered.

"Beasts will not forage and birds will not fly during a storm like the one that is coming." Lorek chuckled. "I'm simply amused how only men are foolish enough to dare such a passage. To tell the truth, Samen and I were on our way to Bandoon. A beyaless cath'en has come down from the mountains and they're worried it may pay them a visit." He set down the wet stone and grinned. "Something to your taste, Bedistai." Turning to Peniff, the smile fell away and he said, "I meant no disrespect. By comparison, this should prove somewhat more exciting."

"There is one thing bothering me," said Tahmen. "Any child can locate Monhedeth. Finding barakMis should not be hard either. But once we are there, how do we locate your family? And even if we manage that, how do you propose we free them?" He laughed. "Come to think of it, Orr will probably escort us to the prison himself, if only for having the audacity to attempt to break in. He might even place us in cells near your loved ones. So maybe that part won't be so hard after all." His tone became serious. "But answer me this. Even if we manage to free them from their cells how do you propose we leave?"

"The same way we will enter," said Bedistai. "And we will not require Orr's assistance for that either. Peniff broke into the prison in danHsar, rescued Darva and myself, then took us out unharmed."

Tahmen regarded Peniff askance. "You do not have the look of either a warrior or a hunter. What is your trade?"

"I am a miller," said Peniff.

Tahmen clapped his hands on his thighs and looked at each of the others in the room.

"Now *that* I believe. Except for the lack of flour on your face, you do have the look. I am loath to call you a liar," he said to Bedistai. "But except for our blood tie and the fact you are in all other regards honorable, I cannot accept your story. My entire pod could scarcely manage to extract ourselves from the sort of fortress barakMis is reputed to be. But this one?" He jerked his thumb at Peniff, then paused. "I am at a loss." He looked his brother in the eyes and said, "Convince me."

"I do not appreciate how you insult my friend," replied Bedistai, "and I would hate to come to blows over your rudeness. I will only say that he possesses a skill none of us have, without which, I agree, this entire expedition would be folly."

"And what is that?"

When Bedistai brought up the legend of Assan Bey, Tahmen laughed.

"And carpets can fly," said Tahmen. "You have been drinking kethna," he sneered, and the rest of the pod mimicked his amusement.

Bedistai appeared unruffled by the response. "People's thoughts are laid open to him like the pages of a book," he said. "He can determine the layout of the fortress before we enter. He can detect where the guards are going and whether they are aware of us."

"Come on, Bedistai," laughed Dorman, nearly falling from the rafter on which he was perched. He turned to Peniff and asked, "Can you tell what I am thinking? Right now?"

"You mean, do I know you broke Bedistai's target bow while he was gone and, even as we speak, you are trying to figure out how you can repair it or make him a new one before he notices?"

Everyone looked to see Dorman's mouth fall open. The youth was holding his breath as a look of astonishment spread across his face.

"Bedistai," the young man began.

"You should see your face," said Samen to Dorman, as Bedistai balled his hands into fists. "It is redder than Mahaz at dusk."

The pod broke into howls.

"You think Dorman looks shocked?" said Lorek. "Would someone please find some polished glass and show Bedistai his reflection?"

Bedistai appeared to be rising from his chair, but the corners of his mouth were already turning up.

"All right," said Tahmen. He waited for the room to settle

down. When they had quieted enough to hear him, he said to Bedistai, "It appears the legends are real." He nodded thoughtfully. "And though I would still require another demonstration if you were to insist carpets can fly ..." He turned to Peniff. "I have to ask why, after all this time, is your family suddenly in danger? He is keeping them alive until he learns the results of your mission, isn't he? Since the first pigeon is dead, and the storm will prevent the second from arriving until after we do, it will be a while before he learns what you have done."

"As the days go by, Orr grows increasingly nervous," replied Peniff. "He is distrustful of me and Hath Kael as well. Wouldn't you be, if you were in his position? Isolated, days away from everything that is transpiring, I suspect he has considered disposing of them more than once already. In fact, after I departed, what need did he have of keeping them alive at all? Assuming I had cooperated and delivered Darva to him, what could I have done if I returned and they were dead? He is keeping them alive only because he is unsure how much I can perceive at a distance.

"On the other hand, if he changes his mind and reacts to some delusional fear, what can I do to stop him, even if I know what he is thinking? I am hurrying to get there before he decides to do something rash. So, if you don't care to help me, and although I stand little chance of freeing them myself, I will go there alone if I must and I will do what I can."

"That won't be necessary," said Bedistai.

"No," Tahmen agreed. "You will not go to Monhedeth alone. We will accompany you. I was only questioning the urgency of this mission and you have answered me."

Peniff looked around the room, surprised to see every head nodding.

"Thank you," he said. "But, before you decide, I want to make clear you do not have to risk your lives for my family. You don't know me, and you have no ties to them."

"No, I don't," said Tahmen. "None of us do. And there are still many good arguments against our going. But of all the things worth doing in life, it is important to stand up for those things one values most. For me, for Bedistai and all Haroun, we place family above all else. Besides," he said, then smiled and his tone softened a bit, "it will certainly be the most interesting thing I have done this year. When do you propose we leave?"

"Mother and Nessra are preparing our provisions, even as we speak," said Bedistai.

"So you really do intend to depart now," said Lorek.

"If we leave at once, we can be at Orr's gate by midday the day after tomorrow. I doubt he will expect anyone to come calling, especially through the storm. That alone increases our chance of success."

"I will come along," said Dorman

"Not you," Bedistai replied. "You are too young."

"I am not afraid. I want to come with you."

"I am not questioning your courage, but you have yet to pass into manhood. You are still an initiate. Even when you pass your initiation, it will take several years for you to acquire enough experience to have any chance of returning home alive from something like this. As it is, some of us may perish in the attempt. This is a dangerous undertaking."

"But we are Haroun," Dorman protested. "Surely no coward in Monhedeth can harm any of us. When you were not much older than I, you slew a beyaless cath'en with only a knife."

"Enough!" demanded Bedistai. "I will hear no more."

"But, Bedistai ..."

"I said enough."

Just then, the door opened and Salmeh and Nessra entered carrying satchels in their arms, while others hung about their shoulders.

"Here is your food" Salmeh said. "I think this will suffice."

"By Vashta's blood!" Tahmen, sitting up to look. "You have been busy."

"We had help, my love," Nessra said. "Josah and Mardit lent their hands."

"Thank you," said Bedistai. "And thank Josah and Mardit as well."

"Yes, thank you," said Peniff. "We will certainly need this."

"As I said," Salmeh replied. "You are one of us, and we take care of our own."

Peniff smiled and averted his eyes downward.

Just then, rain began pelting the roof. From the sound, the drops were large and the intervals between the strikes quickly shortened until the pelts became continuous. The din grew so loud they had to shout to be heard.

"I have a sandiath skin jacket and trousers in my home. Extra sets if anyone needs them," offered Lorek.

The rest had their own, but Bedistai said, "I know Peniff needs a set. Please bring them." Turning to Peniff, he added, "I also have sandiath boots that should fit. The skin is waterproof. It will not do for you to take ill, especially in your current condition."

He spoke to the rest. "I want each of you to bring the greatest length of rope you possess. I suspect we will have to scale the fortress ramparts, so we will need whatever lengths you can provide.

"Now, aside from Dorman, unless any of you choose to remain at home, you should fetch your endaths and begin packing at once. This storm will not abate any time soon and I would like to leave within the hour."

TEN ENDATHS STOOD before Bedistai's house, Chawah and Chossen and the eight belonging to Tahmen's pod. And though it was difficult to discern even nearby homes through the downpour, the hunters made sure their equipment was secure as they prepared to set off.

Samen eyed Bedistai with bemusement. "I see you have become accustomed to carrying a sword in your travels."

"It serves no purpose on a hunt," Bedistai replied, "but it is invaluable in a fight."

"Let us hope stealth will make swordplay unnecessary," said Samen. Then, to Peniff he said, "What have you learned about Orr's fortress?"

"Nothing yet. Orr's thoughts are jumbled. Nor have I been able to gather anything useful from other minds I have touched. Something seems to be interfering. As we draw nearer, I will begin to acquire the information we need."

Samen nodded. "Shall we go?" he asked Bedistai. "Conditions are not going to improve any time soon."

Bedistai nodded.

As he went to help Peniff onto Chossen, the rest of the pod mounted up. Peniff marveled at their courage, these men who owed him no allegiance, yet were willing to risk their lives because of what he stood for. That he was risking his own that his family might live was reason enough for these Haroun to give their all. He gave it no more thought because, were he to do so, he feared the immense responsibility might cause him to cower in the face of it.

Once Peniff was in the saddle, Bedistai leapt onto Chawah. The others were ready and awaiting his command. So, with a hand he motioned the pod to follow and turned Chawah into the gale.

CHAPTER FIFTY-FIVE

L ight rain sprinkled Monhedeth, wet, gray, and persistent; it was no longer an assault, but neither had it finished. Traffic had resumed between the city, danMis, and the fortress, barakMis, but the heavily laden wagons and carts were forced to avoid the quagmires of the highways, traveling instead on their vegetated shoulders. Released at last from the wind's buffet, flattened grasses strained to unbend, and a messenger pigeon resumed its flight.

The name barakMis means Fortress of Blood. When Tahmen's pod emerged from the Ahman Forest, they saw one of the things that had lent it that name. Built entirely of blood red stone, the stronghold stood apart from the land it dominated. Intended to be imposing, with taller towers and higher walls than any other castle in Ydron, it had been erected in the center of a vast field of grass. There was no way to approach it unde-tected, and scaling it seemed almost impossible. Occasional patrols came and went at irregular intervals, making crossing the expanse a gamble.

"Perhaps if we were to send a few endaths galloping across the field, they might distract the patrols," Lorek suggested.

Bedistai shook his head. "That would only serve to announce that the Haroun have arrived. Let's circle northward while keeping within the woods. We can draw a bit closer and reduce the amount of open space we'll have to cross. The patrols don't seem to be looking for anything. In fact, they seem almost bored. That may work to our advantage."

When they had drawn as close as cover would permit, Bedistai noticed something peculiar.

"Tahmen, look at the stones that make up the wall. Instead of a smooth, tightly-fitted face, they are deeply engraved with designs. I have heard Orr is vain and fond of ostentation. In this case, his vanity is providing us with handholds and footholds. How considerate of him."

The remark generated laughter.

"I do find it curious, however, that there doesn't appear to be a watch on the parapets, and so few squads patrolling the perimeter."

"Do you think it's an invitation?" Tahmen asked.

"It could be a trap, although I can't see how Orr could have anticipated our arrival. On the other hand, his lack of precaution may only be due to the land's remoteness. The lack of immediate enemies can foster apathy. In any case, we should be on guard. We must assume he set these patrols for a reason. Whether they share his concern is something else."

"Bedistai," said Peniff, "I'm worried. The walls may be easy for you to climb, but even if I weren't injured, I don't think I could manage it. I certainly can't climb with my leg like this."

"I've already planned for that. We will drop a length of rope. I will fashion a seat at one end and we will haul you up." He put a reassuring hand upon Peniff's shoulder. "You're as good as in."

"One more thing," said Peniff. "I have been trying to learn the fortress's layout, but have been unable to learn anything of use. It's as if my efforts are being blocked, though I cannot see how that would be possible."

Bedistai frowned. "Perhaps once you're inside, your luck will improve."

As if luck would have anything to do with the outcome, thought Peniff. He understood Bedistai was trying to be helpful, yet this was unlike anything he had ever encountered. Nonetheless, he tried to sound hopeful, and replied, "Perhaps."

They were waiting for an opportunity when a patrol, chatting and joking among themselves, occupied more with conversation than surveillance, passed by their hiding place. Once they had passed, Bedistai turned to Chawah.

"I want you to go deep into the forest and hide," he told her. "Take Chossen and the others. Later, when you sense we are leaving, return to this spot and wait."

She blinked and dipped her head, then turned and loped into the woods. The other endaths followed and the hunters returned their attention to the patrol. When the guards had gone perhaps a hundred yards farther, Bedistai, Tahmen and four of his pod ran towards the fortress, while Peniff and the remaining three waited in the trees.

They reached the wall without incident. Once they had scaled its face and disappeared over the top, Peniff placed his hand on Samen's shoulder and said, "I don't think this is going to be that difficult after all. Once they lower the rope ..."

He stopped in mid-sentence as the three beside him collapsed with crossbow bolts protruding from their backs. He whirled to see a squad of uniformed soldiers. Half had their weapons trained on him while the rest were reloading.

"Don't move and don't make a sound," said the one in an officer's uniform. "Lord Orr requires your company."

"But how ...? How did you know ...?" Peniff asked, unable to complete the question.

"That you would be here?" the officer supplied.

Peniff nodded.

The officer laughed. Then, as his expression soured, he said, "You can ask Orr yourself when you see him. For now, shut up, turn around, and put your hands behind you."

CHAPTER FIFTY-SIX

Bedistai was the last one up. He had remained at the foot of the wall until all of the rest had ascended. Lorek and Tahmen lent him a hand and hauled him over the battlement. He halted on the parapet walk, grasping his side, and Tahmen noticed a blood smear below his vest.

"Are you all right?" he asked.

"It's nothing," Bedistai assured. "Something minor. It must have torn open."

His brother nodded and gave it no further mention. Even if it were serious, there was nothing they could do for it.

Bedistai glanced at the grassy expanse they had crossed and was pleased to see how the wind was blowing away all traces of their passing. Although no alarm had been raised, and though he could not see the others waiting in the woods, he was nonetheless concerned.

"I'm still surprised there's no watch on these walls," he said. "This feels too easy. Keep your eyes open."

"I agree," said Tahmen. "As few as we are, we can't afford surprises. We'll check the stairs while you ready a seat for your friend. Once he is up, we'll see what help he can give us.

"Here," Tahmen said, reaching for the rope that was coiled across his chest. He lifted it and handed it to Bedistai. "This should be more than enough."

As Bedistai took it, he thought he heard footsteps. He pointed at a small stone house on the roof, through whose door a party of armed guards had begun streaming.

"Soldiers!" he cried.

The pod reacted quickly. Nocking arrows to their bows, they spread out laterally, ungrouping the target they presented and releasing arrows as they went. Two shafts found their marks. One soldier fell with an arrow lodged in his windpipe. The second arrow embedded itself in the sword arm of another. The shield of a third deflected Tahmen's and, as an advancing guard raised his sword, Tahmen tossed his bow aside and unsheathed a hunting knife half the length of the guard's weapon. The swordsman swung and Tahmen ducked. Then, with his free hand, he held the guard's arm as he drove his blade up and under the chest plate.

Lorek and Natal killed two more, leaving seven to contend with. Bartok and Assah followed Tahmen's lead, discarding bows in favor of hunting knives.

The remaining soldiers broke into two groups—one moving left, the other to the right—as they attempted to isolate and overwhelm individual opponents. One trio confronted Bedistai and attacked him in unison. Although Bedistai caught a heel on the edge of a stone and fell backwards, he managed to release one arrow before he hit the pavers. His target stumbled as the shaft embedded in his thigh. As Bedistai leapt to his feet, Tahmen stepped up beside him and together they grappled with the remaining two.

A pair came at Natal and Lorek, who by now had also abandoned their bows. Encumbered by their armor, the soldiers could not move as quickly as the Haroun, who maneuvered to position the guards between them.

Lorek stepped around one man's shield, away from the sword arm. He grasped the shield arm and drove his knife under the breastplate and into his heart. Natal, on the opposite flank, dropped to the ground. Planting two hands beneath him, he swept out with his legs and knocked his opponent's feet from under him. As the man tumbled, Natal sprang up, knife in hand, arms and legs spread for balance.

Bartok and Assah were confronting the last two, waiting to see what course they would take. As the guards rushed to meet them, each Haroun grasped an opponent's shoulder plates. Then, as if choreographed, they fell onto their backs, pulling the soldiers on top of them. With one foot planted against each attacker's stomach, they pushed skyward, using momentum to launch each man over the battlement wall.

The guard Natal had upended was attempting to pick up his shield and sword, but he fumbled them badly. When he bent to retrieve them, Natal leapt forward and impaled him with his knife. In the same instant, Bedistai and Tahmen slew their attackers. This left the one with the arrow in his thigh as the last one remaining. Seeing the hopelessness of his situation, he dropped to one knee, clutching the wounded one, gazing helplessly, and begging for mercy.

"What do we do with him?" Natal asked, as he wiped his knife on a dead guard's tunic.

"Cut a few lengths of rope, bind him securely and leave him here," said Bedistai.

"But if someone finds him ..."

"I am more worried about the two you sent over the wall and the alarm they will raise when someone notices their bodies. Besides, Orr already knows we are here."

"What do you mean?" his brother asked.

"These guards didn't come upon us by accident. They were ready for us. They knew we were here before they ever laid eyes on us. I don't know how they knew, but this one will not give us away. Our problem is how to finish what we came here to do, then escape with our lives."

As Natal and Lorek stood watch, Tahmen cut two lengths of rope to truss their captive. Meanwhile, Bedistai fashioned the seat for Peniff by forming two loops, one for each leg, at one end of the line Tahmen had brought. When he was sure the arrangement would hold, he dropped it over the wall, securing the opposite end through a trefoil in the wall. The seat reached the ground with length to spare and Bedistai whistled. When Samen did not respond, Bedistai glanced to be sure none of the patrols had heard, then whistled again.

"Where is Samen?" Bartok asked.

"I don't know. I don't like the way things are happening."

Bartok took hold of the rope and swung his legs over the wall.

"If these guards were expecting us, perhaps there were others waiting in the woods. I'm going to take a look. If I don't return quickly, don't come looking after me."

Fewer than five minutes elapsed before Bartok shinned up the rope and reported what he had found.

"The thought gazer's body wasn't among them," he said. "There were tracks of a large party leading away to the south, back in the direction we had come. My guess is they took your friend to the fortress."

"Since you were unable to find his remains, we must assume he's still alive," said Bedistai. "We will continue with the original plan, minus Peniff, and hope for the best."

CHAPTER FIFTY-SEVEN

A residence reveals much about its occupant to the astute observer. The fortress of barakMis was no exception and stated with great eloquence Orr's contentment with his situation. While Hath Kael, Obah Sitheh, and the other warlords battled daily for the very soil on which their encampments or fortresses stood—their ragged tents or pockmarked stone walls stained with the blood of countless lives taken—barakMis was a temple to opulence, pristine and secure within its borders. Its walls and floors of white and pink marble were polished to a high luster. Banners made of the finest fabrics and colored with the rarest dyes hung from its ceilings, while tapestries proclaiming his glory and deeds—likely fabricated—adorned the palace walls. And before those depictions stood sculpted likenesses in as many noble poses as his artisans could conceive.

Yet, not all was as tranquil as might first appear. Only a few yards separated the citizens and merchants, who had come seeking audience, from the prisons and horror chambers lying beneath their feet, places where Orr kept, tortured, and executed the subjects who had fallen from favor.

It was Monhedeth's remoteness that permitted such an accumulation of wealth, rather than force him to exhaust his revenues on weapons and armies. Only tiny Dar, far to the east, could have posed him any threat, were it not for the fact its army was so much smaller. Miast or Yeset had no extra forces to turn against Orr as they held off their neighbors' offensives, and the River Em defended Monhedeth against any other would-be conqueror from the south. In fact, Peniff wondered, had Kael not offered Limast, would Orr ever have done anything more than fantasize about acquiring it?

Under other circumstances, the fortress's magnificence might have awed the former miller. Its grandeur was far beyond the scope of his experience. But with the plight of his family tearing at him, the thoughts of those assembled here assailing him, and the captain of the guard repeatedly prodding him in the back with the staff of his halberd, Peniff was only vaguely aware of his surroundings as his escort hurried him along.

They paraded him through the room—if anything so cavernous deserves such a modest descriptor—past clusters of subjects who turned and scowled at this curious limping man with the armed escort. They took him to the head of the queue of those awaiting Orr's audience, and forced him to kneel at the foot of an elevated dais. At that very instant, trumpets sounded and curtains at the rear of the dais parted. Sabed Orr, resplendent in furs and jewelry, emerged and stood before the throne at its summit. As the room fell into silence, a herald announced, "Ladies. Gentlemen. Let all draw near who would be heard by the Monarch of Monhedeth, His Royal Highness, Sabed Orr."

He fancies himself king, thought Peniff as, for the first time ever, he regarded the one who had altered his life. He was surprised how diminutive the man was. This man who wielded so much power was nearly the size of Broodik. One would never glean that from the statuary. The face was the same—the contemptuous sneer, the tiny close-set eyes—but nothing about him approached the mythic proportions of torso and limbs of his marble depictions. Here was one to be feared, Peniff realized. Fragile ego and soaring ambition were a dangerous combination.

Peniff had raised his head at the fanfare, but when the captain of the guard took notice, he dashed it again to the floor with the sole of his boot. Stifling a cry, Peniff put his hands to his skull and sensed Orr smiling. The lord acted as if he were regarding the assemblage, but all the while his attention was wholly on Peniff. He silenced his subjects with a wave, then said to the aide at his side, "One of our patrols has captured a rodent. Bring him to me. I would learn more."

The aide, a tall, white-haired man clad in the white robes of a priest, motioned to the captain who, in turn, directed two of his men to retrieve Peniff. Placing one hand under each armpit and the other on a shoulder, together they lifted him to his feet. They were starting up the stairs when Peniff came to his senses and tore free.

"I can manage on my own," he gasped, behaving less cautious than was prudent.

One of the men had started to object, when his counterpart nodded and motioned Peniff to proceed. Even so, as he ascended, the two stayed close beside him.

Breathing deeply as he climbed, trying hard to clear his head, Peniff examined his captor. Although Orr's face appeared placid, Peniff could sense his uncertainty over the threat this thought gazer presented. Clearly, he had some idea of Peniff's abilities, but his doubts failed to match his apparent confidence.

As Peniff approached the dais' summit, Orr's aide commanded, "Halt and kneel before your master."

So, at the third step from the top, Peniff knelt, struck an obeisant pose, placing both knees on the second, then bowed his head onto the platform.

It all comes down to a confrontation with a narcissist, thought Peniff.

While he doubted he could win this encounter, he knew he could make matters worse. He would monitor Orr's thoughts carefully and hope he could keep his anger in check.

Orr looked past Peniff to the captain of the guard. "What have you brought me, Captain?"

The man saluted and said, "This is the marmath you predicted, my lord. We found him at the edge of the woods, exactly where you promised. Following your orders, we killed the Haroun who were with him and brought him directly here."

The admission startled Peniff. Even though it had seemed as though the ambush had been planned, he could not imagine how Orr could have foreseen his arrival. Something beyond his senses was at play. If he were to stand any chance of surviving, let alone free his family, it was imperative he arrive at an understanding quickly.

"Thank you, Captain. You have done an excellent job. You will be rewarded appropriately. And you," he turned to Peniff. "How shall I describe what you have done? How shall I reward you, my little traitor?"

Peniff raised his head, but had the good sense not to stand. "I did what I had to, my lord. I did what my conscience dictated."

"What your ..." Orr broke off. He rolled his eyes upward and started to laugh, then cut short the guffaw and glared. "Quite obviously those delightful little children—that sweet little girl and that handsome young boy—mean nothing to you. And that proud, loyal woman you took for your companion, her trust mattered naught to your—what did you call it?—ah yes, your conscience. As for your regard for your lord and protector, do you expect I will hold my promise to you as lightly as you held yours to me?"

"I did not take my promise lightly, my lord. Harad lied to

me. He swore there would be no killing, but after he murdered several youths and an innocent old man, I had no confidence he would keep Darva alive."

"And so you return here without her."

Before Peniff could answer, the aide directed Orr's attention to the foot of the stairs. Obviously irritated by the interruption, Orr nonetheless whispered to his aide, who in turn motioned to someone waiting below. When the man arrived beside Peniff, he knelt and announced, "A carrier pigeon has arrived from Liad-Nur bearing a message, my lord."

The man extended his hand and Peniff studied him. He was holding the message, but knew nothing of its contents.

The aide went to meet him, took the scrap of paper from his palm, and said, "Your lord is grateful for your service. You may go."

The man departed, and the aide handed Orr the message. Without reading what it said, Orr crumpled the tiny sheet and discarded it.

"It is from your friend," he said to Peniff. "We already know what it says."

Stunned, Peniff hurried to examine his thoughts. The lord was clearly not telepathic nor, so far as he could tell, was his aide.

"No," said Orr as if in response. "I cannot read minds, but I must say your puzzlement delights me." He smiled briefly, then scowled. "As for the promise I made concerning your family, I intend to keep it, for I do not appreciate treachery, whatever the reason. You may not see the importance of keeping your word, but I do. It is how I hold this land together.

"Hear me well, Thought Gazer. Tomorrow you shall see your precious children and your faithful wife one last time. You shall watch as I take each of their lives in the most exquisite manner I can contrive. I shall probably take yours as well, though not right away. I intend to let you live for a while, remembering their deaths and their parting screams. You will exist like that for as long as it suits me. It will only be when the horrors dim, no longer serving to torment you, that will I be done with you. How soon that day comes, of course, depends on how great is the conscience to which you alluded."

Orr raised his head as a murmur arose in the hall. Then he smiled and announced, "In fact, this day is full of delights. Surprises abound. I would like you to rise, Thought Gazer, and behold what has become of your plans."

Dread crept over Peniff. As he stood, the image in Orr's head filled his own. He gasped, then he turned. A party of soldiers was leading Bedistai and the remaining five Haroun—all of them bound—into the hall.

CHAPTER FIFTY-EIGHT

How had Orr known?

Peniff could not shake the question. Had Harad found a way to warn him, even before the pigeon arrived? Granted, he and Harad had recently touched minds, but that had required two adepts. Since today's audience precluded Orr as telepathic, a major piece of this puzzle was still missing. He wondered if the way they had been captured offered some clue to Orr's precognition, but there was no way to tell. The Harouns' thoughts were a jumble he was too distressed to sort through.

Orr's guards were leading them down the stairs to the dungeons. An accumulation of grime and mold darkened the walls and the air was becoming dank. Cries of despair and the stench of misery wafted up from below and he suspected no one ever left this place alive. His dejection deepened as he considered the fates of all who were here because of him. Of the Haroun, the three who had elected to remain behind were the lucky ones, having died almost instantly. Bedistai, Tahmen, and the rest of his pod did not deserve whatever Orr had in store.

"Tell me what happened," he begged.

"There were just too many," Tahmen replied, shaking his head. "And they were expecting us."

"Do you have any idea how they knew we were here?" Bedistai asked Peniff.

"No," he said. "I have been trying to ..."

"Silence!" barked the captain of the guards. He kicked Peniff for emphasis, and he tumbled down the flight to lay sprawled across the landing. "I'd watch myself if I was you," said the captain. "You fall and break something and that's how things will stay. There's no doctors here."

The bruises Peniff sustained were the least of his worries. As he struggled to stand, he reached out to his family and learned that earlier, around the time he was captured, Broodik and Halli had been taken from their mother. They were now in another cell—where, they did not know—and they were terrified. Except for his exchange with Harad, Peniff had never been able to communicate with thought, so it was comforting when he could tell that they sensed his mind touching theirs. They calmed at the contact and he remained with them for several minutes before reaching out to Miened. She was where she had always been, in a small dark cell, furnished with only a cot. Like her children, she sensed his proximity. Hope rose within her and he was determined it would not be unfounded. Although it was born of desperation, with no apparent solution, he knew if he stopped looking for a way to help them, they would certainly be finished.

The cell the guards tossed him into nearly extinguished that hope. It was so short and so narrow he could not lie fully extended. It lacked a cot and the only amenity, should one choose to call it such, was a hole in the floor's center. The door slammed shut behind him, plunging the space into near total darkness. What little light remained came through the door's barred window. He could hear the guards incarcerating the hunters as six doors slammed in succession. With nothing else to do, he sat against a wall, drew his knees to his chest and waited.

CHAPTER FIFTY-NINE

Good morning, Peniff."

He opened his eyes and looked up, raising an arm to shield them from the unexpected glare.

"Did we sleep well?"

Backlit by torchlight, a man's silhouette loomed in the open doorway.

"So many years have passed since the time I first saw you," said the man. "Had we met on the street, I would never have recognized you."

The man's mind touched his and the contact made him jump. Peniff extended his own in response, only to find himself shoved back. Never before had another mind shut him out, and the rebuff baffled him.

"Surprised, are we? I should imagine so." The man laughed. "But I have had so many years to refine my gift while you probably never felt the need."

Curled on the floor, Peniff tried to sit, but yesterday's bruises and the stone floor he had slept on made him stiffen.

"Who are you?" he gasped.

"An old acquaintance. One of your first I might add,

although I scarcely believe you will recall our initial encounter. You gave me a similar start on that occasion ... and a blessing as well, I might add, though it took a while for me to appreciate it. Nonetheless, the gift you gave is the reason Lord Orr has kept your family alive. You see, I wanted so much to meet my bene-factor, and I thought that if Orr were to do as he intended before I had the opportunity ... well, I don't think you would have been in the proper frame of mind."

"I am sorry," said Peniff, rising to his feet. "I don't understand."

"No? I suppose you don't. Well, we will get there by and by. I see, however, that a number of questions are troubling you. Perhaps I can answer one or two—clear up some of the mystery, as it were."

Peniff rubbed his face with his hands. While there was nothing to indicate what time it might be, he suspected morning had arrived on what would become his life's most crucial day. He had, in fact, slept poorly and now was struggling to clear his head and identify the man in the doorway.

Once he was sitting upright, he could see that the man was taller than he. His features were still masked in shadow, but he had a deep imposing voice and an equally imposing frame. The backlight showed him to have a thick shock of closely cut white hair, the same color as his robes. As his head cleared, Peniff began to recognize him.

"You were with Orr in the Grand Hall," he said. "His aide, I believe."

"Oh, I am much more than an aide. Keep guessing, if it pleases you." The man chuckled and went on. "The first ques-tion on your mind is how Orr was prepared for your arrival. That answer is simple. I told him.

"I lost track of where you were not long after you set out. Although my mind isn't as far reaching as yours, it is quite acute close at hand. I suppose we all differ in the particulars of our abilities. Nonetheless, I watched and waited for your return. When you finally entered Monhedeth and I could tell you were coming through the Ahman Forest, I alerted him. Then, as you neared barakMis, I told him where you would emerge and, with his permission, I sent a company of guards to intercept you. Unfortunately, they arrived a little late, and I had to make other arrangements for the Haroun who actually did reach the fortress. Nonetheless, all is well. We have all of you now."

While Peniff was reluctant to believe the man's account, there was no other good explanation. Besides, he could not deny that the man was psychically adept, so he continued to listen.

"You were chosen to pursue your mission because you are special, Peniff. You have qualities the sum of which few, if any, possess. My psychic shortsightedness ruled me out as a candidate. That and the fact that, frankly, I'm a coward. Not you, however, and I admire you for your bravery.

"Back then when I tested you, I could tell that your mind is very far reaching. Of course you had no sense I had entered you, like your family does when you touch them. Another difference, I suppose. But, because I have the ability to visit another mind while remaining undetected, as you approached, I was able to block all your inquiries as you sought out information about the palace.

"I will answer another of your questions. I was the one who nominated you for your undertaking. Orr had no idea you even existed until I told him about you, and I would have had no idea of your abilities were it not for our initial meeting. So there we are again, back where we started."

Peniff folded his arms across his chest, trying to sort through the maze of information. A hazy outline began to present itself, but he needed more.

"When was that?" Peniff clarified. "Our initial meeting."

"Ah," said the man, and Peniff could make out the white of a smile break across his face. "That is the crux of it. Come a little closer. I believe, with a little effort, you may recognize me."

Peniff took a step, then halted.

"A little nearer, please. The torches don't cast very far." He turned to the guard and asked, "Do you suppose you might bring your lantern closer and shine it over my shoulder?"

The guard moved behind him and raised the lamp as he had been asked.

"Thank you." Then, turning to Peniff, the man said, "Please. This won't take long. Just another step or two."

Compelled by curiosity, Peniff obliged.

"Thank you, Peniff. With your permission, I would like to look into your eyes," the man said. "Allow me that small favor and all your questions will be answered."

Suspecting what the man was after, Peniff retreated a step.

"Don't waste my time," the man growled. He stepped forward and grabbed Peniff's face with both hands. When Peniff attempted to resist, the guard rushed forward.

"Leave us!" the man commanded, all the while holding Peniff's eyes with his own.

The guard halted just inside the doorway.

"If you won't go, then hold up the lantern and give me more light," said the man.

When the guard complied, the man tilted Peniff's chin upward and peered inside. Peniff gasped. His knees nearly buckled, but the older man held him so tightly he could not pull free. Sure of victory, the man gloated. Using thoughts, instead of words, the man asked, *Do you remember me now? Eliénor brought you to me.*

You! Peniff gasped, unable to speak. *You are the priest my mother told me about.*

306

WHEN PENIFF WAS but an infant his father, Hamm, and his mother, Eliénor, had taken him to the temple to be named and consecrated. He did not remember the occasion firsthand, but he had studied his mother's memories as she related the event.

Hamm and Eliénor were standing together while the priest conducted the ceremony. All of her family, all of her friends had come with them to celebrate. At the designated moment, the priest had extended his arms towards Eliénor, beckoning. She gazed serenely at her newborn, then at her husband who returned her look with adoration. He glanced at his son and nodded his consent. She returned his smile and surrendered her baby to the priest who, in turn, accepted the proffered bundle. He passed the tiny body through the cloud of incense rising from the acolyte's thurible, then elevated the boy for all to see.

"Behold what Siemas has given us," the priest proclaimed, invoking the supreme deity.

He lowered the boy, turning him so that he might behold the child's face, and peered serenely into the little one's eyes. Peniff, heretofore clucking and gooing, fell silent in response and engaged the priest's eyes with his own. Suddenly the priest shuddered, transfixed at the contact. His body grew rigid, his mouth contorted, lips curling in revulsion as he struggled to tear his eyes free. With a jerk he averted his face and blindly shoved the infant towards Eliénor.

"Take him," he gasped, waving the tiny body at her.

"What is the matter, Father?"

"Take the beast!" the priest cried, nearly dropping the boy, juggling the child like a hot bun fresh from the oven.

"What?" she stammered, reaching for her son mechanically.

"Bury it," the priest shouted and shoved it into her hands.

"Father?"

"Burn it. Put the cursed thing into a hole and bury it," he screamed and ran from the chamber.

Eliénor stood open-mouthed. Her dream was now a nightmare. She glanced from shocked face to shocked face for an explanation, but they offered none. Humiliated, desolate, wounded, she stood in that great hollow vault with no direction, too numb to cry.

THOSE MEMORIES WERE his mother's, but Peniff recalled the priest's mind.

*You were not like this. Your mind was not...*thought Peniff.

I didn't understand it myself at the time, the priest replied. *That first contact terrified me. You terrified me. I still do not understand the whole of it. You were trying to do something to me, or I thought that you were. Then again, what might an infant attempt, I asked myself. Nonetheless, you frightened me, and I fled.*

As time passed, however, I underwent a change. I began to perceive people's thoughts. At first, I thought I was imagining it. But as my perceptions grew stronger and clearer, I understood that what I was observing was real. I began paying attention, and over time I gained mastery over this strange new ability. Today, I am not only aware of people's thoughts, but I can communicate mind-to-mind. More important, I can influence their thoughts. You gave me quite a gift and I wanted to thank you.

Peniff saw that the priest did not intend this as a mere opportunity to express gratitude. He had something else in mind.

How perceptive! I do have something else in store, the priest acknowledged. *You see, I have recently developed another skill, something I would like you to observe firsthand. You see, I have learned that thoughts can ...*

Kill! Peniff finished for him. *But why me?*

I want Monhedeth. And I am nearly strong enough to take it. You would be a formidable adversary, a great threat, so I cannot allow you to live.

With that, he insinuated himself into Peniff's fundamental essence. Peniff gasped at the intrusion, as if punched in the solar plexus. His body went limp. The priest held two fistfuls of tunic and Peniff dangled from his hands. When his head fell forward, the cleric shook him until his head flopped back, and resumed his gaze into Peniff's still open eyes.

Peniff was no longer alone in his body. Like the fingers of a cancer, the priest's mind invaded, crowding him out from each new place he intruded. His intentions were clear. Soon he would be alone within the body's husk, all trace of Peniff obliterated. Then he would withdraw, leaving nothing in his wake.

Somehow, Peniff hung on. He did not cringe or cower, understanding at an intuitive level how fear would be his undoing. Instead, he did what came as naturally as what had occurred on that long ago first meeting. He grasped the priest's mind as tightly as the man held his and penetrated the priest in return. He felt the cleric startle as the tables slowly turned. The priest halted his invasion, fighting instead to retreat.

When the priest attempted to turn and run from the cell, Peniff grabbed his robes and held him. Eventually, when the priest realized he could not break Peniff's grip, he began pummeling with his fists. Peniff, however, was now beyond feeling. So, although blows rained upon him, he was all but oblivious to the assault. Taking his cue from what he had learned moments earlier, he began to eradicate the priest. Element by element, he extinguished that sentience. He obliterated one part of the man's essence, then another and another until, bit by bit, the priest ceased to be. Gradually the punches' impact diminished and the body began to wither. When the priest's life force had vanished, Peniff let go and the husk that had been his body collapsed.

CHAPTER SIXTY

S till holding his lantern, the guard stared in wide-eyed silence at the priest's remains. He was beginning to back away when Peniff, returning to the world, reached out and grabbed him. He needed the guard's cooperation, if he were to accomplish his task. From the corner of one eye he noticed the ring, bristling with keys, suspended from his belt.

What is the time? Peniff demanded.

Too startled to realize Peniff had not spoken, the guard replied, "Nearly the eighth hour."

Two hours past sunrise, thought Peniff and realized the palace must already be awake. If Orr were still sleeping, he would not be for long.

Release the Haroun, he commanded.

When the guard resisted, Peniff began to apply pressure. Gradually altering the technique, he began to instill fear.

Suddenly, he halted, realizing how abhorrent this was. He knew the priest's actions had begun to transform him. It felt as though parts of him were missing while others had changed. He did not yet understand what he was becoming—certain, however, he was somehow not the same—but he refused to become like the priest.

Now, he tried imparting understanding. He informed the guard how his family had been abducted and showed him all that had happened since. Because Orr's mistreatment extended even to those laboring within these walls, the guard required no further persuasion. While Peniff held the lantern, he began freeing the Haroun.

"There must be weapons," Peniff said, after the guard had unlocked the last cell. "Where do you keep them?"

The guard led them to a room filled with swords, knives, and other arms. He showed them where their own had been placed. Then, as the Haroun shouldered their bows and strapped on their knives, Peniff presented images of Miened and the children.

"They're not far from here," the guard replied, "but I don't believe they'll be there for long. Orr wants them executed an hour after he breaks his fast."

"When does he eat?"

The guard's face twisted into a scowl, then it fell. "An hour ago."

"Then we must act quickly. Take me to them."

Peniff was unprepared for the sight when the cell door flew open. He had never looked through his family's eyes, so he had never really placed them within the prison's horror. Huddled in a corner, filthy and terrified, his children clung to one another.

"Halli! Broodik!" he called. He choked on their names and the sudden upwelling of tears made it hard for him to see. When they did not respond, he added, "It's Daddy." He wiped his eyes with the back of his hand as he dropped to his knees and held his arms toward them. "Don't be afraid," he begged, when they remained huddled in the darkness.

He reached out with his mind and assured them with a thought, *It's Daddy*.

That was the touch they recognized. They climbed to their feet and ran to him. Halli tripped on the hole in the floor as her brother ran past and flew into his father's arms. Her face struck the pavers and she wailed with all the pain, all the rage, and all the terror she had amassed during the weeks of her imprisonment. Peniff clasped Broodik to his breast and kissed his cheek. He lifted him, then dropped to his knees beside Halli. Setting Broodik on his feet, he grasped his daughter and lifted her into his arms. As she screamed her hurt and indignation, he embraced her and rocked her. Then, pulling Broodik close, he told them both how much he loved them, how much he had missed them. All three, with their heads close together, began to sob.

After a moment, Bedistai approached and placed a hand on his shoulder.

"We need to find your wife," he reminded and Peniff nodded.

Peniff struggled to stand, but encumbered with his children and with his leg and hip injured as they were, he could not rise.

"Here," said Bedistai, as he lifted the boy. "Let me help."

When they had carried the little ones into the corridor, he asked Peniff, "Which way?"

"I'm not sure," the thought gazer said, and his chest tightened. She was on a different floor. "She's not in her usual cell."

"Follow me," said the guard and turned down the passageway. "I think I know where to find her."

In less than a minute they were passing the cell that she had once occupied. The door was open, and the chamber was empty.

"She is gone. Where have they taken her?" Peniff asked.

"I cannot say exactly, but they will have brought her to the level above. That is where ..." His lips tightened when he looked at the children. Putting his lips to Peniff's ear, he whispered, "I'm sorry. That is where the execution chambers are."

Peniff shut his eyes, then opened them. His emotions had clouded his perceptions, so, once again, he suppressed them.

"She is still alive," he said. "There are several others with her and they are preparing her for ..." Unable to finish the sentence, he said, "We must hurry."

They made their way through a maze lined with cells, then up some stairs. At the top, Bedistai handed Broodik to Peniff.

"Take the boy. We may need to fight, and I will need both hands."

The floor onto which they emerged was lit with torches, so the guard doused his lamp.

"This way," he whispered, and jerked his head towards a passage.

The group followed, increasing their pace until they were approaching a run. Abruptly, Peniff raised his hand and brought them to a halt.

"Shhh! We're close. I don't want them prepared. All told, they number perhaps a dozen."

The guard nodded. "Around this corner the way splits in two. The execution chambers are to the left."

They rounded the corner and made their way towards a cluster of doorways ten or so paces apart, three on either side of the passageway. The ones on the right were all lit, and they could hear voices. They paused and clustered together.

"Which one is she in?" Bedistai asked.

"First on the right."

"Can you tell yet how many there are?"

"I count eleven: Miened, Orr, a jailor and eight soldiers."

Bedistai began issuing orders. "We will need to enter quickly. Ideally we should all be inside at once. Since that is impossible, stay close together, Haroun first then Peniff, then ..." He paused to look at the guard. "Are you with us?"

The guard hesitated, then shook his head. "Orr will kill me."

"You have given us more help than we had the right to

expect," said Peniff. "But please, I must ask one more favor. I cannot bring the children. Can you watch them for me?"

The guard nodded. "I have young'uns at home. I will tend to them as if they are my own."

Peniff nodded a tight-lipped thanks, then set the children on their feet.

"We are going to get Mommy," he explained. "It may be dangerous, so I want you to stay with my friend. You may hear shouting. There may be a great deal of noise. But I want you to stay with him until Mommy and I come to get you. Do you understand?"

Broodik and Halli were on the verge of tears. Still, they nodded.

The guard looked at them and said, "I am going to help your father by waiting with you. Will you be brave and stay with me?"

Clinging to one another, they nodded again.

"I love you both," said Peniff, kissing each on the forehead.

The guard remained well behind while Peniff and the hunters bunched together by the door. They had all drawn their weapons, the Haroun their hunting knives—the better to engage in close quarters—and Peniff his sword, and were about to rush inside when they heard Orr speak.

"Sergeant, bring the thought gazer and his children. It's time they joined us."

At the sound of boots, Bedistai flicked his hands towards two doors across the hall. Peniff hurried the guard and children through one, while Bedistai and his tribesmen slipped through another. After a moment, when they were certain the soldiers were gone, the Haroun returned to the hallway and Bedistai fetched Peniff.

As they regrouped, Bedistai whispered, "We won't have much time before they realize the children have vanished and come looking. Let's get your wife."

CHAPTER SIXTY-ONE

O rr was instructing the jailor and his back was to the door. Miened was lashed to a wooden scaffold. Her dress was torn, her head was down, and her hair hung about her face in greasy tendrils as she hung motionless. The sounds of the rescuers entering caught her attention and she raised her head.

"Peniff!" she gasped.

The jailor looked past Orr and grasped his sleeve as he pointed towards the door.

"My lord!" he said.

Orr had started to brush his hand away when the intrusion caught his attention as well. He glanced towards the door, paused, then ran to his prisoner. Stepping behind her, he put his knife to her throat.

"Drop your weapons!" he commanded.

The pod looked to Bedistai, but he motioned them to wait. Slowly, he stooped to place his knife upon the floor. With equal deliberation, he unshouldered his bow and set it alongside, indicating to the others they were to do likewise. Although the Haroun followed Bedistai's example, Peniff hesitated. Then, finding no good alternative, he placed his sword with the others.

"You don't have to hurt her," he said. "It's me you want. My wife has done nothing. Let her go."

"Are you telling me what to do?" Orr pressed the blade against Miened's neck and blood trickled from the spot. Turning to the jailor, he ordered, "Take their weapons."

The jailor, eyeing the intruders, stepped cautiously to obey. Bending low, he slid each blade and bow, one-by-one, across the room. When he had finished, he backed away until he was again at his master's side.

"My men are bringing your children," Orr told Peniff. "Once they are here, I will decide what to do with you. Until then, move away from the door and stand against that wall."

He gestured with the blade and the group complied.

"Not you," said Orr, as Peniff moved with them. "Stay where you are. I want to look at you."

Peniff paused.

"Your gall is boundless. I cannot imagine what drives it. When all you had to do to keep your loved ones safe was find one woman and deliver her to me—something well within your means—you chose first to betray me, then come before me and flaunt your disrespect. And now you have the nerve to ask me not to do what I have promised?" Orr snorted. "The only thing that prevents me from slitting your wife's throat right now is, if I do, I would be left at a distinct disadvantage. That will soon change. When it does, you will see what an honorable man does to those who betray him."

Peniff laughed. "Honorable? Do you call the kidnap and imprisonment of innocents honorable? You extort my services, then call yourself honorable? If that is not gall, I must confess I do not understand the word."

"You are too stupid to recognize that forces beyond your own petty interests are at play. Treachery has its price and you will pay dearly." Taking a handful of Miened's hair, Orr yanked back her head. She had begun to cry, and tears traced paths down her dirty cheeks. "She used to be pretty, didn't she? Loyal, too. Such a waste."

Peniff knotted his hands into fists.

"Even now, you would harm me," said Orr as he noticed the gesture. "Even though doing so threatens her life. How pathetic. But that is about to change." He looked towards the doorway and smiled. "Can you hear? My men are returning."

It was true. Peniff could hear voices down the corridor and the Haroun began exchanging glances. Knowing there wasn't much time, Peniff reached out and examined Orr's mind.

Orr started at the contact. His eyes widened and he looked around the room.

Fascinated by the pronounced reaction, Peniff delved deeper and was surprised he could feel Orr tensing the hand that held the knife. This was new, he thought, unlike reading minds. It was almost as if he were Orr. Almost, because when he tried to relax Orr's fingers and make him drop the knife, Orr tightened his grip. When he tried to move Orr's arm away from Miened, Orr resisted.

"What are you doing?" Orr demanded, glaring when Peniff suppressed a smile.

Peniff suspected, given enough time, he could do many things with this newfound ability. Unfortunately, time was one thing he lacked. The approaching footsteps told him as much. Still he had to try something, and killing Orr, were that possible at all, was not the solution. With Orr dead, there would be nothing to prevent the returning soldiers from slaughtering his unarmed friends. He could sense Orr's increasing discomfort, could sense him beginning to panic. If he could not figure out what to do before Orr could react, Miened might die.

The voices in the corridor were growing louder. They were

almost at the door. Aware that his rescue was imminent, Orr pressed the blade against Miened's neck, then stopped.

"They are gone, my lord," the captain announced as he entered the room, then halted and stared at the surreal tableau.

Although Orr held a knife against Miened's throat and a sheet of blood streamed beneath it, he stood motionless. His eyes were wide, his mouth was agape, and the tip of Peniff's sword pressed against his side.

"Drop your weapons," commanded Peniff.

"My lord," said the captain, looking to Orr for direction.

"He cannot respond," said Peniff.

It was true. Lord Orr stared into space, unable to reply to the captain's call. He did not blink, nor did he look at the soldiers who were standing in the doorway. Instead, he stared blankly into space, motionless except for his breathing.

"If you wish to spare his life," Peniff said, "enter slowly and place your weapons on the floor."

When their master maintained his statue-like pose, and Peniff's sword did not waver, it became clear how delicate, though bizarre, the situation had become.

"You won't kill him," said the captain, arriving where Peniff had moments ago.

"No, I won't," Peniff agreed. "But I can cut off an ear, then the other one. Perhaps his nose. And I promise you, when he awakes, he will remember how you could have prevented all of it."

The captain scowled, then responded as Bedistai had done minutes earlier. He unsheathed his sword, set it inside the doorway and his men followed suit.

"Now move over there," instructed Peniff with a jerk of his head.

One at a time, they moved to the wall opposite the Haroun, who had begun shouldering their bows and retrieving their knives.

CHAPTER SIXTY-TWO

W hat Peniff did to Orr took only seconds to complete. Through it all, the jailor's gaze repeatedly passed from Peniff to Orr and back again. He was clearly off balance, uncertain how to respond, and probably would have remained fixed to the spot had Peniff not taken charge. Uncertain how long he could maintain this control, Peniff looked to the Haroun for assistance. He glanced toward Tahmen.

"Put the jailor with the others."

Tahmen did as requested and Peniff took Orr by the shoulder. Keeping his sword against Orr's side, with his other hand he pressed Orr's shoulder. Orr tilted, and as he leaned, the knife moved away from Miened's throat. Still unfamiliar with this new form of control, but believing he could do more, Peniff exerted himself. Orr's fingers opened, and the knife clattered to the floor. When it did, the lord's chest began to heave, and his breathing became fierce.

"Is he all right?" asked Bedistai.

"He is fighting to free himself," Peniff explained. "I have taken control of his body and he is struggling against me. I don't know how much longer I can continue. Is there some place you can lock up his soldiers?"

"I took these from the jailor," Tahmen said, displaying the key ring. "If I can find one that fits one of the doors across the hall, we can throw them inside."

"See if you can," said Bedistai, "while I cut down Peniff's wife."

Tahmen set off while Bedistai severed her bonds. Miened's legs refused to support her and she collapsed. While Peniff struggled with Orr, Bedistai examined her wound.

"The cut is not deep. The knife did not completely penetrate. I cannot staunch it, but I think it will eventually stop bleeding on its own," he said. Lifting Miened into his arms, Bedistai asked, "How do you feel?"

She nodded weakly and looked at her husband. "Peniff?" she murmured.

"He will be fine," Bedistai assured her, though in truth, he could not know. "Once we put the soldiers away, he can rest."

A few minutes later, Tahmen returned with good news. When the soldiers and jailor were all locked away, Bedistai told Peniff it was safe to release Orr. Peniff staggered when he did, and Orr fell to his knees. Peniff braced against the frame, breathing hard from the exertion.

When Miened whispered into Bedistai's ear, he placed her on her feet. She went to her husband and embraced him. "Peniff," she gasped. "Are you all right?"

"Are you?" he asked, as he struggled to regain his breath. Then, noticing how weak she appeared, he wrapped an arm around her and felt how thin she had become. He brushed the tendrils of hair from her face.

"I'm fine," he said. "You are alive and that's all that matters."

She nodded and smiled, then sobered. Her eyes widened, and she grasped his shoulders.

"The children. We must find the children."

"I've already found them. There they are," he said and pointed towards the door.

Miened turned to see a Haroun entering the chamber, flanked by her little ones.

"Halli! Broodik!" she cried, and they ran to her. "My babies!" she exclaimed, as she knelt to embrace them. She sobbed in relief, then pulled back and examined each one, appraising their faces and bodies for signs of harm. "Are you all right?" When both children nodded, she clasped them to her breast.

"Their guardian has gone to safer parts," Tahmen told Peniff.

He nodded, then turned to Miened. "I am sorry, love, but this is not over. We need to find a way out as soon as we can. So long as we are inside these walls, or anywhere in Monhedeth, we are not safe."

"Are you strong enough?" Bedistai asked.

"Yes," replied Peniff and took a couple of steps to test his legs, especially the wounded one. "I am feeling better. Nearly myself. Let's leave. I can recover as we go."

"Good," said Bedistai. "Natal. Lorek. Each of you, carry a child." Then to Miened, he said, "Do you require assistance?"

"Peniff will help me."

When he saw Tahmen and Assah holding Orr, Bedistai said, "Bring him with us. We will use him to ensure our safe passage."

CHAPTER SIXTY-THREE

They ascended by way of the less frequented stairwells and passages that Peniff selected. Now that the priest no longer interfered with his perception, the palace's interior unfolded itself. They encountered no guards, no palace visitors, and there was a complete absence of the resident dignitaries and staff one might otherwise expect. Even so, the increasing illumination that should have lifted his spirit as they ascended from the gloom left him uneasy, expecting to be ambushed at any moment.

Bedistai led the way, followed by Tahmen and Assah, who had been assigned to restrain Orr. If they ran into danger, he would be their bargaining chip. Behind them came Peniff, Natal, and Bartok, followed by Miened who insisted on carrying Halli, and Lorek, who carried Broodik.

It was shortly after they ascended one stairwell that matters began to go bad. As the shaft they were climbing ended and they emerged onto an upper floor, about to traverse to another set of stairs, a pair of guards confronted them.

"Identify yourselves!"

Struggling to break free, Orr called out. "Help! I'm being kidnapped."

Outnumbered, but armed with halberds—over-sized, double-edged axes topped with spearheads—the guards interposed themselves between Peniff's party and the next flight of stairs. In response, Bedistai, Natal, and Bartok unsheathed their knives, ordering the rest of the party to hold back. In an attempt to maintain control, the guards moved to isolate Bedistai, who was standing apart from the others. Natal and Bartok outmaneuvered them, however, and the three now stood as one. The guards hesitated. While halberds can be deadly, they are large and unwieldy. In close quarters they are a poor match against large hunting knives of the sort the Haroun used.

For a moment, the guards only feinted, offering half-hearted stabs or swings. When it became obvious the hunters were not about to back down, at the urgings of their ruler the guards attacked, swinging their blades in broad sweeping arcs.

Bartok ducked under one attempt, then, dancing opposite the halberd's momentum, captured the shaft with his left hand and buried his knife in the attacker's abdomen. When the second guard hesitated, witnessing his partner's demise, Natal took advantage and knocked his weapon away. It clattered to the floor and the guard retreated. Alone and unarmed, he looked at his master.

"I will bring help, my lord," he shouted before he fled.

Orr sagged when he left and Bedistai called to the rest, "We don't have much time. We must get to the roof before he's able to find help. Lorek, carry the boy and Bartok, you take the girl."

To Peniff's relief, Miened surrendered Halli without objection. For when Bedistai ordered them to run, it was all she could do to keep up. Several times on the ascent, Miened stumbled. It was only because of how tightly Peniff held her that she remained on her feet.

Tahmen and Assah led the way, lifting the diminutive ruler

as they bounded upstairs. Lorek and Bartok followed, while Bedistai and Natal held back until Peniff and Miened had passed them.

They were all gasping for breath when they broke into daylight. Shouts and the concussion of boots grew loud behind. By the time Peniff and Miened had arrived, Bartok was already straddling the wall with a rope in one hand and an arm around Halli.

"I can manage the girl. Lorek will follow with the boy," he called to the others.

As he and their daughter disappeared over the edge, Miened broke from Peniff's grasp and ran to peer after them. When she arrived and had time to look, she turned back to her husband, eyes wide with fright and disbelief.

"I can't go over like that," Miened gasped. "Not like that, Peniff. There has to be another way."

As Lorek went over the side with Broodik, Peniff went to her. He took her hands into his, reminding her, "Our children need you, Miened. Now more than ever."

She turned to look once again. Then grasping his tunic with both hands, she pulled him close and looked at him beseechingly.

"I can't!" she exclaimed as she broke into tears. "Help me, Peniff."

Bedistai approached with a rope in his hands. "I have fashioned one end into a seat," he explained, displaying his work. "This pair of loops is for your legs. Step into them and hold the free end with both hands. Close your eyes if you must. We will lower you over the side and you will not have to look until your feet touch the ground."

Peniff smiled reassuringly, but Miened's face was now ashen.

"They are almost here!" Tahmen called from a place near the stairwell. "We don't have much time."

Peniff grasped Miened's shoulders and peered into her eyes.

"You must be brave for Halli and Broodik and for these courageous men who are risking their lives. I know this is hard, but there is no other way."

Trembling and in tears, she clenched her teeth and gave several short quick nods. "All right," she gasped in a voice not much louder than a whisper.

Bedistai dropped to his knees and said, "Step into the loops."

With a hand on Peniff's shoulder, she stepped first into one loop, then into the other. Bedistai stood and pulled the rig to the tops of her thighs.

"Good. Now, take this," he said, as he handed her the running portion.

"Hurry!" called Tahmen. "They are almost upon us."

With deliberate calm, Bedistai instructed, "Now, close your eyes and hold tight. You will be safe with your children in less than a minute."

She did as he instructed and Bedistai, now urgent, motioned to Natal and Assah.

"Lift her over the edge," he told them. "Peniff, help me lower her."

Natal and Assah raised her over the wall and Miened, now nearly paralyzed, let out a yelp. Hand over hand, Bedistai and Peniff lowered her as fast as they could manage.

All at once, there were voices behind them, and Tahmen was shouting, "Stop where you are, or we will kill your lord!"

Still working frantically, Peniff glanced past his shoulder to see two of Orr's guards standing in the stairwell, the helms and weapons of others visible behind them.

"Are you all right, m'lord?" one guard called.

"I will be, when you do what I am paying you to do," the tyrant yelled.

As Peniff unsheathed his sword, he reached out with his mind to assess how many they would be facing. He counted six in this unit, but dozens were streaming up the stairs behind them. His family would escape, but he doubted that he, Bedistai, or the other Haroun would survive.

The rope went slack and Peniff looked to see Lorek and Bartok helping Miened from the harness as the children ran to embrace her. Now that his family was, for the moment at least, safely outside barakMis, he turned to prepare for the inevitable as Bedistai hurried to secure the free end of the rope to the masonry.

"How many have you brought?" Orr demanded as he strained to break free.

"All of us, m'lord. Everyone is coming."

Orr glared at Peniff. "This is where it ends, Thought Gazer. Tell your friends to throw down their weapons and let us be done with this farce."

There must be a way, Peniff told himself. After escaping two prisons and avoiding capture on the journey home, his effort could not simply end here. He knew he could not allow Orr's guards to simply slaughter them. He would face them as he had faced up to Harad and die fighting if he had to. He steeled his nerves and prepared himself for battle.

Bedistai and Natal were sheathing their knives in favor of bows and arrows. As the soldiers amassed in the stairwell, their eyes on their master, Tahmen and Assah dragged Orr to the fortress wall.

Suddenly and without warning, Orr tore free, crying, "Kill them. Kill them all!"

Soldiers began pouring onto the rooftop. Natal and Bedistai downed the first two, but even as they fell, the ones behind stepped over their corpses and the cries of the following tide became jubilant.

Tahmen and Assah were unshouldering their bows when Orr came from behind and stole Assah's knife. Before either Haroun could react, he slashed Bedistai across the middle.

Grasping at the flow of crimson, Bedistai doubled over. Orr bared his teeth at Peniff, and for a moment the two stood staring. Then, without warning, Orr lunged, aiming his knife at the thought gazer's heart.

Peniff swung his sword in a counterclockwise arc. Steel rang against steel as his weapon deflected the smaller blade. As the sword arm completed its circle, Peniff's left hand joined his right and, with both hands, he brought the blade in a horizontal swing with the full weight of his body behind it. It severed Orr's neck, barely slowed by resistance. He watched Orr's expression change from anger to surprise, just before his head bounced across the pavers and his body collapsed. Peniff side-stepped to avoid it, then stared at the remains of the man who had altered his life and brought him to this moment.

He hated Orr, not only for what he had done to his family, but even more, for transforming him into a killer. Scant weeks ago, he had been a husband and a father. He had been a miller and part of a community of gentle lawful people. Yet, in the time since he had set off on his mission, he had taken how many lives? What was he now?

CHAPTER SIXTY-FOUR

In an instant, his reverie was over. The world returned, and he was aware again of the battle around him. Two guards bounded forward with another pair close on their heels. And though Haroun arrows found each of them, the rest of the horde had arrived. They forced their way onto the rooftop and over the bodies blockading their path. Peniff realized that, however fast the Haroun reacted, they could not release their arrows fast enough to make a difference.

Two guards ran at Bedistai and Natal, two more at Tahmen, forcing the Haroun to drop their bows and engage them hand-to-hand. As more poured onto the battlements, the situation became ever more hopeless. Assah had fallen victim to the sword and Tahmen was now wounded. A soldier stood over Bedistai, poised for the kill.

As many as had died today, however many more would fall before this battle ended, Peniff resolved not another of his friends would be among them. In the instant he made that decision, he realized there was a way. He understood how reading someone's thoughts allowed him to inhabit that individual the way he had inhabited Orr.

All the time they had been making their escape he had kept his mind open. It came to him that he held everyone's mind in his—both Haroun and soldier—separate, yet one. Just as the priest had invaded his body, he could invade others. And though the prospect of even more killing was a horrifying thought, an abomination unlike anything he had ever known, in the end it was no more terrible than what was already happening around him. It had to be stopped.

Dropping his sword, terrified at the prospect of what he was about to do, without further deliberation he committed himself. He grasped the living center of every guard and visualized himself holding each of their hearts in his hands. He visualized squeezing them, visualized stopping their beat, and when he did, their heartbeats halted abruptly.

All around, on the parapet walk and in the mouth of the stairwell, the bodies of the guards and soldiers began shuddering spasmodically. Their knees buckled and, one by one, they began to collapse. As more rushed through the opening, he repeated the process, agonizing over the loss of so many. His heart ached, but there was no time to reflect. As subsequent groups arrived, he murdered those as well. When one soldier fell and his helmet came off, Peniff saw he was only half again Broodik's age. Was he also killing boys?

Please stop, he begged. *Go back from where you came.*

Yet they continued to arrive. And as they came, he continued his deadly task, until one group finally halted at the top of the stairs. They regarded the bodies piled before them. Faced with dozens of corpses heaped one on top of another, arms and legs akimbo, with no apparent reason for their demise, they stood and stared.

They had seen the ones before them fall, yet no weapons had felled them. Those Haroun who were not wounded were standing apart from the recently fallen. Only one man stood before them, knee deep in a mound of the recently deceased.

Standing with folded arms, he stared at the new arrivals, as if challenging them to approach.

The ones in the stairwell backed away, arguing among themselves, motioning those who were following to do the same.

Peniff was dimly aware of Tahmen and Natal, who were standing in silence among the dead, not daring to move.

So many dead, yet not one drop of blood, they were thinking.

When they turned to regard him, he was standing among the corpses, chest heaving, tears streaming from his eyes. A long keening wail filled Peniff's ears, the sound of anguish and horror commingled. It quavered on a high note, broke off and began anew. Over and over it repeated until Peniff realized the sound was his, pausing when he took a breath, then resuming.

Murderer, he called himself. *What kind of monster are you?*

Even though there had been no other way, the taking of so many lives was more than he could bear. He clenched his fists, inhaled deeply, screamed one last time, then fell to his knees and passed out.

CHAPTER SIXTY-FIVE

Daddy. There is Dorman. Can we go see him?" asked Broodik. Halli was jumping up and down beside her brother, hoping her father would agree.

"Of course you can."

Giggling and laughing and dressed in the furs and hides of their new home, the children turned and bounded in pursuit of their friend, their laughter filling the air. They had arrived in Mostoon only three days before, yet each day brought such changes in the young ones as to astound Peniff. By the second day, they had begun making friends. Shortly thereafter, they began to smile, then laugh and play games. Their resiliency was a pleasure to behold. They had already begun to forget their captivity, and Peniff hoped that, over time, their wounds would heal and they would begin to forget. Memories fade, even the bad ones, he told himself. Perhaps someday, the memories of their captivity would vanish altogether.

It was not so for Miened who clung to his arm, a shadow of her former self. She had become frail and fearful, and he wondered if he would ever see the strong vibrant woman who had once been his family's anchor. He thought back to the beginning. How had it begun? As he wondered, his mind returned to simpler times.

It was during Fourthmonth—the time that marks the beginning of the Warm Months—during Peniff's twentieth year, that Podat the baker began sending his daughter, Miened, to purchase barrels of flour from the mill. At the outset, when she began making her weekly trips, Peniff would roll out the barrels and place them onto her cart. Semed, the miller to whom he was apprenticed, handled the actual transactions, either accepting payment or entering the purchase into the accounts receivable ledger. In Seventhmonth, however, Miened made her call on a week that found Semed away on business. She arrived early in the day and pulled her cart alongside the loading dock. After setting the brake, taking the extra precaution of hobbling the horse to make sure the mare would not wander off, she went around to the front, up the stairs and into the mill to conduct her business.

Peniff had started well before dawn. He had completed the morning's milling and was busy shoveling flour intended for household purchases into sacks. It was then that Miened entered the millhouse office. It was not necessary for anyone to announce her. The door always banged shut after anyone had entered.

As Miened stood waiting, Peniff agonized over what he should do. He wasn't shy in the usual sense. He never worried what others might be thinking about him and he knew Miened did not think ill of him at all. In fact, he knew her thoughts mirrored his own about her, and those were not bad thoughts at all. What worried him ... No! What frightened him ... was the prospect of looking into her eyes. The fear was part of an ancient memory he would not allow to surface. It was one he had buried, refusing to examine it.

This morning, she was not about to give him time to decide what course of action to take. When it became apparent he might leave her standing at the counter for the rest of the day, she strode into the millhouse to confront him.

"Good morning, Peniff," she said, then paused to study him.

He knew he did not look the way she had expected. He knew this, because whenever she appeared, he could not resist the temptation of seeing the world through her eyes.

This morning, he was chagrined. His hair was tousled, and his clothes looked as though he had slept in them. As he stood there, looking sheepish, shovel in hand, arms, face and clothing covered in flour, she broke into a smile at his disarray.

"I'm ... I'm sorry," he stammered, suddenly feeling cornered. "Semed has gone to town. I'm afraid he won't be back until tomorrow."

"Are you saying you want me to leave?"

The fact she was grinning embarrassed him all the more.

"Oh, no! No. That isn't what I meant. It's just that usually ..."

"Are you unwilling to help me?" she demanded, clearly delighting in his awkwardness. One did not have to be a thought gazer to see her glee at his discomfort.

"I'm sorry. I didn't mean it that way. I will be most happy to help you. I'm just not very good with words."

"It sounds to me as though you can speak very well."

Suddenly he reminded her of a little boy whose shoes were undone. What came next aroused him beyond words. She couldn't stop herself. She walked up to him and placed her hand on his trousers.

"I've been told," she said, "you can read minds."

Another step and her body was against his.

"Can you read mine?"

He didn't need to. He understood exactly what she meant. He tossed the shovel aside, put his arms around her, and held her tight. Here was a heart he could trust. Here was a place so safe that, if he could but trust himself, he would never be lonely again.

She shoved him onto a pile of empty sacks and began undoing her blouse.

THAT WAS GONE NOW. It was falling to him to hold her together and he wondered if he was up to it. Only three days had elapsed since he had returned to Mostoon, only three days since the killings, and Peniff felt fragmented.

"Do you think she will mind?" Miened repeated.

He had barely heard her the first time she asked, even though he was trying to keep his attention planted in the moment. They were nearly at Salmeh's door and his thoughts turned to Bedistai.

CHAPTER SIXTY-SIX

By the time the killing had ceased and Peniff had returned to consciousness, only he, Tahmen, Natal, and Bedistai remained alive atop the battlements.

Natal was tearing the sash from one soldier's body, while Tahmen cradled his brother's head in his lap. It had not occurred to Peniff that Haroun men could cry, but tears were streaming down Tahmen's face when their eyes met.

"Can you help?" he begged.

Struggling to clear his head, Peniff ran to Tahmen's side.

"We have to stop the bleeding."

Only then did Peniff see how badly Bedistai had been hurt. By then, Natal had arrived. As he began wrapping the sash around Bedistai, he turned to Peniff.

"Call others," he said. "Get Bartok and Lorek. We need them to help us take Bedistai down."

Peniff remembered going to the wall and summoning frantically. He remembered watching Bartok and Tahmen on two parallel ropes struggling to hold onto Bedistai as Lorek and Natal feverishly lowered them to the ground. And he remembered seeing Bedistai tied to Chawah's saddle as she and the other endaths bore the survivors back to No'eth, running as only those creatures can.

"I'm sure she will enjoy seeing us and I'm sure she will appreciate our help," Peniff replied.

"I hope so," said Miened, welcoming the opportunity to be of use.

Peniff was looking forward to the visit as well. He needed to see how his friend was progressing. Bedistai had been barely alive when they had brought him here. They had traveled from Monhedeth in just over a day. With nothing but the sash to staunch the bleeding, and nothing by way of medicine, Bedistai was barely breathing when they pulled him from the saddle and carried him inside.

Salmeh had striven to keep her wits about her when they had placed him on the bed. Even so, she could not mask the fear she would lose him. Even now, as Peniff raised his fist to knock, he sensed she still dreaded his eventual demise.

"Welcome," she said when she opened the door. "Both of you, please come inside."

Her eyes were cratered and her face, deeply lined, showed she had slept very little, if at all. She clasped their hands and drew them through the entrance, leaving the door ajar allowing fresh air and sunlight to dispel the mustiness.

"How is he?" asked Peniff, glancing at the bed on which Bedistai was sprawled.

"I don't know," Salmeh answered, choking back a sob. "He has not improved much, but neither has he worsened. It is as if his heart, as well as his body, was wounded. Still, were he not Bedistai, he surely would have died by now."

Miened took Salmeh's hands in hers and asked, "Is there something I can do?"

Salmeh paused, taking time to consider the new train of thought, then managed half a smile. "Yes, child. Yes, there is. I am heating water. Could you watch it until it comes to a boil? My neighbor, Nooleh, is preparing a broth. I want to fetch some and would be grateful if you could keep an eye on my son and the water ..."

Salmeh fought back a sob.

"Of course I will."

Salmeh gathered herself and added, "And if it boils before I return, I have herbs ground and mixed for a poultice." She pointed at a mound on a nearby table.

"I know how to prepare it," Miened assured. "Go. Everything will be fine until you return."

At that, Salmeh's features relaxed and her body seemed to sag.

"Thank you," she said. "I will not be gone long."

"Take as long as you need," said Miened. "I will take care of everything."

"Let me walk you to the door," Peniff said. Then, turning to Miened, he added, "I need some time alone. Do you mind if I walk for a while?"

"No. I will be all right. Come back whenever you've finished."

Peniff managed a smile, then accompanied Salmeh outside. The two parted ways, and Peniff found a path that led towards the village outskirts.

So much had happened during the preceding days and weeks, he had not found time to sort through and come to terms with those events. He took a deep breath to fill his lungs, then exhaled deeply, wondering where to begin.

What troubled him most, he decided, were his recent changes beginning with the encounter at the supply wagon. Prior to that, he had only been able to read another's thoughts, although the word "experience" was closer to the truth. He had certainly never been able to take action against anyone with only his mind. Before his encounter with the priest, he had certainly never been able to communicate. Since then, however, he could instill horrible fears and even take a man's life. He recoiled.

The priest had not actually taught him these things, nor had he learned them in the ordinary sense. Somehow, when the priest had entered his mind, Peniff had spontaneously gained that understanding—not only how to accomplish all these things, but also about the interconnectedness between a person's mind and soul. That knowledge progressed at once to a comprehension of the life within a person. From there it was just a step to realizing how that life could be halted—within the priest, the guards, within anyone, even himself.

He wrapped his arms around him as he walked.

Did that, then, lend any insight to what had happened to Harad? He knew he had wanted to cause the man harm and had touched many aspects of his being. He wondered if his interaction with Harad had imparted his own abilities, or instead, had awakened latent powers the man already possessed. The priest had intimated as much.

Furthermore, he wondered, what was it that had driven him to reach out to these three and to no others? Each instance had one element in common: the individuals in question were all sociopaths. Was there something within him that was either so attracted to or so repelled by such people that forced him to act as he had? He certainly had not consciously chosen to do so, but he found it hard to believe there was an attractive force at work. In any case, he had been helpless to resist the impulse to reach inside each of them. And while he sincerely believed he had not deliberately set about to destroy either Harad or the soldier, he could not say what would have happened had Darva not interrupted. Consider, he thought, what he had done to the priest.

The fact remained, in the case of both the priest and Harad, he had created monsters. Had he also done so with the soldier? He could not say, although he feared he knew the answer. What then? The world was full of sociopaths. Would he be similarly attracted to each one he met from this point onward? Would he continue to create monsters? If so, was he so dangerous he should consider ending his own life? Certainly, the world was a more dangerous place now than it had been before. In fact, he had become a monster in his own right, as the events atop barakMis had evidenced.

Hoof beats broke through his funk and he gradually returned to the world around him. Several mounted horses were approaching, and he wondered what these creatures could be doing in a place where endaths were the steed of choice. Then, as they drew nearer, he recognized one of the riders.

"Darva!" he cried.

Her face brought a smile where, seconds earlier, a pall had descended. He waved his arms overhead until she spotted him. She beamed. Swinging a leg over the pommel, she sprang to a run almost before her foot touched the ground.

"Peniff!" she called as she drew nearer.

She ran with such determination, he thought she would either knock him down or else leap into his arms. He was relieved when, instead, her feet pounded the ground to arrest her momentum, bringing her to a halt scant inches away.

"Peniff," she grinned. "I am so glad to see you. What are you doing here?"

He explained, then asked her the same.

She looked embarrassed, but there was no way around the answer.

"I have come to see Bedistai." Then noticing how Peniff was peering over her shoulder at the eight men accompanying her, she explained, "Obah would not let me come alone, so he sent bodyguards. But tell me, where is Bedistai? Is he here?"

Peniff's face must have revealed more than he intended, because Darva's expression turned from joy to alarm. "He is all right, isn't he? Tell me he is all right."

He shook his head. "No," he said, then recounted what had happened. "He is at his mother's. Come. I will take you there."

"I know the way, but come with me anyway."

Peniff nodded.

After she had instructed her companions where to find the communal area so they could feed and water their mounts, Darva and Peniff hurried to Salmeh's. By the time they had entered, Salmeh had returned and was trying to get nourishment into her son. As light from the open door announced their arrival, she turned. When her eyes fell on Darva, the two women smiled.

"So, it is your turn to be the nurse," Salmeh said.

Darva approached the bed and her smile became a frown. She knelt and stroked Bedistai's brow, saying, "What kind of trouble have you gotten yourself into?"

Bedistai opened his eyes and a faint smile appeared.

"He recognized your voice," observed Salmeh. "That is the first real sign of life he has shown since he arrived."

"Here," she said, rising from the hassock. Extending the bowl and the spoon, she added, "You feed him. A mother's touch is one thing, but I cannot provide what you can."

While Darva tended to Bedistai, Peniff accompanied Salmeh to the kitchen where Miened was working.

She took the poultice Miened was wrapping and said, "That is enough work for now. Why don't you two go outside and get some fresh air? Bedistai will be fine now that Darva is here. Your time will be better spent caring for each other. I suspect you have much to do in that regard."

They looked at each other, then back at Salmeh.

"I suspect you are right," Miened said.

The two women embraced, then Peniff led Miened out into

the afternoon sunlight. They strolled in the direction they had last seen Halli and Broodik wander off.

After a moment, Miened turned to him and said, "We can't go home again, can we?"

"No. Even though Orr is dead, I suspect Monhedeth will be dangerous for a long time to come."

He knew the reason. A voice in his head was telling him it was so.

Hello, Peniff. I'm almost home.

It was Harad.

ABOUT THE AUTHOR

Raymond Bolton lives near Portland, Oregon with his wife, Toni, and their cats, Max and Arthur. He says this about his life: "I am of the persuasion life is too short to squander. I enjoy fine food, so I have learned to cook. I am endlessly curious about the world around me, so I read and I travel. I like people—who else is there?—so I talk and listen and try to understand what I hear. Over the years I've driven trucks, been an FM disc jockey, produced concerts, served as a mainsail trimmer on racing yachts, piloted gliders, written software, worked as a hair stylist, and owned and operated my own business—all with varying degrees of success, but all have imparted a wealth of experience and taught great lessons. In the course of these doings, I have had the privilege of meeting very accomplished individuals in the areas of music, movies, sports, technology, industry, finance, and politics. Ultimately, all of this background comes together, struggles to find coherence, and emerge in my work."

His goal is to craft gripping stories about the human condition, whether they are set here or another world. He has written award-winning poetry and four novels. *Awakening*, an epic, was released in January 2014, and *Thought Gazer*, an adventure and first volume of a prequel trilogy, was released on January 1, 2015. The trilogy's second volume, *Foretellers*, came out on March 1, 2016. *Triad*, the saga's concluding volume, was released on January 1, 2017.

Awakening has been translated into Spanish and was released as *El despertar—La saga de Ydron* on July 1, 2015. Amazon has already listed *El despertar* as the Number One New Release in Ciencia Ficción. As of this writing, *Awakening*'s English version is being made into an audiobook and is expected to be available on Audible's website in the early to mid-summer of 2018.

IF YOU LIKED ...

THOUGHT GAZER, YOU MIGHT
ALSO ENJOY:

Awakening
by Raymond Bolton

Minotaur
by Alex T. Singer

Griffin's Feathers
by J. T. Evans

OTHER WORDFIRE PRESS TITLES BY
RAYMOND BOLTON

Awakening

(Coming soon to WordFire Press)

Foretellers

Triad

Our list of other WordFire Press authors and titles is always growing.
To find out more and to see our selection of titles, visit us at:

wordfirepress.com

CPSIA information can be obtained
at www.ICGtesting.com
Printed in the USA
FSHW022340061019
62725FS